# Francesca Multimortal

# FRANCESCA
## *Multimortal*

V.C. Peisker

ASHWOOD
PUBLISHING

ISBN: 978-0-6452045-7-5 (paperback)
ISBN: 978-0-6452045-8-2 (ePub)

ASHWOOD
PUBLISHING
Cradoc, Tasmania
www.ashwoodpublishing.com.au

Front cover: image of the statue 'Madonna dell'accoglienza' by Biagio Governali (Studio d'Arte Governali Biagio) exhibited in the atrium of the Duomo di Monreale, Palermo, Sicily. Used by kind permission of the artist. Photograph taken by the author.

 A catalogue record for this work is available from the National Library of Australia

NATIONAL LIBRARY OF AUSTRALIA

# Contents

# 0: Not Growing Old

### Francesca, Melbourne, 2021

WITH NO EXPRESSION ON HIS fine-featured face, the greying oncologist delivers my diagnosis: stage four ovarian cancer.

'Stage four . . . ?'

'A year left to live . . . on average.'

The training provided in Australian medical schools: administer the bitter truth to the patient, no sugar-coating.

I cannot tell him that this is my sixth life; he would think I had lost my mind upon the bluntly delivered bad news. Besides, he seems a busy man. No time to chat. If I mentioned my six lives, he'd offer a nondescript smile and lift his eyebrows, as if hearing a joke he didn't understand. Probably glance at his watch as well – a glinting, expensive-looking one – hinting that our appointment should be over soon. So I just smile and wait for him to continue.

'The chances of a cure are slim because the cancer has spread from its original source. Tests have shown small but certain lesions in your lungs and liver,' the oncologist explains. 'And possibly elsewhere: the pelvic tissues and the lymph nodes. Given the disease is so advanced, your only option is total abdominal hysterectomy . . .'

'The removal of the womb?'

'Yes, alongside ovaries and fallopian tubes, and then aggressive chemo and radiation therapy, which could extend your life for several years. But no-one can say for sure.'

I smile. I never cry in public. I only cried at my mother's funeral. That was de rigueur.

'I don't need my reproductive tract anymore. But the rest does not sound too good. I had friends who "fought cancer" in recent years and I know what they went through. Years of hell, for their families too, and then they died. Is there a point?'

The doctor waits, his handsome brown face – Indian ancestry – frozen for a moment. Then he realises this was not just a rhetorical question.

'That really depends on the patient, Mrs' – he peeks into the printout on his desk – 'Ionescu. Some people don't give up the fight until their last breath. Most people, actually. People hope for a cure, for recovery. Sometimes, they hope for a miracle.'

'Have you seen any? Miracles?'

'No . . . I cannot say I have. Some people last longer than expected, some tolerate the treatment better. Miracle stories have appeared in the news, shared on social media . . . most later proven fake. But I cannot say with absolute certainty that none of them are true.' He shrugs.

Hoping for a miracle? Isn't that sad and pitiable? I don't say it aloud. I don't want to sound pessimistic, or too proud. Both attitudes are frowned upon in Australia. But last-minute reprieves were not a feature in my previous lives.

'Death is an unavoidable certainty. Why choose to suffer beforehand?' One of my bad habits: insisting on getting an answer. Impolite in my adopted country. The doctor waits again, sensing more is coming. Or perhaps he doesn't know what to say.

'What if I don't want anything done . . . but to just . . . wait?'

'That's unusual, but if that's what you want, we're here to

help you with palliative care when you need it.'

'Morphine patches . . . ?'

'Possibly, but usually at the very end.'

He clears his throat. For a moment he seems uncomfortable with our conversation. Is that likely? He's probably had hundreds of these. He is only a little younger than me, if at all.

'There are various things,' he continues, 'but it is perhaps too early to talk about it right now. I suggest you give your cancer cure a proper thought first. We can talk again then.'

'Right . . . I don't want to seem stubborn or rushed, but, you know, I've thought about this before. My mother died of cancer. I've seen what cancer cures do to people. And I don't mean losing hair, even though that in itself must be frightening. Being nauseous for months and years on end . . . that's not life.'

He smiles. 'People are different.'

'I feel like you're talking about someone else. I guess I'm still "in denial". Isn't that the first stage of . . . grieving? An unwillingness to accept bad news?'

He doesn't answer. This is a matter for psychiatrists and counsellors, not his specialisation. I am taking his precious time. He shrugs again.

'Is someone with you? Are you okay to go home?'

'Sure . . . a year gives me plenty of time to get there.'

A lame joke, I know. But what do you say? The alive and the dying do not have many jokes to share. The grim reaper that stands guard next to the chosen one limits the range of topics.

## 2

At first, upon receiving the diagnosis, I thought the knowledge would soon sink in, with terror. But it hasn't. At least not yet, after a couple of months. I am not sure whether to wish for a little more time. 'A year' is just the handsome doctor's educated guess, an average. But the diagnosis brought clarity: here's my final, natural death foretold. And I'm not going to resist.

Do people really admire those who have a 'battle with cancer'? Journalists have promoted it into a dull, sentimental cliché. Shall my quick surrender be judged? It's deemed proper to be troubled by the thought of one's own death. It shows that one values life, and this is a normal way to be. Be grateful to be alive! Yet life is suffering, the Buddhists got that right. But perhaps it's natural to choose *something* over *nothing*, even if it is suffering. *L'être et le néant*, the insoluble puzzle: it's now about me.

I am fifty-eight, not properly old yet, perhaps not old enough to have the whole world's permission to die sooner than absolutely necessary. I've already lived a five-year bonus over my mum, who died of breast cancer. Because she was only fifty-two when diagnosed, we all pressured her into living, into the 'battle with cancer'. After six months, she was a shadow of her usual self. I felt we were wrong about urging her to try everything. She should have died the way she lived, by her own decisions, a strong woman, rather than weak, defeated, emaciated.

Because, you know what? Not trying to extend your life as much as medically possible gives you an upper hand in the game of life and death. It's like walking out of a relationship. Being a dumper is always easier than being a dumpee, right? When it's your own decision, the feeling is different, it is easier to bear the consequences. If I decide not to beg my treacherous body for a few more years or months on Earth, then I'm in charge.

Am I being mean, am I missing something? Some of my friends probably see my take on death as a haughty attitude, or hiding my true feelings, or even not understanding something important. Perhaps it would be nice to have faith, then it would all be clear, but having grown up in Eastern Europe in the heyday of communism, this has not been my lot.

People have the right to want to live, it's natural. Us rich Westerners are even a step ahead, we're at the cusp of wanting to be immortal! All these super-treatments and spare parts! Even senolytics! So why the hell not? Someone has to use them, be a test case, a guinea pig for medical science. Live on and on, as an embodied triumph of scientific medicine. I'm being ironic. Perhaps even sarcastic. It's not appropriate. In Australia, people call it 'cynical', and it is only rarely meant as a compliment, despite the nation's highly developed sense of humour, the dry variety, which I love. I've never figured out the difference between a 'wry sense of humour' (good) and 'cynicism' (bad). Is it just a matter of who's talking (men are better tolerated than women) and whether we like them?

I won't live to be truly old, leaning over a walking frame, long grey hairs growing out of my chin because I cannot see well enough to pluck them out or I just stopped caring. Arthritic fingers picking through my pill tray each morning and night. Being given a long list of forbidden foodstuffs. It may be a good thing to skip all that and proceed to the next stage. In which you, body, will become pale, still and stiff, having moved to the realm of no pain. Switch me off, stop the ticker, fine by me.

An unexpected diagnosis though. I did all the right things. I fought hard against bodily entropy: healthy eating, exercise ... but it creeps and spreads nonetheless, invisibly, in the murky depths of the body machine and then one day – snap! Have I somehow abused my ovaries? I had several pregnancies in my twenties. One abortion, two miscarriages before Bruno was born as the happy ending. I'll never know. But I'd like to know – there is a reason for everything, there must be. My boyfriend

Bertie, a scientist, says things can happen randomly. But this does not satisfy me.

## 3

Four years ago, at age fifty-four, as my periods became irregular, then entirely unpredictable before ceasing altogether, I started having vivid dreams. In every dream I was a young woman, Francesca, a name that assumed national varieties because each life I lived in a different country. I always inhabited a similar body, tall and slim (not necessarily an ideal of beauty centuries ago) and an inquisitive mind (which has never made the life of a woman any easier).

At first, shards of dreams started cutting into my consciousness during the day, at random moments, sometimes stopping me in the middle of a sentence, distracting me during my waking hours. A sudden déjà vu, a shadow whispering and tugging on memory, but hard to catch. The sequences from the dreams mixed with everyday reality. Gradually, I could retrieve and remember not only isolated images, feelings and fleeting episodes, but longer sections and chains of events. I could recall conversations especially clearly, like listening to a recording. The memories were the clearest in the morning. Just as well there was no-one around to distract me, and going to work could almost always be delayed. After a few weeks of such practice, I could lie in bed with my eyes closed, focus my attention, and see stories unfold, like movies playing under my eyelids. It became nearly effortless. I would wander into the study in my pyjamas and write notes – encounters, impressions, feelings, landscapes – the raw material for the story. Sometimes it felt as if the text forced itself out through my fingertips as they flew across the keyboard. I barely had to think.

It was exciting: I had a secret parallel life. Occasionally, I worried I was losing my mind: early-onset dementia, or the wires shorting and sparking, pressed by a tumour? I didn't talk to anyone about my dreams; the whole thing was just too weird.

And now, after my diagnosis, if from time to time I feel a pang of existential angst about my impending exit, I remind myself that I have lived a great deal. I've only ever lived as a woman though, which is unfortunate. It is easier to be a man. I've said this many times, with some conviction, but then who knows? It's unknowable. I lived as a woman for 186 years – a young and attractive one for most of that time, but, as it turned out, that did not make things any easier. Always married, as a matter of course, but only one truly happy marriage. Boris was a dream, a breeze from wonderland. He was sparking with creative energy in bed and outside it. We were never bored with each other, never indifferent to each other's presence. Was it because we were still young when we died together? One in all the six lives – is that below average? Marriage was not invented to make women happy. No, I'm not bitter! I probably had a better deal than most.

Six lives, spread over several centuries. My current life began in 1962 in Ceausescu's Romania. I married westwards, to a Croatian, and ended up in Australia, one of the strangest but most predictable countries on Earth. No wars, no revolutions, no political assassinations. Who is to complain about that? The greatest excitement, a notch above Footy Grand Finals, takes place if the Reserve Bank lifts the interest rates by a quarter of a per cent. I do love you, Australia, and your polite people patiently paying off their mortgages. I got a good deal with you.

In my first life, I was a Sicilian midwife accused of witchcraft in 1692, then reborn into the Amsterdam bourgeoisie some decades later. Next, I was a Provençal country girl suffering

7

through the aftermath of the French Revolution. Reborn again in Victorian England, my dream of becoming a doctor seemed close, but fate intervened. In my fifth, Russian life, I lived under Stalin, a wife of a dissident artist. Stalin, then Ceausescu – a rather poor choice by whichever higher power delivered me there.

Why were events, people, thoughts, feelings, presented to me in dreams? Who chose the episodes? It was a great gift, no doubt, to discover that there was life after menopause, and not just one, but six! A gift from whom though? How did I deserve it, not the lives themselves, perhaps everyone gets reincarnated, but the revelation? I tend to think one has to deserve everything – cosmic justice. A nice thought, but a rather silly one, I suspect.

Time is running out. I need to write down my story, the six lives, without delay. I've been planning to do it, but I procrastinated. I was busy, a full-time job, and it is all too easy to get distracted these days. The end-of-life practicalities are being sorted: a legally certified last will, and I need to finish decluttering my house. It would be embarrassing to leave behind those decades-old clothes and shoes, a pathetic elegance from times and places past. I'll be ready soon. Shall I choose my funeral music? It won't be a proper funeral anyway, just a few friends seeing me off at a crematorium. Still, one cannot risk some cheesy music chosen by a funeral director. Am I being vain beyond the grave?

# 4

I don't see many people these days. Even when we're not locked up by our vigilant government, the pandemic is a great excuse not to visit a terminally ill person. I announced I didn't mind seeing people but they would not have it. Sonia is one of those caring, responsible people who agrees with our government that no-one should die from Covid.

'No problems with Covid as far as I'm concerned, Sonia. I'll die soon anyway.'

'Oh, don't say that, Francesca!'

'Why not? It's true. Look, death happens to everyone. And I'm sure it's fairly easy to be dead, don't you think?'

Silence on the other end.

'Sonia? Are you there? I am sorry! I didn't mean to be . . . whatever I was just then. I hope you don't mind.'

'No, no, of course not. I'm just sorry.'

'Oh, don't be. Sorry about what? I have lived quite a bit and had some good times. I have no debts; my child is a grown-up; and I buried my parents. Therefore, no huge drama. The world can continue without me.'

'I'd better let you have some rest. Sorry if I've upset you.'

'No, you didn't upset me! I am not upset, Sonia. I'm just like that. Ironic. Cynical. Sarcastic. Rude . . . whatever. But death is inevitable. It's just that mine is already visible on the horizon and yours is somewhere in the hazy distance. I'll avoid old age, isn't that a bonus? I'm sorry, I see I'm digging myself into a deeper and deeper hole!'

I suspect that, at that point, Sonia did not feel sorry for me any longer.

'Oh, okay then Francesca. I'd better go. Paul will be home any moment. I need to put the dinner on. Take care, I'll talk to you soon.'

'Bye Sonia! Say hello to Paul. Thanks for calling!'

I take a deep breath. She did upset me a little, actually, and I probably upset her too. That's what friends are for, among other things. I feel a little sad and alone for a moment, but I get over it quickly. I trained myself over the years. Sonia's conventional, almost robotic manner is widespread, it's not her fault. But I like to talk to real human beings, not to culturally programmed robots, who abound among my highly educated friends. A personal approach, please – if you're my friend, then know me. See me, feel me, touch me, instead of carefully avoiding mentioning death because 'it is not nice'. And if I mention it, I come across as rude or unpleasant or God knows what. I hate elephants in rooms. What a great concept, especially useful among Anglo-Australians. When they talk to each other in polite understatements, there is often an elephant in the room. In formal situations, nearly always. At work, at nearly every staff meeting. In Romania and Croatia, there are fewer elephants in rooms. Those rude, blunt people from the Balkans shoo them away quickly. With my old friends, we'd talk freely, without tripping over the beast. But I'm not there and it's much harder to do it over the phone.

Those less persistent, less dutiful, less empathetic, or perhaps just less masochistic – they send text messages. 'How are you today, Francesca? Hope you're feeling well! I hope you get out to the garden – the weather is just lovely! Love, Suzana xx.' An easy cop-out. I say this without bitterness, such is life! Filip, my ex-husband, keeps forwarding jokes and funny little videos. I appreciate this honest admission that he himself has nothing interesting or useful to say.

My favourite Biblical story, the deepest story: Adam and Eve being expelled from paradise. From the paradise of not-knowing to the 'human condition': convulsing in the solitary confinement of our minds, condemned to think, to know our decline and mortality, doomed to unrelenting consciousness. Even those who manage to cushion the inevitable misery with money, love, duty, meaning, good deeds, debauchery, or just some happy brain chemistry, even those are at least dimly aware: humans are cursed with the eternal, all-encompassing loneliness. Each one of us in their own self-contained universe. Singularity. The stuff inside our heads is all there is: the only reality, each different from another. Many years ago, a counsellor told me to learn to meditate. It seemed a good way to have regular breaks from the hamster wheel of consciousness, but I've never succeeded.

# 5

I am on sick leave. My boss cannot disclose my medical condition without my consent, which I have not given. I'm trying to avoid tedious phone calls and free my colleagues from the duty to offer interest and sympathy. It has worked so far. It's peaceful at my place. I'm alone, well, mostly alone. Bertie visits regularly and this gives me a precious sense of not being *really* alone. I have valued his part-time presence over the past decade, and now I value it even more. He comes over three times a week, brings groceries and cooks. We eat together. He always leaves the kitchen nice and clean. I find the title 'boyfriend' somewhat ridiculous for people of my age, but I also dislike 'partner', it's too businesslike for my continental European ears. His status is now harder to define, because he is now paid to take care of me. I am leaving him a hundred grand in my will. There is no inheritance tax in Australia, so this is a better way to do it, and it is decent pay for a part-time job over a year. He promised to hang around as long as needed in case a year was an underestimate. Of course, this arrangement was my idea. If he suggested it, it would be a tacky deal. But given I suggested it, it seems a great idea. Curious, isn't it?

Bertie was shocked and saddened by my diagnosis. He didn't say *that* of course; this is what politicians say after mass shootings and other national and international catastrophes. But he truly was. I was touched – someone is sorry about my impending exit. Does everyone get this much? The 'bereaved families' certainly put on a show of feelings but ... Anyway, Bertie even uttered the word 'shit', which he barely ever does – he is genuinely polite and never swears, never raises his voice. His real name is Norbert, his European mother's choice, but luckily, as soon as he started kindergarten, a sensible teacher decided she'd put him out of his pompous name's misery.

Bertie gave me a hug, a long, warm hug. It felt like true compassion, and sorrow. He seemed confused too. What now? We were planning to start living together when I retired. The look of fear on his face could also mean 'Will I get cancer too?' But perhaps not – it's easy to be wrong about other people's feelings.

'Don't worry, you don't have ovaries,' I said.

'But I have a prostate!'

Indeed – he's taking his time in the toilet lately.

He must be at least a little repulsed by my news. He knows very well that cancer is not contagious but then the ovaries, of all things! And what about sex? Do terminally ill people still want and have sex, and women with ovarian cancer more specifically? Suddenly, from a comfortable and well-practised *pas de deux*, we are thrown into an unmapped land.

Was he tempted to succumb to a male instinct and run off, block me out of his mind? I know of more than one such case. Perhaps men are just not as emotionally resilient, rather than simply being uncaring bastards? And how do you ever tell the difference? The older I am, the less sure I am about anything. But Bertie wouldn't do something so shabby, even without our arrangement.

I felt sorry for him, he'll soon be abandoned; that's why I suggested the new deal. He accepted after a moment's hesitation. It was a clear and honest deal, expressed in numbers, no tricks and traps. Bertie is Anglo-Australian, and he recognised this instinctively as fair and appropriate. The deal provided a clear blueprint for my last year of life and his role in it. Because, deep down, I wasn't sure I could count on his love transforming from eros into agape on cue. He might have started avoiding me. I couldn't risk the disappointment and bitterness; it would distort my writing. I would have left him some money anyway, so why not also use the money to serve both of us while I'm still around? Bruno has a good job and he's not greedy – he won't mind. Bertie has struggled with the money side of things in recent years, and I knew he'd welcome an opportunity to 'have a job'. And I know from experience that even an extreme scribbler could not spend a year alone, inside their head; there would be crisis, the writing would stall. Only Proust could do it that way, the miserable bastard! And I need some domestic support in order to have enough time to finish the book. Towards the end, I may need more than just time-saving support. But I promised I'd keep that stage short.

## 6

How was I able to make such a promise, you may ask. Well, a large part of my peace, if peace it is, comes from a lucky encounter about a year ago. At a Romanian movie night in one of the colourful little bars that abound in downtown Melbourne, I bumped into Moira, an outgoing, feisty, no-nonsense woman, slightly younger than me, and we clicked instantly. Moira will be my death-on-call. She will provide a barbiturate injection. We have a plan. She'll visit when the end is near (deciding when will be my call, I hope I'll recognise the signs!), we'll have a brandy, clink our glasses and say *noroc,* have a chat. Is small talk possible just before a lethal injection? I'm not sure. But we've covered the meaning of life and death many times over the past months.

I'm sure neither of us will go shmaltzy. Moira won't fall apart, she isn't a person who indulges in sentimentality. If you grew up under Ceausescu, you're tough. We agreed it would be like seeing me off on an overseas trip. And then, just a little pinprick and it will be over. There will be no traces of her visit, no witnesses, no fingerprints. She'll prepare everything with surgical gloves on, wash her glass and put it back in the cupboard. She must cover her tracks, lest a coroner make a fuss over 'assisted suicide'. I'll ask her to make sure my eyes and mouth are closed so I don't look scary and grotesque when Bertie arrives. I must think of a way to prewarn him. He has my keys and will be due to visit the next morning, we'll plan it that way. He may be shocked to find me dead and cold in my bed, but I cannot tell him in advance. He supports euthanasia in principle, but I know he'd prefer not to be involved in the illegal business.

Moira is not an old friend, she doesn't owe me anything, and I'm immensely grateful she agreed to do this. My oldest friends, Monica and Sofia, are in Romania. Sofia is the head of a hospital department: high enough up the food chain to be able to procure just about anything. Sofia administered morphine to my mother many years ago so she could go peacefully through her final night. Perhaps it is easier to have a plan like this with a not-so-old friend. Moira works as a vet in the horse racing industry. What can kill a horse will kill me too.

## 7

Until then, a collection of pills is at the ready to keep me going. I didn't ask for any pills. It's assumed that you need them if you have a terminal illness. For a start, knowing you'll be dead soon is considered depressing. Doctors are not misers when it comes to handing out prescriptions. GPs now work on fifteen-minute appointments: a conveyor belt of worried little people wanting attention, trusting white-coated expertise and even hoping for compassion. All that in fifteen minutes? Not a chance!

What I got instead was a script, or several. I smiled at my GP, a woman a decade younger than me. It wasn't her fault. I sloppily folded the prescriptions, three in total, and dropped them into my handbag. Sleeping pills, anti-anxiety pills and Oxycodone, just in case.

'Yes,' I said. 'I understand: Xanax is not to be taken together with the Oxycodone. The opioids should not be mixed with benzodiazepines.'

Why give them to me together, then? I didn't ask.

Anyway, I pop a Xanax each day, half in the morning, half at night. I was reluctant at first, I feared it would dull my thoughts, but I found it made my mood more stable. It eliminated the darkest layer of melancholy. Some days I feel a lump in my stomach or tightness in my chest. The oncologist, looking at scans, says that, for now, this is all psychological. Emotional. So perhaps I'm not accepting my death with a philosophical peace after all, as I'd like to think. Or he may be wrong, and the cancer has already engulfed my vital organs like a noxious weed taking over the garden, strangling rose bushes and fruit trees. The parasite always wins; a cellular wisteria adorning everything with a sinister purple bloom.

Perhaps I'll be one of those miraculous cases ...? Oh no. No, no – I really shouldn't fool myself. I wouldn't even want to live to a ripe old age. I'm not prepared for it. I'm too vain, too proud to be an overlooked old lady people listen to out of politeness.

Now that all my friends know I have little time left, it would be rude to live on and on, exhausting everyone's patience.

## 8

It's nice to connect with clever people, dead and alive, whose thoughts are carefully considered, filtered and edited: I read. Books. Stories. Even an occasional well-written blog or essay. A pity people in the flesh cannot be as refined and interesting as the written-down people, and we still need the former, the warm-blooded herd animals that we are. Our sophisticated minds are just one huge aberration.

At the very end of my time, I want to claim it for myself, unencumbered by duty to others. A hard thing to achieve for a woman: not serving others, and even harder, not worrying about them. Menfolk, children, elderly parents, cats, dogs. Does that change when you're terminally ill? I still feel, sometimes, that I'm being selfish. But my child has flown the nest, my parents are dead. I don't have pets. I am free to do whatever I want, and I am free to die. I want to use my newly acquired freedom, the nothing left to lose (remember Janis Joplin, dead at twenty-seven?) to write down my six lives. If I want to make it a story, stories rather, comprehensible to others and worth reading, why shouldn't I? I'm yielding to my inner call, the luxury that's finally achievable.

While I write, all is good. It makes me feel kind of normal, like everyone else, doing something, rather than being a professional patient. I write in the morning while I'm rested, fresh. As fresh as a 58-year-old woman with terminal cancer can be. I read in the afternoon and at night. I'm rushing to finish reading several books by Stanislaw Lem, a Jewish-Polish genius whose philosophic sci-fi stories are funny and wise. Isn't that the highest calling, to make people laugh … while also making them think? I struggle to understand all Lem's Latin expressions, many of them newly minted by his feverish, overdeveloped brain.

But would anyone want to publish Lem these days? His pitch would probably be rejected, and if he sent a manuscript and they bothered to look at it, they would go 'Oh no. Made-up words, Latin sentences, long explanatory passages! Dense prose! Meandering plotline! Who wants to read that?' Or Italo Calvino, another one I had to read before dying, who I loved but who irritated me at the same time, like an old husband; his most famous novel consists of ten chapters, each being the first chapter of a different novel. A mess today's publishers wouldn't look at for more than thirty seconds! Literary fashions change, and why wouldn't they? Buildings and cars were different a hundred years ago, fifty years ago, thirty years ago, so why wouldn't novels be? People want to be entertained these days! Fast-paced prose, dialogues, cut out descriptions, now called 'info-dumps'; simplify, cut out thinking! Think lite! But then why read books at all, when there are plenty of cat videos and celebrity gossip on YouTube?

My mind, meant to stroll down memory lane, keeps getting entangled in thorny-bush topics. What is hidden under the bushes? Golden nuggets of wisdom or cockroaches of shame, spiders of regret, venomous snakes of guilt, pretty bubbles of nothingness? Is this what the weeds of oblivion are supposed to hide, so they're better left alone? Doctor Freud would disagree. He thought it was worthwhile searching and digging away, excavating one's past, that it was curative. You cannot cure people from the human condition, Dr Freud! The case is lost.

The weeks are whooshing past faster than ever before. The sense of time has always been a mystery to me. It's late August, and it's starting to feel the year is drawing to a close. Christmas is already being mentioned. I am struggling, not against the illness, but against time, against the idea of time itself. I've never been able to just live, breathe, walk, sleep, eat, relax. I've not been one of those lucky people that can fall asleep on the couch any time, or sleep on the train, on the plane, or sleep like a log in their own bed. I'm a victim, a full-blown victim of the vain struggle 'not to waste time'. Time is all we have, and I used to think my father was wise when he instilled this fear in me. Do not waste your time, do something with it . . . something useful! But what is 'useful', Dad? For whom? I've suspected all along that the real wisdom is to abandon oneself to time, to the present moment, to live in time like a fish in water, without noticing it. But I am only able to do this in rare rapturous moments, often when I write. People invented time to be continuously tortured and eventually devoured by their own invention. The cruel god Kronos eating his own children. The human condition.

But the whole story must have a conclusion. And if there is *one* story, in what way it is one – in one life or over six of them?

# I: The Fire

## Francesca (1667–1693), Sicily

ON THE EVENING MARIA WENT into labour, she could hear a distant rumble. She first thought it was thunder, but it continued. In the small village of Croce Vallone, it could have always been *La Muntagna*; its steaming peak could be seen from the eastern end of the courtyard. Etna erupted often – everyone, even young people, had seen or at least heard it. The god Vulcan was hard at work.

With an effort, Maria got up from the kitchen table and opened the front door of the cottage. It was mild outdoors – not a biting winter chill, but a warm breeze, a gentle prelude of spring. The moment of unforeseen pleasure was followed by a sharp pain that cut through her belly. Maria knew what was coming, it was not her first time. She knew childbirth was nothing to look forward to, and motherhood could bring true heartbreak; she had lost an infant girl the previous year. No wonder childbirth was part of the original curse apportioned to women. She held onto the doorway. Grit your teeth and bear it, Maria!

'Lorenzo, I think it's time,' she half-whispered. Lorenzo was still sitting at the table collecting the last drops of *sugo* from his plate with a piece of crusty bread; a rocky-land peasant's habit not to waste any food. 'Go and get Nina and Aunt Margherita.' Lorenzo emptied his glass of red wine and rose, silent.

Nina was Maria's older sister, her rock and confidante, although they had little chance to see each other after they both married and lived with their husbands' families. Nina's first baby was due in summer. Better not to talk about it too early, older women advised – miscarriages were not rare. A woman had to be fortunate not to experience any, and to have no infants die. Margherita, Maria and Nina's aunt, was old, over fifty. She helped many women in the village give birth. Midwifery was the most respected but also the most mysterious female trade. Nina was about to finish her apprenticeship with Aunt Margherita, who would retire once Nina felt ready to take over.

Maria was lucky she had Margherita and Nina to help. Margherita's fingers were knobbly and her stooped back ached, but she was skilful and confident. Childbirth was fraught with danger. Some women bled out and died. Some died in the days after their baby was born, first shaking with chills, then falling peacefully asleep, their cheeks red with fever, until they stopped breathing. Some women became weak, quiet and dispirited after bearing a child, a shadow of their earlier selves.

## 2

The baby born that mild March morning was me. My mother told me that during her hours of agony, the tall dark headboard of the marital bed shook repeatedly. My birth was accompanied by *La Muntagna's* rage, but the strongest eruption anyone could remember happened about my second birthday. Whenever she told this story, my mother's eyes and arms would open wide, showing the enormity of the mountain. In March 1669, *La Muntagna*, magnificent and dangerous like fire itself, destroyed ten villages in an avalanche of rocks and hot mud, but our village was miraculously spared. To my mother, I was therefore *la bambina di fortuna*, 'luck's baby'. A thick layer of ashes covered Croce Vallone, but no damage was done. It only took some heavy spring rain to wash it all away for the world to regain its colours. Each year around my birthday, swallows and storks returned from Africa and remade their nests under the eaves of our roof and on the top of the chimney.

When I turned twenty-one, still unmarried, my mother said I was much like my Aunt Nina. Not only was I preparing to be a midwife, the third generation in our family, but I also shied away from marriage.

Nina married late, just short of twenty-five. She'd already been written off as a spinster. She could have remained unmarried and looked after her parents, but what life is that for a woman? Her mother felt sorry for her. No-one wants an unmarried daughter – it is not a family shame, but it is a failure. But then one summer's day a young widower from the next village turned up at a local fair with his horses. Horses! Most people were happy if they had a donkey or a mule, enough sheep to keep the family fed, one 'domestic' sheep at home for milk and chickens for eggs and holiday roasts. Those better off would buy a piglet in early spring and feed it until late autumn, then slaughter it and eat it, sparingly, throughout the winter.

Uncle Giorgio was mild-mannered and a little shy, an unusual man. His wife had died in childbirth and the baby boy did not survive his first day. When Giorgio learned that Nina – pretty, a little too thin perhaps but that could be helped – was not married at twenty-four, he talked to her parents and that was it. This is how it happened, no courtship, no frills. Nina's parents – my grandparents – were delighted.

Nina was diligent and skilful in several female trades, and

a good daughter to her ageing parents. They had no son who would bring his wife to the family home to take care of them in their old age. But it was high time for Nina to marry; Maria, her younger sister, was already married, she was often reminded. Nina reckoned taking care of a man, a house and any number of children that God gives one must be harder than staying with one's parents and taking care of them when they are old. But a woman could not choose. If a decent man was interested in marrying her, this is what she had to do when she had come of age. It was normal. It was natural. A woman was in the world to bear and rear children and to take care of her husband. Aunt Nina was lucky with Uncle Giorgio. He was better off than most, a caring and gentle husband and a good father to their son.

My mother was right to compare me to Aunt Nina. Having learned midwifery from her, I also hoped to follow her example and marry a widower. A few young men expressed interest to my parents, but they were peasants – quite prosperous, like my parents, but rough and not personable. If I married such a man, I would have to work in the fields and tend domestic animals. It would be unlikely I could continue my midwifery trade. The work gave me independence; not only was I my own person, known to villagers for my skill, but I also earned. Most men did not like their wives to earn, even less as midwives. As they grew older and more experienced, midwives were sometimes considered peculiar, even witches, especially if they were not married. Unmarried women were the easiest target of gossip and malice.

Young widowers, with or without children, were not rare. Being a little older, they were usually better off and also more skilled at marriage. So that was my plan, refined by Aunt Nina's advice. I managed to linger on unmarried for another two years; during that time Aunt Nina and family moved to the outskirts of Catania, too far to see them more than once or twice a year, which saddened me. Aunt Nina understood me so well and loved me like her own child. I started working independently in Croce Vallone and nearby villages. My father was not happy about this and often grumbled about me having to marry while anyone still wanted me, but my mother defended me and often reminded him how important a midwife was for local women and families.

## 3

I met my fate one sunny day in May 1690. I accompanied my parents to the Pentecost Fair in Adrano to celebrate the day of the Holy Spirit. Not long after we arrived, a well-dressed man of thirty, the first grey hairs on his temples, appeared before us with an urgent expression on his face.

'*Buon giorno, Signuri*, I'm Andrea Cavallaro, I live nearby.' He was talking so hurriedly I could barely follow. 'I need help for my wife. *Per favore.* They say *la Signurina* is a midwife.'

His eyes rested briefly on me, but his gaze stopped at my father.

'My wife gave birth yesterday, but she is not well. I could not find the town's midwife. I apologise for accosting you like this, it's urgent. Perhaps *la Signurina* could help.'

'I do not have any tools or herbal remedies with me . . .'

'Please, I am sure you can help!' Don Andrea gasped, addressing me directly. The man was desperate. I did not know what to do. It was not appropriate for me to just leave with a stranger. I looked at my parents and they looked at each other.

'I have a horse and a two-seater. Please let *la Signurina* come with me. I will bring her back here as soon as possible.' He looked at my father again.

My father nodded. My mother moved towards me as if to

accompany me, but my father grabbed her forearm. '*Stare con me.*' My mother went limp and stepped closer to her husband.

Don Andrea's house and workshop were at the end of town, not too far from *Ponte dei Saraceni*, where densely packed houses start to give way to larger homesteads with farm-houses, workshops, spacious courtyards and gardens. Don Andrea anxiously flogged the horse and it took us but a few minutes to get there.

Rosa, his wife, was in bed, pale, breathing fast and shallowly. I touched her forehead; it was hot, but she was shivering with fever chills. Her mother had folded a pillow under her daughter's thighs to elevate her hips, hoping to stop the bleeding, but of course it didn't. The pillow was soaked in blood.

I knew what it was but could not help her without my long spoon with sharp edges, the *curetta*. Her womb needed cleaning; sometimes the placenta did not come out, or a piece of it was left inside, and this was almost always fatal. Bleeding, fever, death. Rosa had little chance of seeing the next day.

The string on Rosa's shift was loosened and her mother was placing wet rags on her neck and chest to cool her down. I sat down, pulled off the sheet, removed the bloody pillow and asked for another blanket to be placed under her buttocks. I crossed myself and pressed her womb hard with both hands. Dark blood gushed out, together with little pieces of tissue. Rosa woke up from her mortal slumber and groaned. Her watery blue eyes opened for a moment and met with mine but there was no light in them; she did not see me.

'How long has she been like this?' I asked.

'Since yesterday morning, may God help her.' Rosa's mother crossed herself.

My heart sank. There was nothing more I could do. I sig-nalled Andrea, who was standing next to the window, that

Rosa was in God's hands. Her mother started sobbing. The baby girl, barely more than a day old and hungry, was whimpering weakly. I took the baby from her grandmother's arms and placed her on her mother's chest, opening her shift. The baby found a nipple and started sucking greedily. She could not breathe face-down on a soft breast, so I asked Rosa's mother to help me turn her on her side. The sobbing woman propped another pillow under Rosa's back. The baby could now suck freely. Rosa opened her eyes again and her mouth twitched. Was it a smile, or did she want to say something? She took a gasp of air. Her last. The baby was sucking her dead mother.

Rosa's mother shook her gently.

'Rosa, Rosa, *mia ragazza!* Stay here! Stay with us!'

Rosa did not move. The baby, who lost the nipple for a moment, attached herself to it again. The three of us fell to our knees around the bed and prayed. Rosa's mother was shaking with sobs and her tears dripped onto the bedcover from her closed eyes. She threw her arms around her dead daughter. Andrea looked stunned. He had told me on the way there that Rosa asked for a priest last night when she started feeling weak. She did not want to risk departing this world without the last rites. Now the baby girl needed to be baptised.

'Mamma, please go find Padre Giovanni. For Rosa and for the child.'

The weeping woman rose on her feet and pulled herself together; there was work to be done. The baby was asleep. I lifted her from her mother's deathbed, wrapped her in her baby blanket and put her in a cot next to the bed. A wave of sadness and love washed over me at the sight and touch of the motherless child.

'You need to find a wet nurse, Signuri. She'll be hungry again soon.'

Andrea got up to his feet and crossed himself again.

I did the same. This could have been me. Any luckless woman.

'You don't need to pay me,' I said. 'I could not do anything. I'm sorry. I am sorry for your loss. *Povera Rosa! E povera bambina!*'

'*Grazie, Signurina, che Diu vi protegga.* I'll take you back to your parents.'

I nodded.

We walked out of the house and to the carriage in silence. The harnessed mare was fidgeting and stomping; there had been no time to free her when we arrived. We travelled back to the fair slowly and without a word, like a funeral.

# 4

Two weeks later, Don Andrea's envoy appeared at our door announcing his visit at a time suitable to us. This could mean only one thing: that an offer of marriage was coming. My father did not seem surprised. A widow was not allowed to marry again for at least a year, while she was in mourning and wearing black, but for a man, especially if he was left alone with children, remarrying as soon as possible was considered a proper thing to do.

The envoy was a widow from Adrano who knew everyone and who did matchmaking among other things. My parents inquired about Don Andrea's circumstances and gave satisfied nods to the answers they received from widow Salineri. Andrea was a son of a saddler and, having learned the trade from his father, developed it further into carriage building.

I made up my mind quickly. Regardless of the speed of events, in some ways I knew more about Don Andrea than most people knew about each other before they married. I had visited his home, been inside his marital bedroom. I knew his wife in her last hour. I held his daughter in my arms. He seemed a decent and hardworking man, and not unattractive. He had been devoted to Rosa and clearly saddened by her death, but a stepmother for his baby daughter was an urgent need, probably more urgent than a new wife for him, I thought. I felt I could embrace both roles with this man.

My parents sent their thankyous to Don Andrea and an invitation to 'visit our modest home'. My mother embraced me tightly after the envoy was gone; I think it was a mixture of happiness and sadness.

Our house was smaller than Don Andrea's, true, but it was well furnished and clean, with whitewashed walls. My family was more prosperous now than when I was a child. My father was a hardworking carpenter who built his repute in the village and further, in Adrano. He received more orders than he could satisfy. My mother kept his workshop and the house spotless and was like a mother to Paolo, my father's taciturn apprentice who, at fifteen, was still barely big enough to handle heavy planks and lift wooden chests for polishing.

I'm not sure if I've ever seen my mother sitting down to rest. She was always tending to everyone's needs, even needs we didn't know we had. For Andrea's visit, she prepared a feast of lamb meat *sugo* and *gnocchi*. I helped her make *cannoli* with the freshest ricotta we could find in the village. My father brought up a bottle of his best red wine from the cellar.

Just before noon on Saturday, Don Andrea turned up in his two-seater, dressed in his Sunday suit. He shook my father's hand and bowed politely to my mother who was, to my surprise, visibly awkward. He turned and took presents from the carriage: a beautiful piece of wine-coloured silk for my mother and a lovely straw hat with a white ribbon for me, as if foreshadowing my soon-to-be passage to the class of ladies.

Peasant women wore scarves and ladies wore hats. Everything about Andrea's arrival seemed right to me, with the sound of church bells ringing in the background, telling the faithful the day was at its middle and it was time to eat and then have a little rest. The sound of church bells made me happy three times each day – it was like leaving the earth and flying up to the heavens on their song.

The wedding was at the end of July. It was a small affair, away from the curious eyes of the townsfolk. Since this was Andrea's second marriage, we did not pass through the village in a loud procession, with musicians in front of the cortège, and people lining up the street throwing *confetti* at us, wishing us a fecund union. Andrea showed his care for his baby daughter by securing a stepmother for her sooner rather than later, and his respect to the memory of his late wife by having a subdued wedding celebration.

Andrea's wife had been dead for less than three months, so only close family on both sides were invited. A rich lunch was served on a long table arranged on the shady side of Andrea's spacious courtyard. It was hot, and a loud chirping of crickets accompanied the toasts. My mother wore her new wine-coloured silk skirt made from the fabric Andrea gave her. Little Antonia was in the village with a wet nurse, supervised by her maternal grandmother.

# 5

During the first year of our marriage, Andrea's trade flourished. He thought we should move to the centre of town. This would not just show off the success of his trade but also bring him closer to potential customers, the well-off townsfolk and their friends from nearby towns who needed his saddles and carriages.

He now employed four people and spent most of his days in the workshop on the outskirts of Adrano.

We bought a two-storey stone house in Via Spirito Santo, close to the church. Not quite a *palazzo*, it nonetheless had two balconies with wrought iron fences at the front and a larger terrace with stone balustrades at the back, on top of the stable. The main entrance had a stone arch that framed a heavy oak door with ornamental flowery relief. The seller was an older widow who had recently lost her husband, a town notary, and was going to live nearby with her eldest son's family. I was happy with our new house because from our attic window I could see *La Muntagna* again. I loved the magnificent mountain with its often-fiery edge brightening the north-eastern horizon.

We employed a maid, a girl of fourteen from Croce Vallone. Anna was recommended by my mother as industrious and modest, from a poor but well-regarded family with eight children. Even though she learned household chores and simple cooking quickly and was good with her hands, she didn't seem too bright and did not say much. Perhaps she was just a quiet type. She appeared scared most of the time; I wasn't sure why. I treated her well, like my younger sister. Her mother must have told her stories about corrupt townsfolk who would try to take advantage of her, to make sure she didn't give in to the charms of some sweet-talking young man before she knew what she was doing.

Married life did not put much strain on me. Andrea was polite and undemanding though he often looked troubled. I couldn't see any apparent reason for this. We lived in harmony, with no voice ever raised. Our intimacies were rare. In our marital bed, he would approach me without a word, and I would yield to him readily – after all, we were husband and wife. Andrea was neither rough nor passionate. Often, he seemed to me to be doing what was expected of him, rather than what he wanted to do. This suited me fine. I neither desired the *amore naturale* nor found it repugnant. I wondered whether our marriage would be blessed with children. During the first year of our marriage, little Antonia was mostly with the wet nurse or with her maternal grandmother who lived close-by. We saw her every Sunday and I grew very fond of the sweet, happy baby girl. Andrea of course expected we'd have more children, and I wanted that too even though, having seen other women in childbirth, a shudder of dread sometimes shook my body at the thought of going through the same.

On Sundays, when we were together, Andrea was usually absorbed in his own thoughts. I assumed his business gave him plenty to think about. He travelled a great deal in his light two-seater to neighbouring towns and villages to visit his clients, and further afield to Catania on his horse. I often asked Andrea about his trips, but he never said much, which sometimes frustrated me. I would have liked for us to talk to each other more, for our souls to be closer. My mother and my childhood friends were in Croce Vallone, Aunt Nina was in Catania. I didn't have anyone close to me to talk to.

Andrea was an honest and pious man. He never forgot to say a prayer before a meal. He would close his eyes when crossing himself and I knew he meant it. He believed God was giving all and taking all, as we deserved. A man, *Il Signuri*, ruling our lives from above, making fair decisions, punishing and rewarding us mortals? I was not so sure.

I wondered how Andrea felt and why he often looked melancholy. Did he miss Rosa? What sort of wife was she compared to me? I couldn't ask. I asked if he worried about his business, did he work too hard, were his workers good? He said all was going well. He told me not to worry. He'd come home from his workshop for lunch and sometimes had a little siesta afterwards. In the evening, he was tired, understandably. Usually, I told him which family had gotten a child if I was helping the wife, and he acknowledged the news, without much interest.

Andrea had reluctantly agreed for me to continue my midwifery trade. I presented it as helping others rather than a job. He was satisfied with this – women had to bear children and skilled help at childbirth was essential – as long as people did not pay me. If I worked for pay, people could think I was not a proper wife fully devoted to my husband, family and household. It was not right for a *Signura* to work for money. So instead of paying me, people gave me presents. For peasants this was the only way – they rarely had any money. But everyone was generous – happy and relieved – after they had gotten a healthy child. Usually, it was a whole *prosciutto*, or a large *fiasco* of their best wine, or a freshly slaughtered lamb. '*Per Don Andrea, per la casa*', they'd always say. My clients always delivered these heavy objects to our house and thanked Andrea personally for my help. Therefore, it was not my job but rather a family affair; I was happy for it to be this way as long as I could work, help other women and have a life beyond the idle life of a town lady, filled with concerns about a beautiful new hat or a fashionable dress made in Catania. My upbringing did not prepare me for such a life.

My newly acquired status as a town *Signura*, a *Donna*, was a source of some awkwardness. Most midwives were ordinary working women and by marriage I was propelled into a higher station. My husband had a well-earning trade, we lived in a fine house with nice furniture and a maid, we could hire a coach and a cook for special occasions, I dressed like a lady. Yet everyone knew I came from a humble family from Croce Vallone. Andrea himself was a self-made man. I was not status-conscious and formal, and people who didn't know me usually relaxed after a few awkward moments. They sometimes apologised for their modest circumstances. I always entered their house, and the room of a mother-to-be, with no interest in anything else but the woman about to give birth. I helped peasant women and ladies deliver their babies. After a year in Adrano, people were saying good things about me, and I was quite busy. This gave me a quiet but steady satisfaction and pride. I was grateful to Andrea for letting me continue my trade; not every husband would have. Perhaps it was the way we first met that convinced him it was good that there was more than one midwife in town.

My cool head in difficult situations and my propensity for light-hearted banter that helped people relax made me more popular than the other midwife in Adrano, Signurina Marcella. This was probably unfair, because she had decades of experience and a spotless record, and I had only worked independently for a few years. But people are ungrateful and superficial creatures. She had a significant limp that was getting worse over the years as her hips and spine suffered from the unevenness of her gait. She was skilful, ready to help and worked for a modest fee, but people said she was too serious and always looked worried. We greeted each other once, in the churchyard after Sunday mass, but I didn't know how to start a conversation, and she didn't seem enthusiastic. We couldn't discuss the secret women's business of giving birth, and somehow it seemed inappropriate for us to become friends even though I would have liked to have a friend like her. I was hoping to need her one day though. I'd been married for over a year, and I was nearly twenty-five, by which age most married women had several children. The dear little arms of my stepdaughter Antonia around my neck often reminded me of my own barrenness. My mother always asked, and I was sorry to disappoint her by having no news to report.

# 6

On a mild and sunny autumn morning, as Anna accompanied me to the market, a breathless, apprehensive young woman caught up with us, abruptly ending our moment of peace.

'*Scusi*, Donna Francesca ... my name is Angela, I serve at Don Peppo's ...' In a hurried, desperate whisper she asked if she could have a moment with me alone. I told Anna to wait and retreated with Angela to the windowless back wall of the nearest house.

'*Molte grazie*, Donna Francesca! I am a chamber maid at Don Peppo's.' She looked to the ground.

I knew the name – Don Peppo was a silk merchant and one of the richest men in Adrano.

'I think I am pregnant,' she whispered. Her arms were firmly crossed on her chest as if defending herself from an invisible attack. Her eyes welled up and a tear rolled down her cheek.

'I have told Don Peppo. The child is his. But he ... he will not help me.' She gave a sob. 'Once my mistress realises I'm pregnant, I'll be thrown out of the house and unable to find another job. And I'd never be able to marry well ... if at all. I will have to move to another town, away from all the people I know, and with a child, where will I turn?' She pulled deeper into the shade and turned to the wall. 'Don Peppo, he said, he said I must ... I think he has done this before ... Signura, you are skilled, you must know a way to ...' She looked up, facing my gaze for the first time. 'I have to get rid of the baby.' The tears now rolled freely down her face. '*Mi dispiace, Signura.*' She took a deep breath.

'I dread such a terrible sin, Signura Francesca, killing the fruit of my own womb, but I have no other choice. I was told you were a nice lady ...' Encouraged by my patient listening, she met my eyes again. 'I beg you, help me!'

Yes, Don Peppo was a middle-aged man, and this may not have been the first time that he caused trouble for his house staff. For a moment, I did not know how best to respond to Angela. Could I take the risk? I knew an abortion was possible, but it was painful and dangerous. What's more, I had never done it before, I explained to Angela.

But if I didn't help her, what would she do?

'I'm a wretched girl! You are my only hope – please, please help me!' she implored under her breath and grabbed my hand with her shaking hands. 'I do not dare ask Signurina Marcella … you're young … and a married lady …' Angela was trying hard to supress sobs, but tears rolled freely down her face.

I pulled out of her grip and straightened my shoulders. 'I cannot promise. I must think what to do. Come and visit me next Monday, during siesta, when fewer prying eyes are around.'

By then I'd have time to properly consider her request, I thought, and prepare, perhaps even seek advice from Aunt Nina in Catania, if Andrea should travel there during the week.

# 7

When Angela knocked on my door she looked pale, scared and even younger than the last time. I invited her in.

'How old are you, Angela?'

'Sixteen last month, Signura.'

'When did you last bleed?'

'Over two months ago … it was still summer … very hot.'

I rolled out a thick blanket onto a long chest in the sitting room for her to lie on and sent Anna to bring a pillow from upstairs and a washbowl of hot water from the kitchen. I prepared my tools and cleaned a long knitting needle and my *curetta* in hot water. The unfortunate girl seemed terrified but determined.

Her lips were bloodless. She had missed two months' bleeding, her breasts were ample, and she often felt queasy, especially in the mornings. There was little doubt about her state. She pulled a small silk purse out of her pocket.

'Five gold *scudi*, Signura Francesca, from Don Peppo.'

I knew he was buying my silence rather than paying me to help Angela.

Angela lay down on the bench and lifted her dress, visibly shaking. I sat next to her and squeezed her arm gently.

'*Coraggio*, Angela, it will not take too long. Take a few deep breaths. It is important that you calm down.'

I gave her a folded cloth soaked in *grappa* to suck and bite into. 'It will hurt, but you must be very still.' I inserted the needle as far as it could go and pushed, slowly. She twitched and whimpered into the cloth. But the worst was yet to come. As I scraped inside her womb, turning my *curetta* in all directions, Angela groaned, and fat drops of sweat appeared on her forehead. In less than a minute she started bleeding profusely. This was a good sign, provided it did not go on for too long. After I finished – I was hoping I had – I wiped her with a wet cloth and pushed another dry one, tightly rolled, between her legs.

'It's over.' I pulled down her dress and covered her with a blanket. 'Just lie there for a while. Make sure you keep warm.' She nodded, took a deep breath and closed her eyes.

When I came back to check on her a quarter of an hour later, her cheeks were rosy and she was fast asleep. A good sign. I let her sleep for another half an hour but then I had to wake her up, as Andrea was going to be home soon.

'Anna will take you home. Walk slowly.' I helped her to the door. 'Don't hurry, Anna, Angela is unwell. Let her hold onto you.'

The girls left arm in arm. Two sixteen-year-olds, both tall

and well-developed. Peasant girls usually put on weight when they started domestic service. Even if their mistress was mean, there was always more food available than at their homes, where they had to compete for their share of each meal with several ravenous siblings. Domestic service was not easy, but never as hard as toiling the fields. I looked at them as they walked away, hoping Angela's young, healthy body would heal itself.

The following afternoon I visited Don Peppo's. His manservant was in the corner of the courtyard chopping wood. There was no protocol for an unannounced visit, so I introduced myself and said I needed to talk to his master. He glanced at me, nodded and obeyed without hesitation. He disappeared into the house and reappeared a minute later.

'Wait here, Signura.' He pointed to a stone bench under a large oleander tree. The bench was cold, and the breeze was getting cooler at the end of September. I shivered. I was tense. Would Don Peppo listen to me, would he be offended by my intention to return his money? It took a few minutes for him to appear at the door.

'Signura Cavallaro.' He opened the door wide. 'Come inside.'

We sat down on a green satin-upholstered bench in the entry hall, under the stairs. He sat so close to me that I could smell wine on his breath.

'I am sorry to disturb your siesta, Signuri.' I edged away from him as much as I dared.

'Thank you for helping Angela with her . . . illness.' He was keeping his voice low. 'She seems to be well. My wife gave her a day of rest.'

'That's very good to hear, thank you. She needs to recover. She was in a lot of pain yesterday.'

'You're very skilful for such a young lady,' he said, looking at my breasts instead of my face. 'I know your husband, he's a master of his trade. I bought some excellent saddles and straps from him this past summer.'

'*Grazie*, Don Peppo. I would not like to keep you from your rest, I just wanted to—'

He seemed not to hear me. 'My daughter will soon have her first child. We may call upon you when the time comes. She lives nearby. They will move to Catania next year.'

'I will be glad to help.'

I got up and reached into my pocket for the purse with the gold *scudi*, but Don Peppo also rose from the bench and put his arm around my waist, leaning towards me. This could have been an innocuous gesture of affection if we knew each other well and other people were around. But we had only just met for the first time and here, in Don Peppo's deserted entry hall, it meant something else.

'*Buon pomeriggio*, Don Peppo!' I tore myself from his encircling arm and rushed through the door into the windy afternoon. Dark clouds were gathering, and it seemed like dusk even though the church clock had just chimed four times. I realised I was still clutching the purse in my hand. Clearly, Don Peppo was a man who did what he wanted and was used to getting away with it. Trying to return the money would have been taken as daring to contradict him. He would have taken offence. Now the coins in my hand testified to the secret I had to keep from my husband. A secret I shared with Don Peppo. Ah! I groaned in disgust and frustration.

I would have to hide the money from Andrea, because how would I explain why I agreed to be paid, and quite generously as well? I could not have argued with Angela about the money – she had no power to decide on anything. Some other secret would not have worried me perhaps; man and wife could have their own confidences . . . but this was a dark, pitiful secret.

Andrea was a devout man, and he would have been horrified if he knew I agreed to perform an abortion. I felt I'd fallen into a trap.

Sharing the secret with Don Peppo made me feel like an accomplice in his callous use of a young servant girl. Having met him, I was sure Angela was not the only one. Rich men were entitled to all the women in their house, save their daughters and daughters-in-law. And other women, if an opportunity presented itself – as I had just experienced. Rich men could sin with impunity. People talked, rumours and stories got out, but money could erase their sins one way or another. Their wives, if wise, turned a blind eye and kept quiet about it.

Two days later an errand boy knocked on our door. Andrea had just gone back to his workshop, and I was at the upstairs window, daydreaming about flying on top of *La Muntagna* and looking down into its fiery crater. Anna opened the front door and then rushed upstairs and knocked on my door.

'Donna Francesca, Don Peppo sent a message. He needs to see you at once!'

'It must be about that poor girl Angela.' I tied my hair with a needle clasp and grabbed my hat and cloak. The rain had just stopped, and the street was wet and empty. The few minutes to Don Peppo's *palazzo* were all uphill, and I was catching my breath as I knocked a brass lion head against the heavy oak door. Don Peppo opened himself and ushered me in, smiling widely. He didn't look like there was an emergency in his house. He grabbed me by the hand and led me to a room on the opposite side of the entry hall.

'*Grazie mia bella Signura*, for coming so quickly.'

'*Prego*, Don Peppo. How is Angela? What can I do?'

'Angela is fine, not to worry. Only, I'm not!' No sooner had I given him a quizzical look than he grabbed me around my waist and pressed me tight against his body. I felt his hot breath on my neck. He smelled of wine again. I jerked my head away, alarmed and repulsed in equal measure. He was shorter than me but thickset and strong and I had no chance of wriggling out of his grip.

'I keep thinking of you since we met two days ago ... Mmm, you smell sweet.'

'Don Peppo! What are you doing? Let me go!'

There must have been people in the house, probably his wife too, having her afternoon rest upstairs, but his grip was unrelenting. His hand slid down over my buttocks and upper thigh. Don Peppo was not used to being rejected.

'Leave me alone!' I screamed. He hesitated for a moment.

'So tall and proud, aren't you? Come my dear, don't be silly. No-one's yet regretted getting cosy with Don Peppo. I know how to please women, and I'm generous.' He pressed his moist mouth on my neck and then headed upwards seeking my lips. I groaned with disgust, turned my head aside and pushed him away with strength I didn't know I had. He must have realised at that moment that I was not going to let him have his way with me, and his grip lessened. He stepped back, looking at me angrily.

'So you're a virtuous woman, are you? One who doesn't mind killing a child in another woman's womb?'

'And you didn't hesitate to get your young servant in trouble, did you? You should be ashamed!'

I stood aghast. I suddenly realised how much smaller his sin was than mine in the eyes of the world. People would just shrug hearing about it. This is what happens! Such is life! A young woman tempting her red-blooded master around the house. No master has ever been ashamed of doing such a thing.

I rushed out of the house, overwhelmed by revulsion.

I realised my hat had fallen off when Don Peppo grabbed me. At home, I walked through rooms not really knowing what I was doing or what to do next. Now I had another secret with Don Peppo. One he would not be keen to divulge. Instead of yielding to his lust as he clearly expected, I was insolent and proud. I had offended him. He was the most powerful man in Adrano, more powerful than Padre Giovanni and the Mayor, Don Russo. They both valued Don Peppo's charitable donations. Don Peppo knew important people in Catania, and beyond. Andrea would be very unhappy if he knew that I was involved in such an unfortunate train of events.

I couldn't sit still or focus on anything else. I called Anna. She came upstairs from the kitchen.

'Anna, please make me some sage tea. Put a bit of grappa in it. I feel unwell.'

'*Subito Signura!* Can I do anything else?'

'No, *grazie Anna*. I'll lie down here on the couch for a little while. Just bring my slippers and a blanket *per favore*.'

# 8

After my unsettling visit to Don Peppo's, I made an effort to learn more about him, inquiring discreetly and asking Anna to do the same within her circle of servant girls. Don Peppo was known as a spiteful and volatile man. A feeling of niggling unease would not leave me.

Every Sunday I hoped not to see Don Peppo in church – perhaps he would forget about me? I certainly didn't want to be reminded of what had unfolded. It was November and the days were short. It rained nearly every day. I stayed at home as much as I could, and in brief moments when the clouds lifted, I'd go to the attic window to see *La Muntagna*. The magnificent mountain provided solace. One especially dark evening, no moon, no stars, just dark clouds and endless rain, Andrea arrived home quite wet and asked Anna for a change of clothes. After I greeted him, he started talking, which was uncommon.

'I heard from my apprentice that Don Peppo's eldest daughter gave birth to a dead baby this morning. A boy. Signurina Marcella was there but she could not help. Did you hear anything?'

'Donna Cosima? No, I was at home all day. *Povera Cosima!* How is she?'

'I assume she is well – I heard nothing about her.'

The people of Adrano, and even more those in surrounding villages, were a superstitious lot. Someone's misfortune was always an opportunity to spin stories. Cosima had been taken good care of during her blessed state. She was a healthy young woman, and her father was the church's greatest benefactor. The next day, rumours had it that her misfortune could be nothing else but an evil spell, the dark art – a witch's deed!

When Anna came home from the market with this story, I told her not to believe everything she heard. Still births happened, usually without an obvious reason.

A couple of days later Anna and I walked down Via Santo Spirito to the market and as we were passing three servant women talking, they went quiet, and when Anna greeted them, they only reluctantly nodded, looking awkward and scared. As we passed them, in the corner of my eye I saw one, and then the other two, cross themselves quickly. People did this, women much more often than men, to repel evil and call God to their aid. Yet what was there to repel, on the main road of Adrano, on a quiet morning?

I remembered this encounter a couple of days later when Anna came home from an errand upset and confused. She sat down on the bench next to the entrance without a word.

'What's wrong, Anna? Are you tired?'

'No, no, Signura Francesca ... What happened is ... I've just been accosted in the street by an older woman who I don't know. She told me ... I am so sorry Signura, but I need to tell you ... she told me I needed to leave your house at once because you were a witch ... a witch who killed Cosima's child in her womb.' Anna burst into tears.

So. The suffocating fog of nasty rumours was settling on me. I slowly sat next to her and put my hand on her shoulder.

'That's just a wicked gossip, Anna, it is not true. I am not a witch.' I didn't know what else to say to this simple peasant girl who visibly stiffened under my touch. 'Calm down. You do not need to worry.'

But I knew very well there was a reason to worry. In Adrano, the gossip spread like a forest fire. The next day, I went to visit a woman who was due to give birth soon, and women who would have greeted me politely in the street now turned away from me and crossed themselves.

More distressing detail arrived home with Anna: I was a girl from the village who was now a lady in town! Clearly, I was a witch who killed Andrea's first wife and enchanted him to marry me before his wife was properly cold in her grave. Antonia, the poor innocent angel, did not remember her mother and loved me because she was bewitched too – what else? At Don Peppo's, Angela was apparently coerced into admitting it was me who killed a child in her womb. She described what happened, without mentioning it was Don Peppo who sowed the seeds. Angela's reputation was smeared in order to ruin mine.

The story reached Andrea the following day, a week after Cosima's stillbirth, via his apprentice on an errand: I was a witch who could kill unborn children, and who also killed young Angela's child. I was therefore responsible for the death of Don Peppo's grandson. Who could know how to kill a baby in the womb better than a midwife who knew the secrets of pregnancy and birth and was also an evil witch?

Andrea burst into the house at midday.

'Francesca, is this true?'

'Of course it's not true!' I grabbed his hand. 'I didn't harm Cosima or her child! How could I? And why?' Andrea just sat there with his hands firmly clasped together and looked at me. Was he not convinced? I realised I would have to tell him all that happened. There was no other way.

After hearing the full story, the look of dismay on Andrea's face only deepened.

'So it is true ... You killed the baby in Angela's womb. It's a mortal sin!'

'Not out of malice or evil, Andrea! Angela was desperate and I was sorry for her. And don't forget, Don Peppo paid for it. Wait!' I rushed to the attic and brought the purse with the gold *scudi*.

'Look! It is from Don Peppo! Does not this make him a witch's accomplice?'

'It may well be,' Andrea conceded, 'but he will never admit it.'

Andrea was right. If it was Don Peppo's word against mine, I had not the slightest chance in front of any authority in the land.

We both knew the accusation of witchcraft was a serious one, especially when it came from an influential man such as Don Peppo.

Two weeks later, early one morning, there was a knock on our door. It was still dark outside. Andrea was about to leave the house. As Anna opened the door, I could hear a man's voice, and then Anna's hurried footsteps on the stairs. Then a quick knock on the bedroom door.

'Signura, they are here from Catania ...'

I rushed downstairs, my chest tight with bad premonition.

An envoy in a full horseman's outfit, his back very straight, stood at the door.

'Signura Francesca Cavallaro?' I nodded. 'The wife of Signuri Andrea Cavallaro?'

'Yes.'

'Is your husband present in the house?'

'Yes.'

Andrea appeared behind me.

'*Buon giorno, Signuri.*' The envoy greeted him with a nod and a click of the heels. 'I am here to serve you with the notice of summons from the magistrate of Catania.' He opened a scroll bearing a royal stamp.

'*In the name of His Majesty the King of Spain and his Viceroy, the ruler of the Kingdom of Sicily! On the 20th day of November, Anno Domini 1692, we have received an Edict of Faith from a pious citizen of Adrano in which your wife, Signura Francesca Cavallaro, has been denounced as a witch. A testimony to her evil deeds has been given. It will be necessary that she presents as soon as possible in the Catania Magistrates Court for interrogation, together with any witnesses that may be invited. The Court will decide whether she needs to be delivered to the Tribunal of the Holy Office of the Inquisition in Palermo.*'

He paused and lifted his eyes from the scroll.

'*The Magistrate of Catania will send a carriage tomorrow morning at this same hour. La Signura is to be ready to travel. Undersigned: Honourable Giacomo Paolo Asciolla, Magistrate of the province of Catania. 27th day of November, Anno Domini 1692.*'

He turned the scroll towards Andrea for few moments.

I felt a chill spreading through my body and my legs suddenly felt weak at the knees. I stumbled but I managed to sit on the bench next to the front door. I regained my composure after a few moments. Andrea and the envoy stayed silent. No-one moved.

'How long shall I stay in Catania?'

'I cannot say, Signura. As long as it takes for the magistrate to reach a decision whether you should return to Adrano or be delivered to Palermo.'

Don Peppo denounced me as a witch to the magistrate in Catania. I looked at Andrea. His face was tense but no other emotion was showing.

'Can I take my wife to Catania?'

'*Si Signuri*. It has to be tomorrow before noon.'

I understood Andrea could not just let the court take me away, not knowing where exactly and for how long. This would be seen as weak and negligent on his part. The husband had to protect his wife in good times and bad. I belonged to him.

I was not sure whether he was convinced of my innocence. He was a man of few words, and he rarely expressed his opinions or emotions. In truth, I had never been sure how much he cared about me. He was occupied by his business during the day and distant in our marital bedroom. Equally distant whether he slept in another room or when he decided to be carnal with me. His lovemaking was impersonal and even when there was no doubt that he enjoyed my body, he did not seek my soul. I did not feel he was making love to me, Francesca, but rather to a female body, to satisfy his natural urges and hopefully continue the family line. Perhaps he liked Rosa better than me? It was because of this restraint I never loved him in the way described in Neapolitan love songs. These songs were beautiful, almost always sad, and they made people cry. But marriage was not meant to be either beautiful or sad; there was work to do, children to bring up. Did it even matter now what each of us thought and felt? It might be too late.

In the morning Andrea took me to Catania. The two horses pulling our covered carriage were lashed by cold rain. There was no time to visit Aunt Nina's; Andrea would visit her later and tell her what had happened. When we arrived at the fortress that housed the Magistrates Court, a guard took my name, name of parents, of husband and the dates of birth and marriage. They then accompanied me to the cell. Andrea followed behind. When we arrived, I turned and looked at him. He came closer but did not hug me or kiss me. He held and squeezed my shoulders tight and looked at my face. I felt as if he saw me, Francesca, for the first time.

'*Coraggio, Francesca.* Stay strong. *Buona fortuna!*' Our eyes locked for a couple of seconds. This was our most tender and intimate moment. He turned back and left. My eyes welled up.

Andrea cared about what people said about him and his family. This was hard for him. When a suspicion that I could not bear a child was added to this shame, Andrea did not get a good deal with me. We had been married for over two years and I had not fallen pregnant. He was well-off and if I did not return, he could easily find another wife who could bear him children. Antonia was now in her third year and I loved her dearly. She called me Mamma. The thought of losing her, and her losing me, tore at my heart.

My cell in Catania was an austere little room. I was not locked in, but I could not leave the fortress. I was not charged yet, just under suspicion. After two days of waiting, I was called in front of the judge.

'Signura Cavallaro, you have been accused of witchcraft. This court of justice wants to hear your side of the story. I will ask you some questions.'

'*Si.*' I nodded. Was I expected to say something? I'd never been to the court of law before, least of all as the accused party.

'You are a midwife. You help women give birth. How did you know how to perform an abortion?'

'Cleaning of the womb the same way is sometimes needed after childbirth.'

'How do you know this? Not even doctors do. Who taught you?'

'My aunt, who lives here in Catania, is a midwife. She learned the trade from her aunt. My aunt and my great aunt taught me all I know about midwifery. My aunt Nina has a book written by doctors at the University of Bologna,' I explained. 'A sailor obtained it in Napoli ... in a brothel' – the magistrate winced – 'and when he returned to Sicily, he wanted to give it to a doctor but he came across my aunt, who was helping his sister give birth, and gave it to her.'

'Your aunt can read?'

'Yes.'

'And you?'

'I can read and write too. Aunt Nina taught me.'

'I see. Do you own other books?'

The judge seemed to be searching for a dark source of my knowledge. It was mid-December when he, after two weeks of investigative detention, decided I was to be transported to the prison of the Spanish Inquisition in Palermo.

# 9

I barely survived the hardship and humiliation of four days on a sailing ship. I was kept in a small cell, in fact a wooden cage under the deck. If I stretched diagonally, my feet would still stick out between the bars; in that sense, a cage was an advantage. A weak oil lamp that burned out of my reach could barely penetrate the darkness. The flickering flame was blown out every time a sailor opened the hatch to descend into the ship's bowels.

I had a blanket that smelled of rotten fish and a bucket that was emptied in the morning. I was grateful to be spared unwanted closeness with sailors; they avoided me, a witch, just in case. They rushed past in their sloppy coarse shirts kept close to their bodies by wide belts holding knives and cutlasses. The midwinter swell rocked the boat without cease. I was seasick most of the time, with short breaks for uncomfortable sleep while the ship was berthed overnight. I arrived in Palermo weak, barely able to stand on my feet. They transported me to the nearby Palazzo Steri on a cart and chained me to the wall by the ankle in a spacious, empty subterranean cell. My bearings gradually adjusted to the firm ground, and I could finally take a deep breath of the fresh air coming through a tall window. I was able to walk a couple of steps dragging the chain behind me.

Palazzo Steri, which housed the prison, was in Palermo's harbour. Through a high barred window, the breeze brought the salty smell of the sea. I could not see outside but I soaked in the view when we arrived: the sparkling blue sea and tall hills in the distance. The breeze also brought in voices from the harbour. It was cold, but at least there was fresh air, unlike in the bowels of the ship. At dawn, at noon and at dusk, I heard the bells from the nearby church of Santa Teresa. Church bells gave rhythm to daily life but also intimated a spirit beyond the mundane, a sphere of beauty, harmony and solace. They soothed my pain three times a day.

Sometimes I heard the guards talking about the important people upstairs. There were some locals among them, but the main inquisitor was due to arrive from Spain. They mentioned a priest who volunteered to help save the church from heresy and devil's associates, witches and sorcerers. I learned that the

Palazzo Steri had been the head seat of the Holy Office in Sicily for fifty years. Since before my mother was born.

It was to be my abode for the next four months. This was the most dreadful, but also the most blissful time in my life. The appearance of the Inquisitor General, my official interrogator, was not what I expected, not even something I could imagine beforehand, not in my strangest dreams. It caused the most acute upheaval in my body, heart and mind.

During cold January, they brought a bucket of hot embers to the large cell every morning. The days were short, often grey and rainy. One bitter evening, when it had been dark for a long time already and the heating bucket had lost any effect hours before, I was awakened from an uncomfortable slumber by a tremor; the bench under me was vibrating. For a moment I thought I was in Croce Vallone, under the erupting Etna, but it was just my dank stone cell in Palermo. The next day I overheard the guards talking about the earthquake, and over the following days I learned more details from their exchanges: a strong quake had destroyed Catania and many other towns in eastern Sicily, close to the Calabrian coast. Was Aunt Nina alive? Was she hurt, homeless? She lived in a big stone house on a hill. My parents in the village were more likely to be able to flee, but who knows? Did our house in Adrano withstand the calamity? Was Andrea well? Little Antonia? The stories mentioned thousands of dead people, buried under the rubble of stone houses. I could not think of anything else for days. I tried to learn more about the disaster, but the guards ignored my questions.

## 10

A couple of weeks after the quake, I was told that the Inquisitor General, my official interrogator, was to arrive on a ship from

Spain in early February. With a priest who served as Inquisitor Teólogo and a Jurist, the Inquisitor General made a Council that was soon to decide whether I would live or die. A guard told me that my inquisitor, known in whispers as the Black Moor, was renowned for his great success in interrogating witches, making them confess terrible stories about their orgies with the devil and their other evil deeds. After weeks of bad dreams triggered by the worry about my family, the anxious wait for the interrogator – would I be tortured? – added to the physical discomfort and aches and pains that multiplied in my body suffering from the cold and the poor prison food.

The same disgusting *zuppa* arrived every day, just enough to keep the prisoners alive. I could barely eat it. When all was quiet overnight, the rats scuttled about. Their squealing would wake me up and sometimes they ran over me. I yelped and shuddered with disgust when it first happened on the ship, but one got used to everything. Perhaps the rats were checking whether I was still alive, or already dead and edible. Male prisoners were upstairs; sometimes, when the clamour of the port subsided, I heard them swearing loudly. Perhaps at rats? Or just at their bad luck in being here?

When it rained, water came in and made the floor damp and muddy. The wooden bench that was meant to be my bed was too short for me, so I slept on the floor on a heap of straw covered by a rough, smelly blanket that a long time ago must have been the usual off-white colour of wool. When the floor was wet I had to use the hard, narrow bench. Two months into my imprisonment, the wind blowing in through the high window was becoming warmer and the days noticeably longer. But the temperature in the cell – originally the castle's cellar – had changed only a little. It was hard to sleep while cold. I asked a guard whose face seemed gentle, and who had never spat on me, to bring me another blanket, and he obliged. He left it on the wooden bench without a word. This was a little miracle that warmed not only my body but also my heart.

About that time, they brought in another *sfortunata*. Chained to the rough grey wall opposite me, she cried and yelled for hours, protesting her innocence. 'Why, why, why, what did I do? Please let me go, I'm an honest God-fearing woman, not a witch.' And so on, until she finally grew tired and fell silent.

'*Da dove sei?*' I asked quietly once she was silent for a while. She flashed her eyes at me angrily but did not respond. Did she, by some great irony, believe I was a witch? She looked like a peasant girl; her hands were rough and her nails dirty. The next day she started talking to me. Her name was Lucia and she was from Monreale, up a steep hill from Palermo. She used to prepare and sell herbal potions to help her parents' fledgling finances, but something went wrong and one of her clients died. 'He was very sick, he vomited blood, he would have died anyway,' she explained. 'It wasn't my potion that killed him. He was beyond help and I shouldn't have given him anything. But he was desperate and was paying well.' She sighed from the depth of her chest. 'I am a wretched girl! Even if they let me out of here, who will trust me to buy anything from me, who will want to marry me ...?' Her eyes filled with tears and sobs shook her body. I felt the weight of the world on my chest.

In early spring, the sun shone through the narrow window once a day. A moment of light, almost hope. Each day, as the sun climbed higher in the sky, the sunny patch was becoming shorter but lingering longer inside the cell.

How could Andrea give me up so easily? Did he have any idea what it was like in here? At the same time, I was dreading the moment when they would put me on a cart and drive me to the Foro Siciliano in the harbour, in a coarse shapeless dress, in chains, for execution. My Aunt Nina saw it once and could not forget it. She told me the woman's bare feet, scabby and bloody, were sticking out of the dress and her greying hair was in a messy bun. Would Andrea be there? If I were sentenced as a witch our marriage would be annulled and he could remarry even before I was executed. Did he really believe I was a witch? Did little Antonia miss me? Perhaps she did at the start, but young children forget quickly. She was two days old when her mother died; I was her mother, she knew no-one else. But it had been at least three months that I had been chained to this cold stone wall.

Oh, how I wished it would all be over soon!

## 11

It was early, just after the morning bell, when the Black Moor first visited my cell. He was tall, dressed in a black priest's robe and a black cape, with a large silver cross on a chain resting on his chest. Long curly hair covered his shoulders; it was silver in front, black at the back. When he came close and leaned forward towards me, a smell made a jolt of pleasure pass through my body. His hair smelt of sage, which I loved. I looked down, as if blinded by light. My heart was pounding.

'*Guarda me!*' he said firmly, in a Spanish way. 'Look at me.'

I lifted my eyes and looked at his face. What a face it was! I had never seen one like that before. In the light of the torch held by the guard I could see his green eyes shine. The torch was reflected in his eyes: flaming emeralds. His forehead was smooth; he only had two long curved lines around his mouth. He smiled at me and showed a line of good white teeth. He smiled! Why?

No-one had smiled at me for months. People in Adrano had

started avoiding me as the rumours spread. In Catania and on the ship, I was feared, despised and shunned. Here in Palermo, the guards sometimes swore and spat at me as they passed by, while crossing themselves at the same time. Sometimes they came threateningly close with their torches. 'You will burn, burn like this!'

And now the Black Moor smiled at me! His breath smelt as wonderfully as his hair – a mild, sweet, intoxicating smell of tobacco mixed with the natural smell of a man. A clean one. Peasants always smelt of sweat and sheep. The city men smelt of tobacco, and richer patricians, those who could afford the expensive potions, sometimes of perfumes that arrived from France via Naples. But no-one smelt like this, like a fragrant plant, with no trace of man-made potions. The Black Moor's skin was light, walnut brown, not dark as Don Peppo's Moorish coachman. He was neither black nor a Moor. Moors were not Christians. But his face had a hint of Africa. Spaniards were often dark and unusual-looking like that. His nose was noble and straight with large nostrils and his lips full and smooth, the upper lip slightly more prominent than the bottom one. His high forehead and chiselled chin gave his face a dignified, regal beauty; it was a face fit to adorn a gold coin. Yet when he smiled, his face acquired a slightly mischievous air. He asked my name and age, where I was from, whether I was married and had children, and how long I had been there.

'I will see you again tomorrow, Francesca.'

He then disappeared as quickly as he appeared, in several lissom, springy steps across the cell and up the dark, curving stairs.

I felt like I was under a magic spell. My inquisitor looked like a wizard, a person out of this world. A few minutes with him turned me into a tangle of curiosity, apprehension and anticipation. What would happen tomorrow? I did not know, but somehow I trusted he would not order investigation under torture. Thinking of him made me forget my miserable, uncomfortable state.

## 12

The day after my first encounter with the Black Moor, I was taken upstairs to a small, clean room. I was given a tub of warm water so I could wash myself. I was noticeably thinner; I could count my ribs and my shoulders and knees looked pointy. My left ankle was badly bruised by the metal clasp at the end of the chain. I washed my hair with the olive soap they gave me. It took a while to make a good lather and get months of dirt out of my hair. I rubbed hurriedly, fearful it was all a mirage that would vanish in a flash. They had given me a clean dress, a not too coarse pigeon-grey cotton frock. It was too short and too wide for me, and my thin ankles and long narrow feet were showing.

I had just finished untangling my hair when a guard came in, bringing some supper. It was already dark. I could immediately smell something better than the revolting daily *zuppa*. It was a large bowl of proper winter minestrone of beans, dried meat and *farfalle*, and a hearty slice of bread. The guard put the food on a small wooden table next to the bed, lit up the oil lamp in the corner and left without a word.

I ate greedily. That meal was the strongest pleasure of my life, thus far. When I had finished, I stretched on the bed, which had a comfortable woollen mattress and clean covers. Was I dreaming, or this was indeed a day of surprise pleasures? I was clean, properly fed, alone in the room, in a clean bed! I had started to doze off when a brief knock made me sit up quickly. The Black Moor quietly entered the room.

Without a word, he sat on a wooden chair opposite me and smiled, just like when we first met. I smiled back and waited, anxiously; there was nothing else for me to do. He looked down at my feet, bent forward and slid his fingertips gently along my leg, above my bruised ankle. He sat back again and looked at my face for a few moments, smiling. His green eyes penetrated my mind: I felt as if I was being drawn inside them. Leaning towards me again, he ran his hand further up my leg and over my calf to the knee, slowly. This was odd but exciting. I forgot to breathe. No-one had ever touched me like this.

'Did you lose very much weight? You are thin, and your knees stick out.'

'Yes, I did. Tonight's minestrone was the first decent thing I've eaten here. Thank you.'

He pulled his chair closer to my bed and bent towards me. He slid his other hand gently down the back of my hair – my clean hair! – and stopped at the back of my neck.

I started to feel hotter by the moment, even though my cotton dress was barely adequate in the cool room of the stone *palazzo*, with damp hair, on a March evening. He then sat on the bed next to me, carefully turned my head towards him, holding it with both hands, and kissed my lips. The smell of his breath and his hair made an intoxicating mixture. Was I dreaming? He was an inquisitor, my interrogator, and I was a prisoner. But the kiss and touch transported me to an entirely different land, a land of pleasure where nothing else mattered. He stopped and looked at me with a smile, then pulled me towards him and kissed me again, brushing his lips against my cheek and stopping at my mouth, which accepted his eagerly. The ecstasy of that moment was like nothing I'd known before.

He lifted his black habit, revealing his slim, muscly legs; then he sat me on his lap, facing him, and lifted my dress. He lifted me and gently pulled me towards him again, and I felt him slowly sliding inside me. When he slid in fully, I heard myself moaning and a few moments later my loins burst into a surge of pleasure waves. It was all utterly beyond my control; I was swept along by the sensation. The Black Moor inhaled deeply and pushed himself deeper inside, pressing me tight onto his chest. A few moments later he pushed me away gently and smiled at me again. He slid his hand over my breasts which enjoyed considerable freedom inside the sloppy dress. 'We did not have time for them.' His lips touched my neck. 'Next time!'

I was stunned and speechless. The contrast of what happened over the past couple of hours – the bath, the food, the lovemaking – with three months in a damp, cold, rat-infested cell could not have been greater. My body felt alive from head to toe; every inch of my skin tingled with pleasure. I thought I could as well die there and then: there was nothing more life could offer.

He left me in the upstairs room. I wallowed in the recollection of his touch, his smell, the shape of his lips, the warmth of his hands, the feel of his chest pressed against mine. I curled under the blanket with my hand pressed between my legs and was soon fast asleep.

I was now given a decent meal twice a day, and I could wash myself every day. Most days, they let me out into the courtyard for an hour. I could sit in the sunny corner protected from the cool sea breeze or walk around. There were no other prisoners outside; the guards and servants went about their business, flashing curious glances in my direction, but they left me alone. The Black Moor visited my cell daily, usually in the afternoon, for a 'special interrogation'. And indeed, every day he used a different technique, but everything he did was perfect. He could not have spent his life celibate! He was gentle, imaginative and attractive beyond what I'd ever imagined a man could be, even though he must have been over forty. Unlike many men of the robe at his age, he was slim-waisted, agile and strong. His exquisite face and penetrating eyes kept me enthralled. His next visit was all that mattered; life, death, the trial, the execution – it all faded into the background. I felt supremely alive, as if years of life were condensed into days.

It was not just the incredible skill and sensuality of his lovemaking. There was a sense of strength and peace about him. After realising I was educated and could read and write, he started telling me stories about his life in Spain and the cautious game he played with his employer, the Spanish Inquisition. He carefully built and maintained his status as an expert interrogator and was sent all over the Mediterranean to make witches confess. I could not imagine him using torture. Did he make love to them all?

He also told me about Palazzo Steri, where cages holding the heads of nobles who rebelled against Charles the Fifth more than a century earlier still dangled from the tower. I could stand up on a little table and see them through a tall window: the skulls were left high up there as a warning. When they were first placed there, he told me, ravens visited. Smaller birds could get inside the cage and peck out the eyes and the soft flesh from the cheeks, until they became clean bones bleached by the sun.

I was riveted by the Black Moor's story about his travels to the New World and always wanted to hear more. He baptised savages on tropical islands and taught them how to pray and worship the Christian God. He did not like those expeditions.

He travelled with rough, ignorant sailors, soldiers and officers who had little idea about what else to do with the natives but whip the men and rape the women. And worse when they were drunk, which they were much of the time. The missionaries travelling to the Americas were not the sophisticated theologians he kept company with in Spain. There was no-one to talk to, and his companions' behaviour was often sickening. Their most inoffensive pastime was teaching the parakeets to swear in Spanish. Upon return to Spain, after nearly a year in Las Indias Occidentales, he raised the issue of indulgent cruelty with the Spanish Crown. He was ignored. As long as the voyages brought back gold, silver, tobacco and spices, the royals did not care what their subjects did in their name in those faraway lands.

I did not think I had anything to tell him in return, anything that would be worth listening to, but he wanted to hear about my work as a midwife. The miracle of birth was outside men's reach and knowledge, he said. He listened without commenting. What should I tell him? That it was an agony to bring a child into the world? That women groaned, cursed, screamed, sweated, bled and not so rarely, died? Everyone knew this, I thought. Should I disclose that, for most women, the first sight of their baby was a moment of intense tension rather than bliss: is the baby breathing? Is it healthy and normal? The surprise about a tiny human that came out of their bodies. Usually, they had no energy for happiness, just the relief that it was all over. *Grazie a Diu!* A woman would always cross herself in deepest gratitude. All this seemed mundane to me, but he was intently focused on my words.

'Tell me more.'

I told him about Andrea's first wife Rosa, who died two days after giving birth to little Antonia, and about young Angela who was carrying her master's child, and how I freed her from the unwanted fruit of her womb. Then I told him the whole story, about Don Peppo wanting me to yield to his lust and my rejection of him, and his daughter's stillborn baby shortly after, leading him to accuse me of witchcraft. He nodded without commenting. He looked at my lips moving.

'I am not a witch,' I said. 'I wish no evil to anyone ... but the decision to help Angela was probably proud and foolish. I am paying for it now.'

He nodded again.

I was pleased that I could tell the whole story to someone who seemed to believe me. He was my official interrogator after all. He should know my side of the story.

## 13

The 'interrogations' continued for over a month. They started in March, the month of my twenty-sixth birthday. One sunny morning – we must have reached April by then as the days were already long and warmer – the Jurist entered my cell. He wore black robes and a dusty white wig. Two guards stood tall and straight behind him, expressionless and staring at an imagined distance. One of them liked to spit on me downstairs. I rose from my bed. The Jurist did not address me directly but opened a scroll and started reading.

*'In the name of His Majesty the King of Spain and his viceroy, the ruler of the Kingdom of Sicily! Their protector of faith, the Tribunal of the Holy Office of the Inquisition, in their seat of Palermo, announces on the 10th day of April, 1693: that all the witnesses have given their testimonies in the case of*

*Francesca Cavallaro of Adrano, born Francesca Lonante in Croce Vallone on the 11th day of March Anno Domini 1667, and that the interrogation of the accused has been completed. The truthfulness of the Edict of Faith received on the 20th day of November, 1692, has been confirmed. The accused is to face the final sentence in front of the Council of the Inquisition on the 11th day of April.'*

The Jurist then looked directly at me: 'Tomorrow.'

He turned around, the guards stepped aside in unison, and they all left. I heard the cell door locking this time.

Would the Black Moor visit today? I doubted it. A grave sadness sat on my chest so that I could barely breathe. My life was over. Instead of his visit, in the afternoon I heard terrible screams coming from downstairs. There was a different type of interrogation going on there. Was it poor Lucia? Or one of the more recent arrivals? I was spared the torture. Who knows why he chose me? There were three other women downstairs, he had told me. They were all older than me. Perhaps that was why? He chose me as a pastime on his Palermo mission. I was lucky. 'Luck's baby', my mother used to say. What were they going to tell me tomorrow? *The truthfulness of the Edict of Faith received on the 20th day of November 1692 has been confirmed.* This could only mean one thing: 'guilty'.

In the morning, not too early, the two guards came to escort me upstairs to the courtroom. It was a large, mostly empty room. The three men of the Inquisition Council sat in tall chairs, behind a long dark table like three black ravens: the Black Moor as the Inquisitor General, a priest serving as the Inquisitor Teólogo, and the Jurist who had visited me the day before. There was a notary, a small thin man also dressed in black sitting at the edge of the table, and two armed guards behind me. I stood in front of the Council, in the middle of the room, in my sloppy grey dress and ill-fitting black shoes. The Black Moor avoided my gaze. The Jurist read the sentence.

After I was proclaimed 'guilty of witchcraft', my attention drifted in and out. I looked at the stone walls with a large painting of the Last Judgment behind the Council, and dark-coloured tapestries on each side wall between large windows. I could see dark clouds gathering outside the window on the right and then, a moment after the verdict was delivered, a violent crack of thunder opened the skies and sent down the rain with a turbulent fury. The Black Moor twitched in his tall seat.

I had not left the building for months. I imagined how wonderful it would be to get out and walk the streets, rain or shine, among other people, unnoticed, on some unremarkable task, going to the market to buy fish, artichokes, tomatoes ... But my next outing was likely to be very different: me, the centre of attention on a cart, being driven to the harbour to be burned at the stake. I thought not so much of my imminent demise, but of my parents who stayed behind, if they had survived the earthquake, in pain and with the stigma of a witch daughter; Andrea ... was he going to remember anything good about me? And my sweet little Antonia ... I hoped they were all well.

I had not bled in March. Andrea and I could not conceive, but I could be carrying the Black Moor's child. Tears rolled down my face.

'Do you regret your evil deeds?' I heard the loud voice of the Inquisitor Teólogo.

'*Si*.' I had no desire to talk. What could I possibly say to the three powerful men who had already made up their minds?

'You are granted a visit by a priest. You can confess your sins, repent, and ask for God's forgiveness. Given the enormity of your sins, you will be committed to cleansing by fire on Sunday.'

Sunday? I did not know what day it was.

'The day after tomorrow,' said the Jurist as if he could read my mind.

At least there would be only two days of dreadful anticipation. The interrogation was over, the sentence delivered. I knew my exotic lover would not visit again. He never said goodbye. He did not say a word at the Court and his eyes did not meet mine. This hurt more than the sentence just delivered. The connection was severed. I was about to die, and he belonged among the living.

He never told me his Christian name. I never asked.

The priest who came to absolve me of sins and give me the final sacrament was a young man. He was visibly uncomfortable. I was likely his first witch. He did not dare to meet my eyes, and I found it hard to call him 'Father', but I made an effort. I was not scared of hell; my conscience was clear.

'Father, I will die young and my parents, or at least my mother, will be desolate. My aunt too, she loved me dearly ... I will be in their dreams many a night. But when they die, who will remember me then? My stepdaughter, Antonia, is too young; she must have already forgotten about me. My husband will want to forget, and he will, as soon as he finds a new wife. Twice widowed, the poor soul! And the inquisitor who made love to me day after day ... I was just one more to him. I will be forgotten ... and therefore, truly dead.'

The priest turned his head towards me in a sudden burst of resolve and looked straight into my eyes. 'Repent for your sins, my daughter, and do not burden your soul further with lies and imaginings on the solemn occasion of your last confession.'

## 14

My hands were tied together by a rope behind my back. The cart was barely needed – Foro Siciliano was only a few paces from Palazzo Steri – but this was the rule. The condemned was to be brought there on a cart, accompanied by two guards. When the guards put me down on the ground, the young priest who took my confession the day before came forward and gave me a large wooden cross to kiss. I turned my head away instinctively. A murmur passed through the crowd; otherwise, the spectators were unusually quiet and restrained. There was no bloodthirsty passion in the air, no yelling out abuse. Perhaps this depended on the weather, who knows? I knew they all stared at me. I looked above their heads, onto the sea, and thought about flying above its surface, as people thought witches were able to do. Then I turned my head back, where I thought *La Muntagna* would be, and all that I knew in this world during my brief time in it. The executioner held the end of the rope wrapped around my wrists and pulled me in the direction of the stake. I climbed up five wooden stairs. He then tied my ankles together and wrapped the end of the rope around the stake. His helper was approaching with a flaming torch. The crowd let out a louder murmur.

The Black Moor appeared to the right of the pyre, wearing a raven-black robe and a large silver cross on his chest. The shiny silver of his hair was lit red by the setting sun. He placed his left hand on the cross on his chest and made the sign of the cross towards me with his right hand. A blessing.

'We will meet again, Francesca.' His deep, soft voice was like a final caress.

I turned back towards the sea and Monte Capaci on the northern side of the bay. The smoke was billowing from the woodpile, wet from recent rains, badly stinging my eyes and filling my throat, forcing me into a painful, rasping cough. I could not see anymore. I could not breathe. My legs buckled and the rope cut into my wrists bound together behind the stake; the final pain before the darkness fell and silence welcomed me.

## Post Fabulam I
### Melbourne, 2021

I WILL BE CREMATED. *AUTO-DA-FÉ* IN the first and in the last life: a nice little symmetry. The purifying fire in both cases: for a witch, cleansing of evil in a public spectacle of execution; for an ordinary dead body, after an ordinary natural death, preventing unsanitary decay. Burning is better: I don't like the idea of maggots eating my flesh even though it may be nobler to push up daisies.

Ashes to ashes, dust to dust.

While Sicily was under Spanish rule, Palermo was an important seat of the Spanish Inquisition. For over 150 years, from 1623 to 1782, the headquarters was in the Palazzo Steri. Early this century, a Museum of the Holy Inquisition was opened there.

I visited the brooding, enigmatic city of Palermo years before my dreams of past lives started. I walked along the main street, Via Vittorio Emanuele, leading to the harbour. My friend refused to enter what she assumed would be a gory museum, but I felt I had to visit it. I knew about the horrors perpetrated by the Spanish Inquisition, but the Palazzo Steri was a real place where the horrors happened. When I got out of the building, I sat on the bench in the harbour looking at the sea. I did not move for a long while. I was petrified. Now I understand why: this was my own history, the museum, the harbour. This was where my first life ended.

In the sixteenth century, just as the continent emerged from the 'dark Middle Ages', the persecution of witches became a popular obsession all over Europe – ironic, don't you think? For nearly three centuries, it was easy to become a victim of prejudice, cruelty or revenge. The women who stood out by their intellect or independence were the ones most likely to be accused of witchcraft.

Even today, a woman has to think carefully about following her interests and passions, lest she offend or neglect someone, lest she be seen as selfish or downright outrageous. For a woman, it is not easy to be unconventional, let alone 'eccentric'. When the word 'eccentric' is used, it is almost always about a man. A quirky, interesting man, perhaps a creative spirit, or a usefully mad scientist. A man who dares to stand out from the crowd: he is tolerated, even admired. A woman, not so. Yet I managed to have it my way, eventually, in this life. Perhaps even most of the time; this is hard to say. But I feel I'm in control now. For over a decade, I've been a self-governing person as much as this is possible, socially and metaphysically. Perhaps that's why I feel reconciled with my impending death? I have, kind of, arrived in my modest little version of nirvana?

How much do my past lives and deaths inform this attitude? They seem to have cast a shadow over my consciousness even before the vivid dreams started. When I first learned about volcanos, in primary school, they exerted an intense pull on my imagination. It was odd to learn that something as wild and dangerous as an active volcano – one that erupted every few years – existed in over-urbanised Europe, on an island with millions of inhabitants, many thousands living just under it, on its wide slopes, within the reach of its rage. A hot mountain with bunker-shelters for tourists near the top. My first incarnation, the Sicilian Francesca, was deeply fascinated by the fiery Etna. She felt she belonged to *La Muntagna*. The word Etna has always sounded magical to me, like a woman with special powers. If I had a daughter, I would have named her Etna.

I wonder what happened to sweet little Antonia, three years old when I was taken to Palermo, never to return? Did Andrea find a new wife who loved him and bore his children? I will never know.

# II: The Stairs

## Fransje (1711–1737), Amsterdam

ONCE WE WERE MARRIED, JOHAN and I were to move to a new house on the western side of the Oudezijds Voorburgwal. A narrow lane, the Enge Lombard Steeg, led west from our house towards the Rokin and further into the network of concentric Amsterdam canals. Our street stretched along a straight canal for nearly a kilometre to connect the Athenaeum Illustre, the highest school of Amsterdam, with the port. We were at the very heart of the city.

The reddish-brown stone façade of our five-storey house contrasted nicely with large, white-trimmed windows, three on each floor and one on top at the steeple. Stone friezes radiated from the top edge of the windows, as was the fashion of the day. A prominent '1735' was divided in half by a pole affixed to the top of the house for hoisting furniture to the upper floors.

It was a beautiful home at a good address, built with the financial help of Johan's father. I was excited to see our furniture lifted up. A small group of maids and errand boys gaped upwards, assembled at a safe distance. We could not move in for another month while carpenters were doing their finishing work. I was invited in on their last working day, to instruct tradesmen where to hang pictures and tapestries on the plastered walls, and where to place oil lamps and candela-bras. I had chosen some stylish silver cups and cutlery to be used when we entertained important guests, and a porcelain water jug decorated with brushed blue stones. The furniture was good quality polished oak. My parents gifted a few nice old pieces as part of my dowry. Some of the furniture was from my maternal grandparents, previously my mother's dowry, and a few new pieces were ordered to match the old. The carpets were Persian, in pretty, lively colours; my favourite was the one with cobalt blue flowers in the dining room.

Our newly employed maid was by my side on this first visit to our new home. Geertje was a tall, stout, sweet-faced girl of sixteen from the village of Bovenkerk, south of Amsterdam. She was even more excited than I, her big green eyes shining with pleasure and her honey-coloured plait of hair flying left and right about her shoulders as we inspected the rooms and looked curiously into every corner. We discussed the details of decorations and lights, and she had some good ideas. I had chosen restrained decorations. No person of taste sought dis-tinction through ostentation.

My mother had obtained a written reference from a daughter of Geertje's previous employer, the widowed Mrs van Krieken, who lived only a block away and had recently departed this world. Geertje was described as 'obliging, discreet and precise', and I noticed immediately that she was not too shy to state her opinions. I was glad about this; I did not know how to handle too-shy people, especially servants. Geertje had been in domestic service in Amsterdam for two years already, and she knew her way around, including many people, both from her class and ours, which was a bonus. Talking to her felt easy and natural.

'My lady, I promised my mother to visit three times a year.

I hope you will be willing to let me keep my promise,' Geertje explained as we inspected the kitchen together.

Her respectful but determined attitude made me smile. 'I am sure we can accommodate your mother's wish. When we travel or visit our families, you can have a free week to spend in Bovenkerk.'

Geertje clapped her hands and looked at me with a big, happy smile. 'Wonderful, thank you so much, my lady.'

Our cook, Sarah, was recommended by one of my mother-in-law's acquaintances. She was older, in her early thirties, married to a coachman who was away much of the time. They did not have children, and at this time of their lives it was becoming unlikely their union would be blessed with offspring. Sarah was more reticent than Geertje, but she seemed able and honest.

'Each evening, I may suggest a menu for the next day, if that suits you, madam. You may tell me what and when you and Mister Johan like to eat.' She smiled shyly.

'That sounds like an excellent plan, Sarah. I will give you a list of our favourites when I speak to Johan. But we'll like to keep it quite simple, apart from special occasions.'

'Of course. Thank you, madam.' Sarah nodded and disappeared downstairs. Staff rooms – many people would say 'servant rooms' but I did not like this – were on the first floor. A steep, gently curving staircase bypassed it, leading straight from the *Voorhuis* – the entrance hall – to the second floor, into our living quarters. There was a sitting room with an elegant and comfortable ottoman in the reading corner, and a dining room.

My parents visited two days after we moved in. A year previously, they had moved to Sloten at the western outskirts of Amsterdam, to a quieter life away from the hustle and bustle, as well as the stench of the canals of the Amsterdam Centrum.

Climbing the tall stairs to our living quarters was quite a feat for poor *Maman*, who had become plump in her middle age.

'My dear Fransje, you are young, but these stairs make me breathless climbing up and dizzy going down.'

Papa had to hold her firmly under her arm. My mother often switched to a Dutch version of my name even though she named me Francesca, quite unconventionally, as homage to the elegant Italian women she encountered during her trip to Italy with her parents and sister as an eighteen-year-old. Her father, who started as a humble miller but made good during Amsterdam's Golden Age with a chain of baker's shops, left his successful business to his two eldest sons upon retirement; he was only going to help with advice, if needed. The ageing paterfamilias decided to reward himself for the life of hard work with a trip to the sunny southern land with his wife and two youngest daughters nearing marriageable age. This was also a claim to a higher status than his class was usually granted.

Two months in Italy were indeed life-changing for my mother, who was perceptive and a fast learner. It helped her achieve a distinction in her style and attitude, from clothes and grooming to understanding art and architecture, and made many eligible Amsterdam bachelors from good families take notice. She had quite a few offers, she'd sometimes remarked with a mischievous wink, and she used her ability to choose well by marrying my father. He was a young entrepreneur with a broad range of interests and modern views. He lived up to the promise; he had been a respectful husband and a loving father. And curiously, as if my mother's love of the warm South and her choice of an Italian name for her first-born influenced the fruit of her womb, I was born with dark curly hair that later turned into gently waving hazelnut. I was Papa's favourite daughter and allowed to marry later than usual. He always called me

Francesca. It was heart-warming to see that he still looked at my mother adoringly as he helped her upstairs.

Our marital bedroom was on the third floor. A four-poster bed dominated the room and a dressing table with foldable mirrors was in front of a large window. I had my own bathroom. It was beautiful! A silver-framed Venetian mirror, a part of family history, was hanging on the wall. It was obtained during my grandpa's trip to Italy, solicited by his wife and daughters. I could not wait to show it all off to my visitors.

We planned to buy a summer house by the Haarlemmer-trekvaart. This was the best way to escape the smell of the Amsterdam canals during the warmer months. On humid days in August, the stench could be so nauseating I could not eat. But we could not buy a summer house on the water just yet; for a young businessman like Johan this would be considered foolish and premature. For the time being, my parents' country house with its shady garden and lovely pond would be our summer escape.

Johan had to be careful with his business plans. His family was well-off, but he wanted to be independent and show his business prowess. Times were tough in the Dutch lands. London and Hamburg had become major ports, and Amsterdam shipbuilders were not getting as many orders as before. With them, down went carpenters, upholsterers, sail makers and other trades. Many people left on ships to look for their fortune in the Dutch East Indies, but this was no easy life. Dutch travellers were dying from tropical diseases and ships coming back had to be quarantined. Amsterdam had gotten rid of the plague only recently and the city feared unknown diseases from faraway places.

## 2

Johan volunteered as an assistant treasurer for his textile guild. Whatever happened, people would always need clothes on their backs, he argued, and surely that was right. This afforded a small additional income but required much work, scribbling in his small study by the light of the oil lamp most evenings. It could lead to bigger things, he thought, and having these skills was useful in running his own business. He had his mind set on the bourse, investment and money lending abroad, or even direct investment abroad once he was confident that he knew where to look and what to do. Johan was ambitious: within five years, he aimed to join the 'chosen': the few thousand Amsterdamers whose income was over six hundred guilders a year.

He was a hard worker, not like some others who looked to marry an heiress and enjoy a life of relative leisure. I brought a considerable sum to the marriage, and this gave me a bit of a say, even though Johan seemed to only tolerate my opinions rather than being interested in them. I was sorry about this even though it was not unusual. Johan did not show much enthusiasm for my father's advice either. I think he listened, but he preferred not to seem like a novice in need of advice. He was twenty-nine, and by that age a man should have been established in his business. Usually also married with at least a couple of children, needless to say. Johan was a little behind his peers. Just like me, he delayed getting married even though he was a desirable bachelor. This made our courtship brief; we were an excellent match and there was no reason to delay. My parents and I accepted his offer of marriage enthusiastically – everything about him seemed right.

Unlike most of the Amsterdam bourgeoisie, Johan did not shy away from knowing Amsterdam's Jewish merchants, many of whom were skilful investors. Some were new to the city, having fled from Poland or Germany. My father knew some of them too. The Jews spoke a mellow-sounding vernacular, Dutch mixed with Yiddish. Most of them learned Dutch quickly. Their modest houses were in abandoned wharves, but those who had successful businesses were allowed to live in established parts of the city close to the synagogue at the Houtgracht. We could not really be friends with them or invite them over for dinner. In fact, we could not do this with Catholics either. Johan hosted Jewish businessmen in his study downstairs and talked with them over a glass of brandy or port in the evenings, hoping none of our neighbours would notice. Gossip spread fast in Amsterdam, and there was little mercy for social blunders.

Luckily, Geertje was loyal to us. She knew that my only real diamond, adorning my wedding ring, came from David, a Jew from Saxony, as a present to Johan for some favour received, but she did not share this knowledge around. David traded in precious stones. I did not know what the favour was that Johan bestowed on David – perhaps it was for the respect that people like David rarely received from Protestants of our station.

Amsterdam society was becoming more diverse and with it more tolerant. Mixing with Jews, short of marrying them, was not as frowned upon as it used to be. If everyone was doing business with everyone in a proper and honest way, people were satisfied.

## 3

My parents were pleased with our new location. The Oudezijds Voorburgwal was where good families lived, so I'd be in the genteel company of local ladies. Like most houses in Amsterdam, our house overlooked a canal. From my room's eastern window, I was often transfixed by the still, murky waters. During daylight hours, the human traffic was heavy – gentlemen and ladies, maids and errand boys crossed Lommertbrug, a small wooden bridge reflected in the black water of the canal. The maids crossed briskly on their way to the market and back, bringing home food in baskets carefully covered with cheesecloth, the shoots of leek and green onions often sticking out. The maids lowered their gaze as they scurried past the gentlemen, but somehow they still saw everything. I knew they were not as demure as they made out. Geertje knew more than me about each family in the neighbourhood. Maids must be gossiping about their masters at the market. Who knows what they were saying about me? '*It's been over a year, but still no sign that she is with child,*' I could imagine them whispering.

Perhaps this was why Johan was not as interested in me as he was in the first months of our marriage? Sometimes, after lunch, he used to run his hand down my back, and then a bit lower still. His shop was close to our house, and he was usually home for lunch. After asking softly into my ear whether I was 'clean', meaning I was not bleeding, he used to whisk me into our bedroom after the midday meal.

'Milady has a headache. I will pull the curtains, do not disturb her.' Then, a second later, he would press me against his chest, lift my dress and slide his hand underneath, squeezing my buttocks.

Johan was handsome, and I could see ladies noticing his tall, straight, broad-shouldered figure and thick blond hair framing his serious but pleasant face. I often admired his piercing blue eyes and his full lips. I never told him so, because a man was not to be admired for his beauty. But I did not really like his carnal zest, his abrupt advances. I liked it when he languidly ran his hand along my back, while others were still around, so he could not proceed to the forbidden parts in haste. I would have liked a slow exchange of intimacies to continue when we were alone. But a well-bred wife could not talk about such things with her husband because she was not supposed to care about physical love too much in the first place. She was there to please her husband and bear him children. And ... I was a reasonable woman, and I knew he was a busy man and he had to hurry back to his silk shop after he had finished with me.

The headache excuse gave me an opportunity to stay in the darkened room and have a snooze, but often I thought about my life, the married life, and what would become of it if I did not fall pregnant soon ... and what if I did. I wanted sweet little children greeting me and kissing their *maman* in the morning, but I was also fearful. Mrs de Vries in the house next door, her main entrance facing the municipal house, fell sick and died shortly after the birth of her second child. I heard from my Geertje that the children, a baby and a two-year-old, were now in the care of maids but Mr de Vries would remarry soon. My godmother's niece died in childbirth even though she was attended by the best midwife in Amsterdam; even the highly respected Dr Hofstadter could not save her.

Johan was a careful and polite man, but in the second year of our marriage, when he joined the civic guards, he would often return home late, and after a few drinks with his comrades he could be querulous and mean. I felt a little uneasy around him sometimes. The civic guards patrolled the streets, marching along the canals fine-looking and upright, with their guns at the hip. They were important and powerful, a tightly knit men's cabal, which suited Johan's ambition. They had become even more important in Amsterdam after Master Rembrandt van Rijn painted their group portrait, *The Night Watch*, nearly a century earlier.

The painting was exhibited in the Town Hall, and we went to

see it shortly after Johan joined the guards. I loved paintings, all art in fact – Johan not so much. He was impressed by the colossal painting with nearly life-size human figures, but even more by the price Master Rembrandt was paid for the commission that took him three years to complete. The art and beauty did not take Johan's breath away; his gaze was fixed upon earthly goals, power and money, and as a natural addition, an adoring wife and children to inherit his name and estate.

As we walked home from the Town Hall, I could not help expressing my admiration.

'You know, Johan, I often think of Master Rembrandt, every time I pass by his house in Jodenbreestraat. He had to sell that house to pay his debts and move to a rented home. But in this modest home at Rozengracht he was visited by a Florentine prince, one of the grand de Medici family – this is how great an artist he was!'

'He lived beyond his means. Luxury and excess that leads to bankruptcy, that's reprehensible. A Catholic sort of behaviour,' Johan remarked.

'I suppose that's what the burghers of Amsterdam could not forgive. He was expelled from the Painters' Guild and lived in relative poverty in his later years.'

Johan shrugged. 'Why feel sorry for someone who had talent, good fortune, and a noteworthy income but failed to accumulate wealth and at the end even lost his house?'

Perhaps Johan was right? 'The stern Calvinist God surely punished him, don't you think, Johan? Both wives died young, and even his remaining son died before him.'

'Well, he rarely attended church or contributed money.'

'Yes, he was unconventional. He did not seem to care about his own salvation or the glory of God. Tall trees catch a lot of wind! He used Jewish people, men and women, as models for his paintings, did you know that? Such closeness would be frowned upon even today, let alone a century ago. He was famous across Europe, but only properly recognised at home after all the people who knew him were already dead, and all their petty gossip and envy buried with them.'

'Don't get carried away, Fransje! His life is a good cautionary tale: nothing is guaranteed, and hard work and modesty are the only way to respectability and contentment in this world, and salvation in the next. Don't you think that's fair?' Johan took my arm and quickened his step; he seemed to have had enough talk of Master Rembrandt.

Johan and I were different, but I was proud of him. He was dashing in his Night Watch uniform with a weapon against his slim thigh. He worked hard and had a vision for his family's future. No-one reasonable should object that he liked the social life of patrician militia men at their guild rooms more than paintings and music. And I was a reasonable woman.

At the outset, Johan drank with the civic guards after his weekly evening patrol, but before long he started going there more often. He was thinking of a political career, even though this was not something he'd discuss with me. Why else would he invite the *Burgemeester* and his wife to dinner? This was not just a social call; they were much older and more prominent than us, and I thought there had to be a specific matter to discuss.

The dinner caused a big fuss. Geertje and Sarah were instructed in detail by Johan's mother, who visited especially for that purpose. I was considered too inexperienced to plan such an important occasion, hosting a dinner with the *Burgemeester*, all by myself! Inevitably though, I was responsible for keeping the *Burgemeester*'s wife entertained, and this wasn't the easiest of tasks. The esteemed couple were about fifty, almost our parents' age. Mrs van der Veen was mainly talking about her ailments, fragrant salts and massages she was prescribed to alleviate aches and pains in her limbs and her back. Johan and Mr van der Veen were discussing politics, the civic guard, business, and the intricacies of investing in the Dutch East India Company. Once the dessert was over the two men retreated downstairs to the *Voorhuis*, and Geertje followed with a bottle of brandy and glasses.

# 4

I was a little disappointed that my enchantment with our new home and the harmony of its décor kept me interested for only a few months. Once everything was done and every little thing was in its proper place, I felt I needed another occupation, something more. The house started to feel like a comfortable cage.

I often remembered those happy years when my three siblings and I were let loose in the country. We were allowed to run out of our summer house in Haarlem any time we wanted, except at mealtimes, and to roam the swampy fields scaring the chickens and cows with our shrieking and splashing. At age fifteen, my life became more restrained, with learning of music, languages, geography, history and even mathematics taking more time than before. My tutor, a young Jesuit monk, had a way of making things interesting and acknowledging my progress, and I always looked forward to his lessons. The same could not be said for a matron who taught *bon ton* and comportment to young ladies. We attended her house in small groups. She was always disapproving and would not let us have any break for a conversation. Tittering was met with a stern stare.

All this was preparation for adulthood, and my parents took it seriously. My family was not old money and, just like my mother before me, I had to earn a good husband by fitting into a social stratum a notch above my own. I had to achieve the right balance between being attractive and modest, between being educated and ready to defer to my husband. It seemed that my parents' plan succeeded: they were delighted about my marriage to Johan and they liked his family.

But being a grown woman and a lady meant that my nice clothing did not leave much room for movement, apart from a ladylike stroll while keeping a good posture and showing off my feminine figure. If I walked fast, my stays would start to feel too tight on my chest and I could not take a deep breath easily. I could not really do as I wished.

Apart from playing the piano or lute, the art of being pretty and for those more daring, seductive, was the only art allowed a lady. Keeping a nice home and being able to deal with servants was de rigueur. A respectable woman was allowed to have skills, volunteer in local civic initiatives or engage in charitable work, as long as her pursuits did not jeopardise her reputation or take too much time from family duties.

Perhaps because of my tutor, Brother Cornelis, the life of a lady soon left me wanting more. We knew Mrs Bakker, one of the governesses of the Burgerweeshuis, the city orphanage, through her husband, who was Johan's militia captain. We belonged to the same congregation at Nieuwekerk. One Sunday after the service Johan chatted with Mr Bakker and I had an opportunity to talk with Mrs Bakker, a tall woman of about forty in a black laced hat, whose dark blue eyes dominated her pale and somewhat gaunt face. She told me about her work and the orphanage itself, which gave me the idea I could help as a volunteer teacher in the orphanage school. After some persuading, Johan agreed this might be a good idea. I sent a message to Mrs Bakker and she said we could have another chat after the Sunday service.

Mrs Bakker greeted me cordially, visibly more animated than the week before. We agreed I could help by teaching reading, writing and music. She asked if I could visit the Burgerwee-shuis on Monday morning at eight; I could be introduced to the children after they finished breakfast.

'Yes, of course Mrs Bakker! I am thrilled by the prospect of making myself useful in the Burgerweeshuis. The excellent reputation of the orphanage transcends Amsterdam, and indeed the Dutch lands ...'

Mrs Bakker smiled. 'Thank you, Mrs Hoekstra. Be warned though, our children are no angels. Until tomorrow, then!'

We bid the Bakkers goodbye, I slipped my arm under Johan's, and we left.

'I hope you'll like the work in the orphanage, Fransje,' he said in a measured tone. 'And I hope it will be what you expect. Teaching is hard work, especially when your pupils are not likely to be ... the brightest.'

Johan's remark made me think. Were orphans less bright than other children, or less well behaved? If so, why? My tutor had always encouraged me to think about why something was the way it was and not to take all that people say for granted. He seemed amused by my enthusiasm for learning, and we'd sometimes slip into a philosophical discourse. He warned me, though, that this habit could be seen as inappropriate in a young lady. I remembered this quite often, but keeping a cunning tongue was not my natural instinct. On this occasion, I made an effort not to query Johan's remark.

The next morning, I wore my most serious dress, barring the black one for funerals. As a teacher, I had to project some authority. I was twenty-five, but people often told me I looked younger. The dress was a dark emerald green, matching the colour of the first leaves of spring on my silk scarf. I found a discreetly laced fawn-coloured hat that blended nicely with my hair, a couple of shades darker. I knew I should not look coquettish, but there was never any harm in proper grooming. Well-travelled people often told me I looked Italian; it was in my hair, not just in the name. Being told one 'looked French' alluded to style and elegance, but 'looking Italian' mostly meant looking different from the majority of blond or red-haired, blue-eyed, pink-skinned Dutch. Was I vain, admiring the clothes, smiling back at the pleasing reflection in the elegant Venetian mirror?

What could I teach the children? To read and write for sure, music perhaps if they had any instruments, or at least singing if they didn't, but what were the virtues they could learn from me? Did I have any? I must have had some – I married well, and I didn't want to be just a lady, occupying her time with the beauty of her home and her own comeliness. Was this just vanity in another form, wanting to be seen as a useful member of Amsterdam society?

Geertje interrupted my train of thought by appearing on top of the stairs with two umbrellas and my dark brown pelerine. The morning was grey and drizzly. Geertje was to accompany me to the Burgerweeshuis. It was not proper for a well-bred young woman, married or unmarried, to wander the streets of Amsterdam alone early in the morning, at least until the neighbourhood learned where she was headed. But I knew that, with Geertje's help, all our neighbours would know about my work in the orphanage within days.

# 5

The Burgerweeshuis was on busy Kalverstraat, less than a five-minute walk from our house. When I arrived, the drizzle had cleared and the sun shone through the clouds, so the children were out in the courtyard. Wet leaves were glistening on sunlit trees and raindrops sparkled on the benches. It was a lovely scene; I imagined a painting of it. I enjoyed seeing the girls wiping the benches and choosing where to sit, talking under their breaths and giggling. Mrs Bakker, who had come out to greet me, followed my glance and smiled.

'On warmer sunny mornings the girls do their needlework here in the courtyard. They may chatter if they wish, as long as their hands are not idle.' The older girls were making white lace collars for themselves and others, to use on special occasions, and I could see them teaching younger girls. They wore neat dark dresses with collars high up on their necks, with red inserts on the shoulders and hips and white caps that covered most of their hair and ears; those small slivers of red prevented the uniforms from looking monastic.

'We have more orphans on the Burgerweeshuis' books every year,' Mrs Bakker told me as she showed me the dormitories. 'If a working-class man's wife dies and leaves young children behind, with no daughter old enough to take care of her younger siblings, he cannot cope and they often end up here – the fathers pay for part of the upkeep if they can. Boys and girls sleep in separate dormitories, grouped by age.'

I listened carefully and nodded, while observing the children in the courtyard.

'We teach the children trades suitable for their age – cooking and other kitchen work for the girls, as well as cleaning, sewing and embroidery. The boys learn carpentry and metalwork, or just stable work if they are not too bright, or good with their hands.'

Mrs Bakker smoothed her skirts and gave a satisfied look at the girls in the sunshine.

'Dedicated hard work is the only habit that will get them

through life, which did not start too well for these children.' As a married, genteel woman with a family, Mrs Bakker volunteered in the orphanage in the mornings, keeping the books in order and receiving visits from the benefactors as well as those who sought to commit children to the orphanage. She also sat on the board of governors, which met fortnightly.

The orphanage was clean and well maintained. I was impressed by the rather small but well-appointed kitchen with a spacious sink under a tap coming out of a bulky water tank. A set of shiny pewter plates was stacked on the side shelves above the sink. A large stove took up most of the opposite side.

'Older girls help in the kitchen and laundry. They also clean their own rooms. From twelve years of age, most girls are able to earn their keep. Boys take longer to grow strong and be able to work in trades ... at about fifteen, typically,' Mrs Bakker explained.

There were three resident staff who supervised and taught the children. Miss Kok and Miss De Graeve, one a round older woman with bright pink cheeks and the other tall and sallow, both dressed in black skirts and white blouses with lace collars, seemed pleased to meet me and hear about the plan to help with the teaching. They were unmarried women; I thought they were lucky to have a respectable and probably decently paid job. Mrs Bakker had to meet a visitor, so they took over and showed me the rest of the Burgerweeshuis. Miss Kok had to supervise the girls tidying the kitchen after breakfast, and I was left with the tall Miss De Graeve – it was nice to look another woman in the eye without stooping.

'I hope you like it here, Mrs Hoekstra.' Miss de Graeve smiled. 'We teach the girls practical skills as well as counting and simple sums, so they can handle money and go to the market when they are old enough. They first come with one of us several times, then go by themselves. They like to be given the responsibility—'

'Oh yes, I can imagine that.'

'And once they know domestic chores and can read, sign their names and calculate the exact change at the market, they're ready for life . . . for domestic service, which is what most of them will do. After they learn the basics, the bright ones can advance their skills quite easily.' She glanced at my silk scarf. 'You know, we do not polish silver and wash silk finery here. It's nice to hear about our girls having good lives after they leave us. Some drop by to see us and tell us their news and bring some apple cake. Others never do – perhaps they prefer to forget that they spent years in an orphanage. But we hear what became of them sooner or later.

'But I am talking too much and taking your time.' Miss De Graeve suddenly changed her tone from chatty to formal. 'I will introduce you to the older girls, who must have finished with the kitchen by now. I should be going to the market at once.'

I nodded and smiled. 'Of course, Miss De Graeve. I know you are busy. I enjoyed your introduction; my time was well spent in your company.' I felt Miss De Graeve really cared about the orphan girls.

The orphanage school ran for two hours after breakfast and two hours before dinner. With me acting as a teacher, the morning instruction was to be mainly scholarly, with the practical classes in the afternoons. The girls made the majority of my students, joined by younger boys who were not yet committed to apprenticeships outside the Burgerweeshuis. The children seemed respectful and well behaved.

It took only a few days for several girls to become quite attached to me. In the morning they would greet me with unrestrained joy, jumping around like bright-eyed puppies, before they sat down with their tablets and chalk. I was not there to secure discipline and hard work, but to read interesting tales to them and teach them to read, write and talk properly. The brighter ones appreciated this; apart from the mental amusement, I think they sensed being literate and well-spoken would give them distinction in the world they were soon to face. It could be their entry ticket for a better life, for some girls through a propitious marriage. Those less bright seemed somewhat scornful of my efforts. They had no light in their eyes; they knew they were going to be maids and the only thing that mattered was that they could count money and not get cheated in the market when procuring freshly slaughtered chickens and best cheese from Gouda for their masters' meals.

I sometimes spoke to the girls in their own vernacular, showing them I was not necessarily better than them and that they could perhaps become educated young ladies like me. I often wanted to tell them they should keep their hopes high. At their age – thirteen, fourteen, fifteen – anything was still possible; even the wildest dreams should not be dismissed. But I never said it. I could not find the right words, a right moment. I was surprised to learn that these girls, all under fifteen, were keenly aware of the society outside the Burgerweeshuis. I felt sorry for them, caged in their sober realism, but I also understood this was an attitude which would protect them from disappointments and life's many snares.

The orphan girls and my Geertje made me contemplate the social hierarchy. People like Johan and I had more money and influence, but how was my life better than the life of my maid? Maids were free to go to town on their own, be themselves out there in the real world, argue and barter with men and women in the market, get to meet young men they liked, and at the end, if they were pretty enough, they usually chose their own husbands. Their parents were far away and could not control them. They were freer and more independent than I.

Of course, they had to work hard and serve and obey others. They were on call all day and had to curtsy in front of their ladies ... but they could also make naughty gestures, gossip and giggle behind their backs. I was educated but barely allowed to work in a society which only respected people who worked hard and secured their salvation by earning money. I was lucky to have Geertje. Rather than respecting or fearing me, I think she liked me and perhaps felt a little sorry for me. The life of a lady was limited, devoted to pleasing one man, her husband, and making her family proud by excelling in embracing social conventions and constraints, in the gilded prison of a bourgeois home.

# 6

My work in the orphanage was a valuable addition to my married life. My marriage had not developed the emotional or intellectual intensity that I was hoping for and our home, taken care of by Geertje and Sarah, required little effort on my part. Once we were settled in our domestic life, Johan and I did not seem to have that much to talk about. I was excited about masterful paintings and people who could play music or sing beautifully; he was excited about making money and mingling with important people. Perhaps we were just a normal couple?

But now, three mornings a week, I had a mission. I knew what to do: make myself serious-looking and walk across to the Burgerweeshuis with some books and scores under my arm, just another busy person in Amsterdam. I enjoyed seeing my students again and noticing their progress. Walking back home at eleven, I would choose a different path each time, meandering through the streets and along canals, sometimes dropping inside a church for some silence and otherworldliness, on other days having a chat with the owner of a newly opened shop. Shops were many and varied, appearing and disappearing quite quickly. People from smaller inland towns and those coming from outside the Dutch lands were trying their luck in Amsterdam.

One morning, while passing one of these new shops, an enticing smell made me stop and peer through the wide-open door. This must be coffee, the drink I had heard of but had never tried. I stepped in, and a couple at the counter turned and smiled at me, both looking at me a little longer than necessary. It was unusual for a woman to walk alone into a café – that's what they called these places in Paris – but the sight of two ladies at the corner table, who also smiled at me as I entered, encouraged me to stay. The rest of the guests were men talking business. I noticed David, Johan's Jewish friend, sitting at a table with a Dutch gentleman. David rose from his chair and bowed politely, acknowledging our acquaintance. I smiled and nodded back.

'Would you like to try our coffee, madam?' The woman at the counter smiled at me again.

'I would indeed! I am on my way home from the Burgerweeshuis, but this delightful smell made me come in.'

'Ah, isn't it excellent that our product advertises itself?' the man at the counter interjected, leaning towards me with a broad smile.

I smiled back. 'Yes, it most certainly is! I hope your business flourishes!'

The coffee was hot and tasty. It was served with a pinch of chocolate powder and a teaspoon of sugar – they called it a 'mocha'. This was revealed to me in return for the sigh of enjoyment I made after the first sip.

'Glad you like it, madam! Ladies usually like this version. We make pure hot chocolate as well. We source all our goods from the island of Java in the Dutch Indies.'

'I see! I may try the chocolate next time then.'

# 7

I came home in a buoyant mood. Geertje greeted me with her usual friendly smile, a nod and a quick curtsy that always seemed a little ironic because she knew I did not demand or expect it. Johan arrived a few minutes later. He kissed me on the cheek, and we proceeded to the dining room.

'I saw David in a café at Rokin,' I volunteered. 'He was having a beer with a Dutch gentleman over some papers they must have been discussing ... business, likely.'

'Did you, Fransje?' Johan asked, with more than his usual polite acknowledgment of his wife's idle chatter. 'So you frequent Amsterdam cafés now ... you never told me.'

'The smell outside the shop was so enticing, I had to step in. I tried the coffee. A "mocha", to be precise.'

'You'd better be careful, my dear! I hear coffee is addictive and some people have been known to have problems with it ... and with spending too much time in cafés, too! Who has time for that? I am surprised David does! He is a serious businessman and business is best discussed in the privacy of one's home or office.'

'You are too strict sometimes, Johan! Perhaps this is the way of the future. And you do know that business is often discussed outside home, like you do in your militia guild rooms.'

Johan remained silent for a few moments. He did not like me finding flaws in his argument.

'That's quite different, Fransje, our civic guard club. We discuss matters of public importance. And given we are all businessmen, spending time together sometimes leads to business deals ... though we don't discuss them there.'

'There seem to be plenty of matters of public importance to discuss then! It often takes late into the night. And a few drinks!'

I knew I had stepped onto thin ice with my comment, but I could not resist. Johan was biased and old-fashioned. Why would having a coffee or a beer in a café in the middle of the day be less appropriate than drinking in guild rooms into the small hours of the night? Did people's social status make whatever they did respectable, did it turn their personal opinions into wisdom?

Johan riposte was terse. 'I'm a grown man, Fransje. I don't need anyone telling me what to do.'

The rest of our lunch passed in silence, apart from Geertje commenting on the menu as she was bringing the food upstairs. I thought of men and women while I munched the roast without much enthusiasm. Did a grown woman need to be told what to do? Was a woman ever 'grown' the same way a man was? Clearly not. Not a married woman. Not a lady. Perhaps those unmarried women working at the orphanage were; no men to hover over their decisions and censure their opinions. But then, everyone pitied unmarried women!

As soon as he finished eating, Johan stood up precipitously, wiping his mouth with a starched white serviette.

'I'm off Fransje. I shall be later than usual tonight. Don't wait for me for dinner.'

No kiss on the cheek, let alone the 'lady has a headache' script. I felt a little disappointed, perhaps frustrated too. I loved Johan, but our marriage seemed to be growing progressively cooler. I think Maman was right. I remembered her saying, with a sigh: 'For a woman, the marriage and the family are of utmost importance. A man always has more important things to do. That's just how it is.'

I retreated to my reading room upstairs, determined to distract myself with a good book. Instead, I ended up staring through the window into an undetermined distance. Geertje found me with the book resting on my lap.

'Here is your tea, my lady.' I lifted my eyes thinking of something nice to say back to the fresh-faced, smiling lass.

'We may buy some coffee and chocolate powder, Geertje. I tried something called "mocha" this morning and it was excellent.'

'Oh, the mocha, yes, of course! It's very popular these days.'

Geertje was again one step ahead of me.

'You know everything, my dear girl!' I laughed.

She blushed a little. 'I tried it only once, madam ... a short time ago a gentleman ... a sailor ... a naval officer, I think ... who had just arrived from the Dutch Indies, treated my friends and me to a hot coffee drink at the markets. There is a street vendor there. He explained coffee could be mixed with chocolate. I think it was quite expensive. Given that others accepted, I didn't refuse either ... such things don't happen often. The sailor ... the officer ... was very jolly and kept repeating that he'd "struck gold". We thought he was being generous because he was celebrating getting rich in the colonies.'

'You are a smart girl, Geertje, and I'm sure some lucky man will snatch you one day soon, and we'll lose you. Ah, such is life, things never stop happening! So ... given we both like the drink, let's buy some coffee and chocolate. This will be our vice of choice!'

Geertje's face suddenly darkened.

'What's wrong, Geertje? You look worried all of a sudden.'

'I am not sure how to say this, my lady, and whether I should say it at all. But there's something that's been preoccupying me for weeks, maybe months, and it is not my business ... but you have been so nice to me, you treat me like family ...'

She stopped, swallowing tears. After a few moments' break she composed herself and continued. She looked tortured.

'I noticed today that Mister Johan and you had a ... conversation during lunch, and then there was a silence and then he left saying he'd come home late ...'

I was still stretched on my reading ottoman with an unopened book on my lap. I looked up at Geertje, not understanding why she was talking about Johan and me. This indeed was not her business.

Geertje blushed, and red blotches appeared on her neck and chest.

'I am really sorry, madam, you now think I am a nosy servant, but honestly, I'm not. I just happened to have seen something that haunts me, and I feel I must tell you. I'm so sorry ...'

'What is it, Geertje? What are you sorry about? Stop apologising and talk straight and clearly. I haven't got an idea what you're trying to tell me.'

'Oh yes, yes,' she stammered then finally collected herself. 'For sure. Well, some time ago, while you were visiting your parents for a few days, Mister Johan behaved strangely ... he ...'

'Geertje, please say it finally, I'm getting nervous. He didn't try anything with you, did he ... ?'

'Oh no, no, never, he's good to me, he respects me, madam. I've heard of gentlemen who pester their servants, other girls talk about it ... but not Mister Johan, he's not like that.'

I took a deep breath. A sigh of relief.

'What is it then? How did he behave strangely?'

'Well, he was coming home very late, for a couple of nights not until dawn ... and then one night, Mister David was here.

Before taking my leave for the night I dropped past the *Voorhuis* to see if they needed anything.'

Geertje was talking fast and breathing heavily as if she'd just climbed the tall stairs. 'You know the double door to the *Voorhuis* is never closed, but this time it was almost fully closed. I could not hear voices, so I thought Mister David was gone. I peeked through the gap just to make sure there was no-one there, but they were both inside' – at this point she instinctively lowered her voice – 'embracing.'

I straightened myself on the ottoman. Geertje swallowed, took a breath and quickly continued, as if concerned the story would run away from her.

'Mister Johan's shirt was hanging down his trousers and Mister David's arms were bare . . . I . . . I took my clogs off and fled to my room . . .'

I could well imagine Geertje running upstairs, clogs in hand. Momentarily, that stood as a barrier to a mental image of David and Johan embracing.

'I didn't tell anyone . . . I would never tell such a thing to anyone. People would never stop talking.'

Indeed. No doubt about that. It would be ruinous to Johan's reputation and business. I remembered hearing about the scandalous trials that had started in Utrecht a few years back. 'Unnatural tendencies' were not forgiven even in free-thinking Amsterdam, which prided itself on its tolerance. Among sailors, this sort of activity was a matter for lewd jokes, but it would be taken very seriously among respected, married men of substance, those serving as civic guards and having political ambitions. Doing business deals with Jews was one thing but this was quite another. It was unfathomable.

'I'm sorry to have upset you, madam! I thought about it for a long time and I thought in the end that you should know . . .

so you don't blame yourself for ... for ... Mister Johan's lack of ... attention ... perhaps.'

Of course, domestic staff knew everything! Their masters' marital bedrooms were not a secret to them. They changed our bedlinen, washed our clothes, cleaned our rooms, listened to our conversations, witnessed our moods.

'Perhaps you are right, Geertje – perhaps I should know. Although my mother thinks it is better for a wife not to know what her husband is up to, given she may worry about it but not be able to do much ... She may be right too, *ma chère maman.*'

I wasn't sure what to do with this unexpected and unwelcome knowledge. I felt numb. Perhaps I felt a little bit of a relief, even ... a strange feeling I did not expect. It explained Johan's coldness. Perhaps the pain would come later.

Geertje stared at me wide-eyed, her eyes welling with tears. 'I'm so sorry, madam, so sorry to worry you and disappoint you. But you can be sure I'll never tell anyone else, even if you dismissed me ...'

'I am not going to dismiss you Geertje. It's not you who has disappointed me.'

'Oh, your tea has gone cold!' she cried, finding a way to end this difficult conversation. 'I'll bring another one for my lady.'

Geertje wiped her eyes quickly with the back of her hand, like a child, and rushed downstairs to the kitchen before I could stop her. My desire for tea or reading was entirely gone.

# 8

I didn't see Johan that night. I tossed and turned in our large bed until the small hours of the morning. After I heard the Nieuwekerk bells chiming twice, I finally fell asleep. I didn't hear Johan returning home or getting into bed; I only heard him getting up in the morning. I pretended to be asleep. I had no idea what to say or how to act.

He left without trying to wake me. He'd be home at midday. This was going to be twenty-four hours in which we did not exchange a word. It had never happened before. After Geertje's revelations, I could not even remember what yesterday's tension and subsequent silence between us were about. It seemed irrelevant now.

I had no idea where to start with this new knowledge about Johan. What did this mean to our marriage? Should I do anything? Confront Johan, announce I knew his secret? I had no gut instinct, no internal emotional guidance. I could not analyse the problem because I knew nothing about it. Surely, it was unnatural. Telling Johan what I knew would not be like confronting a husband over his concubine, or his visits to a brothel. I sensed it was more complicated. But whatever the case, no-one liked to be confronted. That would not help. I knew what Maman would say: 'Do not argue about things that you do not have the power to influence.' Another piece of her incontrovertible life wisdom! Should I share my secret – mine and Geertje's – with her? She'd be worried and unhappy, and her advice would be to pretend nothing happened. Could I do that? I was not sure. I felt unsure about almost everything. Shaken.

Johan and I were due to go on a long trip soon. Perhaps this time together might draw us closer ... but the more I thought of it, the more the trip I had been looking forward to so much looked merely like something that would have to be endured. My excited anticipation was reduced to trepidation about being alone with a distant, indifferent husband; Johan going about his business and ignoring me as much as he could.

I couldn't stop thinking about what Geertje had shared with me. Perhaps that night had been a one-off episode fuelled by too much drink? I knew David was a sober type. Protestants liked to unburden their soul with a glass or two though. And Catholics, to be fair! But the Jews were known as cautious people, not prone to letting their self-control slip.

I racked my brain: what did I know about this sort of relationship between men? I had heard about servant girls sharing a bed and being seen to kiss and caress each other, but that was seen as harmless, if indecorous, conduct. People turned a blind eye. What did it matter what servant girls amused themselves with late at night? Or the sailors on long sea voyages? But for the men of the propertied class, paterfamiliases, those who ruled the city, the land, this was quite different. Their habits and tastes mattered!

And then I remembered! I did know something about this! My tutor, Brother Cornelis, told me about ancient Greek philosophers who made love to boys and this was considered normal. Was this how Socrates 'corrupted the youth'? Surely not? But whatever the case, yes – Mister Cor, as I often used to slip into calling him, or even just Cor, for I felt so close to him – I should definitely talk to him. He was a most captivating teacher. He was less than ten years my senior but he knew a great deal and he was a man too! A celibate one, presumably, but I was sure he could tolerate my confession and questions. Catholic priests were trained to listen to people's confessions, and these had to be a source of deep knowledge about the human race.

The urge to see Brother Cornelis made me restless. I wandered through the house like a disoriented ant looking for its anthill. I was thinking hard. Where would I find him? He always came to my parents' house, and I never asked where from. In my mind, he was a smiling, pleasant but otherwise disembodied source of knowledge. I never thought of him as a person that eats, sleeps and attends to his bodily, and not just spiritual needs, like the rest of us. His monastery must be not too far from the place where we lived back then. My mother was the person to ask. I could easily make an excuse for wanting to see him: he was a great teacher, and I was myself a teacher now, a novice in need of advice.

But then another thought flashed in my head. There was a hidden Catholic church, a *Schuilkerk*, in our street, just a short walk along the canal. It had been a century and a half since Calvinists took over the grand old churches and altered them for their purposes, while Catholics went defensively underground. Yet everyone knew where they were – usually hidden behind an unassuming façade. I stomped downstairs to the *Voorhuis*. Geertje appeared from below with a teapot and a cup on a tray just as I was putting on my cape.

'I am afraid this tea will also go cold, Geertje.' I smiled at her. 'Where has my hat gone? Ah, there it is, high on that hook!'

'Oh, my lady, you're going out . . . ? Can I help you? Shall I come with you?'

'No need, Geertje! I'll be back in a flicker . . . just a short walk along the canal. If it weren't so smelly today, I'd say I was going to get some fresh air!'

Geertje smiled. She seemed relieved that I acted as usual rather than being shattered by her revelations.

'See you soon, Geertje! I'll have my tea in half an hour!'

'Very well, madam.' Geertje performed a comical little curtsy. 'I'll have it ready then.'

A gust of warm south-westerly reminded me that living in Amsterdam Centrum was not always an advantage. It wasn't even summer yet, but the air was heavy and putrid along the canal. I put a scarf on my nose and mouth, watching my step on the cobblestones. In a couple of minutes I was in front of the heavy wooden door that only had a small iron cross in the upper left corner to signify this was a holy place. I knocked but did not expect anyone to hear it. I pressed the round iron handle and pushed the door. It wasn't locked. Even though it was grey outside and about to rain, my eyes needed a few moments to adjust to the nearly complete darkness. Past a small lobby, there was another door, also unlocked, and I found myself in a large room with rows of pews and hassocks. A few candles provided sparse light; there were no visible windows. No sooner had the door slammed behind me, than I started to discern paintings and crucifixes on the wall. A man in a priest's robe appeared from a side room, carrying a burning candle on a candlestick. He bowed his head respectfully.

'May I help you, madam? You do not seem to be of our congregation?'

'No, indeed I am not, Father. But I live nearby, and I would be grateful if you could help me find someone.'

He nodded hesitantly but said nothing, waiting for me to continue.

'Some years ago, I was lucky to have an excellent tutor, at that time a young monk, Brother Cornelis. He made learning a pleasure and I've been forever grateful; no money can pay for such charity! I am a teacher myself now, at the Burgerweeshuis. I would love to find Brother Cornelis and have a conversation with him. He could teach me about teaching. Do you know where I could find him?'

The priest's face lightened. 'I know that Brother Cornelis has become Father Cornelis, a member of the Society of Jesus. You might find him at De Krijtberg, only a few minutes' walk from here . . .' He waved his hand in its general direction.

'Oh, I'm so lucky . . . I could not hope for better, could I?'

'Father Cornelis may not be in Amsterdam at the moment,' he continued quietly after my rushed interruption. 'It's been nearly a year since he left for the Dutch East Indies, and his plan was to proceed to China, to continue the spiritual mission of the Jesuits in that vast country. I have not heard that he has returned.' He bowed again. 'I am afraid this is all I am able to tell you.'

'I see.' My mood darkened. 'Would it help if I asked at De Krijtberg?'

'They may be able to tell you more, madam. God bless you.' He made a nearly imperceptible sign of the cross in my direction.

'Thank you, Father. May God be with you too.'

I left the building and faced the dark windy afternoon again. Large raindrops had just started to fall, pockmarking the stagnant surface of the canal. I suddenly felt tired and melancholy. I turned left, going home, instead of right, to the Singel. I yearned for the shelter of my reading room and Geertje's hot cup of strong tea.

# 9

Visiting De Krijtberg at the Singel the next day required a small detour on the way home from the Burgerweeshuis. A young deacon was just lighting the candles when I entered. He readily informed me that Father Cornelis was due home next month.

'A ship from the Far East arrives every two weeks,' he explained. 'Father Cornelis announced his return in June, so we are expecting him on the next one. But on such long trips unexpected things can happen. If you leave your name and address, madam, we will advise Father Cornelis of your visit and your desire to talk with him.'

'You are very kind, Father. Unfortunately, my husband and I are leaving on a trip to Antwerp and Paris on the first day of June. It seems I will have to visit here again upon our return.

In the meantime, can you please pass on my message and my best wishes to Father Cornelis? So that he will not too surprised to see me this summer.'

I attempted a smile through my disappointment. Suddenly, talking to a knowledgeable Jesuit seemed more exciting than travelling to Flanders and France. Could I stay at home? This thought provided no relief.

Over the following two weeks, Johan and I grew even more distant. The silences between us lengthened. Johan only talked when he had to, and I did not know how to bridge the distance between us without starting the topic that was stuck in my mind, obscuring everything else. Why was he silent? Was it that he'd always just responded to my conversation starters? Did he even notice anything was different, or wrong? Or did he suspect I knew about his relationship with David – if this was a relationship . . . ?

If it was, did it have to be in competition with our marriage? Wasn't marriage something different? But what was it? What, if not closeness? Talking to each other? Sharing a life together? Perhaps that was just the conventional story about 'being one in sickness and in health'? Perhaps it was normal that we lived next to each other, even close to each other, but never touching, like parallel lines? Enjoying our own pursuits while heeding our common business as necessary? The common work of marriage: children, property, a respectable family image shown to the world? Did I have a right to expect, or even demand, anything more? There were 'marital duties' of course, but that had also sunk into oblivion in recent weeks. My mind was going around in circles of torturous rumination. I had no answers, just more and more questions, like ants crawling inside my skull. I ached to talk to Father Cornelis!

But instead, I supervised Geertje as she packed our bags for the trip. Clothes, shoes and hats for different occasions, toiletries, a letter-writing pack, Johan's business papers, books, umbrellas. He was to meet some businessmen, several well-known financiers and share traders in Antwerp – David's connections – and some potentially large buyers of silk in Paris. This was primarily his business trip, but it was also to be our common pleasure, something to remember. I felt too listless to even imagine trying to win back my husband, or just to keep myself amused. After all this gloomy contemplation, I decided not to be a burden to Johan, no matter what. I felt unwanted and sad, but I had to preserve my dignity. I felt sorry for him too; he might have been torn between his ambition, the fulfilment of which demanded conventional propriety, and his desires.

## 10

We arrived at the harbour mid-morning. The sun had already bounced high in the sky and the wind was picking up, which would help our sailing. The northerly breeze was going through my bones – what a contrast from last week when it looked almost like summer. The Flemish ship that would take us to Antwerp was berthed right in front of the Customs House. The beautiful white building, harmonious and peaceful, contrasted with the dark sea of the harbour. Perhaps seeing beautiful buildings and new things would be pleasant after all, and everything would fall into place? Could *the problem* disappear? Could I forget what I knew? I sometimes felt a little annoyed with Geertje. Did she have to tell me? I was sure she meant well; I could not, I should not hold it against her.

A handsome officer with a honey-coloured waxed moustache, in an impeccable, tight-fitting uniform, told us we would take two days at the most to sail to Antwerp, and if we had a good wind in the sails all along, a day and a half. A hazy red sun was still well above the horizon when we sailed into the Antwerp harbour the next day, through the wide estuary of the river Scheldt. The city impressed me with grand port buildings visible from afar, and an elegant white fortification built by the Spaniards who ruled the city in the past century. As we sailed through the vast port, we stood at the deck and Johan chatted about Antwerp's business tradition with the first officer, a native of the city. The officer talked enthusiastically about the centuries-old diamond, sugar, pepper and cinnamon trades that attracted people from all over Europe, the Mediterranean and even India. The city was the world centre of the diamond trade with the unique Jewish-dominated diamond bourse. Sephardic Jews had been arriving during Spanish rule; they were undesirable in Spain but tolerated in Flanders.

I felt a flicker of enthusiasm; perhaps wandering through a cosmopolitan city where French, Spanish, Portuguese, German, Greek and even Arabic could be heard in the streets would make me forget my marital woes. Amsterdam was an open city, businesses-driven and diverse, but still so supremely Dutch. Antwerp, in contrast, struck me as a European city, a world city even. Doing business with everyone saved us from the worst of wars and destruction, according to Johan. It seemed this idea guided the city of Antwerp too. If it was either business or war, business was better – who could argue with that? Does that apply in marriage? – the thought flashed through my head.

As the ship approached the quay, a sailor threw a thick, noosed rope across to a port officer who hooked it onto a mooring. I could see people waiting, clumped in small groups. It was a more colourful crowd than the sombre Amsterdamers: a man with a turban, another wearing a fez, two Indian women in shiny saris, and all European races, from Italian and Spanish-looking ladies to the local Flemish folk. By the time we walked across the plank and handed our luggage to a porter, the streetlamps were being lit. I felt the thrill of travel again, seeing new places, new people, the anticipation when turning a corner on an unknown street. I glanced at Johan as we were climbing into a coach; his face had a stony expression. Was he excited, interested? He was not giving anything away.

The streets of Antwerp were wider than ours, and houses were not as tall, narrow and tightly packed along the canals as in Amsterdam. The coachmen's Flemish Dutch had a melodious lilt. The Noble Antwerpian inn was in Joodenstraat, around the corner from the Rubenshuis, which had beautiful gardens designed by the master painter himself and open to visitors, the driver told us. I decided this would be my first sightseeing point.

The guest room at the inn was smaller than our bedroom at home, with a dark, heavy wooden bed and starched white sheets that felt a little rough to touch. We ate downstairs and Johan drank nearly a bottle. I had several sips of the strong Spanish red wine that tasted of the warm South, and the heat settled into my cheeks and my body.

During a somewhat silent dinner, I had suggested a short walk in the endless June dusk to get to know our new surroundings, perhaps the Rubenshuis gardens, but Johan was not enthusiastic and I had no good reason to insist. 'Let's get you pregnant,' he suddenly suggested as we stepped back into our room. I was a little wary and felt almost shy; we had not shared marital intimacies for a month. The thought of David sprang to my mind, but when Johan pressed his body against mine and lifted my dress in search of the bare skin at the top of my stockings, my body responded, tingling with desire. I helped Johan unfasten my dress. As the heavy fabric slipped on the floor, he embraced me again and I felt his hard manhood pressed against my thigh.

Johan kissed me passionately, pushing my mouth open with his tongue in a new way. His hand fondled my buttocks under my silk petticoat while undoing his trousers with the other hand. He was in a hurry, even more than usual, only this time I felt the same.

I uncovered the bed and we slipped onto the pristine bed-sheets. I loosened the cords of my bodice and Johan got there in a moment, sucking my breast which he had freed with an urgent hand. I embraced him on top of me. He grabbed my ankle, lifted my bent leg and slipped deep inside me, forcefully, with a grunt. I usually disliked his abrupt lovemaking but this time I was as ready as he was. The coupling was smooth, and the usual tinge of pain was instead an extreme pleasure. I heard myself gasping. As he achieved a good rhythm, I felt waves of pleasure rising higher and higher in a perfect progression, not the usual chaos of pleasure and pain colliding. As Johan regained possession of both my breasts with one hand, I felt my body tightening into a spasm and then bursting into a fast sequence of delightful contractions. Johan grunted loudly with his last push, staying inside this time, his full weight collapsing onto my damp body. 'Francesca,' he uttered, as if checking the sound of the word. He'd never before called me by my 'foreign' name; he preferred the ordinary 'Fransje'.

A moment later he had already fallen asleep. I eased myself off his heavy, limp body and stood up looking for a clean shift. The room was warm and saturated with our smells. We had not washed since the morning before we boarded the ship in Amsterdam. I opened the wooden shutters and the glass panes of the window. A French party was exchanging loud farewells in the street below. I returned to bed and covered myself and gently snoring Johan. Perhaps Antwerp and Paris wouldn't be so bad after all, I thought before falling fast asleep.

On our last morning in Antwerp, the inn's errand boy knocked at our door with a message that our hired coach had arrived. He offered to take our bags downstairs. Johan tipped him unusually generously. We waved to the lady at the reception, who was displaying her ample bosom in a low-cut dress that morning, and stepped outside into the cool damp air. It was going to be a nice day once the late spring sunshine burned off the mist. Farewell Antwerp!

## 11

I couldn't wait to arrive in Paris! The trip from Antwerp was hard. After four days of ceaseless rocking and shaking in a confined space of the coach, I felt as if I had spent time on a ship in rough seas. I could not eat when we stopped for meals, and I slept poorly at night; the bed appeared too still and the room too quiet. We had to stop more often than planned because of my motion sickness. Patiently, Johan helped me in and out of the carriage, whose soft velvety seats unfortunately carried smells of previous passengers, making my nausea worse. Johan agreed to seek a different return trip, by sea from the closest port of Le Havre.

Paris was all that I expected, and much more. Amsterdam was quiet and orderly in comparison. Wide streets were packed with carriages to the point that crossing them was a challenge. At night, we had to close the windows of our hotel room on the bank of the Seine to block out the noise. The clatter of horses trotting on cobblestones mixed with loud voices of inebriated passers-by and an occasional shriek from ladies of the night. Overnight, the sloping grassy banks of the Seine hosted vagrants and amorous couples. The traffic of carriages started again at dawn.

The city showed its splendour ostentatiously and its misery

shamelessly. Quite different from Amsterdam where both extremes were restrained and invisible, perhaps even non-existent? The hotel staff explained that the elegant part of the city was behind the hotel, away from the river. Over there, the streets were astir with life and movement, the calling of vendors and the rattling of coaches. Meticulously made-up ladies in ornate dresses, often holding coiffed little poodle dogs whose hair colour mimicked their owners', accompanied by gentlemen or maids, rubbed shoulders with expensive *courtisanes*. It was hard to tell them apart.

It was a fascinating world which I marvelled at for a few days, but I soon began to feel saturated and a little out of place. My clothes, elegant in Amsterdam, were bland and even austere here, amid powdered wigs, brocade dresses, heavy make-up, strong perfumes and sparkling jewellery. I felt underdressed but not keen to shop; Parisian-style outfits would be considered excessive in Amsterdam society anyway. I had to bring something from Paris, so I bought perfumes in beautifully shaped little bottles for myself, Maman and Johan's mother.

While Johan had his business meetings or spent his mornings observing the workings of the *bourse*, I spent several days in the Palais du Louvre, not so long ago the royal residence, admiring its luxury salons. After the royal court moved to Versailles, the Louvre became a home to the *Académie Royale de Peinture et de Sculpture*, which was teaching, making and exhibiting art. In the Louvre, I felt at home again: I could immerse myself in art and talk to artists from several workshops, most of them producing painting and statues commissioned by rich patrons. A kind young gentleman took me around and explained the exhibits; he was keenly interested in Master Rembrandt and his subdued, dark-hued portraiture. The *Académie* had two Rembrandt pieces, both self-portraits. Pascal was impressed by my knowledge of Rembrandt and his peculiar style, which he saw as testifying to a 'lack of vanity'.

'Oh, the French are so vain.' Pascal laughed. 'Including artists, even the best of them! There has to be colour, movement, brilliance, red, gold, bright blue . . . surely not just the shades of brown!'

I was glad that Pascal offered his company the next day, too. He was a young *Comte* studying painting and specialising in portraiture, knowledgeable and talkative, but also listening carefully to my responses. Pascal told me his father was not happy about his interest in art. Art was not manly enough, and nobility was not supposed to mingle freely with *artistes*. It was too much like work as well; the nobles could enjoy art, and they owned valuable pieces, including portraits that projected the family status. But getting one's hands dirty with paint? *Bon Dieu!* Pascal's father was hoping the art school was his son's passing infatuation and he would soon come to his senses; a military or political career was a proper pursuit for a noble son. He suspected his mother suggested a softer approach to her husband: sit tight and wait until the problem went away. Hours flew past in Pascal's company.

Johan became interested when he heard I was acquainted with a young nobleman, so he joined me on my last visit to the Louvre. It was not jealousy that prompted him, even though I would have perhaps liked that. Rather, this was his unique opportunity to meet a member of the French nobility. Unfortunately, Pascal was absent that day. We cut our visit short and had an early lunch. I felt a desire for a coffee sold on the street, but Johan suggested that we not rely on street vendors. This was the usual cautious Johan, and it was only reasonable of me to agree. He thought Paris was more advanced with textiles, fashion, perfumes and food, but much behind Amsterdam with banking and finance. The Parisian *bourse* had been in existence for a mere fifteen years.

'You're right!' I said. 'The food has been delicious so far; I've put back on all the weight I lost during the trip. And their mocha is even better than in Amsterdam!' An excellent lunch of chicken and asparagus, with a dessert of *les petits fours* with coffee, added to our appreciation of the city. Johan was more relaxed and talkative than usual, as if he became a little bit French himself. I enjoyed his company as much as at the very start of our courtship, and our marital intimacies became regular again. I was reprimanding myself for my anxiety and started to think Geertje's revelation was just some sort of mistake, one way or another.

I also visited the Notre Dame, a short walk across the bridge from our hotel. There was plenty of exquisite art there as well. The Nieuwekerk's austere interior invited contemplation of death, God and eternity, but the highly decorated Notre Dame reminded the faithful of this life with its joys and sorrows. Next to the splendid church was the Hôtel Dieu, a shelter and hospital for the poor and the sick. Johan reluctantly agreed to accompany me there. He was baffled by my interest in the less fortunate in society – the orphans, the homeless, the poor and the sick, especially when this was not my recognised charity work.

It was clear as soon as we entered that this was nothing like the Burgerweeshuis. As we progressed through the long corridor, accompanied by a nun in a white robe with light blue apron, the stench became overpowering. I hated to appear precious, but my stomach could not take it. I was grateful when Johan suggested we leave. The nun spread her arms in resignation, half apologising, half protesting.

'It is overcrowded,' she explained. 'We cannot refuse sick people who come to our door. They fear they will die on the pavement without God's mercy. This is the result.'

'This is not healthy, Fransje!' Johan grabbed my arm and urged me out. 'You'll have to imagine the rest instead of seeing it with your very eyes.' He was right, I thought as we rushed out.

'It is a sad place, Johan. There are many destitute people in Paris. A great deal more than in Amsterdam, would you agree?'

Both the splendid and the sordid were glaringly on display in the metropolis of Paris.

## 12

We arrived back in Amsterdam at the end of June, as planned. Geertje was excited to see us back. The house was immaculate: the floors polished, rugs clean and fresh looking. Geertje had visited her parents for two weeks while we were away. She had helped with farm work and looked tanned and healthy. Sarah rushed to the kitchen to prepare a light evening meal of mashed carrots and potatoes and cheese omelette. So simple and Dutch, I thought as I tucked into it. The dusk seemed endless, noticeably longer than in Paris, and the sky was still dark pink above the canal when we finished our supper at eleven. I remembered Brother Cornelis's geography lesson about latitude, the tilted Earth's travel around the sun and the seasons. The city barely slept around midsummer. People were crossing Lommertbrug at every hour. I loved the midsummer season – it was magic, even though I could not sleep much and often spent time at dawn at my window looking at the red and grey clouds flowing and overlapping, reflected in the dark water of the canal.

When Johan retreated to his little office and Geertje came in to clean the table after supper, I told her she would do some errands for me in the morning. She was to visit the Burgerwee-shuis and tell them I'd be there the next day. On her way, she'd drop by De Krijtberg at the Singel and inquire whether Father Cornelis was back in town, and if he was, when and where I could see him. Geertje nodded eagerly, looking forward to resuming her usual duties.

The next morning, I again woke up far too early. When I sat up in bed, trying not to wake Johan, I felt nauseous. I swallowed and lay back; the feeling faded. I tried again a few minutes later. It was now even more intense. Instead of enjoying my morning contemplation at the window overlooking Lommertbrug, I rushed to the bathroom and dry-retched. There was nothing to throw up; my stomach was empty. I drank a sip of water and returned to bed. My mother was expected to visit that morning and I remembered her explaining morning nausea was what pregnant women often experienced. I had never been sick otherwise. I had not bled since before the trip. This must be it, I thought; an Antwerp baby was growing inside me!

Should I tell Maman? Of course, I must! She should know. To whom else would I tell such a thing? The nausea didn't leave much room for positive excitement, and I felt a tinge of anxiety. How would Johan react? No doubt he'd be pleased.

But then I remembered David. Would a baby change anything for us? Would the prospect of being a father prevent Johan, who highly valued respectability and social convention, from succumbing to his errant desires?

I couldn't wait to talk to Father Cornelis. He was back and happy to see me the next morning at eleven.

'You are pale, Fransje!' My mother rushed to me and pressed me against her soft bosom. She smelt of roses. 'Is anything wrong? You're not ill, my dear child?'

'Oh no Maman, don't worry, just a bit queasy this morning.'
'Queasy . . . ?'
'Yes, for the first time today . . .'

My mother's eyes sparkled. 'You mean, you're pregnant?' Her face beamed with an irrepressible smile.

'I don't know, Maman. It is possible. I have not bled since before we left Amsterdam.'

'Possible, you say! I think this is it, my sweet Fransje! *Voilà!* I will soon be a grandmother! That's wonderful! It was about time! You've told Johan, ya? He must be pleased!'

'Well, no, I haven't actually. It was only this morning that I felt sick, and I remembered this might be because—'

'How have you been, *chère maman?* Any news during our absence?' Johan entered the living room and greeted my mother before kissing me on the cheek.

'Well, my dear Johan, the news seems to be at your end! You will become a father in about eight months!' Her grin was the widest I'd seen in years.

Johan turned to me with his eyes, and his whole face, wide open with anticipation. I had hardly seen such an expression of genuine interest on his face before.

'Um, yes, it seems so . . . but we shouldn't rush to celebrate just yet. Let's wait for few weeks. It's too early to know for sure.'

'Yes, Fransje, I understand, perhaps it's better to be a little cautious. But I'd be very happy if we are to become a family.' He got me up from the chair, embraced me and kissed me again. 'This is going to be our foreign child then!'

Geertje appeared at the door and curtsied. By the look on her face I was sure she had heard Johan's last remark.

'Geertje, please do not spread the news before we know whether we have any news. Do you understand?'

'Of course, my lady.' She smiled. 'My lips are sealed.' She made a sign of a cross over her lips. 'I shall bring your lunch upstairs if you're ready?'

## 13

The next morning, I felt nauseous again, but getting ready for the Burgerweeshuis took my mind off my discomfort, and by the time I arrived there, I felt steady again. My pupils were happy to see me back and I was glad to be needed and liked. It was uplifting to see the children cheerful and chatty. The older girls wanted to know about Paris. I told them about the crowd-ed boulevards with their hawkers selling brandy, coffee, bread, water, just about everything – including sex, but of course I did not mention the latter. I told them about fashionable ladies with huge hairstyles carrying small dogs, but also about paupers, beggars and children that wandered through the city streets and did not seem taken care of, or even noticed by the passers-by.

'I think Amsterdam is a better city than Paris,' I ended my story. I was amused that the children were visibly disappointed with such a conclusion.

We then read stories and sang. Singing always led to laughter because not everyone had an ear for music and some of the boys' voices were breaking, producing unexpected, comical sounds.

Children could usually absorb me fully, but that morning my thoughts kept straying towards Father Cornelis: a hope was burning hot in my chest that his knowledge and generosity of spirit would help me, guide me, show me the way out of the cage of the doubts and worries that were, after our return, again besetting me.

Father Cornelis appeared as soon as I entered the house of De Krijtberg at eleven, as arranged. He nodded and pointed towards a side room. When we were close enough to the door, he smiled and extended his arm, letting me enter the room first.

'Francesca, you have matured and you're a real lady now! I hope you're well and happy. I should address you as a lady. What is your married name?'

0

'I am now Mrs Hoekstra.'

'Mrs Hoekstra, what a nice surprise that one of my students thought it worthwhile to see me again after ... how long? Five, six years?'

'Yes, six years, Father. Six years that separate the curious youngster and a married woman who ... well, has some problems.'

'I am sorry to hear that! I thought you wanted to talk about teaching?'

'Well, yes, I've been helping with teaching in the Burgerwees-huis since last year. But ... something else is foremost in my mind right now.'

I took a deep breath and told him about my problem and how I learned about it. It took longer than expected. I told him about my thoughts and dilemmas, about the person Johan was, and our somewhat distant relationship. I told him I was probably pregnant. I finished with questions: what did he think about Johan's 'unnatural tendencies'? Should I talk to Johan or pretend not to know anything?

Father Cornelis remained silent for a few moments.

'This is not what I expected, and I must admit no-one has ever asked me similar questions. I'm not sure Greek philoso-phers are much to go by; the world has changed in the past two thousand years' – he gave me a broad smile – 'and all Christian churches regard homosexuality as repugnant; moreover, as a serious transgression which warrants excommunication.' He paused, looking pensive.

I waited for him to continue even though questions multi-plied in my head.

'As to the "unnatural tendencies",' he continued, 'they may not be as rare as we think. Perhaps they are not even as unnatural as we think. Of course, a man and a woman are a natural couple, united in marriage so that the next generation can be born and raised. But not everyone fits into this mould, and only those who have no sins should cast the first stone...'

His view did not surprise me. Father Cornelis taught me to think with my own head and he did the same. I was hoping to hear some more. I stayed quiet. He lifted his head and his eyes met mine. It was my turn to speak.

'What should I do, Father? I need your guidance!'

'I am sorry, but I cannot give you such advice. We do not know whether this is a new thing in Johan's life or something quite old which you did not know about. It is unlikely a man of thirty has only just discovered this side of himself. If you think you can live with your husband as he is and has been over the two years of your marriage, and be a good mother to his children, then this may be enough. From all I know, hearing people's confessions, no marriage is perfect, Mrs Hoekstra. You are too intelligent to have expected eternal bliss, as some people do, am I right? Perhaps your relationship changes and improves with the arrival of children. Often, men open up and become warmer and closer to their families through children.' He paused. 'Only time can tell.'

'But I cannot get it out of my mind, Father. The questions nag inside me day and night. Do you think I could talk to Johan about it?'

Father Cornelis took a deep breath.

'You know your husband, Mrs Hoekstra, and I do not. If he is a reasonable and mature man, perhaps being open would help your relationship. He would know you can tolerate his ... tendencies, and perhaps this would give him peace of mind. He is probably quite concerned himself. It is difficult to have such a secret. If you spoke about this, you could have a secret together, rather than having a secret between you, one that pulls your marriage apart. This may not cure him though.'

'Thank you, Father Cornelis. I think this is good advice. I cannot live with this secret weighing on my heart. I will talk to Johan.'

'Good luck, Mrs Hoekstra. May God be with you.'

## 14

A loud thump awoke me, then I heard a man swearing. My heart pounded. The darkness in the room was nearly complete. The small hours of the morning; in the sultry night of early August there was no sign of dawn yet.

'Johan . . . ?'

No reply, just a painful grunt, then swearing again. I had never heard Johan swearing, but it was his voice, words pushing through pain. I sat on the bed and lit up the oil lamp on the bedside chest as fast as I could. I stepped barefoot through the open bedroom door; it was never closed when Johan was not in bed with me.

I lifted the lamp. Johan was sprawled on the wooden floor of the landing, trying to lift himself on his elbow, as after a fall, his left foot still overhanging the last stair. He must have tripped. Next to him was a puddle of an indiscriminate colour. Vomit!

'Johan, are you all right?

'No, no . . .' He lifted his head and his hand upwards towards me; his expression was pain and disgust combined.

I put the lamp on the floor and squatted next to him. I could smell alcohol.

'You were drinking!' I felt my stomach lifting. I felt sickened and disappointed.

'Yes, I was drinking . . . and worse . . . !' His voice was low and hoarse.

'Worse? What happened, Johan?' Contrary to my overall feeling towards him, presently I felt little compassion for an inebriated husband lying in his own vomit – a new low of his drinking habit. A feeling of disillusionment and loss settled on my chest like a physical weight. Then a thought formed in my mind, one that perhaps most women have when their marriages go wrong and their men misbehave: 'Did I somehow deserve this? Is it my fault?'

'Yes, worse!' Johan's voice was full of scorn. 'Someone saw me doing things that no-one should have seen. Prepare for a scandal, *Francesca*.'

He was slurring his words. My foreign name came out of his mouth with a sarcastic inflection.

I stood up and Johan managed to lift himself from the floor too.

'With David . . . ?' I had to force the words out of my throat.

Johan growled in return. 'How come you know everything, you witch?'

He grabbed me by the shoulders and shook me, holding me close to him.

'So you know too,' he hissed into my face. 'Perhaps everyone knows! I'm ruined!' His breath smelt of vomit and alcohol.

He then pushed me away. I stepped back, but the floor of the landing disappeared from under my foot; just the empty space above the steep stairwell curving down two floors to the *Voorhuis*. I lost balance and hit the wall along the stairs sideways, then bounced back onto the stairwell.

'Oh, God, no!' I heard Johan's scream before my back hit the angular wooden edge of the stairs. Then I rolled down head-first. I felt a lightning strike of hot pain at the back of my neck and then there was darkness first, then silence.

## Post Fabulam II
## Melbourne, 2021

Life's ups and downs!

Two young lives ruined in a moment of tension and confusion. Drinking husbands – how many marriages, how many lives marred, diminished, ruined this way? How many deaths? And those steep stairs in tall, narrow Amsterdam houses! Most of the houses were built over three centuries ago; how many people have died by falling down the stairs during this time? Perhaps someone's done the research, offered an estimate? Some of those stairwells soar two floors up without as much as a landing. They are too steep and narrow to carry anything bulky up or down, including sick people and dead bodies. They have to be hoisted through the window.

As a rare distinction from ordinary mortals, I can remember my own deaths. Five unnatural deaths. Is it a terrible thing to have one's life 'cut short'? I don't know. But it made me remember George Orwell's musing on the matter: 'It's better to die violently and not too old. People talk about the horrors of war, but what weapon has man invented that even approaches in cruelty some of the commoner diseases?'

I read these words in my twenties and was gripped by them. And now I'm awaiting death from a 'commoner disease'. My own death has never been my worst fear. But perhaps that's just me, who has lived and died before? For most dwellers of the 'First World', dying is much better than in Orwell's times: modern medical conveniences make the passing painless, peaceful, perhaps even pleasant; add morphine, and one may not return from a wonderful dream! So why not give up the ghost peacefully, without protesting too much, and leave room on Earth for others?

*Now that I know*, thinking about death invites a whole assortment of feelings. It's inspiring. There is even some enjoyment in the mix. People who live very long lives watch their friends, all the people dear to them, die one after another, and feel increasingly alone, left behind. I've heard this first-hand, more than once. In recent years, I've often thought about ageing. It cannot be fun to live in an old, worn body. Patronised. Handled when you become rickety. Others waiting for you to die. Old: when people think you're dead if you don't pick up the phone when they call.

But most oldies do everything possible to repair, renovate, regenerate their achy, creaky, shaky bodies. People cling to the last minutes of life. Yet death is a problem for those who remain, not for those who leave. Will Bertie be sorry when I'm gone? He is polite and thoughtful, but not wearing his heart on the sleeve. He is not neurotic, not prone to love his suffering. Good for him. And Bruno, my only son? He's a grown-up and it's normal to bury one's parents, so . . .

It would be hard to argue in polite company that dying violently, and young, is not as bad luck as it may appear at first sight. And yet . . .

# III: *The War*

## Françoise (1791–1818), Avignon

WE LIVE OUTSIDE THE WALL. *Paysans.* People of the land. The townsfolk of Avignon look down on us. But our *faubourg* is a heathier place to live than the city of smelly, narrow streets and damp buildings inside the medieval ramparts. We have fresh air, sun comes to our windows, and our village rats are happy enough in the corn shed without visiting the kitchen. In the walled town, windows are nearly always shaded by the walls of other houses across the narrow streets. Ships coming up the Rhône have brought rats and plague to the town several times. The cemetery had to be extended. It is now as large as the town itself. It is easier to survive an epidemic outside the walls. And naturally, we are better fed in these years of war. The starveling burghers must take a purse bursting with gold francs to the market. The maids of Avignon always taste-check our fruit, cheese and olives, even though they know very well what it all tastes like, the clever girls! We then wrap the freshly slaughtered chickens in their cloths or large vine leaves and fill their jugs from our milk pails. They think they are better off, the haughty folk of Avignon; yet they depend on us to feed them.

Twice a week, I rise with the first light of dawn and load our produce onto the small cart. It is hard without Jules. I leave baby Simon with my mother, rushing to fit market day between nursing him. On Wednesdays, the market is on the elm-shaded square in front of the southern town gate. On Saturdays, it's beside the Rhône, in a paved space reclaimed from the mud of the riverbank, at the foot of the Pont d'Avignon and partly shaded by the forbidding walls of the Popes' Palace. My father helps me to harness Louis, our tall black donkey. Louis isn't named after our hapless king who lost his head under the guillotine nearly twenty years ago, *non!* He's named after the mayor of Avignon, who has adopted the regal name. His stiff and affected manner is in line with his name, but both are beyond his natural station. His big ears and small stature, alongside his unpopularity, is why in winks and whispers, people call him 'donkey'; in turn, our donkey is named Louis.

'Let's go, Louis!' I murmur in his ear. He pricks his ears and sometimes stomps his hoof. He understands me! I don't make his name public; people can be mean and vengeful, so better not to give them ammunition. These days one can be fined for 'contempt of the public office', I've heard at the market – so serious we French have become about our Republic! A republic, ruled by an emperor? Ah, the politics and the powers that be! It's better not to even try to understand it! You just nod and feign respect but live by your own rules as much as you can. Their rules change all the time, as those who make them come and go, rise and fall.

I often wonder why Jules was so ready to leave. We'd been married less than a year; I was six months pregnant with Simon. Maybe he wanted adventure? Jules came to live with my parents because I had no brother to bring in his wife, and Jeanne, my older sister, married and moved to her husband's family home in another village two years ago. But my parents adored Jules. My father and Jules got on like a house on fire, especially over a glass or two of red wine in the evenings. The farm was doing well; we never went hungry, and our market garden provided a steady income.

Jules seemed happy, content. But when the Mayor's courier delivered the conscription letter one early morning in March, he looked at the Emperor's signature and didn't curse or protest. Within a week he was ready to go. Jules thought he would fight for France and its great revolution that would free the whole of humanity. Do all men have their heads in the clouds?

Town criers are busy these days announcing new laws; they passed through the market to announce to all and sundry that French is now our official language, and that is how we should speak, not Occitan or Provençal. 'How can they decree how we speak all of a sudden?' people were saying. 'We cannot speak French even if we wanted to!' I agree! Those officials drumming this line, and generals who trot through with their armies, paid by our taxes, they can speak it, rather than ordering us, who feed them, not to say 'Avinhon' and 'Avinhonen' but 'Avignon' and 'Avignonians'. Why should we, who spend our days watering vegetables and milking cows, give up our language, my father says. And I wonder, would Louis the donkey understand me if I started to speak French the way they speak in Paris? It was even decreed that the *Courrier d'Avignon* be written in French, not Occitan. People are complaining. And I, *je m'en fiche!* What worries me more is that since before I was born, Provence, and the whole of France, have not had peace. Will the war ever end?

Federalists, royalists, republicans, papists: army after army march through the town and around it, bringing fear and hunger because not only do we have to display our respect and loyalty, we have to feed them too! They sweep through the village like a swarm of locusts; sometimes officers 'collect contributions' half-politely, but at other times they just let their soldiers loose to demand food and hospitality as they see fit. Avignon, at the crossroad of kingdoms, is even more exposed to marauding armies.

The generation of our fathers fought in the 1790s and now it is our turn, they say. Making women widows and children orphans, that's what war does! For the peasant youth, the war is a way to escape the everyday tedium and backbreaking work, and to see faraway places and foreign lands which the poor folk would never see otherwise. But what a price they pay for it!

Jules may not even know that he has a son. I sent him a letter, but only God knows whether he received it. I don't even know if he's alive. I hope he is because we have received no letter with a golden signature from the Emperor Napoleon. Many unfortunate families have received it. The conscription letter has an ordinary black ink signature; for the death of a soldier, it is in gold.

## 2

I was five or six when I first heard people at the market arguing about the great general, Napoleon Bonaparte. He was flying on the wings of the people's great revolution, and spreading the seeds of freedom, equality and brotherhood around the world, the story went. *Liberté, égalité, fraternité*! I remembered the words immediately, without knowing what they meant. I learned later they meant France was the greatest nation, the nation of free people. We were to be ruled by reason, our own reason, not superstition and religion! Three years after the revolution broke out in Paris and before the King's head fell into the basket at the guillotine, the Church was reined in. Holy orders were disbanded, and monks and nuns expelled from abbeys and convents.

Here in Avignon, the wartime started with a massacre in the Palais des Papes. That forbidding popes' palace, rising menacingly above town, what else could happen there but horror? People still talk about mutilated bodies tossed onto carts like firewood and taken to the graveyard. Some of the distraught relatives managed to take their dead back home to have a proper Christian funeral with a requiem mass, to commend their sons and husbands to our Lord. Others never found their murdered menfolk; the executioners were in a hurry to bury them, to hide the evidence of the atrocities.

My mother was pregnant with me at the time, and the shock and fear upon hearing about it nearly made her go into labour. Like most women she loathed war and military glory and was suspicious of the revolution. Lucky my father had the sense not to get involved in the quagmire of local politics. Only a few *paysans* did; political intrigues were the province of the burghers of Avignon, those whose shoes were seldom smeared in mud.

When I was a girl of thirteen or fourteen, I was told many times that I was too old – but also that I was too young – to wander around on my own, especially at the time of war. I was not fifteen yet when a solitary soldier, a straggler, possibly a deserter, turned up at our doorstep. His uniform was torn and tattered, his hair dirty and dishevelled; he explained he was lost and hungry. Maman offered a meal and a glass of red wine and Papa offered him the hay shed to rest in overnight. He said he had to go, try to find his regiment. The soldier didn't take his eyes off me while I served him, and asked me to see him out of the village. I hesitated; I looked at Maman and saw that she was alarmed, but he insisted and started dragging me out of the house. We both cried out and Papa came back from the yard to see what the commotion was about. The soldier left me and pointed his gun at Papa, who was composed enough to say: 'So will French soldiers now shoot the honest French folk?' The soldier cursed, spat on the ground, pushed him aside, hurting his shoulder with the butt of his musket, and ran away. Bewildered and frightened for his own life, he was a danger to others.

My mother mentioned this incident many times, as I started to collect herbs, first for our own kitchen, then for sale. I was so good at it that she relented, and we added the herbs to our regular market offer. Little fragrant bunches were popular with the city folk. At the time of wartime austerity, people clung to these precious little luxuries. I often wondered why they were ready to pay for them even though they could easily collect the herbs on a short walk along the river, just outside the ramparts. But the city folks did not like to make their shoes dusty, let alone muddy – that was below the status they had to uphold. Just like most *paysans*, they did not seem to care to hear the birdsong, the sound of the flowing river, the noise of the wind in pine trees, or the burbling of a creek. The clicking of fashionable wood-and-leather heels on the stone paving of narrow city lanes was the sound they recognised and liked to hear, the sound of respectable people outfitted in their elaborate frocks, or civil servants in their long black coats. The maids did not make noise; they were expected to tread softly in their leather slippers and be able to run if needed. But in this modern war, living inside the ramparts could also mean deprivation and trouble, not protection and privilege. Roaming free in the meadows and bosquets was so much better than worrying about my appearance, subject to curious, judging glances of the uppity burghers.

I was a wild child, a tomboy, using every free moment to run out to the fields, along the Rhône, and into the wooded hills. Those moments were not many, as there was always work to do in the house, in the barns and in the vegetable garden. If I wanted some time to myself, I had to make up my mind quickly.

Once, I ran all the way to the river Durance and was caught in the dark on an unfamiliar part of the riverbank, lined by goat willows. I slipped in the mud and ended up in the murky shallows, wet up to my chest. I ran back home through the fields, under the moonlight, cold and scared but also happy and excited. Nothing could happen while I ran – I thought I could run away from anything and anyone! But there was no-one. Just scared rabbits scurrying in the dark and dogs barking in the distance. When I arrived home, breathless, my mother stared at me for a couple of moments and when she was sure I was just wet but otherwise unharmed, she slapped me so hard my ear was ringing for a while.

'Oh *maman* ... *pourquoi?*! I've just ...'

'You're *not* to roam about alone after dark, Françoise – never again! Have you learned nothing from what happened last year?'

I was nearly fifteen, already as tall as a grown woman, taller than most and well-developed. Everyone thought I was older and ready to be married, but my mother thought I was childish because I was happiest when running through the fields or hiding behind my favourite tree, a tall, broad elm on the bank of the Rhône. I used to embrace it and whisper to it, just like I later did to Louis the donkey. The tree was struck by lightning when I was a small child, but it recovered. It lost one large, charred branch coming straight up off its trunk; a long black scar was there now, and a hollow where woodpeckers liked to feed.

I used to wander far beyond the back fence of our farm, along little tracks and narrow water canals, among garden beds and larger fields, intoxicated by the smell of sage, my favourite herb, whose sticky leathery leaves I used to rub onto my hands, arms and neck to keep the fragrance on my skin. Rosemary, wild oregano and thyme, fennel and wild roquette plants up to my chest, mulberry trees and olive groves, vineyards and fields of sunflowers framed by rows of cypresses enchanted me. I felt part of it all. All I wanted was just to be there. Most villagers were indifferent to the sights, smells and sounds around them. They treated plants and animals as no more than a way to provide food for their families and sell surpluses to the Avignonians.

For me, plants and animals were not just things to grow, kill and eat; they were my friends. Not just faithful Louis the donkey, but also Vachine, our fawn-and-white milking cow, and the two pigs in the sty: Aubin, a white hog, and Babou, a mother of eight piglets, which soon ended in the Christmas ovens of well-to-do Avignonians. Aubin and Babou responded to their names – they turned around when called. Sometimes they looked at me as if to check that it was a familiar human bringing them their usual feed. They seemed to be thinking and wanting to say something, but all they could do was grunt. They surely were saying things to each other that I could not understand. Maman waved her hand dismissively when I told her, but she hid her smile and did not scold me. I knew she did not mind, but my father disapproved.

Each year, in early December, the terrified screams of pigs echoed through the village. During the slaughter season, the animals were restless and scared; they put up huge resistance to any movement or approach by humans. They were terrified when they heard the scrape of knife-sharpening, long before a razor-sharp blade approached their throat. When tied with a rope and taken out of the pen by two strong men, they knew what was coming to them. I am sure they did! Why otherwise their desperate screams? As a child, I used to run away, all the way to my elm tree shelter and hold my ears tight shut, which angered my father.

'You are a peasant girl, Françoise, not a lady! We raise and slaughter animals because we must eat. You have to eat too!

We also feed other people. Stop being silly and do your work.'

Yes, I had to eat. My job was to chop loads of onion, garlic, and herbs for sausages, and apples for the *boudin noir*. I ate the sausages, which were rolled and hung in the shed to dry; Maman cut them in small portions before the meal. Roasted on an open fire, at the end of a long fork, they tasted divine. I ate them as a special treat and in my thoughts, I thanked our hog for his sacrifice, after only a short life, so we could enjoy good food. I remember how happy our pigs were to see the daylight when they were let out into the small corner of the yard outside the pigsty. They dug and turned every patch of land into mud, but that's all they could do in a small space, in the service of humans. Their wild cousins in the forest are better off, free to roam, like me.

Papa was a hardworking man, or at least so he often claimed. He worried I was straying from a peasant girl's proper path: hard work and early marriage. Thinking too much, having odd ideas, might make me less appealing as a bride. I was in no hurry to become a married woman and in fact I felt sick when I thought about it. Once you have a house, children and a man to take care of, you can't just run out of the house and into the field or wander along the river to your favourite tree, can you?

Papa's fears did not come true. I was married at twenty. Jules was a diligent worker, and that was what mattered in a farming family. He was taciturn but amicable enough; his arrival didn't disturb our existing family order too much. We worked together harmoniously, and he did not make much of his husbandly power over me. He was indifferent to anything outside our everyday life, apart from military movements and the politics that directed them. They might affect us any day, he claimed, and he was not wrong. But whether animals had a soul, just like people? Were we committing sin when we cruelly and unceremoniously slaughtered them? This did not interest him in the slightest and when he was not interested, or when he disagreed, his response was silence. I didn't suppose it would be worth asking Father d'Eglantine either. He didn't seem like a man who would entertain thoughts outside biblical stories, or have the patience to talk to a peasant girl about such an unusual subject. I missed Simone.

Once Jules had gone, and with the baby, I barely had time to think of such things myself. At twenty-one, my youth was over. My mother helped look after Simon until she also departed, for good, before I could even imagine my strong Maman could be taken away by an illness. Simon was only one year old at the time. I worked so hard I barely had strength to pray for my mother's soul in the evenings; I'd fall asleep as soon as I stopped moving, often with Simon on my breast.

## 3

Simon was named after Simone. Simone, my lost friend, the only person who took all my thoughts and questions seriously, who taught me to read and write, and many other things. She used to sell elixirs at the market; her stall was behind mine and we became friends. But Simone didn't come to the market anymore, not since she reclaimed her vocation as a choir nun *chez les Chartreux*. I hoped she was well and happy somewhere. The last time I saw her, she'd been worried: Napoleon had ordered that all the religious orders' secret recipes for potions and medicines must be sent to the Ministry of Interior for review. Did the Carthusians surrender the secret of their famous *Elixir Végétal*? I still had some tucked away in the tallest shelf in the kitchen. Simone said it was to be taken in drops, and it could last forever. Sadly, it could not save Maman.

I had been accompanying Maman to the market from an early age, but when I was sixteen, she decided I was able to take over from her. I was tall and strong; I could unload baskets of produce from the cart and as a coach girl I was able to control our donkey – Louis and I had a secret pact – on the short ride from our *faubourg* to the ramparts of Avignon. By then I knew many people who were regulars at the market, either as sellers or buyers. An elegant woman who I knew by sight but not by name approached me on my first independent market day. Her stall had been back-to-back with ours for a while, and she spoke with Maman on occasions. She was selling drinks and potions in small bottles encased in wooden boxes.

'*Bonjour mademoiselle!* You are alone today! I hope your mother is not unwell?'

'Oh no, not at all! Thank God, she is fine! It's just that I will be coming here by myself from now on,' I declared, unable to hide my pride.

'*Très bien, très bien!* Your name is Françoise, *n'est-ce-pas?* I've heard your mother addressing you ... My name is Simone.' Her face lightened as her broad smile radiated towards me. She was beautiful and had nice teeth. Her shiny chestnut-coloured hair was tightened at the back of her head. She was wearing a black dress, buttoned up to her chin, with white lace around her neck and hands, at the end of tight-fitting sleeves. She looked a little austere but not at all like a peasant woman. She did not sound like one either.

'*Enchantée, madame!* Yes, I have seen you here before too ...'

'I would not like to distract you from your trade. There are many people at the market today – perhaps we can talk in the afternoon?'

'Yes, that would be nice!'

At midday, as the crowd thinned out, I remembered Louis

was still in harness. I had forgotten to let him loose to graze on the nearby riverbank, in the enclosure beside the marketplace allocated for this purpose.

'*Excusez-moi*, Madame Simone, would you be so kind to look after my stall for a minute while I attend to my donkey? I forgot about him, I'm sure he's cross with me.'

'*Bien sûr, ma chérie*. No trouble at all!' Her smile flashed again, as she scrunched her face humorously. 'Just call me Simone.'

I hurried to provide some water from the river to the thirsty beast. I patted him affectionately, apologising. Louis moved his ears forward and back a few times. I swiftly returned to my stall.

'Louis the donkey was hungry and thirsty, not being able to reach grass or water. I apologised and I think he forgave me.'

Simone smiled. She understood.

'You're good to your donkey. Not everyone is.'

'Our domestic animals are like us in many ways. And we could not survive without them. While they could survive without us!'

'Yes, I agree! Shall we sit under the tree? My legs are aching from standing up all morning.'

Church bells announced noon; this was a call to the faithful to pause their work and eat their midday meal.

'Yes, let's – I'm hungry as well! Looking at all this food being bought and sold reminds me of lunch much before I hear the bells . . . !'

We sat together on an empty jute bag and some cushions she took from her cabriolet and spread out on the grass.

I pulled out the lunch Maman packed for me early that morning – two fat slices of bread fried in butter and egg and an apple – and started to eat ravenously. I had arrived at the market at dawn.

'What do you sell in your little bottles, Simone?' I asked after I had swallowed a couple of large bites and my empty stomach stopped hurting. 'It was so noisy and busy this morning I couldn't hear what you were saying to your customers.'

'It's a liqueur, mainly. The tiny bottles contain *Elixir Végétal de la Grande Chartreuse*. The larger bottles are liqueur – some people refer to it as 'cordial' – usually called just *la Chartreuse*. It's sweet but very strong, alcoholic. It comes in yellow or green varieties.'

'Yes, I have heard of it. Who makes it?'

'It used to be made in an old convent across the Rhône … *la Chartreuse de Villeneuve-lès-Avignon*. It's a centuries-old recipe, believed to have medicinal properties. People buy it as medicine, as a tonic for their ailments. We also make an elixir, which comes in those small bottles, medicinal, and dearer.'

'How come you're selling it … if you don't mind me asking?'

Simone paused for a moment and straightened the bag we were sitting on with her hand. I noticed her fine hand and a beautiful ring with a blue gemstone.

'Well, many years ago, I was a novice at the convent of Chartreuse in Villeneuve. After the revolution, the convent was closed and the nuns thrown out. Some fled to Spain, some to Italy, some dispersed in France, especially here in the south where the Pope still controlled some parts. I had found a safe haven at Sisters of St Claire in Avignon. But this did not last; their convent was destroyed around the time of the massacre at the Palais des Papes …'

'Oh, yes, I've heard about the massacre from my mother.'

'At the time the Carthusian convent was destroyed, I had only been there for less than two years. I was on the path of completing the seven-year formation needed to become a professed nun. During that time, one must devote oneself to the study of the Bible and learn theology and liturgy. One gradually commits to living in solitude and silence …'

'That sounds difficult . . . were you not allowed to talk to others . . . ?'

'You can talk to others at specified times. Women – nuns – are less isolated than monks because they have more regular duties in the garden and kitchen. As you progress through the Carthusian ranks, you become gradually more devoted to seclusion, also depending on whether you're on the way to becoming a choir nun or a lay nun. First, you're a postulant; this is your trial period. You live like a nun but you have not yet taken your vows. You can change your mind if you find that the life of faith is not for you . . .'

'Do many people change their mind?'

'I don't think so. But I had only been at the Chartreuse for a short time and at the Sisters of St Claire's for another year, so I cannot tell you with certitude . . . The postulancy is followed by two years of novitiate. At this time you start to wear a full black cloak over a white habit.'

'So you did not want to get married and have children?' I immediately regretted asking the question. But Simone did not seem offended.

'No, I didn't.'

Simone stopped and took a deep breath, then continued, her forehead crumpled in a gentle frown.

'I wouldn't want to say things to a young woman like you . . . things that could sway your thinking. It is natural to marry and have children. But some people have a different calling, such as to enter a spiritual marriage with our Lord Jesus Christ. My family encouraged me to pursue my calling.'

'Tell me about the marriage to Jesus.'

Simone smiled pensively.

'I believe living only for one's own pleasures and happiness is a sinful way to live. Being a lady is such a life . . . a life of pleasure, apart from bearing children. Servants, nannies, indulgence in fine food and clothes ... and any intellectual or spiritual pursuit treated as a mere pastime. That was not a life I wanted.'

She paused for few moments. I was curious to hear more. I was not eager to be a wife either, for different reasons. Perhaps Simone would understand that too.

'We all need to contribute to society,' she continued, 'not just seek our own pleasures; or even just seek our own salvation. Useful work gives dignity to a person. I wanted a dignified life. I know the life of a monk or a nun may look easy to a peasant toiling in the field ... we do spend much time in prayer and contemplation of God, but this is not idleness. It is work and discipline. We also take care of most of our own needs ... and often make useful things, like the Chartreuse liqueurs and tonics. Nuns work in hospitals, do charity work ... Monks and nuns are educated so they can provide education to others. Dedicating one's life to faith is a privilege, but also a duty ... a demanding one if one takes it seriously.'

She touched the back of my hand lightly, then continued.

'I ... I was a shy and solitary child. My siblings and I had tutors and I liked books and learning. I especially liked calligraphy and music. My love of solitude had always outweighed my fear of it. When I was fifteen, I told my mother I did not want to marry, but instead to enter a convent and become a nun. In fact, choosing the life of a nun over marriage felt so natural it was as though the life chose me rather than me choosing it ...'

'And your mother agreed? And your father?'

'Yes, they did. In a family like mine, it is not unusual for one of the children to take religious vows.'

'Where is your family? What are they like?' Seeing that Simone did not mind answering my questions, I let my curiosity loose.

'My father died three years ago. My eldest brother lives on

the family estate with his family. In the south, next to Saint-Rémy-de-Provence. My mother is there too. My younger brother chose a military career. My sister is married in Arles. I returned to the family home after the convent of the Sisters of St Claire was destroyed, but there was nothing for me to do there. After less than a year, I returned to the Chartreuse at Villeneuve, which in the meantime became a workshop controlled by the local authorities. The commune of Villeneuve was under the Republican government, while Avignon was still a papal city. I have worked there since. I am hoping one day I'll be able to return to my spiritual calling.'

'What do you actually do at the Chartreuse at Villeneuve, apart from coming to the market? Your hands are white and fine – you're a lady, you do not labour on the land, do you?'

Simone tilted her head and laughed. 'You're quite observant! How old are you?'

'Sixteen.'

'Oh yes, I remember that age – I was in a hurry to grow older.'

'How old are you?'

'I am thirty-one, nearly twice your age.'

'Oh, I would have never guessed! You look young.'

Simone smiled but said nothing.

'During my time with *les Chartreux*, I learned about the liqueurs and tonics they have made for centuries. I know part of the recipe, so I work in the distillery. I know about the herbs that need to be macerated in alcohol to produce the green and yellow liqueurs. We use over a hundred different herbs; I supervise herb collection and treatment. Herbs are essential for the process of maturing the liqueurs, and crucial for the medicinal properties of the tonics. The cordials and potions need to age in oak casks for a long time – the longer the better. Once they are mature, I fill the bottles and bring them to the market. I write the labels too. They always sell well. I come here most weeks.'

'I love herbs too! I collect them regularly and sell them at the market. Mint and fennel, oregano and basil. I also pick wild roquette. I pick and dry camomile flowers. They are easier to dry than fruit – flies are not interested in them!' I laughed. I suddenly felt so happy; we had quite a lot in common, even though Simone was a lady, and I was a peasant girl. It was so enjoyable to talk with her! I had never spoken to anyone else in this way.

'Yes, I have noticed neat bunches of herbs on your stall. We always need herbs at the convent... that is, the workshop. You could trade with us, perhaps? I can check how much we can pay you. You can also swap your herbs for olive oil if you like. We work together with the *moulin de la Chartreuse*, the mill that makes olive oil.'

'Oh, that's wonderful, *merci beaucoup*, Simone! Maman will be impressed when I tell her.'

'And she may be wondering where you are too! We'd better go. We can talk more next week.'

# 4

My mother was indeed impressed. 'The first day trading by yourself, and you get a business offer – not bad at all, my girl!' She hugged me, then she pushed me gently away, holding me by the shoulders and looked me straight in the eye. 'But do be careful, *mon trésor*! There are all kinds of people out there; the revolution and the war have messed up the people and the old customs.'

'You always worry too much, Maman!'

I could not wait for the week to pass so I could see Simone again at the Saturday market.

She arrived early, just minutes after me, and set her stall next to mine. Mist hovered over the Rhône in the cool October morning. We chose a spot close to the water, that would not be in the long autumn shadows of the Palais des Papes once the sun was out. I greeted Simone and had to refrain from embracing her – this would have been inappropriate, as I was much younger and of lower rank, but I felt like we were old friends already.

'*Bonjour, ma chérie*! Nice to see you again!' She smiled and squeezed my hand tight between hers. Her hands were small, smooth and cold. 'It's a nippy morning! We'll have to dance to keep warm until the sun rises!'

I laughed, then sang the first line of an old song that everyone knew.

'*Sur le pont d'Avignon, on y danse, on y danse …*'

'*Bien sur!*' Simone stretched out her arms and performed a couple of light, jumpy dance steps *en rond*. We both giggled.

It took less than half an hour for the market to fill with people. Most trading was done before ten, and a little more before noon; after lunch the stalls were mostly empty. The people could then relax, greet their acquaintances, eat, talk with other traders and buyers, moving from one group to another to hear all the news. The market was the best way to learn the news.

At midday, Simone and I sat under the same tree as the last time. I tucked into the bowl of farm cheese with cream sprinkled with eschalots that Maman had prepared for me. Simone had a baguette, a large slice of blue cheese, and a couple of yellow pears. Upon hearing the pears were my favourites, she passed one to me. I protested.

'Do not worry, *ma chérie*, it's too much for me anyway. I am shorter and slighter than you. I need less food. You work hard and you have to eat.'

'That's what Maman says too!'

'You sold everything! Well done! My bottles are gone too! We could stroll down the riverbank if you have time?'

'Oh yes, let's do that! I can show you my secret hiding place at my favourite tree downstream.'

'A secret hiding place – what an interesting girl you are!'

We collected our things, placed our crates onto our respective carts and left. The cool morning turned into a pleasant, warm afternoon. The Rhône was sparkling in the sun.

'I feel so happy! Everything seems fine in the whole of the world!' I spread my arms and turned a full circle.

Simone laughed. 'Yes, I feel that way too! It is lovely, and it does not happen all the time!'

As we walked along the riverbank, Simone told me about the revolutionary calendar. In 1792, three years after the revolution, the first Republican government introduced a new calendar. This was another move against the Church and especially against the Catholic Church in France being subordinate to the Pope in the Vatican.

Simone explained that the latter part of the year became Year One of the new Republican era. The year started on the twenty-second of September, the day when the French Republic was proclaimed. The first month was *vendémiaire*, named after 'vintage', and the first day was dedicated to grapes. The Republican calendar replaced the Catholic calendar where each day had a protector saint; in the new calendar, days were named after everyday things – plants, animals, minerals, tools – in order to celebrate the ordinary life of French villagers. Months were named after wind and rain, budding, flowering and harvest. I learned that my herbs had their dedicated days and that March, my birth month, was divided between the *ventose*, the windy month, and *germinal*, the month of budding.

I clapped my hands together gleefully. 'What is there not to like in a calendar that follows the seasons and celebrates the gifts nature gives us?'

'Yes! I liked the new calendar too,' Simone agreed, 'even though it was created to diminish faith and the Church's influence. People grumbled for months against having to learn new names. People do not like change. Change is difficult. Following tradition and old customs puts people at ease and makes them feel safe. People fear whatever is contrary to their usual habits. In any case, Napoleon abolished the new calendar and reinstated the old Gregorian calendar last year.'

'Oh, pity! Yes, you are right about people disliking change. My mother always grumbles against new laws. She keeps saying the new regime won't last, and my father seems to agree.'

'Well, your parents are right – at least about the calendar. Three years ago, France stopped being a republic, so the days of the Republican calendar were numbered, so to speak!'

I chuckled.

'Yes – you cannot have a Republican calendar alongside the crowned Emperor Napoleon, can you?

'You are so right, Françoise! You are a smart girl! Napoleon wants to spread the revolution through creating a French Empire.'

'Hmm ... an emperor spreading a revolution ... doesn't that sound strange?'

I relished talking with Simone, and even more listening to her. She knew so much! My father and mother could remember many things, but Simone could also explain them. She talked so enchantingly, so passionately. The sinuous melody of her words stirred not just my mind, but my whole being. I felt a great pleasure in starting to understand the revolution and the wars that followed. For ordinary people like my parents, there were two sides, for and against, black and white, France and others, but Simone made it plain that things were usually more complicated. The times we lived in were idealistic and bold, but also disorderly, frightening and violent. Simone could have talked to a mass of people assembled in a square, or to an army in the field, just like Jeanne d'Arc. But she talked to me, just me. I felt lucky!

'There have been many changes, and too fast. This is why the old laws and customs may return. People need time to get used to changes, they need to be gradual, not violent and abrupt,' Simone argued.

'Here's my favourite tree. Let me show you my secret hide-away.' I was sorry to interrupt her.

'An elm tree. In the Republican calendar, there is an elm day in early March. Didn't you say you were born at that time?'

'Yes! Now I like the Republican calendar even more!'

'I have a copy of the calendar at home. You can have it if you like.'

We sat down in an enclosed alcove created by a low branch, in the narrow space between the tree trunk and the water's edge. In summer, the tree provided a deep shade. In October, as the elm started shedding leaves, a semi-shade was letting in the mild autumn sun.

'Oh, I'm not sure what my parents would say if I brought such a thing home. They are not too pious, just suspicious of the revolution and its novelties. But I would love to see it . . . and learn the names of all the months.'

'Can you read, Françoise?'

'A little . . . not well. I can recognise the words one sees often: 'France', 'Franc' and my own name. I know all the letters, and if I have time, I can put together and understand words, but only slowly.'

'Would you like to learn to read and write properly?'

'Oh yes, I'd love to! Even if my parents don't agree! My father thinks it's not good for a woman to think too much.'

'I've been tutoring several children from Avignon and Ville-neuve. Perhaps you could join the younger group; they learn to read and write. You are older, and you will quickly catch up with them. You could join the class on Sunday after church if you like?'

'*Oh oui, oui! Merci beaucoup*, Simone.' Then, I suddenly remembered I was just a peasant girl. 'But I am afraid I could not pay for your classes. My parents would never approve such an expense. Or even me spending time learning to read and write.'

'Not to worry, *mon amie*! You do not need to pay. You can contribute in herbs. Voilà!' She waved her hand and smiled. Then she looked up at my tree again.

'How did you find this tree? Do you live close?'

'We live north of Barbentane. I like running, and I can be there in fifteen minutes. I often collect herbs close to water, that's how I found this tree.'

'Ah yes, the herbs. Are you able to collect some and bring them over to the Chartreuse next Saturday? We could go there together after the market. I can show you the workshop and we can agree on the terms of trade. We will have to talk to Madame Du Pont. She is in charge of supplies, provisions and accounts. And once we agree on the business, I could take you to the Tour Philippe le Bel. You can see the whole of Avignon and Villeneuve, and the rivers and bridges from high up. Perhaps we could have a reading lesson using the calendar as well?'

'Yes, I'd love that! I've never been to Villeneuve at all. Or to a large workshop like yours! We have a market garden close to the river Durance. Perhaps I could grow herbs instead of just collecting them wild?'

'Yes, you could indeed! I can see you're a young entrepreneur.'

'*Merci*, Simone! You make me think of myself as an adult who can think and make decisions, not just as a girl waiting to get married, which is how my parents think of me. Especially my father.'

'I am delighted by this unexpected gift of friendship, *ma petite amie!* We seem to have more in common than I first thought!'

Simone turned to face me. She reached out and gently stroked my hair. My mother often did this, but the way Simone did it felt different. The pleasure sent a shiver through me. I wished Simone would embrace me, but she stopped, and after a few moments of sweet tension, she started talking again. Her hand rested on my shoulder. 'We could have a little siesta in the warm sun. Soon it will be winter, the wet, cold winter.'

Following Simone's example, I slid down on the jute litter and before I knew it, I dozed off.

A little while later, I woke up to find Simone gazing at me. When she saw I was awake, she pulled me gently towards her and embraced me. Her breasts against mine, her belly against my belly. I felt her heart beating fast and I could hear my own breathing quicken too. Her fragrant hair touched my face. At that moment a breeze blew through the elm tree above us and several dry leaves fell on us, with a gentle scrunching noise.

'Your secret tree is covering us . . .' Simone whispered in my ear.

Our closeness embarrassed me a little, but excitement and joy prevailed.

I did not expect this turn of events. But this was not a secret date with a boy, from which any number of things can ensue: malicious gossip, a marriage proposal, an unwanted sexual congress, and even an unwanted pregnancy . . . Maman had explained it all when I started menstruating two years before.

'You are a woman now, Franny. You should keep away from older boys and men until you are to be married.'

'Also my cousins and uncles? But why, Maman?'

'Oh, do not ask all these "why" questions, my child. Just do as I am telling you. Your cousins and uncles are family. Make sure you do not get lured by other boys . . . or men of any age. Do not let them touch you.'

I vaguely knew this was about something dishonourable; I had heard adults talking about it. I insisted and my mother had to tell the full story. I could see it was not easy for her. I appreciated what she did.

'*Merci maman*. I understand. Don't worry. I'm not interested in being alone with men and being touched and kissed by them. I prefer to be alone with the trees and herbs.'

And it was true. But being close to a sweet-smelling, gentle lady and liking her touch . . . surely this did not fall into the realm of the forbidden deeds? In any case, the elm tree and a wide, slow-rolling river created a perfect hideaway.

# 5

The following Saturday the weather turned cool and wet. There were fewer people at the market and buyers were not in an ebullient mood. Neither Simone nor I sold everything. At lunch time we packed the leftover produce and headed across the bridge to the Chartreuse de Villeneuve. I had never driven my cart across the Rhône; and I was going to Villeneuve on business! I felt important.

'Hey Louis, how do you like the big bridge across the big river? I hope you don't mind doing a few extra miles today. Your effort is for a good cause, and you may get some treats in return.'

Louis the donkey turned his ears backwards to hear me better.

'We may be half an hour or a bit longer to the Chartreuse de Villeneuve. We are following Simone's cart; see the nimble, elegant little cabriolet in front of us? It's just for people, that one, while ours is for cargo as well, so we're a bit slower. Let's not lose her. I know you're being whipped by cold rain, but I am in the same boat, Louis.' I tapped him gently with the whip, just to remind him we were on a mission, and he flicked an ear in reply.

The traffic across the bridge was sparse. We only met one cart headed for Avignon. When we arrived, Simone directed me to leave the cart in their courtyard. I freed Louis from the harness and a place was found for him in an empty stable. He was dripping wet.

I was soaked too. Simone's cabriolet had a retractable leather roof protecting her from the rain. She invited me to her room to find some dry clothes. 'We'll put your clothes to dry next to the stove and you'll have them back in a couple of hours. In the meantime, you will look a little different.' She smiled and pulled a black frock from a trunk in the corner. 'This was my first Carthusian habit; I only wore it for a couple of months. It's been altered into an ordinary dress. It will be a little short for you.'

She turned her back as I dressed. The garment barely reached my ankles; its edge sat on top of my *sabots*, revealing some of my calf as I walked.

'Come, dry your hair next to the stove. Then we'll talk to Madame Du Pont.'

Madame Du Pont was a strict-looking matron dressed in a black two-piece costume with a starched white-and-grey collar on her jacket.

'*Bonjour mademoiselle...*'

'My name is Françoise ... pleased to meet you, *madame*.'

'Françoise can help with our herb supply. We met at the Avignon market a while ago. She has been collecting and selling herbs for some time and she knows them well. She has some samples with her.'

'I can give you a list of what we need most. Can you read?''

'Um, yes *madame*, a little ... I can manage.'

'I will help with the list and make sure Françoise knows what to look for,' Simone offered.

'*Bon!* We can pay a gold Napoleon for a large basket of select fresh herbs. I don't expect you'd be able to collect that much each week, outside summer and autumn. This means we can pay half a *jaunet*, or ten francs, for half a basket, if that's what you bring.'

It seemed a good deal. I could make more than one Napoleon from my weekly market trade only on especially good days.

'*D'accord, madame.*'

'*Merci, madame Du Pont.* I will explain the details to Françoise.'

Madame Du Pont nodded; the deal was done and we could leave the room.

'I will show you the distillery if you like.'

As the rain lessened, we walked briskly across the courtyard into a large hall. Several cast iron and copper cauldrons and pots were heated by fires. Steam and condensation pipes led into smaller tubs and buckets, covered tightly by canvas. Two men were mixing the content of cauldrons with large, flat wooden paddles. The smell of alcohol vapours and spices was overpowering, though not unpleasant. In the next room, somewhat smaller, herbs were spread on a beige-coloured canvas close to the window. At the other end of the room, against the wall, there were wooden barrels, smaller than the wine barrels I was used to seeing.

'This is the right time of the year to see and to smell the process, when the recent harvests of grapes and pears are crushed, fermented, boiled and distilled into a clear brandy.

Then we add different herbs in precise proportions, to get the desired colour and aroma. There are different strengths too. Medicinal potions are made in a hall at the back, but I cannot take you there. Access is strictly limited to the artisans, testers and supervisors.'

Simone put her hand around my waist and gently pulled me out of the distillery.

'I will go and collect the Republican calendar from my room. Together with the list of herbs from Madame Du Pont, it will be a good, practical first reading lesson.' Simone smiled and disappeared into the corridor.

The rain had stopped, and sun shone through the fast-moving clouds. An earthy smell of damp, dead leaves was rising from the ground in the tree-lined courtyard. Most trees still had to shed a load of red, yellow and copper-coloured leaves.

'The weather has improved – we can walk to the Tour Philippe le Bel. You must see the view from up there!'

The tower was a short walk away, at the riverbank, at the end of the bridge we had crossed earlier. Simone was shorter than I, but she walked so fast I could hardly keep up. I was glad there were few people out in the street and not a living soul in the tower; I was conscious of my too-short, ill-fitting dress and my damp, messy hair that I had to leave untied for it to fully dry.

We climbed narrow wooden stairs to the roof terrace. There was a wooden bench at the little platform protected from the rain, next to the bottom of the stairs climbing further up onto the turret and the lookout tower. The view of the bridge over the wide river, swollen with rain, filled me with a sense of awe. Between Villeneuve and Avignon the river split into two currents, Petit Rhône and Grand Rhône.

'I felt like a small speck in the big world, which is a surprisingly nice feeling.'

'I know what you mean, Françoise. That's why we like towers, and all the other tall buildings, churches, castles ... they give us special views and those exceptional feelings. This tower used to be a watch tower, a gatehouse between the French city of Villeneuve and the papal city of Avignon; during wars also a defence tower. A *châtelain*, tower keeper, lived here, and the guards were present most of the time. Since the revolution, it has been abandoned by its minders and it is starting to show signs of disrepair.'

'Oh, pity ...'

'It is now only used by passers-by who suddenly feel the urge to get above the earth and their everyday life for a moment. Like the two of us.' Simone flashed her broad smile at me again.

'I have a strong feeling I'm outside my everyday life. I feel one with the river, the bridge, the sky, as if the time has stopped,' I offered, encouraged by Simone's approval. 'I hope you understand ...'

'I do, I understand very well. One feels like that in meditation and prayer, but some everyday experiences can also lift us above earthly concerns.'

After we had admired the view in silence for a few moments, Simone unrolled a canvas scroll she was holding – the revolutionary calendar. We looked through the illustrations: twelve beautiful women, each representing one month.

'Today is the twenty-sixth of October ... this was turned into the fifth of *brumaire*, the foggy month.'

Simone's finger slid down along the list of days. The day was dedicated to the goose. She pointed to the word. Goose. *Oie.*

'A strange little word to start your reading lessons,' Simone said with a girly giggle. I joined in. Then I pronounced the letters one by one. 'O..i..e.'

The woman representing *brumaire* was carrying firewood

on her back and a lamb in her arms. Her dress was sleeveless, inappropriate for the season. Most of the twelve images showed bare arms and sometimes considerably more, even breasts. I pointed that out.

'Yes,' said Simone. 'I cannot imagine the Church would have ever approved such a calendar. Its intention was to contradict religion in spirit and in presentation.'

The sun was out but a cool breeze made me aware the *brumaire* was deep autumn.

We then went through the whole calendar, tête-à-tête, looking for herbs I knew and those listed by Mme Du Pont. Sage: *Sauge*, twenty-sixth day of the month of *messidor*, which is the fourteenth of July in the old calendar, *La Fête de la Fédération*, so my favourite herb's day was the most important French holiday! We looked at each other and laughed excitedly. *Camomille*, the tenth day of *prairial*, June tenth in the old calendar. *Roquette*, twenty-fourth *germinal*, previously the thirteenth of April . . . I spelled out the words, letter by letter. I forgot about time. We sat close to each other; our thighs and shoulders were touching. I felt as if the sweet smell of Simone's hair and her soft voice were descending from heaven.

After a while, Simone lifted her head from the calendar and looked at me. 'Are you cold, my dear? Your hair still looks a little damp and you are underdressed.' She gently ran her hand at the back of my head and then wrapped her arms around me to warm me. She was warm and fragrant. I could feel her breasts rising and falling, pressed against mine.

'When I was not much older than you, I had a gentle and sweet friend, another nun. We were close, but she fled to Italy after the revolution, and I've never seen her again.'

'She left when your convent was closed?'

Simone nodded. 'It was anarchy after the revolution. By

attacking the Church so viciously, the new regime tested ordinary people too much. I suppose the government really wanted the Church's wealth, but the simple folk need spiritual guidance and the solace that the faith provides. In larger towns and villages, the National Guard had to step in to stem the unrest and protect the 'new clergy', the so-called elected 'Jurors' who took a new oath to the French Republic.

'The *paysans* were confused and angry, especially here in Provence. *Le Midi* never liked Napoleon, a man scornful of tradition. At his coronation, Napoleon took the crown from the cardinal's hands and placed it on his head by himself . . . to show that the authority of the Church was not beyond his own . . .' Simone paused and took a deep breath, looking troubled. 'I think the country was divided the most over treatment of the Church. The *paysans* might have hated the nobles and rejoiced that they lost much of their land, but the Church was a more sensitive matter. The political division penetrated even families . . . my own family included.'

'But you were not hurt? Tell me more. Tell me about the destruction of the convents. Were you scared?'

'I was not hurt. Not physically. My family was well connected. My brother joined Napoleon's army, so my family was on both sides of the barricades, which proved useful, ironically. But yes, I was scared, scared and confused.'

Simone looked into the distance. Her face was flushed. I embraced her gently, as if to protect her.

'Who would want to hurt a woman like you? The new regime needs good and knowledgeable people like you, doesn't it?'

'The country had been in turmoil since 1789. Which other people killed their own king? Then the Queen, and after her under the blade came the nobles, political leaders, lawmakers, writers, philosophers, scientists, even poets! Guillotines overheated after the revolution – hundreds, maybe thousands of powerful and important people were executed. First, you send other people to the guillotine, and then, one fine day, it's your head's turn to fall into the basket. The poet who invented the Republican calendar was also executed, a year after his calendar was introduced. Did you know the guillotine was known as the "people's avenger"?'

'I can see that the ordinary folk might have enjoyed the plight of high-class Parisians,' I said. 'But it's the *paysans*, like my family, who still have to feed the politicians and their armies and go to war and get killed.'

'*Bien sûr, ma chère amie!* You are so right. The little people have suffered the most, as always: high wartime taxes, marauding armies, conscription – many thousands have died already, and more will die.'

We sat quietly for a few moments, deep in thought.

'Are you against the revolution, Simone?'

'I'm against violence. It scars cities, villages, people suffer. The revolution was triggered by extreme grievances and had a vision of justice, but violence is never a way to improve society.' She gently touched my hand. 'In your birth year, two years after the revolution, I was at Sisters of St Claire. Avignon was taken from the Pope and declared part of France. But this only meant that the Papist armies – the army of the Holy See, officially – roamed about, pillaging and raping. Nothing holy about them! In wars, armies are let loose to indulge their lowest instincts. The spoils of war! And the more blood, death and destruction they see, and inflict on others, the worse they become, these unfortunate young men, the cannon fodder. War is never honourable, as they are trying to tell us.'

I nodded. 'Where violence rules and there are no laws – when a bare life is at stake – it is said that people are then like animals.

But I am not sure this is fair . . .'

'People are compared to animals when they behave cruelly – but I know you like animals so you must disagree . . .' Simone smiled at me lovingly, like my mother did.

'Simone, do animals have souls? It seems to me sometimes, when I speak to them, that they understand and would like to respond, but they cannot.'

'According to the Bible, only people have an immortal soul. I can see that you have your doubts. In any case, the way you treat animals . . . and plants . . . with care and respect, is the righteous Christian way.'

She took my hand. 'You remind me of Isabelle,' she said quietly. 'She was beautiful and kind-hearted too. It has been nearly fifteen years since then . . .'

Simone's face was wistful. I drew closer to her. She turned around and kissed me on the lips. At that moment I felt one with her, body and soul.

Simone touched my face gently and kissed me again. Her scent, the feel of her mouth on mine, was delicious and I responded eagerly. She then slid her hand down my thigh and under my dress. Her hand slowly caressing me made my body tingle. She proceeded between my legs, reaching the warm, damp spot with the back of her hand. Her other hand was lightly sliding across my breasts, on top of my dress and stays, which added to the pleasure that was washing over me. She rested her hand on the lower part of my belly that was free of the stays. Then back between my thighs, with a back of her hand, and both sides of her hand, the thumb dipping into the slippery recess for a moment.

I pressed her hand between my legs, as I felt a wave of pleasure overwhelming me. I buried my head into her shoulder and let myself be swept along by it. I gasped. I wanted to say something, express my feelings, but I was lost for words. I took a deep breath of pleasure instead.

Simone moved backwards, pulled her hand away gently and straightened my clothes. She then stroked my hair. 'You're a smart and beautiful girl with a good heart. This is not what you'd expect from someone saying faith is her vocation, is it? But I wanted to give you pleasure. Love, life and faith are more complicated than a Sunday sermon leads us to think.'

Simone was talking softly. 'I have resisted the temptation of the flesh many times over the past fifteen years. But the denial of one's earthly body is not necessarily a life of virtue. It can also be a life of self-mutilation that darkens one's soul.'

'Your faith is strong, Simone. But from time to time, we are all tempted. Father d'Eglantine says "tempted by the devil" in his sermons, the old-fashioned way ... but I'm sure that what you did was not a work of the devil.' I smiled and took Simone's hands. 'My mother explained it all to me ... but I didn't think a woman could give pleasure to another woman.'

We embraced warmly before we noticed it was suddenly much cooler; the afternoon had ripened into twilight. It was time to leave the tower of pleasures and revelations.

# 6

Maman left this world while Jules was away. Always full of life and energy, she became progressively weaker. First, she complained about being fatigued. 'I'm getting old,' she'd say as she threw herself in a kitchen chair or took a rest on the garden bench. She was in her fiftieth year, so in fact not young, but the change was all too sudden. I remembered Simone's potion in the corner of the top cupboard. Maman took a few drops every day. She said it gave her more strength. However, the hope was short lived. Once she started feeling breathless, even over light tasks such as milking a cow, we knew something was seriously amiss. She spent more and more time in bed. I was helping as much as I could, attending to her orders, often given two or more at once, without grumbling.

Papa was sad but he didn't let it show. Instead, he tried to cheer her up. 'You may get plump, Adèle, just like I've always wanted you, if you continue lying about.' She'd give him a faint smile. There was no danger of that at all; instead, she was withering away quickly. In early spring, she was barely able to plant some seeds in the garden, shivering with cold; by early May, she was hardly able to walk. She died a few days later, at dawn. The birds were loudly chirping outside when she drew her last breath, after a restless night of laboured breathing and coughing up blood. My father was pacing up and down the house and in and out of the stable all night, but hardly appeared in the marital bedroom where Maman struggled through her last hours. I was in bed with her, making sure she took sips of milk when she wanted and had a wet cloth between her dry lips. I stroked her hair and whispered comforting words I did not believe in.

'*Françoise, merci ma chérie.*' She held my hand.

I had to hide my tears, and a lump in my throat prevented me from speaking.

'*Je vais mourir*' were her last words. 'I am going to die.' Just like that.

'*Mais non, maman . . .* !' She stopped breathing only minutes after her announcement. I shook her gently, but she did not respond. I kissed her pale cheek and ran out to tell my father. He knew what had happened as soon as he saw me. He came into the bedroom and crossed himself, then knelt in front of the bed, his face buried in the bedcovers. He stayed like that for a long time. I knelt next to him and sobbed. All those tears I held back during the night came pouring out. I let myself go.

After my father left the room, I too got up and washed my red, swollen eyes in cold water. I had to notify Father d'Eglantine of the death and order a funeral mass. I ran – one cannot run and cry at the same time. Running was invigorating, life-giving. My dear Maman was dead, but outside life went on as if nothing had happened. People were opening their shutters to the morning light, others were passing by on carts, shouting orders to their donkeys and mules. Cats darted across the lanes as I ran past. The sun was shining. Life and death: in people's minds, there is a chasm between them, but in fact it is only a thin line; a few short moments.

Father d'Eglantine crossed himself and mumbled a few words of condolence. He noted that my mother had not asked for the last rites.

'This is true, Father, she did not,' I agreed. 'But she also refused to call for a doctor, and we did not know how ill she was. Some people spend many months in bed before they die, and sometimes they even recover. With Maman, it was only a couple of weeks. Her death caught us unprepared.'

'The last rites and the final confession are important. It helps the soul rest in peace and face the last judgment with equanimity.'

He crossed himself again, rolling his eyes upwards.

'She did not have much to confess, Father. She led a righteous life.'

'It is not up to you to say this, my child.' Father d'Eglantine's voice was stern. 'We are all sinners. We sin not only in deed but also in thought.'

'It's true that Maman was not your most devout parishioner, but she was a good mother, a good wife and a hard worker. She earned her daily bread twice over every day of her life . . . and she helped others in need, Father. She . . .'

My voice trembled and my eyes filled with tears again.

Father d'Eglantine was visibly displeased by my uncalled-for argument. His lips were tight. He did not try to comfort me.

'May peace be with her.' His voice was flat. I rarely prayed, but it seemed the right thing to do; what else can one do in a moment like this? Faith gives death dignity and meaning.

I walked out of the priest's quarters through the cool, dark, empty church to face a bright morning outside. There was a sudden sense of peace and relief in my heart. Maman did not suffer any longer. The sun was caressing my face, a simple comforting pleasure. I had to pay a visit to two women, known as 'the spinster sisters', who washed and dressed the dead for a small fee. They crossed themselves and murmured condolences when I told them the news. They said they would come as soon as they could, before the body stiffened, and told me to prepare funeral clothes. They did not say 'for Adèle' but 'for the body', even though they knew my mother; she was not a person anymore, just a body. It was the usual way of talking, but it suddenly seemed wrong. Without a thought about the immortal soul, death is too mundane, too trivial. I crossed myself again and wished there indeed was a God and angels to take care of my mother for eternity. She'd be immortal in my thoughts.

After the funeral, at the wake, Papa barely noticed the people who were approaching him to give condolences, shake his hand or embrace him. He sat down silently and drank until he fell off the chair. We put him to bed and took his boots off. In the weeks and months that followed, he grew quiet and listless. Red wine became his best friend. Sometimes he would not eat properly all day; my sister, my aunt or myself supplied a cooked lunch for him each day but often, most of it was left uneaten and fed to the chickens and geese the next day. Papa just drank and made wooden figures, bowls and handles for tools all day long. People admired his artefacts and they sold quickly at the market. Given he drank continuously, I often wondered how he managed not to cut his fingers off with one of his sharp axes and chisels.

Less than a year after Maman died, my father's stomach bulged out and his legs grew weaker. Since my mother's death, he had only walked from the house to the work shed and back. He refused to go to the cemetery, even on the day of *Toussaint*, when the place was buzzing with people honouring their dead and adorning the graves with bunches of chrysanthemums. We were short of money and short of workers and we had to sell the cows, one by one. Jeanne and I were told to divide whatever was in the house. She took some pots and some of our mother's finer linen. Papa would not hear about taking another wife even though after two decades of wars, there were more than enough widows around. He had another plan. His stomach was hard and swollen and his skin had a yellow hue. He was in pain, but he kept drinking. He seemed determined to kill himself as quickly as possible. I was on my own now, with little Simon. Life was hard.

# 7

I was overjoyed when Jules returned that autumn, only weeks before Papa died. He appeared at the doorstep suddenly, with nothing but a small bundle under his arm. I threw myself at him and embraced him. He responded almost shyly, and his face had no expression. My chest tightened; I knew at once this was not the same Jules who left two years earlier. He was not well, and the turmoil of war was not over yet. Hard times, with slow-moving weeks and months, continued.

One Saturday in November 1814, not long after Jules returned, a rumour went around that a Papist army was approaching the town despite the Pope's abdication of his rule over Avignon. The mob was especially hungry, unruly and ruthless. The maids of Avignon made their purchases in haste and hurried home. By mid-afternoon, stately coaches could be seen on the road alongside rickety conveyances. Avignonians were fleeing. Men, women and children were pouring out of the southern gate as an early dusk started to fall. The crowd was milling among loaded carriages turned in various directions under the old elm trees.

It was a good opportunity to sell food to travellers, rather than having our larder stripped bare by a mob of soldiers. A hazy moon lit up the paved road in front of my cart. By the time I arrived there, icy lines streaked the water in the ditch on the side of the road. A flock of crows, scared by the human clatter, flitted off from their night shelter. No-one seemed to have noticed this bad omen; people were too preoccupied. I sold all that I had: cheese, butter, eggs, and a basket of bread and brioches that I had baked all day. I put the money I brought home in a small wooden box that Papa had made and hidden in a hole he dug in the corner of the stable, under a pile of hay and animal litter. This was our 'safe'. I kept several gold francs on me to give to the soldiers if they turned out to be especially vicious and persistent.

I was tired when I returned, and fell asleep early. I woke in the middle of the night and pricked my ears, but I could not hear anything unusual. No soldiers came to the village. It was a cold night, and the frosty dawn turned into a morning sparkling in the thin warmth of the late autumn sun. The army only arrived after Sunday mass. The soldiers, assembled under the pine trees in front of the church, showed a semblance of impatient respect for the faithful coming out of church in their Sunday finery and left them alone. Just as well: it was the Pope's army. People were anxious; one never knew what to expect. Times were tough; they had been tough for my entire life.

Now that the revolutionary fervour had subsided and Napoleon's power had crumbled, the Church was emboldened again. At Sunday mass, Father d'Eglantine talked about the Reign of Terror. He said the revolution had been in danger of ending in mob rule, but fortunately the great French nation and their kings knew better. Louis XVIII, a brother of the decapitated king, was on the throne. The country was at peace and would prosper, he said. But we knew that the old landowners were returning to challenge the new ones, and the peace was fragile and tense.

The Church reclaimed some of its property; religious orders were reinstated and gathered back most of their dedicated monks and nuns. I wondered what had become of Simone. She left and rejoined her order a year before I married Jules. For all I knew, she might have been back with *les Chartreux*, across the Rhône in Villeneuve, living a secluded life as a choir nun. I often looked around at the market as if she'd appear there, but at the bottom of my heart I knew this was just a vain hope.

I thought of her often with fondness and gratitude. It would have been nice to see her again and tell her how much she meant to me all those years back. I could visit the Carthusians in Villeneuve-lès-Avignon, as it was now called, but what would be my excuse? I could perhaps say that I wanted to do business with them again. They continued to make their famous liqueurs and potions and I continued to collect herbs. But if I saw Simone, what would I tell her? That my mother was dead and my father on his deathbed; that my husband was back from the war but badly damaged by it? That my life had turned from the hopeful youth running through fields, talking to animals and trees, excited to learn to read and write, to the trying life of a *paysanne*, a woman burdened with relentless toil and the care of her men, three of them: one small child and two sick adults? I would not want to tell her I was laden by my husband's sorrow as well as my own, but unable to find solace in faith.

I did not go to church much, especially after Maman died. My mother did not like the local priest and avoided going to Sunday mass whenever she could find an excuse. I was seven or eight when I overheard my mother talking to my father. At the confession, our old priest, Father Bouillier, asked her why she only had two children, especially given they were both girls. Did her husband not want her to bear him a son? I sensed she was upset. My father did not say anything but from the kitchen door left ajar I saw him holding her tight, pressed on his chest, her head buried into his shoulder. I did not know what it all meant, and why I didn't have as many siblings as our neighbours – four, five, even more. I don't know even now.

## 8

After returning from the war, Jules had an absent look. Unlike many other returnees, he had all his limbs, but he moved slowly, like an old man. He insisted he was not ill, just tired and needing to recuperate. He was twenty-six, the prime of life, and I thought it would only take a couple of weeks for the happy Jules I had married to reappear. A few hearty meals, peaceful rest in his own bed, his wife's warmth, his child's innocence, and he'd be cured of whatever malaise weighed down his body and soul. Our little Simon, only a toddler, was cautious; he kept his distance at the start but then attempted to approach his father. For a few days upon meeting his son, Jules seemed awakened from his war nightmare. I could see he was trying to get to know the child, to be a father, but soon he sank back into his melancholy. It seemed as if a thick winter fog from the Russian steppes settled in his mind and would not lift, obscuring everything else. He was distant. 'A boy ... for the next war,' he whispered, looking at Simon chasing snow-white geese in the bottom of the yard. He did not smile.

Late one morning, Simon snuck into our room and climbed onto Jules' back while he was still asleep. Jules woke up with a start and jumped up violently. Simon fell on the hard wooden floor and started wailing. I rushed from the kitchen and held the child to my chest. '*Ça va, mon bébé* ... Your papa just got scared out of his sleep.'

'I am sorry! He frightened me. I had a bad dream ...' But Jules did not try to comfort the child. He did not seem to want any closeness with another human being, neither me nor little Simon. He no longer desired my body. Sometimes, when I reached to touch him during the day or caress him at night, he would recoil from me. One night, a few months after his return, shortly after my father's funeral, I woke in the middle of the night to find him engulfed in sobs that shook his whole body and even our bed. I embraced him and whispered into his ear.

'*Jules, Jules mon chèr*, what is it that is troubling you? Tell me, perhaps it would help you, help heal your soul from the horrors you have seen.'

That was the only time we embraced. And that was the only time that Jules shared his war memories with me.

Jules was among those lucky soldiers – one in ten or even fewer – who survived the Russian campaign. It started in high spirits: in June 1812 *les enfants de la Patrie* thought their day of glory had indeed arrived. But alas! Most families who lost their sons and husbands did not even have a body to bury. Early victims' bodies were returned home, but later in the campaign dead had to be abandoned along the way, buried in Russian soil. Often, buried only by snow.

Jules told me how his company were first baked by the sun, then bogged in the mud during heavy autumn rains. Scores of horses perished, and many men fell sick even before they reached Russia. Many soldiers from the allied troops – Poles, Bavarians, Spanish, Portuguese, even Africans – deserted, on the slim chance that this would save them. At the start, desertion was considered cowardly and shameful, but later on, as the army retreated through frozen desert, it seemed like common sense … which the idea of conquering Russia certainly was not!

Jules paused, his shuddering breaths the only sound in the dark.

'There were two black soldiers from Saint-Domingue in my regiment … tall, upright and strong.' His voice was firmer now, telling the story. 'They were captured and brought to France a decade earlier in order to journey from one war to another. For them, being forced to march to Russia was the last bitter drop. They were older, around thirty, and they knew that Russia was very far from France, and immense. Their sea voyage from Saint-Domingue and local legends about the arrivals of their African ancestors to the West Indies made them grasp the distances between lands much better than the naïve young Frenchmen could. Most of us had only ever travelled to the next village or a nearby town.'

Jules asked me to light a candle.

'Once confidence between us was established, the Saint-Dominguans told me they would escape; their only purpose was to flee the war that was not theirs. One day they simply vanished. Perhaps the Russians spared them or even helped them because they were so obviously not French?'

Initial victories lifted the spirits of young men, Jules' story continued. The battle of Borodino was an important victory, they were told, but all they had seen was a vast field covered by dead bodies and the wounded calling out for help that was not likely to arrive. The remaining troops dug graves for their dead comrades all day. These were large holes in the ground where as many bodies as possible would be stacked and covered by a thin layer of damp clay. Crosses were placed on the fresh graves, one per person; an army scribe went around checking the names of fallen soldiers with the survivors. When they reached Moscow a week later, they learned that more than one-third of the French army were already lost. The Russian army was retreating in front of them. Moscow was evacuated, abandoned. There was no-one there to recognise French victory. And worse: as soon as the army took camp in the capital, the wooden city went up in flames.

'After we had recovered a little, we started to retreat. It was autumn, mid-October I think. First we were a neat file of soldiers with horses and some supplies. Then the supplies dried up and the army turned into a crazed, starving crowd. We pushed west for hundreds of miles, through hunger and cold.' He covered his face with his hands for a moment, then continued. 'The horses ... we ate them soon enough. They would fall from exhaustion and lack of proper feed, and the soldiers would use them as a source of bodily heat. The horse would be still breathing, covered by emaciated soldiers enjoying a short respite on its warm, dying body. Then when it expired it would be cut and eaten. A portion of horse meat was usually our only meal for several days.'

Jules paused for few moments, pulling the duvet higher up. 'A story went around that freezing to death was a nice, pleasant death, like falling asleep in a warm bed. What consolation!'

Jules told me how they slept in tattered tents, huddled together like animals, while the wind howled violently across the steppes. Those in the middle could keep warm but those on the outer shivered through the night. *La Grande Armée* left behind a trail of dead bodies; feverish and exhausted fighters did not have strength to honour their dead comrades with due Christian ceremony.

The ghost army passed through ghost villages. The Russians fled their homesteads and took supplies and livestock with them. Where did they go, where did they hide? Bigger towns were ready to defend themselves. The French soldiers still had guns and some ammunition, but these would-be conquerors only wanted to reach home alive. Home: a land where people spoke their language and saw them as deserving of mercy. *Marchons, marchons!* The revolutionary fervour of a few months before was but a distant memory. The officers on horses appeared from time to time, trying to revive a sense of mission, to no avail.

Jules was young and strong; he survived dysentery with a high fever on his feet. They crossed the Berezina river, a half-point between Moscow and Warsaw, in late November. Once they reached Poland, army supplies were reinstated and a hope of reaching home alive was reignited. When they crossed into German lands, Jules gradually recovered and put some of his weight back on. After a month of recuperation, his division was replenished by fresh recruits and sent to war in Germany. Many went to Spain. The larger war plan was only hearsay. Alliances changed quickly; yesterday's friends were today's foes. Jules survived another battle, at Dresden, but he could not recover his faith in revolution, the military leadership, justice. He came home convinced that he had gone through hell in vain; the revolutionary ideals were fading, Napoleon was dead and the old dynasty was back.

Jules's account was full of pain and despair. I was trying to understand the source of his pain. Was it fear? Was it moral disgust? A despair about the ruthlessness of the powerful and his own powerlessness? Was it a bodily memory of fatigue and suffering? His body remembered his ordeal: even in summer, I had to keep the duvet on the bed. The Russian winter continued to live with us, sucking warmth out of our lives. After all he told me, while refusing to answer my questions, I could not fully comprehend. Something crucial was missing from his story. Perhaps he could not find strength to bring to light his darkest memories or feelings, and they continued to gnaw at his *élan vital*. I could nurse Jules's body back to health, but young Simon and I could not fill the void in his soul.

It was like being married to a walking corpse. I was not able to ease Jules's suffering; instead, we both suffered. I often remembered the years before I was married: wandering in the fields, daydreaming in my secret nook under the elm tree, enamoured and affianced to plants and animals, talking to Louis the donkey as we trotted to the market. How sad and complicated human affairs and relationships were in comparison!

I thought about Simone; meeting her, her naturalness, her knowledge and wisdom, her deep understanding of people, including me, my body and soul. All that was now superfluous, a useless knowledge of a past that had vanished, perhaps even burdensome, making it plain how diminished my life had become. Simone's warmth, liveliness and generosity were in stark contrast to sharing a life with a distant, crippled man. What a penance my marriage had become! Was I being punished? Would a just god punish me for a beautiful friendship with Simone; the friendship that made me so much more than I was before I met her?

# 9

I worked from dawn to dusk, but I had little to take to the market. Animals often went hungry, and the market garden was overgrown. There were day labourers around that I could make good use of, but I had no money to pay them. During my parents' illnesses, our savings had been depleted. The little box hidden in the corner of the stable was empty. Without my mother's tireless work and my father's ability to make and fix nearly anything, our stock of animals was shrinking and the farm was falling into disrepair. Jules had given up most of his daily occupations and slept long nights and whenever he could during the day.

Jules neither agreed nor objected when I suggested we would have to sell the market garden. I was inconsolable about this prospect: it would reduce us to the house, a yard and one little orchard; we would just be able to subsist, if no major disasters – droughts, floods, more wars – struck. This was to be a precarious existence, where little needed to go wrong before we would go hungry. Yet we had no choice. This gave us a little respite, but the proceeds of the sale were modest and they would soon be gone. I wanted to keep some for a rainy day. I was also worried about little Simon; what would become of him? What would he inherit? What would he live on if we continued like this?

I lost sleep with worry. I felt sorry for Jules, and myself. I was angry with the revolution, the country and the government that took a healthy, happy young man and returned a cracked, hollow shell. I remembered Simone's impassioned speech against wars and violent revolutions in the Tour Philippe le Bel nearly ten years earlier – how right she was! Jules's body was healed, he was strong again, but, weighed down by his memories, he drank too much, seeking oblivion. When he was in a state of clarity, out of the fog of alcohol and slumber, he seemed tense and tightly wound like a clock mechanism at breaking point.

One autumn morning Jules set out to harvest our small orchard. He was not back by late afternoon, so I went to check and found him asleep under a tree, in a drunken torpor. I was getting resentful. I had to admit to myself that Simon and I would be better off without him; he did not earn his keep. All he did with clockwork regularity was buy wine in the village, and when he went to Barbentane, he'd always get stuck in a local tavern. No doubt we were a target of local gossip, perhaps some pity as well. I could leave Simon with Jeanne's children – she had three children, two of them older than Simon – but getting there and back was stretching my working day beyond endurance.

'Jules, you're strong, you're able, you have a wife, a son, some land, animals – you must work. It could help you get out of the morass of your memories, perhaps, and cure whatever is tormenting you. Please, try! I cannot cope. We cannot pay any-one to help either. You must help me, and help yourself. There is no other way. Otherwise, we will fall on hard times before long. We may go hungry this winter. Your son will starve or be taken to an orphanage.'

I was getting desperate. After, or during, my increasingly frequent pleas and rebukes Jules would usually walk away and disappear from view; into the house, or out of the house, away from me. He must have known I was right but was unable to break the bad spell. Jeanne was sympathetic, but she could not help beyond having Simon in her care from time to time. I could have asked Father d'Eglantine for guidance, but I knew what he would tell me: 'Carry your cross, my daughter; you must stand by your husband, who has lost his health for France,' or something like that. It had been over three years since Jules returned. Where to find hope that things would change for the better?

My trips to the Avignon market were becoming rarer. I had little to sell and little money to buy anything. In June that year our cherry orchard was especially fecund and a trip to the market was warranted. We picked the fruit and placed it in large baskets with shelves. Simon loved cherries and was smeared red and purple from head to toe on the two harvest days. On Friday evening he suffered diarrhoea, which did not surprise me. It was a small price to pay for his happiness of the previous two days. He fell asleep late and I did not want to wake him early to take him to Jeanne's or with me to the market. I woke up Jules instead. Morning had broken and I was ready to go.

'Jules ... Jules, wake up, please. Listen. I'm off to the market with the cherries. Please take care of Simon. He had a bad tummy last night after gorging on cherries. Don't let him eat any more fruit. Just give him some bread and tea. Do you hear me?'

Jules nodded vaguely and when I repeated the question, he lifted his arm as if to say 'Yes ... I've heard you.'

Louis the donkey was sprightly that morning and we made it quickly to the Saturday market at the Pont d'Avignon. It was going to be a hot day and I was hoping the cherries would go quickly, so I could get home before the heat of the afternoon.

I was lucky; two men stopped next to my stall with a little hand cart and bought most of my crop. It turned out they were from the Chartreuse de Villeneuve and the cherries were going to be used for liqueur. My heart jumped when they mentioned the convent; I could not help asking after Simone. It was over six years since I'd last seen her, just after the convent was reinstated.

The men, who worked in the distillery, told me they had worked with her and remembered her well; she had left a couple of years earlier. I told them I used to supply herbs to the distillery and asked where she had gone. They were not sure, but they had heard Italy being mentioned. Did she go searching for her youthful *petite amie* she told me about, Isabelle? I hoped she was happy wherever she was, the beautiful soul. I felt tears stinging my eyes. There was no time to indulge in sweet memories; I packed up my stall and loaded the cart.

On my way home, the memories flooded back. Our conversations, Simone's stories, the reading and writing lessons, the herbs and liqueurs, her radiant smile, our exchange of gentle intimacies. In comparison, how rough Jules had seemed in our marital bed! But I accepted the inevitable, adjusted to marriage, and our life together started well. It was a simple but peaceful and orderly life. I was joyful with Simone, content and hopeful with Jules, and then the war ruined everything. At the surface of my life, nothing much changed. But in fact everything was different now, so different, so sorrowful, hard!

The yard was quiet when I opened the gate to bring the cart in. The front door of the house was wide open. It was summer, but still, this was unusual. I entered and called Simon. No response.

'Jules! Jules!' No response.

'Simon, *mon chéri*, where are you? Mummy's home.'

No response. I heard Louis bray. He was still in harness, but he was usually more patient. He started pulling the cart towards the stable, ears pointing at the doorway. 'What is it, Louis?' Then I heard a little voice moaning inside.

I hurried in and found my little boy curled up and holding his head with both hands. His hands were red, but it wasn't cherries – it was blood. Simon's own blood, from a deep gash on his forehead, and another one on his arm, just under his shoulder. His clothes were covered in blood. I lifted him up and he started sobbing on my shoulder. He was fully conscious, and terrified.

'What happened, Simon?'

'I fell ... from the hayloft ...'

I turned around and saw garden tools left lying on the ground under the hayloft. Simon must have fallen on the sharp garden hoe, or even the scythe. It could have been worse. His face was unscathed, thank God.

'Don't cry, *mon trésor*, Maman is here. Let's go inside.'

I took him into the house. I sat him on the kitchen bench, next to the copper pail for drinking water, and began to clean his wounds.

'I'm thirsty,' he wailed.

At that moment Jules appeared at the door, looking at his blood-smeared son with a frown, in a mental torpor, not understanding what had happened.

'Jules! Is this how you took care of your son? He could have been killed. He fell from the hayloft on the garden tools left underneath ... Why weren't you watching him?'

Jules did not respond, just muttered something under his breath, turned around and left. The usual.

A flush of anger rose fast through my body and when it reached my head, I suddenly felt hot. I rushed out after Jules and grabbed him by the forearm.

'Do not run away from me. It's enough of this! What kind of life is this?'

My fury gave me the strength to turn him towards me. My face must have been twisted with rage. He grabbed me across the face with his other hand as if wanting to cover it, not to see it, and pushed my head away from himself with all his force. The back of my head hit the edge of the stone door frame behind me hard; the blow brought an explosion of pain, then came darkness.

Before silence fell, I heard a little voice calling me. A moment later I felt Simon's small body next to mine, on the ground, and his little arms around me, as I struggled to draw my last breath.

# Post Fabulam III
## Melbourne, 2021

POOR LITTLE CHILD, HUGGING HIS mother as she lay dying in the dusty yard! Did he run to his father for comfort, or bolt away from him in fright? What did Jules do? Look for help? Make up a story by which he could be found not guilty for my death? Or flee and leave Simon alone with his dead mother?

I cannot bear to think of my little boy in an orphanage . . . I hope ardently that Jeanne took Simon and brought him up as one of her own. I hope my baby had a long a happy life. I could look for church records . . . After the revolution, the French developed a state bureaucracy that kept meticulous records of population, taxes and government expenses, so there would possibly be civil records too. I could go to Avignon and . . . no, no, I cannot do that! I'm running out of time. And what if I learned that my beautiful boy died young? It would break my heart.

The death of a child is the saddest thing.

I imagine him young and strong and happy, perhaps educated and joining the class of the well-dressed townsfolk with clean shoes . . . or even clergy.

Nearly ten years back, Bertie and I travelled through the south of France, as the Franco-enamoured Australians like to do. I was especially attracted to Avignon, the surrounding countryside and its vast cemetery. I remember the wide, slow-flowing Rhône, and the feeling of familiarity, as if I'd been there before. A déjà vu. We cycled across a long bridge, across the islet in the middle of the river. We stopped and looked at that pathetic Pont d'Avignon that seemed to me a monument to all abandoned projects. We then continued to Villeneuve-lès-Avignon on the other side and cycled about town, but we did not have time to climb to the Tour Philippe le Bel before dark. The next day, we visited the

Palais des Papes, which repulsed me with its immense, cold emptiness. There wasn't even a museum there, just a forbidding memorial of the centuries of papal power and its corruption.

Ah, Françoise! Ah, Simone! Lives thrown into turmoil by the revolution and the wars that followed! Armies, battles, wars: men's way to seek grandeur, by spilling the blood of others, if they are generals, and bleeding themselves, if they are rank-and-file soldiers. The honour and the glory ... for whom? Young men do not think two steps ahead; their mothers do, their wives do, but they themselves do not. The women, children and elderly are left behind to struggle along, do all the work that needs to be done. They are granted no honour and no glory for it. And then always the grim finale: the men return from the war maimed and stunned by horrors they've seen – if they are lucky enough to return at all.

The French still venerate Napoleon; one has to bow at his tomb at Les Invalides in Paris in order to see his ornate sarcophagus with curled ends. His army swept through Europe, introducing the secular, modern bureaucratic state at the barrel of a gun. Napoleon's Russian campaign was one of the worst miscalculations in military history, blighted by ambition and a *delusion de grandeur*. Hundreds of thousands of young lives snuffed in their prime, and millions damaged, maimed and ruined: the forgettable fodder of history. Like Jules, and his destroyed little family.

# IV: The Beach

## Frances (1865–1885), Brighton & London

OUR STREET DESCENDS TO THE Esplanade at a right angle. A hundred paces and I'm there, at the seawall: the view opens up and the salty wind fills my chest. On a sunny day, the usually greyish sea sparkles blue. In winter, the sea breeze is frigid, but I love the mighty water even so. It pushes and pulls the pebbles, making a soft, rhythmic sound. On quiet evenings, the soothing noise of the waves lulls me to sleep.

Sometimes, when no-one's around, I cross the Esplanade and look down at the wide beach under the high seawall, the wide, open sea and, on clear days, the distant line of the horizon. My fancy flies to the next land: France! Their sea is bluer and warmer, and the land extends all the way to the Mediterranean. Someday, I will cross the Channel and find myself on the continent. Then I'll go further by train, all the way to the balmy south. If I were a man, it would be easy: I'd walk to a ship on the dock and offer my services. I'd be sent to an officer who'd ask me what I could do and whether I knew anything about ships and sailing. Or if not, then about cooking and cleaning. I could do it now, set off on my adventure straight away, and come back after a few years to tell my tales of foreign lands. Or not come back at all. My cousin Brad left last year. His sister told me he packed a bag of clothes in a hurry and gave a hug goodbye to their shocked mother. The same ship came back two months later, but Bradley was not on it. His brother inquired with a seaman, but he could only pass on a rumour that Brad disembarked in Italy.

A woman cannot do anything of the sort. No ship would take me, and even if they did, it would not be deemed an adventure but rather a disgrace. A woman cannot even stand alone on the Esplanade and gaze at the sea to her heart's content. A neighbour told my mother that she saw me at the seawall, and she warned me, not for the first time, that 'people talk'. They certainly do, thin whispers and eye-rolling glances. Brighton is not a small village, and not everyone knows everyone, but news spreads like a forest fire.

Even the Queen complained about nosy Brightonians; that's why she sold the Royal Pavilion and moved her summer residence to a quieter place. My mother was ten at the time and eager to catch a glimpse of the Queen, but the Queen packed and left before her wish could come true. Too many people had the same wish, to take a peek at Victoria and her entourage, but she thought them 'indiscreet'. But why would she be surprised if people gawk at her? Isn't that the purpose of the whole extravagant royal spectacle?

Since I started my nursing apprenticeship at the workhouse, I often think about the rich and the poor, and wonder whether it has to be like that. Perhaps it does; it seems that many people must be poor for a few others to be rich. Apparently, the royal family was 'too cramped' in the Royal Pavilion built as their summer retreat. Our royal family happens to be quite large, but the Pavilion is a huge palace with a hundred rooms! The poor accommodated at the Spike, as they call the workhouse, sleep a dozen to a room. My cousin Jack, who left for London, says that down here there aren't as many destitute folk as in

London. Splendour and squalor, much of both can be found in the feverish, fashionable capital fifty miles to our north. In any case, I prefer the stillness and infinity of the sea horizon.

# 2

Us Brightonians did not bathe in the sea and only came down to the beach if there were tourists there to do business with. From about the time my mother was born, the railroad made it easy for the sea bathers to come from London, even just for a day. The middle classes stayed in hotels, and the rich and status-conscious in the Grand Hotel with sea views and a vertical omnibus to lift them to the upper floors. Well-dressed ladies in beribboned hats could be seen strolling along the Esplanade and in the Pavilion Gardens. The more curious took a ride several miles into the hills to visit the Devil's Dyke.

But most visitors could be found scattered on the vast beach. Everyone believed bathing in the sea water was good for one's health, and some people even drank it. Sent by their parents or trade masters, local boys roamed the beach burdened with baskets, selling tea, scones, lemonade, sweets and ice cream in the afternoon when sea bathers were peckish after swimming or playing games, but still a few hours away from their dinners. Towards the end of August, the summer season was over. Everyone was gone and the beach was deserted again.

In spite of being enchanted by the sea since my childhood, I tried sea-bathing only once, and even then, barely ... One sultry evening at the end of August, my cousin Emma and I snuck down to the beach. It had to be dusk so people would not see us from the road above, and even if they saw us, they would not recognise us. But it had to be before the darkness fell and the wind became too cold.

Emma was a tomboy and a daredevil, her head always full of ideas; to my mother's dismay, she could usually persuade me to follow her. We were sixteen then, born only months apart, and close to each other ever since we could remember. We ran downstairs from the road to the beach as fast as the wind, clutching our baskets that hid towels and our underwear. We were scared and excited in equal measure and giggled ceaselessly as we hurried across the expanse of pebbles towards the water's edge. The western horizon was red and we could see the contours of the West Pier protruding into the sea, with ice cream shops and merry-go-rounds, erected not so long ago for the amusement of visitors and locals. The sea was darkening fast.

We left our things at a safe distance from the waves and rushed out of our clothes and into the water. The coast was not too steep at that section of the beach, but the seabed was disappearing from under our feet and neither of us could swim. We were careful to stay within a few yards of the shore. The water was bracing; we splashed for a minute, making swimming motions with our feet touching the seabed. We avoided wetting our hair; it would not dry fast enough and our adventure would be revealed.

The flapping about was brief, as Emma was hit by a wave with her mouth open and swallowed some sea water. She coughed, spluttered and spat which made me laugh irrepressibly, only to be splashed across the head by a freak wave myself. It was Emma's turn to shriek. Why is another person's trouble always so funny? We stood in water up to our waists, muffling the sound with hands over our mouths. There was no need really; even though the sea was calmer than usual, the noise of the waves rolling the pebbles back and forth drowned our laughter. We got out and sat on the beach huddled together, shivering as our wet chemises and drawers clung to our tensed bodies.

'Ugh! Why would anyone want to drink sea water? It's bitter and disgusting, it burns in my throat!' Rolling her eyes comically, Emma passed more unflattering judgment on the hordes of Londoners who descended on the Brighton beach in summer. Drinking sea water had just gone out of fashion in fact, but bathing was considered a cure for many ailments.

'Oh, stop Emma, please stop, I cannot stop laughing!' My teeth started chattering with cold.

'Let's change! I'm freezing!' We grabbed our baskets and ran as fast as we could, barefoot, across the expanse of buff-coloured pebbles, a distance of two chains or more, to the high end of the beach where the arcade containing changing rooms sheltered us from being seen by the passers-by up on the Esplanade. The light was fading fast, but our white undergarments could still betray our presence.

Peeling wet underwear off our bodies was not easy and required full attention. We went quiet. Being naked outside, in a public place, was terrifying and exciting in equal measure. Emma, having taken off her chemise, came closer and gave me a hug again. Her skin was cold and I felt her full, firm breasts against my own; we were of the same height. A strong jolt of bodily pleasure took me by surprise. Then she stepped back and passed her hand over my breasts, squeezing them gently at the end. A light breeze was drying my skin. It felt nice. I gave her a quizzical look.

'You can do it, too,' she whispered into my ear. 'Go on, try!' She pushed her bare chest forward, almost touching mine again.

I nearly always did as Emma proposed. We had always stuck together and had much fun as far back as I could remember. Somehow, her impish ideas had never got us into real trouble. I put my hand on her breast and squeezed it. It was hard and soft at the same time, a smooth cushion with a nipple that hardened from the cold.

'Yes, that's nice, Frankie, do it with both hands . . .' I heard Emma's hurried whisper and felt her breath on my ear.

I did as I was told, forgetting the cold, as Emma started rubbing herself between her legs. A few moments later she released several deep and noisy breaths, with her lips apart and her eyes firmly closed. Then she opened her eyes and her whole body, until then tight as a bow, relaxed. She kissed me quickly on the mouth and then on the neck.

'Oh good, nice . . . fine with you too Frankie . . . ?' Emma murmured.

'Yes . . . but let's dress up and go now, it's cold . . . and dark.'

After we managed to pull dry underwear onto our damp bodies, getting on our skirts and blouses was easy. We got dressed as fast as we could and rolled our stockings into the towels instead of putting them on. We hurriedly forced our damp feet into shoes.

'Hey, wait a minute!' Emma said under her breath.

'What?' I was already at the bottom of the stairs that zig-zagged up to the Esplanade, stomping my feet to warm them up.

She waved urgently, asking me to come back. 'There's someone up there.'

I lifted my gaze and indeed, there was a man, one foot on the low stone fence, looking at the horizon where the last evening light was dying off and the stars were becoming brighter.

'Well, we need to go anyway, don't we?' I said. 'Let's just be very serious.' We quickly straightened our clothes and smoothed our dishevelled hair, took hold of our baskets and walked up the stairs with our heads up and straight, next to each other. Emma grabbed my hand. The man turned as he spotted us.

'Aah, good evening, young ladies!' he said with a suggestive inflection, probably after a couple of rounds in one of the nearby public bars.

'Good evening, sir,' we greeted him back gravely, and rushed away as fast as we could, across the wide Esplanade and into the shelter of the narrow street going not too steeply uphill. The gas lamps had just started to flicker. In a few moments, the street lit up, darkening the sky above.

'Emma, I have to hurry! It's dark, my mother will be worried.'

Emma flung herself at me, gave me a tight hug and kissed me under my ear – 'Mmmm, salty!' – then ran off uphill towards her house.

There was no taming Emma – one could take her or leave her. She was not just my cousin but also my dearest friend. I slid my hand over my breasts, remembering Emma's touch, before I hurried home.

## 3

A month later, as the days became shorter and colder and the sycamore trees turned rusty brown, I started helping at the workhouse run by my parents. I was now a nursing apprentice. I had completed my elementary education two years earlier at Brighton's Central National School as a top pupil. I was keen to continue my learning, but voluntary schools and secondary colleges would not take girls. Convent education was the only option for a girl of fourteen, but convents were run by Roman Catholics, and we belonged to the Church of England. My mother championed my wish; in her day, she was only able to attend school for five years, but she was bright, taught herself the best she could afterwards and learned a great deal. She reasoned that having a good education was the way of the future, for men and women alike. 'Those who are educated have better lives.

They cannot be easily misled and defrauded and they garner more respect in society.' She pleaded with my father, but he was reluctant. He was a hard man, but after years of marriage, he had learned that his wife's judgment was worth heeding.

I listened to their discussions with hope, and sometimes with alarm. Years later I realised that my mother was priming my father in gentle instalments. I could read and write well, I was good at the arithmetic and at reckoning too; I wanted to study sciences and languages – all that my cousin Jack was not too interested in, but he was sent to Brighton Grammar as a matter of course, being a boy, while his sister Emma and I could not be admitted. My mother agreed with my father that I was tall, strong enough and mature enough to take responsibilities around the house and, over time, also in the workhouse, but she maintained this could be done while being educated further. Eventually, my parents reached a compromise: I would be responsible for some chores at home and help in Emma and Jack's parents' shop. This would leave a couple of hours a day for education. I could have private tutoring; what I earned in the shop would go towards paying for it. I was delighted.

I studied diligently with two tutors. Mademoiselle Bouvier, a French matron, previously a governess in a wealthy local family with several children, taught me French, Latin and history. She said she enjoyed teaching me so much she could do it for free, yet she charged quite handsomely. She lived in rented rooms nearby, planning to retire to her hometown of Rheims before too long. Emma was also interested in French tuition and drawing, so her parents agreed to contribute to Mlle Bouvier's fees.

Mr Waterfield, an engineer retired from the Rail Works, tutored me in mathematics and sciences. Emma was not interested in this; she was artistic and musical, but there simply was no time and money for her musical tuition. Mr Waterfield was able to handle numbers and formulas even when not entirely sober and distracted by packing his pipe. I defended him before my mother, who was aware of his drinking habit. 'He would not have to do private tutoring if he spent less in pubs,' she retorted.

In any case, he fell sick after a year and left Brighton to live with his widowed sister in Kent. I was over the moon when my mother told me she had found a medical student to tutor me in biology, chemistry and elementary medicine, hygiene and the theory of disease. This was what I really liked! Young Mr Gibbons could only devote an hour a week to our lessons, but he lent me books and I read hungrily; he then explained issues further when we met.

My mother had two books that she often pulled off the shelf. One was the ninth edition of *Every Man His Own Doctor or the Poor Planter's Physician: A Treatise on the Prevention and Cure of Diseases*, originally written more than a century before by John Tennent, an American doctor; my tutor pointed out that its later editions were printed and distributed, perhaps also updated, by Benjamin Franklin. The book explained, in plain English, how to cure various distempers and injuries using simple procedures and substances that most people could procure.

The second book was written by Florence Nightingale five years before I was born and much more modestly titled *Notes on Nursing*. The book contained much sensible practical advice on personal hygiene and the sanitary state of private homes, workhouses and hospitals. My mother revered it more than the Holy Bible. I read the two books and anything that Mr Gibbons gave me cover to cover. I made notes and wrote down questions for my tutor.

'Too much education can get into a girl's head,' my father grumbled, 'and she already has too many strange ideas. We are only middle-class people, and which young man in his right mind will marry an opinionated, overly educated woman? Such women have been known to be trouble, and often not able to have children.'

After two years of this happy life of learning, at sixteen, I started as a trainee nurse at the workhouse. I was squeamish about dealing with sores, wounds and boils, but I liked helping people. My mother was confident I'd gradually firm up. Once I learned to dress wounds and administer potions, the job became somewhat dull. I knew it was a respectable career for a woman, and nurses were sought after, but they were not expected to have medical knowledge about the human body, illnesses and cures. They were skilled and dexterous in helping the sick and the infirm, but not academic and knowledgeable like doctors.

I was attracted to the science of medicine; if nursing was the best I could hope for, and the study of medicine was out of reach, I thought the teaching profession might suit me better, or perhaps charitable work with the poor. I was aware that in such an occupation I was likely to meet widows and otherwise single mothers struggling to bring up children on their own, and families with various problems, the most frequent of which was alcoholism. Many working-class women suffered from their husbands' drinking and gambling, which drove families to poverty. It was not uncommon for the father to brutalise his wife and children. The Brighton Temperance Society and the Society of Quakers advocated abstinence from intoxicating liquors, but their success was limited. For most working men, the temptation to seek relief and relaxation in a pub after a day of hard labour was too great.

My father was no exception. He drank more than his wife could gladly tolerate. Alcohol made his foul temper worse. Once, when I was still a child, I saw him hit my mother. She had just finished cleaning the kitchen when he came home drunk and demanded his dinner. She refused. In response, he slapped her across the face. She looked stunned for a moment, but then she addressed him, her face glowing with hurt and anger.

'Do not try this again, Mark! I am a skilled and experienced nurse, and I can support myself and my children if need be. But if I leave you, you are likely to lose your job. There are people in town who can harm you, and who'd love to see you humiliated. Without me, you won't be voted in by the Board again. Think of that and make no mistake – I am not one of those wives who are happy to be punching bags.' She indignantly shed her apron and stormed out of the scullery.

'You could do with a scold's bridle,' my father griped, and swore under his breath, but even drunk, he understood that she meant what she said. Only then did he spot the three of us children cowering at the corner of the dining table, and he waved his arm towards us, shooing us away like chickens. We darted to our bedrooms. I was worried and sad about my mother, but happy that she stood up to him. We feared our father, and Mother was our rock, our seawall keeping at bay the waves of Father's rage.

Over the years, I often wondered why my mother, an able and lovely woman, married such a brute. Sometimes it was easy to see a reason behind a mismatch of this kind, but not in my parents' case. Perhaps it was the fact that my mother was quite old when she married my father – she was twenty-five, at the edge of the precipice of spinsterhood. My father was twenty-nine, hardly a youth 'showing promise'. Perhaps his temper was less foul when he was a young man? I asked my mother once why she married my father. A simple question. She said she did because she loved him. A simple answer. I could not go on asking – she would have told me off. She did not seem enthusiastic about the topic.

I discussed this with Emma, and with Kate, my older sister, more than once. Emma had a dim view of marriage: 'A woman's youth comes to an abrupt end when she marries.'

Kate had been married for almost a year and was pregnant with her first child, but not thrilled about it. 'Marriage is already too much work! Cooking, cleaning, washing, ironing, pleasing and serving Clive! But you always need to look presentable at home and in town as well.'

Kate hoped Clive would relent and employ a serving maid when their baby was born. 'You may be too diligent as a house-wife, so Clive does not see the point of paying a maid,' Emma suggested. Kate and I both nodded on that occasion; there was a point to consider there.

Clive was a fishmonger, and at twenty-two he had already developed his business enough to have a stall at the markets and a shop in the Lanes. He employed two staff; a man who took care of the market stall and a woman who ran the shop. Clive negotiated the supply and prices of mackerel, and whatever else was in season, with the local fishermen, and transported crates of fish to the shops. As a result, he moved in a cloud of faint fish smell, but he was keen to be well-presented, which kept Kate busy with washing and ironing his clothes. 'Not to worry, my dear, soon I'll have a driver to take over the transport and I'll just take care of the business side of things – and I'll be smelling like a rose,' he told her. There was hoping! My father asked Clive to keep an eye on fishermen's need for menial labour, as some of it could be sourced from the workhouse. On days when the catch was especially abundant, and seasonally, when mackerel fishing was at its peak, the workhouse inmates could earn a few pennies at the Old Steine. Their wages were delivered straight to the Master.

My parents' marriage – and Kate's, to a point – stripped

many illusions about holy matrimony from my mind. I agreed with Emma: this was not something I yearned for. I wanted to learn, earn my living and be independent. Spinsterhood was not an attractive option though, so I hoped I'd come across a man who would somehow fit into my – at that stage still quite blurry – formula of a woman's life less conventional.

Some months after I started my apprenticeship at the work-house, my cousin Jack left for London. After three years at Brighton Grammar, he had spent two years practising accountancy at Mr Sedge's offices. He learned not just how to keep the double-entry ledger but also about the business side of things, and he planned to seek his fortune in the capital. 'It's never too early to make money,' he claimed. He was nineteen at the time, more than two years older than Emma and me.

Emma, Kate and I saw him off to the railway station and wished him luck. The memory of his beaming face at the train carriage window made me smile as the train idled, and then heaved itself off with jerks and hoots. Just as the mob on the platform began moving alongside, it whistled deafeningly and puffed out a cloud of steam, as if telling us to give up the race at once. Jack waved vigorously so we could see him through the steam. For a moment, the metal window frame glinted in the sun and his face was obscured. Kate sighed wistfully when we turned around to walk back home. I think she wanted to be on that train instead of Jack.

Jack came home for a week in late July, fancily dressed in a white shirt with frilly sleeves, a wine-coloured bowtie and a velvet waistcoat of the same hue, no doubt to show off his success. He did look fancy and if he weren't my cousin, I'd think of him afterwards! But he was my cousin, and I thought his vaingloriousness detracted from his appeal. Over dinner in our house, we were all ears as he talked about his London venture.

'It's going well, all as planned, but too early for important moves.' He sounded like a man about town. As we ate and he drank a pint of beer, he told us more; Jack liked to talk and be listened to. He mainly addressed my father, seeking approval.

Jack worked at an accounting firm in Westminster for a decent wage and was able to save a few guineas each week; by now he had worked out his options. He could work hard, distinguish himself and save money to fund his entrepreneurial ideas. Not to start his own business – that was too hard for a novice from the south – but with some luck, he could become a junior partner. Or he could save more money and study law. Lawyers were handsomely paid if their law chambers were on the right side of town. The legal profession supplied the government ranks, so who knows, other doors might open ... ?

I could not quite imagine Cousin Jack hunched over thick books late at night or giving a stunning speech in a court of law or the parliament. I could see him stepping out of a fancy carriage, helping an attractive lady in a low-necked dress. I think this is what he had in mind when he planned a legal career, or a partnership in an accounting firm. Jack told us about the West End, where cultured and well-dressed people strolled, ate in pricey restaurants and went to theatres. It was clear he wanted to join the company of important gentlemen and glamorous ladies.

'Well done, my boy!' My father slapped Jack on the shoulder as we finished dinner. 'You have time. You've only just started.' My father's praise to his children, or anyone else, was rare. I sensed that, like all men, he would like to have a son he could be proud of. He never once praised Kate or myself, even though we won all the school awards and were respectful daughters. Our younger brother Aaron, born a mongoloid, was a blow to our father's pride.

Jack came back home again for Christmas wearing a fine black coat and a tall hat. His boots were polished and his suitcase had nickel-plated corners. In less than a year, London transformed him from a mere stripling to a well-presented young gentleman.

'Breathe! Breathe! In-hale! You don't know what you've got here!' he yelled as soon as he stepped onto the platform. The train bellowed out soot and the air at the station wasn't particularly good – but still much better than in London, Jack insisted. He called for a porter and an older man in a shabby suit and a blue tie appeared out of nowhere. Jack handed over his suitcase and continued his story.

'It is hard to breathe in London in winter! No-one can escape the smog, not even well-off people who do not live packed like sardines in repulsive tenements. Some days it's unbearable; soot settles in one's nose, hair, on one's clothes.'

Cousin Jack liked to enlighten us girls. But I did know what I had in Brighton: the big sea, the big sky, the salty wind that in winter leaves a fine white layer on everything. My mother called it 'good, bracing air'.

# 4

At the time I started my nursing training, my parents were running the Race Hill Workhouse as the Master and Mistress, and another one in Brighton, about two miles inland: the Warren Farm School for pauper children. The East Sussex Board of Guardians supervised both institutions and appointed their masters. My father had been Master of Race Hill Workhouse for over ten years. Yet he was popular neither in town nor in the workhouse; he flew off the handle too easily, consumed by anger that seemed directed at the whole world, only looking for an outlet. The inmates feared the rough and sometimes violent Master. When Mademoiselle Bouvier taught me about slavery on American plantations, only abolished in the year of my birth, I'd always imagined my father as a slaveowner in tall boots, cracking his whip. The master was responsible for the discipline in the workhouse, and for my father this appeared to be the favourite part of the job. He did not have a whip, but he had a cane.

The workhouse consisted of three buildings. My parents called them 'pavilions': one for men, one for women and children under fourteen, and one for the disabled and the sick, including those who were too old and decrepit to work. There were common spaces too, an airing yard and a large kitchen where women prepared food. Women and children were the majority of the inmates, so their pavilion was extended when my parents took over. They were under the supervision of the Matron, which was their stroke of good luck. My mother was firm but fair and for her, Christian charity and mercy were not just talking points; she practised them and was loved and respected for it.

My father and the porter, who doubled as a guard, patrolled and supervised the men's quarters, which included a carpentry workshop that kept nearly half of the men employed. Yet many men needed to be employed outside the workhouse and it was my father's non-trivial task to find jobs or suitable apprenticeships for them. Managing a workhouse, which seemed to me a cross between a factory and a prison, was not an easy job. Adhering to any sort of discipline was not the inmates' strong suit. Many grew up orphaned or in broken families, abused by a drunken father or neglected by an overworked mother. Barely anyone managed any schooling and most of them were illiterate.

Minor upsets happened daily. The work required physical and

emotional stamina, which my mother possessed, or developed over time, I could not tell. As to my father, he was physically strong and free with the use of his cane; his dominant moods were anger and spite, which did not help either him or the inmates. Perhaps his personality was a good match for the job? Could a workhouse be run gently? I often wondered whether instilling fear in the inmates was the only way to keep the enterprise running in the black, to the satisfaction of the Board of Guardians, and everyday life relatively orderly, sprinkled with minor rather than major dramas. My father was required to inspect all wards twice daily, at 11 a.m. and then at 9 p.m. for the final check before the porter turned the lights off and locked the workhouse gate for the night. The inmates scrambled to tidy up their quarters and hide evidence of mischief: smoking, drinking, gambling, brawling, fornicating.

As Mistress and Head Nurse, my mother supervised the housekeeping and the dispensary. She oversaw nursing in the other workhouse too, and helped hands-on at the time of disease outbreaks, which happened with unrelenting regularity. She was in charge of recruiting new indoor staff in both workhouses. My father could thank my mother, whose reputation was impeccable, for having kept his position that provided a decent income; his iron fist was sloppy outside the business of disciplining and punishing, especially with the administration. He often ignored orders circulated by the Poor Law Commissioners and was issued warnings several times. My mother was able to smooth the ruffled feathers and reassure the government inspectors on their twice-yearly visits.

The Board of Guardians expected the workhouses to be run with 'the minimum cost and maximum efficiency', which meant extracting as much useful work from the inmates as possible while paying them the lowest wages. It also meant cutting costs on food and medical supplies and paying staff modestly, which was a constant source of dispute between my parents.

Apart from me, a part-time nursing apprentice, the Spike was visited daily by a chaplain. Father Hubert provided pastoral care, but I was not convinced that he improved the lives of the inmates, unless being chastised and prescribed abstinence and prayer helped them. My mother worked overtime most days, but instead of hiring another nurse, my father employed a bookkeeper to lighten his own workload.

In a similar vein, when Kate and I reached the ages of twelve and ten respectively, our father had decided we didn't need a maid at home, as we were able to help with domestic chores. Our brother Aaron was only eight at the time, and he required extra care. My mother wanted to make sure that Kate and I had enough time for schoolwork and tried to spare us as much as she could. This meant she often worked until late, to the point of exhaustion. My father offered to recruit the help of 'one of the more decent women' from the workhouse, but my mother resisted this idea.

# 5

Aaron's simple-mindedness was a source of sadness for my mother, and wounded pride for my father. For Kate, Emma and me, he was just a human being with his unique features; we were baffled by the constant, lingering regret and even shame, in our family and wider society. Aaron was not a burden; he attended the School of Industry in Upper Edward Street and learned the skill of fishnet making. The fishermen from Old Steine kept offering him more work than he could take. By the age of sixteen he was able to earn his keep.

Aaron was peaceful and seemed happy in his childlike way,

happier than most 'normal' people I knew. All his troubles came from other people treating him badly. Rough boys in his school introduced him to liquor too early. He was good-natured and the more he drank the readier he was to be a clown. He was the butt of jokes, but he enjoyed it when people laughed at him. He was aware that this was more likely to happen after a pint or two of beer, so he was glad to accept drinks from working-class men in pubs, who treated him as entertainment they could buy with a few pennies before going home to face their exhausted wives and unruly children.

One day a small group of local lads offered to introduce Aaron to a 'girlfriend'. He was delighted. He came home beaming and asked to borrow a cravat from our father's wardrobe. I was suspicious and perturbed by the prospect of ridicule, but decided not to intervene; whatever I said, Aaron would do exactly as he wanted anyway. Against my better judgment, I helped him dress up for the occasion. He looked comically handsome with his chubby young face, mouth a little askew, watery blue eyes and an early onset of middle-age plumpness around his waist.

The story reached my parents by the end of the day; my father heard it on his after-dinner inspection at the Spike. The porter who had just come in for his night shift told him that two local lads bought a couple of drinks for Sharon, a local woman of easy virtue, and persuaded her to have a 'date' with Aaron. One of the lads accompanied Aaron to an agreed 'secret' place in the far corner of the St Nicholas's Church grounds. Sharon was already there, sitting on a bench and smiling sweetly. The others lurked in the bushes ready to observe the date from their hideout. It was agreed that if she kissed him the 'French way' a couple of times, for at least five moments, they'd pay her. She did, and as soon as the kissing was over, she wiped her mouth with a back of her hand, jumped up from the bench and rushed to the bush hideout asking for her reward. Aaron realised he was set up and dragged himself home, disappointed, seen off by their laughter, catcalls and lewd comments.

He arrived home looking sad and shed a few tears before dinner. I was silent, not sure how to comfort him. Mother just said: 'Aaron, you should avoid those lads. They are a band of ne'er-do-wells and mixing with them can only do you harm.'

Father arrived an hour later, furious. Of course, the story had to be told far and wide; it was meant for our father's ears, to humiliate the man that thought highly of himself but was ready to criticise everyone else, from the most wretched inmate at the Spike to the Queen herself. The Aaron and Sharon episode triggered father's rage; he started a harsh rebuke, which would be useless in improving anyone, much less Aaron, who shrank to his smallest possible size on the sofa, scared to look up. He started to cry again when father called him an 'imbecile'.

I was not sure that Aaron understood what the word really meant, but he surely understood that it was meant to hurt him. My mother rushed out of the sitting room; she was probably thinking that opposing my father would just add fuel to the fire and prolong his angry rant. She was right, but I could not stand my father's callousness.

'Father, can you please stop chastising him? It is not his fault! Your rebuke is not useful and it hurts us all. It is cruel!'

'Oh, shut up, will you Frances? Your defence of the poor, downtrodden and feeble-minded again, is it? I am fed up with it! You make me look as if I am doing something wrong at the Spike and now in my own house! Let me tell you, miss: if you let those ne'er-do-wells that we house have their way, they'd just sleep and eat and freeload on hardworking people's taxes ... The Spike gives them a roof above their heads. They need to earn their keep. What the council gives us is nowhere near enough to run the place. I work hard: making those layabouts do enough useful work each day is an exacting job! Do you understand? If you're not happy you may leave the comfort of your parents' home, young lady, and see what life is really like when you're on your own, earning your living.'

'I may do just that, Father! Aaron is a simple-minded but good, mild-natured boy and he did not deserve the casual meanness of the local lads. It would be more useful if you confronted them; they are cowards and the real offenders. Instead of being harsh to Aaron, you could use your power to protect him! But you cannot, can you, because you are ashamed of your own son ...'

I knew I had just poked into the hornets' nest. I had dared to say what we all knew was true. Mother came back into the room and was looking at me, then to my father, with her hand raised, eyes wide open and lips apart, as if wanting to talk but not being able to utter a word.

'You brazen hussy!' My father started to shout, red in the face and pointing at me. He bellowed about disrespect, ingratitude, insolence and a proper woman's place and behaviour. His anger was triggered by Aaron's misadventure, but readily redirected to me. Deep down, he knew he should leave my brother alone; among other things, my mother resented his putting down of Aaron more than anything else.

I said nothing more, waiting for his rage to expend itself. But tyrants needed to be resisted; I remembered my mother's stance when my father hit her. I decided there and then to leave home; I would head for London like Cousin Jack. He'd give me shelter for the first few days until I found somewhere to live. I'd find a job. There were many hospitals and workhouses in London and nurses were sought after. Over nearly three years, I had gained ample experience at the workhouse, which was sure to help me find a job.

# 6

I packed my things the next morning. My mother was upset by the quarrel and dismayed to see me go, but she did not try to discourage me. I thought she might have been secretly proud of me and quite confident I would be able to support myself. I was sorry to leave her without dedicated help at home and at the workhouse. They would have to recruit a new trainee nurse; it was probably for the better that this was not a family member. The fact that Jack was in London gave my mother peace of mind about me, a young woman of nineteen, navigating the big city for the first time. She said she would hate it if I were there 'all alone' and insisted I took a letter for Jack where she asked him to 'take care of me'. This was not needed. Even though Jack was focused on his successes and pleasures, and a sense of family duty was not uppermost in his moral universe, Jack and I had been close since childhood and I knew he would not let me down if I actually needed him.

The moment the train left Brighton, my mood turned from anger at my father to positive excitement. The middle-aged gentleman who shared my compartment inquired discreetly about the purpose of my trip to London.

'I am going to train as a nurse.'

'Ah, I see! Very well, miss! Which hospital?'

'St Thomas',' I replied. It was the first hospital that sprang to mind, and I knew it was the largest teaching hospital.

It was not usual for a young lady to travel alone, but it seemed that my short and proper answers satisfied him. In my serious attire I must have looked older than I was; I could pass for early twenties. I asked about the best way to get to Liverpool Street in Islington from Paddington Station, where we were due to arrive. He could not answer my question in detail, as he lived 'more west-way' – where respectable people lived, according to Cousin Jack.

'You could take an omnibus to Islington; you see, cabs, the Hackney Carriage Service, are quite expensive at sixpence a mile.'

There were several omnibus stops around Paddington Station and given my destination, I probably needed to look for one on the north side of the station. My helpful travel companion suggested I hire a porter who would take me there. He seemed pleased when I thanked him for all his advice. The porter took me to the front of St. Mary's Hospital. Another large, imposing hospital! I thought that was a good omen at the very start of my London sojourn. The omnibus took the whole hour to get to Islington, and I arrived at Cousin Jack's at dinner time. I hoped he'd be at home, as no letter announcing my arrival could arrive before me.

It turned out that Jack's address actually belonged to the part of town called Angel. Another good sign, I thought. In my excited anticipation of a new life, the contours of which were still entirely vague, I was ready to succumb, temporarily, to heeding magic omens. Owing to long May days and fine weather, the street was full of people and quite noisy when I stepped off the omnibus. The driver had kindly stopped at the corner, ten paces from the entrance to 52 Liverpool St. It was a neat-looking, two-storey brown-brick town house with a whitewashed entrance, ground floor and basement. Long balconies on both floors had white-framed French doors and ornamental iron balustrades. I dragged my suitcase over four steps from the pavement to the front door and knocked using a brass lion's head. A maid with a white starched apron over her black outfit opened the door at once, before I could even straighten my jacket, let alone inspect the two purple-and-green stained glass panels on the front door. She checked me from my hat down to my suitcase.

'Good evening! I am looking for Mr Jack Cooper. I am his cousin, just arrived from Brighton.'

She glanced at my boots. 'I see. Mr Jack. Just a moment! I'll fetch the landlady.' She closed the door and disappeared. A stout middle-aged lady in a navy-blue dress opened the door a minute later.

'Good evening, miss!' She checked me out too and seemed satisfied with my presentation.

'Good evening, madam. My name is Frances Wood. I am sorry to inconvenience you at this late hour and disrupt your after-dinner rest. I have just arrived in London, and I suspect my cousin has not received my letter advising him of my arrival yet. I was hoping to stay with him for a few days until I find my own accommodation, if that's possible.'

'I am afraid Mr Cooper is not in yet; he told me this morning he'd dine in town. But do come in – no point having a conversation this way – this neighbourhood is not as quiet and pleasant as it used to be some years ago.'

She opened the door wide. Once we were both indoors, Mrs Dadson introduced herself and pointed to a small sitting room to the left of the entry corridor. She waved towards a sofa under the window overlooking the street. 'Please have a seat.'

'I do not think Mr Cooper will be much longer. I'd say he'd be home before dark. We have a guest room for short visits, which I could let to you for a week . . . once Mr Cooper is back and we discuss the matter.'

'That would be excellent – thank you so much for your kind hospitality, Mrs Dadson. You see, I'll work at St Thomas' Hospital. I am a trainee nurse, that is, not certified yet. I worked at a workhouse run by my father . . . my parents for nearly three years.'

I heard the front door slam and Jack entered the salon. At the sight of me his face assumed a comical expression of exaggerated surprise.

'Why ... my little cousin Frances!' He approached and hugged me tightly. He was in an ebullient after-dinner, after-a-few-pints mood.

'Good evening, Mrs Dadson.' He turned around and bowed to his landlady. 'I was walking to the hat stand and I thought I spotted Frances through the door, but I could not quite believe my eyes ...'

Mrs Dadson smiled but remained quiet, observing the meeting scene.

'What are you doing in London, Frances? Just granting me the pleasure of your visit?'

'That would have been nice, Jack, but no. I am here to learn more nursing.'

'Are you indeed? Well, that's great news! Tell me about it!'

'With pleasure! I'm just conscious we're taking Mrs Dadson's time ... and space. She kindly let me in on your behalf, so to speak. There is a guest room I could have for a week if that's fine with you too ...'

'Oh, but of course, by all means! I must show you around town too! This is your first time in London, unless you have more surprises up your sleeve ... ?' He laughed, turning to Mrs Dadson again.

'Thank you so much for letting Frances in, Mrs Dadson – I'd hate to see a young lady like her standing at the street corner!' He turned back to me. 'Why didn't you write about your coming over?'

'I did, only the letter must be late,' I lied. 'And I have a letter for you from my mother. While your mother complains that you do not write often enough ...' I turned towards Mrs Dadson.

'My mother and Jack's father are siblings. Anyhow, should we sort out my accommodation and let Mrs Dadson have her evening peace back ... ?'

'No trouble, Miss Wood. But yes, let me take you to your room. You probably cannot wait to take your boots off.'

## 7

Jack and I talked until late in the sitting room. I explained to him that I would like a job not just to support myself in London by doing what I already knew; I was eager to become a certified nurse and learn more about the science of medicine. I was not sure what my options might be. Jack nodded his head.

'Yes, I understand, my dear cousin! You are ambitious, just like me. You are a woman, which makes it harder ... but why not try?' He thought the large St Thomas' Hospital, which included the Nightingale School for Nurses, might indeed be my best chance.

'Let's be clever from the start, Frances! On Saturday morning, we'll go there together and have a look around, try to find someone to talk to.'

Jack thought a lady, especially a young one, would be more convincing if accompanied by a well-dressed and well-spoken gentleman. I would have preferred a world where a woman could do her own talking and would be considered more convincing if she showed her personal determination. But Jack was trying to help me, so it would have been ungrateful to refuse; and he was probably right.

The next morning, Friday, I accompanied Jack to his office in the City, close to the central Court of Law. I was curious to see the hospital as soon as possible so before we parted, Jack explained how to get there. I needed to walk down the Strand towards Trafalgar Square and then turn left into Whitehall towards the Parliament, then cross the Westminster Bridge leading to Lambeth. A line of large hospital buildings would not leave any doubt about where to turn from the bridge, Jack explained. He warned me to take care of myself and my possessions, look everywhere, not get run over by a carriage, and refuse offers for help even from respectable-looking people.

I nodded and smiled; Jack was perhaps over-explaining again, but I enjoyed his concern – he was playing the part of a good, caring cousin well. Was it my mother's letter? Or the independent life that inevitably made him more mature? I thought the latter was more likely. He was twenty-two and in London for over two years. He enjoyed the role of guide. I was excited; I was at the juncture between two worlds, two realities; the old one that I had escaped already felt far and faded, and the new one was full of possibilities. I knew it was not going to be easy, but there was a promise of a new life and I was in a state of hazy, hopeful unreality.

The following morning I walked down the Strand admiring large, sumptuously decorated buildings: colleges, foreign embassies, churches, theatres, government offices, aiming high with their spires, domes and turrets. Everything in London looked grand and opulent! I reached Trafalgar Square where the crush of people, carriages and omnibuses became even denser. I had been concerned I would be conspicuous – a woman wandering alone, stopping to gape at every building, monument and sign – but I was invisible in the busy crowd. This was not Brighton's Esplanade.

Yet if someone did notice me and took interest – this is what Jack warned me about – it was plain to see I was not going to a specific place on predetermined business, as such people walk at a pace and do not look around much. I was not the usual sort of visitor on a grand tour or just a short holiday, because a young lady would not be alone. I could not be a curious city *flâneur*, because that was a role reserved for gentlemen. This presented a question I thought about as I gathered my early impressions of the imperial capital: who was I now? Just someone trying her luck with sparse knowledge of how to go about it and what her chances were. An adventurer? If that was my new status, so be it – I liked it! The buzz of the big city was thrilling, and the feeling did not leave room for apprehension. At that very moment, I was boldness incarnate.

I turned left into Whitehall; more imposing government buildings, more monuments. Mainly men on horses – kings, dukes, generals, all of them victors in one war or another. The Empire was on display not just in brick, concrete and marble, but also in people; many more types, races and costumes than in Brighton, even at the peak of the southern resort's summer season. Big Ben had just announced ten o'clock as a lush, carefully manicured parkland opened in front of me, and the Thames rolled slowly by on my left. The new vistas excited me. I inhaled deeply. The air was clear. Westminster Bridge was in front of me. As for most people, bridges had a special mystique for me, but given the intense pedestrian and vehicular traffic on the bridge, I had to pay full attention to edging my way across. I could now see the line of eight large, red, square buildings: St Thomas'! As soon as I stepped off the bridge, I was at the promenade in front of the Hospital Gardens. A free bench offered a moment of respite; I needed to think what to do next.

I decided to stroll around the buildings first. The sun was warm and a breeze from the river soft and pleasant. One of the eight large pavilions had a plaque reading 'The Nightingale Training School and Home for Nurses'. I remembered the main message from her book: people's lives and wellbeing depended on the care they received from women – mothers, wives, governesses, serving maids, nurses – and if these women knew how to keep themselves and others healthy, that was an immensely better way than the grim business of curing the sick. The workhouse managed by my parents was known for cleanliness; fleas, bedbugs and lice were kept at bay. Being clean and neat is more than halfway to self-respect and health: this seemed to be my mother's leading maxim. Florence Nightingale pointed out that in wars, many more soldiers died from infectious diseases contracted in unsanitary conditions than from battle wounds.

Circumnavigating the hospital grounds took a good half hour. Now I wanted to have a peek indoors. I entered the first building, next to the little park where my expedition had started. In a spacious lobby, a porter was sitting at a large desk, directing visitors. He was busy talking to a middle-aged couple and I decided not to wait – I would not know what exactly to ask anyway – and instead slipped in and climbed a wide staircase splitting left and right at a mezzanine.

On a whim, I turned right. A sign on a swinging door on top of the stairwell told me I was entering the Gynaecology and Obstetrics ward. I stepped through the door as quietly as I could and found myself in a long hallway, three yards wide, its high ceiling disappearing into a semi-darkness that the gas lamps on the walls could not penetrate. The waxed floors gleamed. Given I was dressed neither as a patient nor as staff, I walked with determination, making sure I didn't appear like an unauthorised visitor sauntering about but rather as someone on a mission.

Most doors to the rooms were closed, but some were ajar, allowing streaks of daylight to penetrate the corridor. I could glance at a line of iron beds with white bedlinen covering motionless bodies. Towards the end of the corridor, a smell of urine filled my nostrils, even though they had modern water closets here at St Thomas', as indicated by a sign on the door. I recognised the ineradicable, native smell of the casual ward for vagrants in my parents' workhouse. I could hear soft, monotonous groaning, a woman's voice. I stopped for a moment but then continued; I could not intrude.

The ward left a mixed impression, not a pleasant place but not dreadful either. Overall, cleaner and quieter than Brighton workhouses, in spite of my mother's tireless efforts and my father's tough-mindedness. The poor people admitted to the hospital were easier to control than those able-bodied in workhouses who exercised their anarchic will and desperately sought whatever immediate pleasures they could come by. For them, life was too hard and deceptive to count on a better future. All that they could hope to enjoy were things they could lay their hands on here and now. Did St Thomas' patients have hopes for the future?

I turned around and rushed back even faster, keeping my footfall as light as I could. As I descended, I noticed the white marble of the stairs was interspersed with light grey veins, rather like human skin. The porter lifted his gaze. I smiled, waved and slipped through the door into the bright spring day before he had time to ask a question.

# 8

Jack started inquiries at his office the same day and found out that a senior colleague's sister had trained at St Thomas' Nightingale School. He learned that it was a tradition for nurses to meet the great woman in person after they completed their training. Florence checked their personal records, including those on their character, and consulted the hospital matron before reaching the final decision to grant their nursing certifications. The bad news was that the school only admitted a small number of students each year. The next admission round was in September. I would need to have some hospital experience and excellent references by then if I were to have any hope of getting in. It was mid-May. I had only the summer to attempt this. 'You will need quite some luck, Frances,' Jack concluded. My mother had always said that one made one's own luck, but in this case, the task was nearly impossible.

The next morning, Jack treated me to a hansom cab to Westminster. 'Your new life should start in style,' he announced half-jokingly, half-solemnly. During the ride, he explained about types of carriages passing us by and pointed at public buildings, adding morsels of metropolitan gossip about their famous occupants. From Westminster, we strolled across the bridge and arrived at St Thomas' Hospital before Big Ben struck ten. I told Jack about my 'visit' of the day before.

We went straight to the porter's desk. I was relieved to see it was a different porter. Jack took his hat off politely. 'Good morning, sir. Is it possible to see the most senior nurse on duty today?'

'Matron is not at work today. May I ask about the purpose of your visit?'

'Well … this young lady – my cousin – will join the Nightingale School for Nurses this autumn, and she would love to have a little look around if possible. She is visiting from Brighton. Talking to someone to gather more information would be extremely helpful.'

'Well, sir, for this you need to have someone to guide you, a pre-arranged appointment. On this occasion, I can only give you this.' He pulled out a brochure showing the Lady with the Lamp image, of Florence Nightingale administering to the sick soldiers, on the front page.

I was standing a step aside from the desk, and a young man clad in a white doctor's uniform came down the stairs. He looked only a little older than Jack. I stepped over to him.

'Excuse me, sir ... might you be the doctor on duty?'

He seemed friendly; his pale, sallow face, with a chiselled chin and a slightly crooked nose, gave a somewhat stern impression, but his kind dark eyes and full lips softened the picture. 'Yes, I am Dr Somerset, on duty today. Can I help you ... ?'

Jack turned around from the porter's desk and nodded politely. I decided to speak in spite of Jack's erstwhile advice.

'I apologise for accosting you like this, without introduction or appointment ... I am Frances Wood, and this is my cousin, Mr Jack Cooper. I wonder if you'd be so kind as to give us a moment of your time and possibly the information we seek.'

'By all means, if this is not something the porter would know better! Feel free to join me in the gardens on my smoking break.'

We exited the echoey entrance lobby and walked to a bench facing Westminster Abbey across the Thames. Dr Somerset sat down and waved to us to join him. The same bench I sat on the day before – another good omen! I sat at the edge of the bench with my hands on my lap. Jack stood by.

'Thank you so much for your kindness, Dr Somerset. I have just arrived from Brighton, where I trained as a nurse in a workhouse,' I said in a rush. 'I would like to train here at St Thomas' by joining the Florence Nightingale School.'

Dr Somerset lit up a cigar and took a puff before answering. 'I see. I don't know much about the School's administration or admissions. You need to talk to the hospital matron, who also heads the nursing school. Perhaps a good first step would be to talk to the ward superintendent next week. Miss Guthridge. I know her well. I could arrange a meeting with her if you wish.'

'Oh yes, that would be most excellent, Dr Somerset! Thank you so much!' I could have jumped up and down with joy, but I remained seated on the bench, of course. I realised Dr Somerset was younger than I had first thought – perhaps the thick black moustache was there to make him look older and more authoritative. I gave Jack a quick glance. He was standing up serious and expressionless.

'I can put in a word for you on Monday morning and ask her to see you for a few minutes without a pre-arranged appointment. She may be able to tell you how to go about your quest. No guarantee though – she may not be available on Monday at all, who knows? I suggest you come here again on Monday about eleven a.m., and I will escort you to Miss Guthridge.'

I clapped my hands together with joy. 'Thank you so much, Dr Somerset – you are the kindest person I have ever met! I will come back here on Monday at eleven a.m. Where exactly will I find you?'

'The Specialty Registrars' Office, on the third floor. I am specialising in obstetrics.'

Jack seemed pleased with the outcome of our visit. He was surprised by the young doctor's open and uncomplicated attitude. 'He must fancy you, Frances! Be careful.' He winked.

On Monday morning, I arrived at the Registrars' Office before eleven. I was full of anticipation and even though I did not feel too nervous, my mouth was dry and my palms were sweating. Dr Somerset was busy at the ward, but he had left a message for me, to wait in front of Miss Guthridge's office on the third floor. At a quarter past eleven, a young nurse poked her head through the door and looked around. I stood up.

'Miss Wood?'

'Yes!' I approached her with a smile.

'Please come through. The Superintendent can see you for a few minutes; Monday mornings are always very busy.'

'Thank you!'

I walked into a spacious, whitewashed room, with a large desk at the corner, next to the window. The ward superintendent's name, Miss E. M. Guthridge, was carved in silver letters on a wooden display on her desk, turned towards the visitors.

'Please sit down, Miss Wood. We must be quick. How can I help you?'

I had practised the speech lines in my head. Being brief would leave a good impression on this busy woman.

'I arrived from Brighton last week. I have over two years of nursing experience at a workhouse run by my parents. My mother is the head nurse for both Brighton workhouses. My ardent wish is to enrol in the Nightingale School of Nursing at St Thomas' and become a certified nurse.'

'The School enrols a small number of students each year, never more than thirty. We receive many more applications than there are places. This year's intake is currently being considered, so you are late. The admissions are advertised in *The Times of London* in March, and applications are due by the end of April. There are other ways of becoming a certified nurse, in other hospitals.'

'Yes, I am aware of that, Miss Guthridge, but the Nightingale School is the most prestigious and it opens the possibility of teaching and even of further medical training, which is what attracts me. After elementary school, I had two years of private tutoring in mathematics, sciences and languages including Latin. I have practical nursing experience and I am prepared to work hard ...'

Miss Guthridge sat back in her chair and looked at me.

'I can see you're a young lady of strong resolve. Given you are well educated and have some nursing experience, you could join our Lady Volunteers team for a start. This will give you a chance to show who you are and what you know. I will refer you to our volunteering coordinator, Mrs Watt. She is here three times a week in the mornings. Please check the roster in the main lobby for exact days. She may be able to see you at the end of her next working day, which is at twelve noon. Please arrive half an hour earlier in case she has time to see you then. I am sorry that I cannot be more precise. I wish you luck, Miss Wood.'

## 9

I decided to wait until Dr Somerset came back to tell him the news and ask for further advice. I was excited: I already knew three people at St Thomas', and two medical staff I had met in person! I was hoping to be enrolled as a nursing volunteer before my first week in London was over. I felt I was getting somewhere. I could not wait to tell my mother and Emma about the news. But I decided to hold off at least until I actually met Mrs Watt and started volunteering.

It was a good half an hour before Dr Somerset came back. He seemed preoccupied but he smiled when he saw me.

'Miss Wood! How was the meeting with Miss Guthridge? Did you learn anything useful?'

Dr Somerset didn't know Mrs Watt as well as Miss Guthridge, but he thought it should not be too difficult to get a volunteering engagement. There was a considerable turnover in the ranks of the volunteering ladies, especially among younger women. Sometimes the job did not meet their expectations, or they proved too squeamish for the grim reality of a public hospital. Or they got married, had children and left.

'Volunteers are chiefly given non-medical duties; sometimes they help with administration or with non-medical care of patients. Volunteers don't usually have medical knowledge or career ambitions; you don't really fit the mould, but you can try and see for yourself. And, as Miss Guthridge suggested, show who you are. There may be a way forward from there.' He shrugged his shoulders, spread his arms and smiled.

'Thank you so much for your help and encouragement, Dr Somerset! There is another thing. I actually need to earn some money, a problem, I'm guessing, that most volunteering ladies do not have.'

'Perhaps you can try the Lambeth Workhouse for paid nursing work? It is walking distance from the hospital. It seems a bleak place; some of our patients come from there, and all my knowledge comes from their comments. You may collect some intelligence yourself once you start as a volunteer.'

Meeting Mrs Watt was easy, almost like a pleasant social visit. She herself coordinated the Lady Volunteers Service in a voluntary capacity. She had a soft, welcoming air, which medical training seemed to exorcise out of people and replace with a hard, unsentimental attitude. Mrs Watt offered me a cup of tea and we chatted effortlessly about my past work and future plans. She explained the rules of service and handed me a blue and white sleeveless volunteer jacket to wear while in hospital.

'Please take care of it and return it when you leave us. I am sure you will be a valuable member of the Lady Volunteers team, Miss Wood. Welcome! Please take this form and my letter of recommendation to Miss Guthridge, whom you have already met. She will provide a brief practical induction.'

I had a job! Not one that could pay my board, but things were moving forward.

Once I became a volunteer, Dr Somerset and I got to know

each other better. He told me he had only recently completed his medical exams and begun his specialisation. Women who gave birth at St Thomas' were those who could not afford a midwife in their own home. Mortality of mothers and the newborn was high in the hospital, even though dropping recently, after new rules of hygiene and disinfection were introduced.

Luckily for me, Dr Somerset was generous and unconventional; I barged into his life and wasted his time, but he did not seem to mind. He was not just a source of practical information about the hospital, its people and practices; fresh out of medical school, he was bursting with medical knowledge. He was also a deep thinker of life and people, and the slight stammer which he bravely ignored would disappear completely when he became engrossed in a topic of conversation. I cherished his company and a chance to chat with him became the highlight of my days at St Thomas'. A couple of animated discussions convinced us both that we were passionate about the same things and should seek the pleasure of each other's company whenever possible. Underneath a critical mind and a dry sense of humour, Dr Somerset was a kind man. But by now I was sure: he did not fancy me, Jack was wrong. That was a relief: having a friend like him was a real boon, and a suitor would have been a burden.

After a couple of meetings, when he perhaps felt sufficiently confident that I was not a young country woman chasing a suitable husband in the capital, he confessed that he did not plan to pursue a medical career for life. He wanted to be a writer and was in the process of drafting his first novel, inspired by his hospital work. He read ravenously, the medical literature as well as *les belles lettres*, and kept pressing books upon me. Given I had a basic knowledge of biology and chemistry, the study of anatomy would bring me within the terrain of medicine proper, he suggested. The next day he appeared with the fifth edition of *Demonstrations in Anatomy: being a guide to the knowledge of the human body through dissection,* one of the first books that medical students had to pore over.

'Do not expect to have fun, Frances,' he said as he handed me the tome. (By now we were on first-name terms, on his insistence: 'We're nearly the same age, and we are namesakes, it must be a sign!') 'It is a dreary and graphic book about humans as they are without the polite, mostly inoffensive cover of the skin. But that's medicine for you – not a pretty trade. Nor a gentle one. This may be part of the reason, or excuse, why women are considered unsuitable for medical training.'

'Oh, I have seen some raw humanity in the workhouse, Frank! Destitute people, neglected children, the old, the sick. It was hard at the start. One toughens up or runs away. I haven't seen deep under the skin though, I only dressed superficial wounds. My mother sheltered me from the worst things. Starting with pictures and descriptions is surely a good way for a novice to study anatomy.'

'It is! But cutting cadavers is another thing altogether: the acid test for medical students. Not everyone passes. Many need a chair, or a bucket, during their initial lesson in the mortuary. Some don't return for the second time.' He chuckled. 'Perhaps that's why anatomy is a first-year subject.'

The working classes who lived in the Borough of Lambeth, just behind the hospital, were the object of his intense interest, their bodies less so than their minds and souls. Frank felt sorry for women exposed to unhealthy work in factories and laundries, doomed to multiple pregnancies, dangerous childbirths and caring for large families in insalubrious tenements or cold and damp houses.

'And as if all that were not bad enough,' he continued his

observation, 'they often endure rough treatment by their husbands. The men are mostly unlettered types with vile manners,
faced with the drudgery of their working lives. Drinking is a way
to endure the lives they cannot escape. Their idea of heaven does
not extend beyond the beer garden, where Lethe, the goddess of
oblivion, awaits to provide deliverance. They do not know Lethe
is a denizen of the underworld, rather than heaven . . . And once
their wives stop being a source of sexual pleasure, which is at
the time of the first pregnancy, they become their punching
bags, a source of momentary relief from the frustrations and
indignities of life.'

'I understand what you're saying very well, Frank. So many of
the women who end up in the Brighton workhouses are there
because of their husbands' drunkenness and brutality – their
children too! My father himself is a brute . . . but middle-class
brutes tend to get less drunk less often than those of the working classes. As far as I know, he only hit my mother once. She
is a lovely woman – she could have done better than him. She
probably waited for too long. I am in no hurry to get married
either.'

'Yes, it seems that way, given your passion for medicine. I hope
you will get there and when you do, not be disappointed . . . in
either medicine or marriage. Not an easy path for a woman; you
will be discouraged and looked down upon every step of the way.'

Dr Frank Somerset did not have too many kind words for
doctors and medicine.

'You may be better off if you start clear of the illusions I had,
Frances. You should know that poorer-class people treated
here – the vast majority of our patients – are often discharged
in a worse state of health than on reception. Women who give
birth here are assisted by doctors, but they have a higher chance
of dying than those who give birth at home with the help of a

midwife! The ones who come here are often unmarried women or even prostitutes; they are treated with condescending pity by nurses and with contempt by doctors. But what they need is soothing sympathy and compassion.'

'It's a shame that all the common prejudices find their way into hospitals . . . and perhaps medicine too.'

Frank nodded vigorously. 'Oh yes! Especially medicine! Professors of medicine bring into their theory and practice all the worst sex and class prejudice one encounters out there.' He waved his arm towards the window.

'The medical knowledge of this century has been a slow and painful progress . . . littered with mutilated bodies and corpses. We have a worse record than the Spanish Inquisition!' He laughed bitterly. 'Imagine: after some insightful and dedicated people spent decades researching and writing about the importance of hygiene and disinfection, still today, in 1884, many doctors find it far-fetched that they should wash their hands before operating or handling the patients! I've seen this with my own eyes, many times. They kill patients by their arrogant negligence – the lives of their hospital patients are expendable!'

Frank paused to catch his breath before continuing his diatribe.

'We now know that illnesses are caused by microscopic germs that are everywhere, on our hands and inside our noses and mouths, but do they care? Some medical professors here still talk about 'miasma'. By defending misguided old theories, they defend their professional status. The cases of childbed fever leading to deaths of young women are intolerably high. If newborns survive, they are left orphaned!'

'Yes . . . everyone knows of a woman who died in childbirth.'

'But it does not have to be like that! Doctors wash their hands when they visit their private patients in their homes, but the poor people here do not seem to deserve the same care. Nurses are better, and easier to convince; being common women, they have no inflated opinion of themselves and are willing to learn. Actually, they are always told what to do; the best nurse has to submit to the worst doctor.'

He paused and looked at me with a pained expression on his face.

'I cannot fight the rigid medical establishment, but I find it too painful to look at it, Frances. I worked hard and received my degree to satisfy my parents, but I will pursue writing rather than medicine. Who knows, perhaps a good novel can change the world more than a scientific treatise?' He laughed ruefully.

Frank told me a heartbreaking story, of a Hungarian doctor who practised in Vienna mid-century. In 1847, Dr Ignaz Semmelweis managed to dramatically reduce mortality of women from childbed fever by introducing the practice of washing hands and instruments with chlorinated lime solutions. His evidence was incontrovertible. Yet his ideas and his practice were rejected by the Viennese medical establishment, and he was ridiculed.

At the time of the 1848 revolution, Semmelweis was dismissed from his post for political reasons and forced to return to his native Budapest, outraged by the indifference of his colleagues to the easy-to-implement practice that obviously saved many lives. He descended into alcoholism and eventually died in a lunatic asylum.

'It's a bitter irony that his ideas became widely accepted only a couple of years after his death,' Frank concluded.

'The history of science seems a terrible battlefield,' I offered, 'rather than a polite scholarly discussion among learned men, as we outsiders tend to imagine it!'

'Oh yes ... ruined careers, broken lives, mental breakdowns, suicides, even executions! Science is meant to rest in cool-headed, logical arguments, but people's emotions, prejudices and selfish interests interfere. People are weak, fallible creatures . . .'

'You sound like a wise, old man now, Frank.' I laughed.

He chuckled too and rolled his eyes. 'Yes, twenty-three years old and somewhat of an old grumbler! I've got evidence of fallibility and weakness I cannot turn a blind eye to – myself. To be a writer, one needs to understand other people, and to do that, one needs to purge a practice of self-deception first . . . engage in self-inquisition of a kind.'

Frank supplied more books. The extraordinary history of medicine made me a little sorry that I could no longer see it as a noble and virtuous pursuit guided by a desire to alleviate suffering. But I was still keen! Frank mentioned Mary Scharlieb, who had graduated barely two years earlier from the London School of Medicine for Women. She was nearly twenty years my senior and only through persistence and good luck had she finally succeeded.

'Oh Frank! Persistence and good luck, but still, she had to be thirty-seven to receive her Bachelor of Medicine! Do I have such persistence, and will good luck be with me?'

'It's not luck, it's society, its customs and mores. Hard work gets even harder for some people, while doors open in front of others. If Semmelweis were Austrian rather than Hungarian, he might have been spared the appalling treatment and the sordid end . . .'

'Yes . . . I am not Hungarian, but I'm a woman, which may be worse! Perhaps it would be wiser to return to Brighton and get married . . . to achieve the nursing certification could still be possible, but a study of medicine is another matter. Robert may wait for me for a year or two, but not longer. Why should he?'

'Oh, so you're engaged?'

'Not quite. My mother likes Robert and everyone expects we'll be betrothed next year, and then married the year after, when I turn twenty-one. But I'm not at all sure that's what I really want. I want medicine, however flawed it may be.'

'There are people who break new ground. It always involves grim determination and sacrifice. Only you can decide whether you're made of that stuff. I know I am not! You're bright and full of energy. Follow your dream, Frances, but be ready for a long battle.'

'Ah, a long battle!' I threw up my hands. 'I don't think I'm an overly patient person. Lister introduced an antiseptic technique in 1877, over a decade after Pasteur's germ theory of disease was published! He was the right kind of person in the right place, neither a woman nor a Hungarian, but he was initially opposed and mocked nonetheless.'

'Florence Nightingale was – is – a woman, of your grand-mother's generation,' Frank said seriously. 'Still, she's been a trailblazer. She never married even though she had many opportunities. Her unbending conviction was that nursing was her calling and that marriage and children would have been intolerable distractions. It was brave of her to defy public opinion like that all those decades ago, wasn't it? Perhaps you'll be the next famous medical woman, Frances!'

'Frank, you are so kind, but I should not deceive myself too much ... she had an enlightened father and a private income that allowed her to be single-minded about her future. My mother would support me in spirit, but my father holds the purse strings ... and even if he were more supportive than he is likely to be, the purse is not very deep.'

I loved the discussions with Frank, but as a result I rumi-nated and prevaricated; I lost sleep torn between two possible futures. Frank instilled in me a feeling that my desire to study medicine was not just an idle daydream. But he did not allow me to keep any illusions. If I took the hard path I could not afford to fail: there would be no-one to save me, nothing to fall back on. Robert would have married someone else, and my ageing parents would not be able, and perhaps not willing, to rush to my rescue. Yet I was only at square one; Frank suggested I take one step at a time, at least at the very start, and I knew he was one hundred per cent right.

# 10

After securing a position as a volunteer at St Thomas', I managed to find a place to live in Belvedere Rd, Waterloo. It seemed a good middling street – neither as busy as most thoroughfares in central London, nor one of those deserted little lanes which one would not dare to step in after dark. I rented two upstairs rooms in a red-brick terrace house. A small bedroom window overlooked the backyard, and a larger sitting room had a street view. I could see the tip of Big Ben across the Thames.

The landlady and her sister, both in their forties, both called Miss Abramovich, lived in the rooms on the ground floor. There was another tenant upstairs, a young teacher in a nearby elementary school, a tall thin chap not yet thirty, with a gloomy expression. On my arrival he introduced himself – Mr Hindrum – and explained that our landladies were not up for a chat because their English was quite basic, as they had arrived from Russia less than a year ago, fleeing yet another Jewish pogrom, but apparently being lucky enough to flee with some capital. 'They are pleasant and discreet, as long as one pays rent regularly. I hope you enjoy it here!' Mr Hindrum concluded his brief exposition, nodded and withdrew to his rooms.

It was a modest but decent house. The outdoor lavatory and the backyard water pump were well maintained. In the mornings, I was awakened by the familiar, soothing sound of cooing pigeons. The place felt like home at once. If an easterly wind blew, the vinegary, but not entirely unpleasant smell of the pickle factory in Newington came through. My place was under a mile's walk to St Thomas', which was a great advantage. Once I had unpacked and settled in, I thought I had enough news to report home.

*Dearest Emma!*

*Where do I start? So many impressions! Jack, London, St Thomas' Hospital, Lambeth and its people ... and the amazing underground railway, which seems to me a miracle of engineering. And my new abode, a whole new life, as you can imagine! I scarcely have time to write!*

*I started volunteering at St Thomas' Hospital two weeks ago. This may be my foot in the door to the acclaimed Nightingale School of Nursing, and it won't surprise you that my plan does not end there. The London School of Medicine for Women is ten years old and my sights are on it. But whatever has happened since my arrival in London and whatever is still possible, none of it would have happened without the generous help of a young Dr Frank Somerset. I know what you think now, so I must reassure you, or perhaps disappoint you: there is no romantic attraction between us. We are just good chums, and he is such a fascinating, knowledgeable and unusual man! A bit of a bookworm, I'd say, but in a good sense. No lady friend or fiancée has ever been mentioned, but he most certainly does not try to woo me.*

*The volunteer work is not challenging, but I am learning a great deal about St Thomas' and the whole public hospital system. And about London. Last week I was helping a woman who had given birth at St Thomas'. Her name is Lisa Jones, she is twenty-six. This was her third child, a baby girl. She has two boys, six and four years old, by her estranged husband, who has paid no support over the past year, ever since he heard that she was involved with another man. This other man, a musician like herself, ran off shortly after he learned she was pregnant. Awful.*

*Mrs Jones was quite well-off with her job in a music hall, but each pregnancy meant she was out of the job for months. Then a couple of years ago her vocal cords start-ed playing up and she could not sing anymore. After she spent all her savings, she started earning a small income by making lace. She is so versatile, with many skills! Towards the end of her last pregnancy, she developed migraine headaches and sometimes could not get out of bed for a couple of days. She could not earn and keep her boys even in modest circumstances; they were taken away from her and placed in an orphanage. She implored me to visit them and see how they were, and to tell them their mother did not abandon them. So off I went, to visit the Hanwell School for Orphans and Destitute Children. Her younger boy has the sweetest, saddest face I've ever seen in a child. His smile, when I handed him a little packet of boiled sweets, was like a ray of sunshine: pure joy, only seen in children! It brought tears to my eyes. I could not resist giving him a hug. Poor little soul! His older brother was quite shy and kept his distance, so I only shook his tiny hand when we were parting. He gave out a quick little smile when I gave him a small paper bag of marshmallows.*

*Upon her discharge, I accompanied Mrs Jones out of the hospital. The Lady Volunteers sometimes do this when there are no adult family members to take care of an outgoing* patient. She was admitted to the Lambeth Workhouse because there was nowhere else for her to go. She wanted to see what had become of her place, so we dropped by. In only one week of her absence, the landlord sold her furniture to recover her rental debt, but this was not enough, we learned there and then. London is a brutal place, Emma! People get sick or unemployed and end up on the streets, including women with children – it is heartbreaking. Many working-class people hail from the country, the succour of their families out of reach. So they end up in a workhouse, like Mrs Jones. The workhouse is bleak, tucked away at the end of a small street, sharing a back fence with a slaughter-house. I decided there and then not to look for work there. When we arrived, Mrs Jones was forlorn and shed a few tears. I was sorry to leave her there, with her newborn, but what could I do? She is such a talented woman; with a bit more luck she could have been a vaudeville star, perhaps a famous actress, or a singer.

As you can see, my dearest Emma, I am filled with strong impressions. Some are good – I have had much luck so far – and some are bleak. For outsiders, Mayfair and Whitechapel are parts of the same city, but in fact, they are two different worlds. Fancy ladies in silk gowns and mink wraps being helped out of their carriages in front of West End theatres are a breathtaking contrast to the homeless vagrants and prostitutes treading on the dirty pavements of the East End. Does it have to be like that, I often ask myself, but I cannot fathom out a response. The hospital work reminds one of poverty and sickness every day, every hour. But it is a good feeling to be able to help.

I now need to find a paying job because my savings are at the end. Jack offered a loan, which is kind of him, but I'd *prefer not to have to take his offer. A teacher who has rooms where I live suggested that our Jewish Russian landladies may need English tuition – they asked him, but he works full-time and has no energy for extra work. I will talk to them about it presently.*

*My dearest Emma, is there any chance you could visit? I have a sofa in the sitting room where I could comfortably sleep, and you can have my bed. I think I'll have to spend all summer in London. I have neither time nor money to visit Brighton, but I would love to see you.*

*Please respond soon with your news!*
*Much love,*
*Frances*

# 11

In response to my admiration of the London Underground, Emma's letter mentioned Brighton's novelties: during my first summer away, 'Volk's Electric Railway' started running along the Brighton seafront. Volk was the German engineer who built it. 'Brighton is hurtling into the *bright* future – what else?' Emma's writing was alive with her playful, mischievous voice. The shops at the Lanes, including her parents' shop, now had electric light. 'One turn of a switch and voilà! The smelly oil and gas lamps are gone!' The Old Town and the streets and gardens around the Royal Pavilion and the Brighton Dome now also had electric lighting.

The news made me feel as if I had been away much longer. Nothing much new with Emma personally, but the shop her parents left her in charge of was doing very well during summer. Her parents were pleased, of course. More and more often, she was being nudged about getting married, having just turned twenty and being a shop mistress, making money. Fortunately, her parents left her alone, and she was quite happy to ignore the others.

Emma not only sold souvenirs, hats, bathing costumes and other beach paraphernalia to the hordes of sea bathers; she made them herself too. Besides, her small drawings and paintings of Brighton's environs were selling like hot cakes to the middle classes who wanted to bring home a small memento from the *riviera*. She also started drawing visitors' portraits on the spot, in the shop. 'People's vanity is endless, Frances! Just make them a little smoother looking, while still recognisable, and a nice tip is guaranteed!' she wrote. I was sure her charm and sparkling personality enhanced her success as an artist and a shop owner.

Doing art and crafts removed the tedium of the shop-assistant's work and Emma sounded happy with her occupations. She was considering whether having her own shop would be a good option for her future. She still wanted to learn art in a proper art school; apart from a few months' tuition by Mademoiselle Bouvier, she was self-taught. Summer was her busy time, but she was thinking of visiting me in September.

Summer turned out to be a busy time for me too. The Misses Abramovich (Leah and Rachel) were delighted by my offer to tutor them in English. It turned out they spoke French better than me, so this was at first our lingua franca. They were fast learners, bright and diligent, coming to each lesson with a richer vocabulary. Once the language barrier came down and we got to know each other quite well, not only their good education but also their colourful personalities shone through.

They were connoisseurs of Russian and French literature and fine arts, and they both played music. They missed the St Petersburg social life and concert season greatly. Leah was outgoing and bold, the leader of the two. Rachel was grounded and practical, passionate in her own quiet way. They had their mind set on reading great English novels and they asked me for recommendations. I made a list of a dozen titles. A week later they proudly showed me beautiful, red-leather-bound copies of *Pride and Prejudice* and *Jane Eyre*, already amply annotated on the margins, carefully and lightly in pencil so that it could be later erased; they had many questions for me. In return for English lessons they considerably reduced my rent; it was a good deal, even without counting the fact that teaching them English was pleasant work, where I also learned many interesting things, including a few dozen Russian words and simple phrases.

My landladies knew many other Jewish people in London. Some of them were newcomers like themselves, and needed language tuition, or their children did. I did not have to look far for paying work; Leah and Rachel wasted no time, and two weeks after we started our English lessons, they supplied a neat list of names, addresses and ages of people needing the same. There were more people than I could take on, given my hospital volunteering three days a week. The Abramovich sisters recommended some families before others, just as I did with the great English novels.

Living at the Abramovich sisters' soon started to feel like home. Leah and Rachel were my mother's age and, not having their own children, they took a keen interest in me and my future plans. I tutored two sons of a recently arrived family they knew well; they were relatives of a surgeon at St Thomas' Hospital. Dr Friedmann was born in Germany, shortly after his parents arrived there; his family migrated further to England after the 1848 revolution, when he was a child. Leah sprang into action again and soon I had an appointment with Dr Friedmann, who was a respected orthopaedic surgeon at St Thomas'. He was a kind man and seemed genuinely interested in my desire to study medicine.

'The Kaganoviches are impressed by your tutoring; they ardently hope their boys will pass the entry exam for the University of London Engineering School. The mother of the family is my cousin, née Friedmann. They did not expect a young lady to be able to help their sons with the scientific terminology and the engineering idiom. Your knowledge of science would be a great asset in the study of medicine too.'

'Thank you, Dr Friedmann, you encourage me greatly!'

'I am not able to help you with getting into the Nightingale School; the matron in charge is a strict and upright lady, not known for letting people skip the queue. But you could conceivably skip the nursing school altogether and enter the School of Medicine for Women on your own merit. You could sit an entry exam in early October if you have a letter of recommendation. I cannot give it to you just because my relatives think you are wonderful' – he grinned – 'but you could volunteer as a medical officer in my ward, which would give me a legitimate basis for the recommendation . . . if you indeed are as good as the Kaganoviches think.' He smiled again. 'I am guessing paid employment would be better, but there is no time to organise that. How does that sound, Miss Wood?'

'That is much more than I could hope for, Dr Friedmann! I am extremely grateful for your kindness. You're offering me a great opportunity. I'll do my best to rise to the occasion.'

'Excellent then! I'll introduce you to our ward superintendent as soon as possible. How quickly can you farewell the Lady Volunteers?'

'Oh . . . well . . . I'll tell the coordinator, Mrs Watt, tomorrow – I'm sure she'll understand. I don't have any ongoing or outstanding patient commitments at the moment, so I expect

I could be discharged as soon as I return my uniform . . .'

'Well then, Miss Wood! Please come by my office tomorrow after you see your coordinator, and we'll move the plan one notch further.'

I left Dr Friedmann's office floating on air. I rushed straight to Obstetrics, hoping to find Frank at the Registrars' Office and share the news. He was there, engrossed in writing an anamnesis for a newly admitted patient.

'What fantastic news! Well done, Frances – we'll be colleagues before we expected!' He laughed. 'The blind goddess Fortuna is by your side!'

'Thanks Frank! I'm so happy I could fly, but I'm trying to keep my feet on the ground. There's hard work in front of me, and it is not certain that I'll be able to do it.'

'Of course you will! You already know so much! I'll bring some more books you can revise from. The medical admission exam is about scientific and medical vocabulary, scientific definitions, some not too difficult mathematics . . . you can do all that.'

The new plan turned September into a frantic month. Dr Friedmann let me borrow any books I found useful from his personal library, and Frank took me to the hospital library to pick up more. I had more volumes than anyone could look over in a month, even if I didn't sleep at all.

Each night I nodded off at the desk before collapsing into bed. I realised I had to cancel the invitation to Emma, about which I was terribly sorry. I also had to reduce my English tutoring hours. My landladies were delighted about my plan to sit the entry exam and offered help with cancelling some of the scheduled lessons, as they attended the same synagogue as most of my students. During September, I only kept up the lessons to the Kaganovich boys, who prepared for the same challenge of entering university.

The month whirled past. In late September, I sat the three-hour exam alongside two dozen other young and not-so-young ladies. I felt that too many medical terms and definitions were crammed into my head, and I was hoping my trepidation would not affect my memory. I could not believe my ears when an invigilator said: 'Ten minutes left, ladies.' I ran out of time and did not answer all the questions, but I answered most. The results were to be announced two weeks later; a list of successful applicants would be exhibited in the School's lobby.

My heart was pounding as I approached the glass-covered notice board. My name was not on the list. My heart sank. I sat on the bench next to the exit, feeling ashamed. Not so much for not being above the cut-off line, but for even thinking I could achieve this so quickly. I felt I had been arrogant and silly. What did others think of me? Frank – he must have known this was an impossible feat. It dawned on me that during my feverish preparations I had not given any thought to the issue of the rather expensive tuition if I were admitted. How would I pay the tuition fee? My savings were miniscule. This was a salutary slap in the face.

Frank was a picture of equanimity: 'Life consists of ups and downs, Frances. One learns from the downs and often becomes deluded from the ups.' Dr Friedmann was unfazed. He offered for me to stay at his ward as a medical officer and learn, keeping my direction until I succeeded. Leah and Rachel comforted me. 'You will do it next year! What's a year? You're not twenty yet.' They told me the Kaganovich boys had both passed their entrance exams and were offered places at the School of Engineering. That made me feel better.

Emma visited in late October, and we had several joyful days together. We walked around the city arm in arm, talking and laughing incessantly, often oblivious of our surroundings. On the Sunday, Jack took us on a 'London from the Thames' boat tour, complete with a three-course lunch, and we visited the Tower of London afterwards. On the last evening, Frank took us to the theatre; dressed in our finery, we played West End ladies for the night. After the play, Frank was charming over a glass of dry sherry – an *oloroso*, he explained, a stronger variety of dark amber colour and a nutty, spicy aroma – and canapés. I felt completely happy in the company of my two best friends.

The drink worked its magic on us all. Emma's cheeks were glowing. She surpassed her usual dazzling self, laughing like a silver bell and attracting glances in the theatre bar. Frank seemed pleased to have not one but two attractive young ladies for company. He declared he would write a play, better than the one we had just watched.

The play was about the unrequited love of a young gentleman for a crude, plain-looking waitress. I found it unconvincing. Why would *he* fall in love with *her*? Frank and Emma agreed. 'How unromantic we all are,' we snickered over our drinks. In most people's minds, the question of 'why' diminished the mystery of love, one that should not be analysed but simply succumbed to. It was widely believed that one could fall in love suddenly and inexplicably. Women were considered more susceptible to such a romantic affliction, but there were also many stories like this play, of men being 'bewitched' by the wrong woman.

'The great mystery of love, straight from the heart, bypassing one's head.' Emma swooned dramatically onto my shoulder.

'You just hear the flapping of Cupid's wings . . .' said Frank mockingly.

'. . . and you hear the *whoosh* of his arrow . . .' I added.

'And your heart now belongs to some bounder you didn't even know the day before!' Emma concluded. We all giggled.

Emma suggested that the 'heart' was just a polite-society

substitution for 'lust'. Frank guffawed. The heads turned towards us again.

Emma's visit was just the therapy I needed after the failed exam.

Over Christmas, Jack and I travelled to Brighton together. I could see that my mother missed me in her heart, at home and in the workhouse. My departure had been unexpected, and I could sense she hoped I might equally abruptly pull up the stumps on my metropolitan venture and come home. Aaron was extra affectionate, hugging me at every opportunity. My father kept his distance, for which I was grateful.

Robert came to our house for dinner on Christmas Eve. We met again on Boxing Day and talked about the future. I did not feel I could promise anything. Robert asked if I would come back if I failed the medical exam again the following year. I said I might, but I thought my failure would be an inauspicious start to our life together. I asked if he would come to London if I passed. He took a deep breath and paused, then he said that his job, the family business, was in Brighton. He could not leave it.

On my last day in Brighton, I crossed the Esplanade to my old haunt. It was cold and wet, and the view from the seawall was shrouded in grey mist. I felt a little heartsore that Brighton did not feel like home anymore. The family, the business, the shopkeeping, the marriage, the small seaside town, the hordes of frivolous holidaymakers ... there were other things that now interested me more.

## 12

In early spring of the following year, my voluntary work at Dr Friedmann's ward became a full-time paid job. This was excellent news. Alongside learning practical medicine on the job, I spent much time with medical books. I also kept tutoring English and saving money.

In late September, I passed the entry exam and was admitted to the degree course of Bachelor of Medicine. I was joyful and proud, but not ecstatic; my delight was quieter and more mature than it would have been the previous year. It was like a warm glow inside. My name was close to the top of the list, and I was offered a scholarship covering tuition and a modest living allowance. I was now inside the ramparts of academic medicine. It was time to start remembering all that Frank told me about it: to be diligent, but also vigilant. This was not a fairy dream anymore, but a solid reality with all its flaws. I was ready for it.

Leah and Rachel organised a celebration as if I was their own daughter. A dozen of my students attended, including the Kaganovich boys. They told me about their university life; they had passed all their first-year exams with flying colours. Mr Hindrum came downstairs and joined us; Frank and Dr Friedmann were there too, stopping their intense conversation when I approached to greet them. *Mazel tovs* and congratulations accompanied the clinking of glasses. I was deeply touched by everyone's kindness. It was an unforgettable night.

There was one dark cloud on the clear blue sky of my new life: the thought of those I'd left behind in Brighton. My mother, Emma and Robert would miss me, although Robert was likely to find consolation with another bride before long. I felt worse about my mother and Emma. I was part of their life in an inerasable, enduring way. It was not just that they'd miss me; I needed their warmth and unconditional devotion, which had been my source of strength ever since I could remember. Brighton was not that far, but it was far enough for these emotionally intense relationships to wither into wistful shadows of what they once were.

## 13

In November, my mother fell suddenly ill, and this drew me back home to Brighton. I was unhappy about having to interrupt my studies after only six weeks and upset to see her unwell. I had meant to visit for just a week, two at most, but her dizzy spells accompanied by nausea concerned me. They were often followed by fainting episodes she described as 'terrifying, like dying'. I leafed through medical books but could find nothing useful. I hoped all this could be ascribed to her change of life and overwork. I suggested she reduce her relentless daily schedule, in the workhouses and at home. Her tired smile in response to my advice did not give me much hope she'd take it. I blamed myself too – my absence had meant more pressure on my mother at home and at work. My luck in being able to pursue my dream meant hardship for her. So on top of helping at home, I started helping in the workhouse too. I came from London to help, after all! I hoped lessening my mother's burden would help her recover faster. I was trying to fit in some time for my medical books as well, and this encroached on my bedtime; I felt rather tired and joyless.

In the workhouse, I was mainly helping with administration. Two days into resuming my work at the Spike, a Mr Grenfell came along with his mother, whom he pushed along in a rickety, makeshift wheelchair that reminded me of a wheelbarrow.

Mrs Grenfell, a woman not yet old, suffered from dropsy, with hips so sore and knees and ankles so swollen she could barely walk across the room, leaning heavily on two sticks. Her son wanted her entrusted to the infirmary. I spoke to her and recorded her details – Mrs Sarah Grenfell, age fifty-eight, widowed for many years, laundress while she was able to work. She and her son lived up the hill in Preston, in one of several large tenements close to the fish cannery. Mr Grenfell declined the chair I offered and stood in the corner of the office, as far as possible from both of us, staring intently at me while answering my sporadic questions. I was not sure whether the look on his face was hostility or anger or something else, but I felt uneasy in his presence. I would not have liked to be left alone with him.

'Could you contribute to your mother's keep at the workhouse, Mr Grenfell?'

'If I could, I'd keep 'er at home, miss,' he responded sullenly. 'I lost me job at the cannery and now I do odd jobs for a couple o' shillings a week . . . if I'm lucky.' He signed the admission form as the 'next of kin'. I noticed his nails were dirty and his fingertips yellow from smoking. His clothes were in dire need of a wash. I forgot about him afterwards, while attending to workhouse issues, but when I came home his image sprang to mind again. Was he married? He seemed an example of those angry, downtrodden working-class husbands Frank had described, who took their frustration out on their wives. But how could one reform such a person, help his family? Curing people's bodies was important, but it was not touching the underlying problems society was riddled with.

It's sheer luck, where one is born, in which family! But the upper classes understood their privilege as their virtue, their own merit . . . ! I happened to be born middle-class, and lucky enough to have an enlightened mother who cared to have me educated . . . and therefore less likely to suffer brutal treatment from a husband, or anyone else for that matter. Which reminded me of Robert. There was an unresolved issue of clarifying things with him. We both knew what would happen: nothing. Each of us would stay where we were. Why bother explaining anything? I was delaying it, hoping to somehow avoid it, but I felt guilty.

By late November, the year had grown into deep autumn. The night was falling early and it was already dark when I left the workhouse just after 5 p.m. Torn clouds sailed above the western horizon, dark grey on the background of fading pink. I shuddered in the cold, stiff sea breeze and wrapped myself tighter in my woollen cloak.

I needed a few moments by myself and some bracing salty air in my lungs before going home to be a dutiful daughter. The sea had always been my ally and consolation. It provided a sense of perspective: immense and indifferent, beyond people's petty troubles. I turned from the Esplanade onto a concrete ramp that, lower down, became a curving stone stairwell descending to the beach. The sea was patchily illuminated by the remains of daylight; the dark swells crashing upon the shore reflected shards of paling pink. It was the exact same spot where Emma and I had attempted sea-bathing some years back. Two silly, happy girls on a warm August night. It was cold now and I was alone, listless and melancholy.

Just as I stepped on the pebbles, two strong arms grabbed me from behind. I screamed in fright, but the sound of the waves drowned out my voice.

'Shut up, miss! No-one can hear you,' a husky voice said right into my ear. I could smell tobacco and alcohol. I tried to turn my head to see his face, but I was in a clinch and I could only kick back. I tried to scream again but the voice was not coming out, as if in a bad dream. He pressed my throat with his forearm and held my wrists together behind my back with his other hand. He dragged me backwards towards the paved area under the seawall colonnade, hidden from view from the street above. I struggled to breathe.

Surely someone would see us from the West Pier? The desperate thought flickered through my head, but under the quickly darkening skies the chance was close to nil. He pushed me onto the ground; I fell hard on the uneven clumps of soil and grass in a small unpaved quadrangle. My hair got caught in a bush. He grabbed me and yanked my hair loose and in that instant I saw his face – it was Mr Grenfell, the man who had brought his mother to the workhouse earlier that week. His dirty fingers and nails were tearing into my flesh.

I jolted sideways and tried to get up before his body pinned me to the ground. He grabbed my upper arm and turned me around like a rag doll. I was now lying on my stomach, my face in the dirt that was getting into my mouth as I was trying to breathe. My upper body was under his bulk and he lifted my cloak and my dress. I could not move at all. He then viciously twisted my neck and turned my head to one side. He wrapped something hard and cold around my neck. A belt! He tightened it with a swift motion; I tried to breathe, in vain, through excruciating pain.

My last thought before the darkness fell was of Emma and me at almost the same place a few years ago, happy and playful, and of human depravity lurking in dark corners.

# Post Fabulam IV
## Melbourne, 2021

WHAT IS IT ABOUT THE English fascination with murder? Has anyone counted how many 'whodunnit' BBC TV series have been made since the venerated broadcaster launched its television service in 1936?

As to actually murdering women, a man of planetary fame, Jack the Ripper, swept through the streets of the East End only three years after Frances's death, butchering and dismembering his victims in the most appalling ways. It was suspected he was someone with the knowledge of anatomy, either a butcher or a surgeon. He was never caught. Would this be the case if his victims were not prostitutes but respectable women? Or even respectable men?

In his essay *Decline of the English Murder*, George Orwell places the great period of the English murder between 1850 and 1925. He lists ten murderers 'whose reputation has stood the test of time', among them two doctors and one woman, and of course, Jack the Ripper. Orwell argues that 'eight of the ten criminals belonged to the middle class', and that the murders were a 'product of a stable society' with its 'all-prevailing hypocrisy'.

Like, it was less harmful for one's reputation to kill one's wife, or husband – provided one got away with it – than to divorce...?

Frances: the worst death of multimortal Francesca. Senseless, unexpected, terrifying, disgusting, bereft of any ideological or circumstantial pretext. And just as she started on the path she wanted so much and worked so hard for! Her mother's heart must have been broken to a million pieces. And Emma's. Frances's death surely stopped the gossip about Robert's overly ambitious fiancée and him not being manly enough to pull her back in line. Now people could feel sorry for him instead. Oh, and the Kaganovich sisters! They were devastated, no doubt. Those lovely, generous, knowledgeable, fun ladies, Frances's spiritual family. Their house was so full of warmth and liveliness. I hope they recovered.

The death of a young person leaves so many people distraught. Those who knew her would have said, 'Poor Frances, she died so young!' But why do people feel sorry for the dead? Apart from the sordid and frightening attack leading to her demise, those few horrific minutes, she was not the one to feel sorry for. There were years, decades of pain left in her wake, in the hearts of people who loved her. And how lucky she was to have had such people, and how unlucky they were to lose her!

I wonder what happened to her attacker. Was he found out, tried, jailed? The wretched man, drunk and numb, devoid of compassion and decency. Who knows what made him thus – a violent father, perhaps, or poverty, squalor, deprivation, anger at those luckier than him … Or a hatred of women who, I imagine, kept away from him if they could.

There has been a spate of murders in Melbourne over the past year, murders under the veil of darkness, committed by strangers, the old-fashioned Victorian way. Victims: very young women, some still teenagers. I have often thought about their mothers, families, left behind in a state of shock to wade through their anguish and sorrow. A bitter, hard sorrow that clasps the heart like barbed wire, encircles it like a crown of thorns in those sentimental representations of the Sacre Coeur, the bleeding heart of Jesus.

Yes, that's truly carrying one's cross: losing one's child so senselessly, through inexplicable violence.

# V: The Volley

## *Francesca (1909–1937), Leningrad*

O H NO! MY LITTLE GOLDEN wristwatch was telling me I was late for Saturday lunch with Uncle and Aunt Nevsky. The tram was so delayed it would have been faster to walk. Later I heard it was because a man slipped on a patch of spilled oil and fell under a tram, his head severed from his body. What horror! It could have been me! But I hadn't wanted a long walk in my brand-new black-and-white lacquer salon shoes, another present from Uncle Vasily. It was a glorious day in early May, and I could finally show them off.

The Grand Hotel Astoria on Bolshaya Morskaya Street was Uncle Vasily's favourite hangout. The occasion was the publication of his new book, a pre-eminent work on the development of Slavic languages, already under contract to be translated into German, English, French and Czech. Given that Uncle Vasily was celebrating his good fortune, he was the one to foot the bill, usually not trivial at the Astoria. True to its name, the place kept its olden-day grandeur. White tablecloths were in harmonious contrast with dark oak chairs upholstered in red velvet, comfortable for long lunches and even longer suppers. Plush old-gold armchairs and glass-topped coffee tables lined the perimeter of the grand dining hall. Large, low windows gave an excellent view of St Isaac's Square. At night, passers-by on the square could also glance at the Grand Hotel clientele lit up by the crystal chandeliers. Sometimes these glances were disapproving, Uncle Vasily reckoned, because the 'ruling proletariat' sensed that it was still shut out from places like the Astoria.

My family arrived half an hour late. Papa was always busy, and socialising was a rare luxury for him. I was glad I had a few exclusive moments with my favourite uncle and Aunt Sonya, who of course noticed the new shoes. Once my family arrived, a low-level animosity between my father and Uncle Vasily dominated the conversation. My uncle, a professor of linguistics at Leningrad University, and my father, a navy division commander, always exchanged humorous taunts, often on the brink of descending into actual insults. What kept them civilised was, above all else, the presence of my mother. Aunt Sonya was more tolerant, or perhaps just more indifferent, to whatever was happening between the two men.

My younger brother Dmitri (Mitya to us), just nineteen, was still learning how to be a Russian male from a 'good family'. On his second vodka before we even ordered food, Mitya was certainly making good progress. Our father was restrained in most things, including drinking, but Uncle Vasily's vodka habits made him a great role model of Russian manhood. My brother was starting at the military academy in autumn, but he was hardly a chip off the old block. I couldn't imagine him as an army officer. Look at him: he had a problem deciding what to have for lunch! How would he make momentous decisions involving the life and death of other people? 'Discipline, my son,' our father often repeated. 'If not me, look to your sister.' Mitya hated me a little for being presented as an example to follow. Envy and antagonism were rightful elements of brotherly love anyway, weren't they?

My train of thought was interrupted by a young waiter in a crisp white shirt, black bowtie and black waistcoat approaching our table. He carried two large round *Rostfrei* trays, filled with bottles, with remarkable ease. I estimated they weighed over five kilos each. The trays moved on his forearm in sync with his stride, his hips swaying among the tables in a semi-comical performance. I pointed this out to Mitya; he glanced at the waiter with unconcealed boredom.

'You must be very strong, carrying these trays like that,' I said when he reached our table.

In return, a row of white teeth gleamed at me, his full lips pointing up mischievously at the corners. 'Oh, the trays are much lighter than a ballerina!'

Uncle Vasily, already warmed up by an aperitif, laughed loudly. 'Well put, young man! What's your name, comrade? I don't think I've seen you around here.'

'Boris Antonovich, comrade,' the waiter responded promptly with a discreet bow. 'I am new here. At your service!'

'You do in fact look like a ballet dancer, Boris Antonovich.' I took the opportunity to continue the conversation.

'In fact, I was, until a few months ago.' He turned to leave, but grinned at me, teeth flashing again. 'I'll be with you again very shortly.' He disappeared across the hall. A young waitress appeared, carefully and laboriously pushing a trolley overloaded with food. What a contrast to Boris Antonovich's fancy-dance waitering routine!

I wanted to learn more about the ballet dancer turned waiter, Boris Antonovich. When he next approached to take our food order, he stopped right next to me, looking down. I glanced at his strong forearm covered with fawn-coloured hairs, his outstretched hand holding the tray of wine glasses. Warmth spread through my body; perhaps just an effect the aperitif had on me.

I looked up, smiling. Unlike in tsarist times, in our new society it was fine to chat to waiters. Servants were now 'household aides' and addressed as 'comrades' by their masters, using the same honorific in return. Not that many people had servants; only members of the Central Committee and a few hundred other high-ranking officials. It was fine to take interest in a man on the pavement who polished shoes for passers-by, sitting on a low stool, rugged up on a frosty morning. We were all equal now: the proud Soviet people doing our different jobs, everyone contributing to building the most progressive society on Earth: my mother teaching Russian in a state high school, my uncle lecturing in linguistics at the university, me pursuing a degree in civil engineering, and these young people, about my age or slightly older, carrying trays and pushing trolleys in a restaurant. All jobs had the same dignity. The salaries were not the same, of course, and residences allocated by state housing commissions were vastly different, depending on the family's job status, but also connections in the right places, and sometimes sheer luck. The fact often emphasised in political speeches was that we were all housed and employed. And indeed: who would not admire that? Western countries had just slid into a deep economic crisis.

'So you were a ballet dancer? Why did you stop? You seem too young for retirement?' I stopped talking and placed my hand over my mouth in mock horror. 'My apologies for being so nosy, comrade – far too many questions!'

'Not at all, miss! I was at the Bolshoi Ballet Academy in Moscow for some years and performed with the Bolshoi Theatre quite recently, but then my Achilles tendons started hurting and I had to retire. I'm twenty-five – not that far from the usual dancer

retirement age.' He glanced around. 'It was a good opportunity to move to your lovely city . . . Excuse me, young lady, I am
needed over there.'

I noted he addressed me 'the old way', not as 'comrade'. 'My
name is Francesca . . . *enchantée!*' I managed to say while he
was still within earshot. He turned around and smiled. I was
gripped by a strange delight.

## 2

Cheered up by vodka, good food and the festive occasion with
himself at the centre, Uncle Vasily was even more talkative
than usual. As a renowned Russian linguist, he often travelled
to Western Europe and was well connected there. He spoke all
the main European languages, most Slavic languages and also,
for a good measure, the impenetrable Finnish. He was lavished
with hospitality and attention when he visited Paris, London,
Berlin or Prague, and always came back with presents and a
handful of anecdotes.

A week earlier, Uncle Vasily had given an informal talk at
The Club of the Society of Writers. He informed the assembled
literati (I could hear the irony in his voice, but I was not sure
why – he was quite proud to be a member) that a little book by
Yevgeny Zamyatin titled *We*, published in 1921 and promptly
banned in Russia, then published in English in 1924, had
attracted a great deal of attention in the West. It was set in the far
future, but the Party censors immediately smelled a rat. Uncle
Vasily argued that they may in fact have liked the book. It was
not only an amusing but also a short novel, and this was why,
ironically, the 'official reviewers', a euphemism for the Party
censors, had actually read it and made their decision to ban

it fully informed, unlike with many other works of literature.

He turned to me: 'I did not say exactly this at the Club, of course – this is for family only.'

Zamyatin was blacklisted, shunned and unable to do much at all, Uncle Vasily continued; he could not publish anything and even *samizdats* became too risky for him. Still, he was lucky; what saved him from exile to Siberia was his pre-revolutionary Bolshevik credentials and perhaps even more importantly, his enduring friendship with some people who were still in power or at least 'in favour'. Uncle Vasily knew Yevgeny Ivanovich personally and liked the man. He had read his short stories and found *We* hilarious: a playful, absurdist satire, as the genre allowed unrestrained flights of fancy. He forged new words and coinages but it was also a precisely constructed work, the work of an engineer as Zamyatin originally had been, Uncle Vasily observed. I agreed; as a budding engineer, I felt qualified to second his judgment. Unusually, my father was listening attentively to Uncle Vasily's little exposé.

'Interesting ... ,' he interjected. 'I know Yevgeny Ivanovich too. We studied naval engineering at Sankt Petersburg Polytechnic at the same time ... umm ... more than twenty-five years ago.'

My mother had been fidgeting on her chair for some time, and at that point she could not bear any more of this. Saying 'Sankt Petersburg' instead of 'Leningrad' was suspect in itself, even without praising a banned book.

'Enough of Zamyatin, perhaps? Can you please change the topic? We're in a very public place,' she urged the two men in a low voice. Like women everywhere, Russian women were trying to save their men from themselves.

Uncle Vasily lowered his voice but could not be stopped.

'He comes to the Astoria sometimes, has a drink ... once I saw him over there, actually.' He nodded towards a table in the far corner of the hall, now vacant. 'He's banned from the Club – not officially, but he knows. People greet him here, even if it's just with a very discreet nod.'

He gave my mother a meaningful stare. 'Or more openly, if they are brave enough. Some stop and chat, risking being called out in *Pravda* the next day, if they are well-known academics or artists, or writers. These days *Pravda* can review you not just out of literary acclaim but also out of your job, or existence itself. You know the mantra: 'Soviet people cannot be duped by abstract paintings and atonal music . . . and formalist poetry . . .'

Uncle's uproarious laughter followed. Boris Antonovich, far away from us at that instant, turned towards our table and grinned. Perhaps he thought it was nice that satisfied guests were having a good time? It made the mindless job of carrying trays around more pleasant, perhaps? I could not help laughing too. Uncle Vasily's defiance, even if it was sheer vodka-fuelled carelessness, was exhilarating, like any danger.

Not my mother's idea of fun, though! Not in public! She had a tight-lipped, tense expression.

'All right, all right, Marya Petrovna, I'll stop! I do not want to worry you, my dearest sister! That expression does not suit your lovely face, Mashenka! I was just going to mention that my young assistant was at the funeral of the greatest poet of the revolution two weeks ago; a huge crowd of people, most of whom did not even realise Mayakovsky had recently fallen out of favour and was effectively executed by *Pravda* before he was actually found with a bullet—'

Mama urgently signalled him to stop before he could finish the sentence.

'Look, Mashenka, there aren't many people around apart from these nice young people serving us, and what do they care . . . ?'

'For such a smart man, you are quite naïve, Vasily Petrovich.' She sighed.

Uncle Vasily might have felt safe because his linguistic treatises were rather obscure and the Party censors would be properly bored on the second page. Professor Vasily Nevsky's books were reviewed in scholarly journals, not in *Pravda*. He rubbed shoulders with European intellectuals twice a year. He could not disappear from the university, or from the face of the Earth, without anyone noticing it.

Uncle Vasily was an exotic creature in Western Europe: Professor Nevsky, a Russian intellectual living under Stalin! His lectures filled large auditoriums in spite of highly technical and, to non-linguists, obscure topics. Everyone wanted to talk to him, as if they expected to smell Stalin on his breath. Western European intellectuals were keenly interested in socialist Russia: its art, literature, politics, economics, society. Was it a working people's paradise or a totalitarian hell? Uncle Vasily told us that these intelligent and erudite people were disinclined to see shades of grey in their picture of Russian life under the Bolsheviks. It had to be either black or white, and the vote seemed split fifty-fifty. Western academics, the bespectacled bookworms, wanted the Russian professor to usher excitement and controversy. But when sober and behind the lectern, Professor Nevsky knew better than to satisfy their hunger for drama. Russian embassy officers were always in the audience, taking notes.

What added to the European interest in Russia was that Europe itself was reeling from the stock-market crash of the year before, while the land of the Soviets was powering ahead. There were no beggars in the street, no people sleeping rough, as in London where my uncle travelled a few months earlier. He was shocked; even though he tended not to praise the virtues of the Soviet regime and often ridiculed Comrade Stalin's 'visionary insights', he came back from London feeling a little more convinced that the Soviet social experiment might have some merit. In Great Britain, the sudden economic collapse rendered millions of people unemployed and in many cases going hungry; it was the same in Germany, France, Czechoslovakia.

'And also, the Germans and the French treat their Jews even worse than we treat ours, I hear,' my father blurted out. My brother chuckled. The black humour surprised me; perhaps my father had a little more vodka than usual?

My mother hissed at him. 'Andrey – don't you have anything better to say? You know walls have ears these days!' she added in a whisper.

'Don't get in a flap, Masha Petrovna! I am not spied on! Perhaps your brother, who has the potential to corrupt the youth and spread the word about us in the West, but not me. I'm just a soldier . . .'

'Of course you're important enough to be spied on, Andrey! A navy division commander . . . !'

My father was being ironic, but my mother was not in a mood for nuances. In the ongoing low-level war between the two men, a scholar and a soldier, I was secretly on my uncle's side. Not everyone was enamoured of Professor Nevsky's smooth patrician talk, even among those who could follow his argument. I did not blame Mitya too much for rolling his eyes at him from time to time. Free-flowing vodka could make him overly talkative and oblivious to his audience's lack of interest. This only happened in private though; at university, he had a reputation as a captivating teacher.

I liked Uncle Vasily and forgave his voluptuary habits because he was a genuine scholar, absorbed in his science, or art, whatever linguistics was, and sincerely excited about words, how they developed and changed over time and how various groups of people used them. He also had a respectable knowledge of art and architecture and excellent taste in all everyday things: furniture, clothes, jewellery, drinks, food, just as one would expect from a *bon vivant*. Had I not been gently pushed into engineering, perhaps I would have followed in Uncle Vasily's footsteps. My school essays were often praised by teachers. As an eleven-year-old I wrote my first poem devoted to the revolution. But my literary knack was not encouraged at school; as a girl who understood mathematics and found physics interesting, I was earmarked to join a legion of young women tasked with proving that we were all the same, men and women, and that we should build our country and carry forth the revolution side by side, shoulder to shoulder.

A cool breeze was blowing off the river Neva when we finally left the Astoria. Uncle Vasily's cheeks had a vodka blush. We had cheered my uncle's long and illustrious academic career, miraculously unhindered by the revolution, and cheering was invalid without vodka. I thought he was headed for an afternoon nap. My father had an important late afternoon meeting at the navy headquarters.

'*Privyet*, Bezymensky!' Uncle Vasily waved to a bearded, somewhat dishevelled man who was on his way into the Astoria. 'Alexander Ilych Bezymensky,' he explained. 'A poet . . . doing well . . .' I smiled. What a name, I thought! Unforgettable: I'll check his poems. Uncle Vasily was in a terrific mood. Mitya rolled his eyes again.

# 3

I had to learn more about Boris Antonovich, one way or another. I found most young men, my suitors at the university, dull. Dull,

dull, dull! Perhaps those studying fine arts or literature were more interesting? As to the budding engineers, their handsome young faces and athletic bodies usually faded in my mind after five minutes of conversation. I started seeing one two years ago because everyone asked me about a boyfriend, and I began to feel I had fallen behind my peers. Perhaps I could say the pressure was subtle, but among Russians pressure is rarely subtle. Vanya and I were a couple for nearly two years, which was, in retrospect, far too long.

My mother was fond of Vanya, who was a dandy and a flatterer. Always immaculately groomed, he stood out among the engineering students. He had never turned up to our house without a bunch of flowers for Mama, and a bottle of French wine. Where did he get the wine? There were queues for basic things, and besides, he was not earning any money. He said he had his 'secret source', but we all knew this meant his father, who was a member of the *nomenklatura*, highly positioned in the OGPU, the State Security. Comrade Stavrogin was paying a generous alimony after leaving his wife and son for a younger woman ten years earlier, when Vanya was only twelve. Vanya's mother, who showed no interest in remarrying, was at his beck and call. 'What would you like for lunch, Vanyechka?' Always that maddening diminutive! Never 'Ivan', or even 'Vanya'. Vanya was expected to become my husband down the track. After a few months together, I knew we were not meant for each other, but it took a while for me to break it off; I had taken my parents' judgment too seriously. I knew Vanya was overdue for army service; his father had been delaying it 'until he completed his studies', but they were dragging on and Comrade Stavrogin had to pull the pin on his spoilt son. He still ensured Vanya was serving in the capital, rather than in some godforsaken place at the Mongolian border. I was finally free.

From my short observation thus far, Boris Antonovich seemed to be an anti-Vanya; definitely worth further investigation. A week later, on Saturday morning, I visited the Grand Hotel Astoria again, alone this time.

Factories worked on Saturdays, but the intelligentsia had more freedom with their work and leisure. Not everyone's pockets were deep enough to dine at the Astoria, but its cafeteria was always crowded on Saturday mornings, peaking at about eleven. This meant my lonely presence there would not be too conspicuous, but it also meant that Boris Antonovich, if he was at work at all, would be very busy. I could have eloped from university during the week and slipped in for a drink, but I wanted to give him time to forget me, if I was forgettable. Or to remember me, if I was memorable.

Shortly after I sat down at the table, my heart jumped a little when I spotted Boris Antonovich swaying his slim hips through the hall buzzing with voices. Around me, people with small round glasses and neat hairstyles in animated discussion, mainly men; some with their drab-coloured coats on their laps or at the back of chairs. My outfit stood out. Uncle Vasily had no daughters and I was his favourite niece, therefore the main present-receiving beneficiary of his travels to Western Europe. A few months ago, he had bought a lovely light red – watermelon colour, he pointed out – cashmere twin set for me in Paris. He was generous; this could not have been cheap and even though his university salary was three or four times that of a factory worker, it could not get him far in Paris. Knowing this, or perhaps just because he was worth it as a scholar, his hosts usually covered his travel costs.

My father was jealous of Uncle Vasily, who had a habit of telling me I was beautiful and giving me presents that I loved; perhaps that was the source of his animosity towards my uncle?

Or perhaps I gave myself too much importance in my father's life? He was not one to express love or even approval, apart from praising my consistently high university marks. I felt I had to earn my father's love; Uncle Vasily was more affectionate. He told me about the elegant Chanel stores in Paris where, with some luck, one could bump into the supremely chic Miss Coco herself. Unfortunately, her prices were beyond his means.

I was not a little self-conscious wearing my bright cashmere twin set and crystal earrings for the first time. My clothes screamed out among the greys, blacks and browns in the room, but I wanted to make sure Boris Antonovich noticed me. His well-trained waiter's eye probably did not need this extra help, but just in case. He danced past the little round table where I sat as soon as he had delivered an order on the far side of the hall.

'Hello! Nice to see you again!'

'Nice to see you again too, Boris Antonovich.'

'Oh, you remember my name!'

'Of course I do! Do you remember mine?' I used my most mischievous smile. It was a risky question.

'Francesca ...'

My heart jumped again. I liked how it sounded coming from his lips.

'I have to go. I cannot serve you today, your table is outside my zone. You are probably waiting for someone ...?'

'No, I came to see you.'

'Oh, I see!' He gave a broad smile. He stepped closer and leaned slightly towards me. 'I finish early today, at noon. We could have a cup of tea together afterwards?' He raised his eyebrows. His dark blue eyes sparkled at me. 'I'll be at the back door, the staff entrance, at twelve fifteen. Voznesensky Avenue, the northern side of the building.'

I nodded almost involuntarily.

'You look like a lone poppy flower in a harvested field. Beautiful.'

I was relieved that he approved of my standout attire. He danced off even faster than usual, with an empty tray on his muscular forearm.

I ordered tea. It was not polite to take a table without spending a few roubles. I drank it quickly, shuffling through the pages of the *Pravda* Saturday edition that someone had just returned to the newspaper stand, but I had no idea what I was reading. I was thinking about my date in forty-five minutes. I had hoped for a date, but the speed of events caught me unprepared.

I gave up trying to read the paper. I paid for my tea and stepped through the door into the bright midday light. The river Moyka was a stone's throw away, but I chose the more distant Neva as I had half an hour to kill. I crossed St Isaac's Square and walked through Aleksandrovskyi Park to the riverbank. Resting my elbows on the high wall-fence separating the pavement from the embankment, I stared at the slow-flowing greyish water. This was all I was capable of now. The water had a calming effect. I was checking Uncle Vasily's little golden watch every five minutes. Exactly at noon, I turned around and took a long route to the Voznesensky Avenue entrance.

## 4

Boris came out of the door at 12.18 p.m., three minutes late, dressed in dull colours like most citizens of Leningrad. Black trousers and a dun-coloured jacket. Ironically perhaps, he lost some glamour without his waiter's uniform: a white shirt, black bowtie and a silky waistcoat enhances every man's allure. He seemed a little shy, almost awkward, a significant contrast to his confident performance in the Astoria's grand hall.

'Hello, Francesca! You're tall!

We were the same height and I was wearing nearly flat shoes.

'I am indeed. One Montenegrin grandmother.'

He smiled at me but said nothing, waiting for the story.

'Montenegrins are a small mountain tribe in the Balkans, the tallest people in Europe, apparently – if my grandma is to be believed.'

'Your grandma wouldn't lie to you, would she?' He grinned, his teeth gleaming. I noticed strong, pointy cuspids giving him slightly wolfish look.

'No Montenegrins in my family. Ukrainians on my mother's side, nothing exotic,' he said with mock apology.

'Do we know where we're going?' I looked up as the sun shone through scattered cottonwool clouds.

'No idea. Not to the heavens just yet! It seems warm enough – lets walk to the Winter Palace Gardens and make a plan there.'

I appreciated the initiative. I was acutely distracted by his presence and unable to think of anything practical. We walked up Admiralteysky Prospekt towards the Winter Palace. Boris Antonovich's stride was just like in the hall of the Café Astoria. I was nearly breathless keeping up with him. I was pleased when we found a park bench in semi-shade, next to a white marble statue of Cupid with an arrow and bow. I noticed the symbolic coincidence, but I bit my tongue and didn't say any-thing. I could detect a young man's scent, like a whiff coming out of Mitya's bedroom.

'Oh, nice.' He sighed like an old man when we sat down. 'It's good to get off one's feet. Waiting on tables is harder on the legs than ballet dancing.'

'Really?'

'Dancing is an intense exercise; it pumps blood through your body and at the end you feel pleasantly tired. Waitering gives you varicose veins.' He laughed and pulled a packet of Herzegovina out of his pocket. 'Comrade Stalin also smokes Herzegovina. In fact, he smokes Herzegovina Flor, a more exclusive variety.'

'You know, Herzegovina is a province adjacent to Montenegro.' My nerves were talking.

He smiled and offered me a cigarette. I accepted, reluctantly.

'Why did you stop dancing?'

Boris Antonovich told me he had started dancing as a ten-year-old at the ballet school of the Voronezh State Theatre. A year later, the revolution swept through the land, but the school, and the theatre, somehow kept going. His favourite teacher, a woman of thirty, disappeared; the rumour was that she and her husband had fled Russia. Many people fled, as he only understood later on.

Boris continued with his ballet practice and at the age of sixteen he started regular performances in Voronezh. He took his *matura*, the final high school exam, a year late, in 1926. Only days later, on the day of his twentieth birthday, one of his ballet teachers suggested he move to the Bolshoi. He thought Boris had promise and should try his luck in the capital. The teacher recommended him to the artistic director at the Bolshoi, who was his friend.

'So, five years ago, I was on top of the world! I was in the famous theatre and Moscow was large and exciting . . .'

'You danced there until a few months ago, right?'

Boris lowered himself on the bench and stretched his legs. 'Yes, until the end of last year. It's nearly six months in fact. I was cast for the *Red Poppy* production and danced in it for a couple of years. I was 'standing out from the rest of the troupe', according to the artistic director. He told me I was going to be given a leading part in last year's production of *The Sleeping Beauty*.'

'Wow! You must have been very pleased.'

He glanced at me. 'Yes, I was thrilled. But . . . at the last moment, I was relegated to a minor role. I was disappointed, as you can imagine . . . I realised I needed connections that I didn't have.' His honesty surprised me. Why did he choose to trust me?

'Yes, *svyazi* – who you know is important . . . often more important than hard work and talent. My father often says that.'

'And what about you, mysterious red poppy? What are you up to? I saw your company at that lunch in the Astoria, I presume some of them were your parents?'

'Yes, my parents, and uncle and aunty, and my spoiled young brother Mitya.'

'And you're disciplined and tough, unlike your brother?' He showed his cuspids again and I felt like kissing him. I didn't, of course.

'Well, sort of. I'm afraid I study engineering. I hope I won't be judged too harshly by you, an artist. To be perfectly honest, I'm bored by all the technical drawing and ultra-practical way of thinking; engineers must have imagination, but it travels on railway tracks rather than flying freely towards the sun. Engineering is important, according to my father, and so is fighting wars. He's an army officer, but a naval engineer by education.'

'And your uncle? He seems a fun man!'

'Oh yes, I like Uncle Vasily! He's a linguist. Perhaps we Soviet citizens could build our bright future without knowing all the details of the Proto-Slavic language branching into a tree of modern Slavic languages and how this tree grew from the same soil as Baltic and Germanic languages. Still, I find it fascinating. I persist with my engineering degree because I'd hate to disappoint my parents. But at least I was able to choose civil engineering. Building roads and bridges may even be fun, you know, getting out of the office, travelling ... !'

'Yes, it can always be worse. That thought provides some consolation, doesn't it?' He suddenly looked serious.

'What about your family? Where are they?'

'My father died when I was fifteen. He was forty. It wasn't long after the revolution. 1921.'

'How did he die?'

'He lost his life in a skirmish with Cossacks, somewhere not too far from Voronezh. He was a volunteer reservist in the local Red Army 'territorial defence' unit. I don't know much detail, my mother wouldn't talk about it. I'm not even sure how much she knows. She received a letter explaining that my father died 'in the pursuit of his military duties'. My mother had suggested he volunteer, as they were otherwise likely to be declared 'bourgeois' and have their shop confiscated. But after he died, my mother lost the shop anyway. She couldn't run it herself and she wasn't allowed to employ other people, so she had to give it up. She received a small compensation from the Voronezh municipal authorities ...'

'Oh, that's so much bad luck! She lost her husband and then her shop. Your poor mother! What kind of shop did she – your parents have? How is she now?'

'Do you really want to talk about my mother?'

'Yes!'

'Okay then!' He stepped on his cigarette butt and turned towards me on the bench. 'My mother is a qualified pattern-maker and a skilful seamstress. She also designed suits with my father, and after the revolution, they switched almost completely to making new Soviet military uniforms. The demand was high and after a short while they specialised in those finer ones for army officers.

'After she lost the shop, my mother was offered a job in a

local clothes factory, but she excused herself on the basis of her health problems, her unsteady lower back. It was likely she would have been given a supervisor's job and hence not confined to a chair and a sewing machine, but she preferred to continue working on her own, doing clothes repairs and individual orders. She also has a knitting machine, so she makes jumpers and jackets to order. She earns modestly, but she can cope. She's good with money. She was able to keep her small flat above the shop. So that's the story.'

'She didn't remarry?'

'No, no she didn't. She rents out one room to a young woman, to keep her company and supplement her budget.'

'So your family is from Voronezh?'

'No, my grandparents migrated to Voronezh, a small town back then, from Ukraine, when my mother was a child. After the revolution thousands of people from the villages flooded into Voronezh to take jobs in factories. In my primary school class, I was the only child whose parents grew up in the city of Voronezh. My mother says that another large wave of people is pouring into town these days. The authorities can hardly cope. Unauthorised building is rife and shantytowns have sprung up outside the city. Petty crime is common, as newcomers are desperate to survive. Black market, prostitution, child labour, you name it.'

He paused and took a deep breath. 'The situation in Ukrainian villages is dire. Starvation has propelled people into towns. You know, the Astoria is a great place to learn about what's really happening. I overhear many 'elite' conversations without even trying. Besides, people are chatty after a few drinks, and less careful about what they say to strangers. I wonder whether the Bolsheviks thought of using vodka and friendly curiosity as an interrogation technique.'

We cackled even though we both knew it was not a funny topic. Boris was expressing freely and fearlessly what most people only dared say in whispers, at home. The truth was, we were alone in a park, but he had only known me for a couple of hours. I could see there was a painful, dark lump of anger in Boris Antonovich's soul, even though his wry humour added a light touch.

'Yes, the periphery of Leningrad is also flooded by incoming villagers,' I said. 'It's ironic that people have to leave their land and farms in order to fill their stomachs, isn't it?'

He nodded, looking pensive. He pulled out another Herzegovina from the packet and lit up.

We left the park bench and, just like our conversation, meandered through the city. It didn't really matter where we went. Water had an instinctive attraction; we found ourselves following the Griboyedov Canal. I heeded the places and people around us from time to time, just as a matter of orientation, but otherwise we moved along in a bubble of two, absorbed by the moment, opening ourselves to one another. Once starvation and food were mentioned, I realised that instead of lunch I had only had a couple of cigarettes. My stomach demanded to be filled.

'Aren't you hungry, Boris Antonovich?'

He laughed aloud. 'I like your style, Francesca Andreyevna! Hmm, not sure . . . I should be. I had a snack standing up about eleven. I can eat or not eat, it doesn't matter. Whatever you like.'

I felt the same way; eating seemed a distraction from more important things.

'I had breakfast before nine, and a cup of tea at the Astoria. So my executive decision is: we should eat.'

'Yes, Comrade Francesca!' Boris clicked his heels together and saluted.

City restaurants were out of the question – this would be

too big an investment of time and money, and I did not know the state of Boris Antonovich's finances. From his story, I was guessing modest. More importantly, if we sat in a restaurant, too much outside reality would invade our private bubble and the magic would be lost. We could have bought a tasty cheese pastry or a sweet pumpkin pie from babushkas selling their produce and home-made snacks at the central open-air market nearby, but at four in the afternoon it was almost certainly too late.

'Oh, I know! Let's go to the university! There's a canteen open seven days – students from the provinces have to eat each day. I don't use it normally, but I'm a student after all. They'll have to feed me.' The survival imperative reinstated my practical sense. 'Vasilyevsky Island is too far to walk, especially on an empty stomach, but we can hop on a tram.'

Boris nodded.

I felt reality starting to invade our enchanted bubble, but it was still holding.

'Where do you live, Boris Antonovich? Is it far from Vasilyevsky Island? We'll have to go home at some stage, I guess. I told Mama I was meeting a university friend for a cup of tea. It's been six hours since I left home. She may be worried.'

Reality invaded further!

'I don't have a mama problem.' He laughed. 'No, I don't live too far. In the industrial part of the port actually.'

An unusual location. I gave him an inquisitive look.

'There's an old residential building where port workers used to live ... mainly those who came from the country after the revolution. Some are still there but the building has been gradually disused. It's meant for demolition, but for now it's still standing.'

'How did you end up there?'

'Well, my mama' – he laughed – 'got involved in my move

from Moscow. You know, mothers! I did not ask for help, but she asked around ... she learned one of her neighbours in Voronezh had a daughter in Leningrad who got a scholarship to study here two years ago, but ended up pregnant and, basically, alone with a baby ... well, a toddler now. She had to move out of the student accommodation and was allocated a small apartment in this building as a temporary solution. She was pleased to take me in. She's trying to study by correspondence, but it's hard, of course. She goes to university sometimes. It's not far from her place. I help her a little with the child, food and bills, but I don't pay any rent.'

'It sounds like marriage!' I said. 'Are you sure you're not married?'

'Yes, quite sure!' He laughed.

Immersed in our conversation, I noticed we had reached the University Embankment only just soon enough for us to jump off the tram. My stomach now rumbled and demanded food. The main canteen was at the back of the building, opposite a grand colonnaded entrance. It took us five minutes to walk around the massive edifice. The refectory was empty – it did not look promising. But there was steam rising from the bottom of the large hall and there was a pervasive smell of cabbage. A flushed, plump woman stopped cutting carrots and looked at us. She did not look friendly, especially not with that big knife in hand. The thought crossed my mind that if I was in her shoes, a young lady in a red cashmere twin set and crystal pendulous earnings would perhaps irritate me too.

'Excuse me, when does the supper start?' I produced my humblest, most polite smile.

No smile back. 'Six o'clock. Are you students?'

I nodded vigorously. 'Yes, we are.' I was hoping she would not ask for our student identity cards.

There was over half an hour to kill. We walked to the front of the building and sat down on the embankment at the point where stone stairs descended into the dark water of the Neva.

Boris Antonovich pulled out another cigarette.

'Now I have to tell you the truth, Francesca Andreyevna.'

My heart sank. He was married after all! What else could it be?

'I am not from Earth, originally. I fell on Earth as a pebble many years ago and took the shape of a man. I do not age the way humans do but I could be recalled to my home planet at any time.'

I could not suppress a giggle. I loved the change of tack his declaration introduced. We – our enchanted bubble – could now shed the weight of earthly problems and fly high, any-where. Boris gently blew a thin wisp of smoke towards me and smiled. It smelled exciting. If cigarette smoke could smell so nice from a man's mouth after hours of neither eating nor drinking, only smoking, then there was a real chance that he might be an extra-terrestrial being. An attractive one! I decided not to disclose this thought right there and then. I sat closer to him; our shoulders were nearly touching. It was time to flirt.

'Do the extra-terrestrial pebbles have magnetic properties?'

He blew some more smoke in the air. He was trying to sup-press a smile, but I could see he was pleased.

'I hope so!'

'What's your planet called?'

He smiled, looking deep into my eyes, buying time.

'*Par-vo-li-tus.*' He slowly enunciated all four syllables.

I laughed. 'Something to do with rocks . . . ? And "parvus" means "small", right? My high-school Latin has gone rusty quite quickly.'

'Yes, you're right. It means a "small rock". Maybe a "small

beach" ... ? Let's say a "small rock on the beach".' He laughed.

'Even in outer space, one cannot escape from Latin.' I rolled my eyes.

'Clever girls are a magnet to me!' He blew another thin streak of fragrant smoke in my direction. He looked a confident person striding through life again; his playful waiter persona re-emerged.

I knew then that I'd like to see a lot more of Boris Antonovich. And I knew he wanted that too.

## 5

Being married to Boris Antonovich was never going to be dull, or even calm. He was intense; he could easily tire out people who did not understand him. The never-ending sequence of whirlwind, often outrageous ideas spiced my days and nights with him. Luckily, he did not insist that we act upon them; as a married man he redirected his adventurousness towards small-scale daily surprises. On a life scale, he seemed happy with the status quo he entered with me by his side: 'You understand me. I am the happiest man!'

I was not a wifely type and my early marriage surprised everyone, including myself. I had not thought much beyond completing my degree and finding a job. This was 'normal'; every Soviet woman was meant to be employed. The revolution virtually abolished the idea of housewife. Marriage certainly had not been one of my immediate goals! Matching this, Boris was not someone you could easily imagine leading a life of coupled domesticity. That was part of the attraction; neither of us was the marrying type so it kind of made sense we ended up married to each other.

Boris was a man of many – too many – talents and electrifyingly interesting, but he was not a steady, dependable type a woman would, following conventional common sense, choose for a husband. I recognised he was a wild card despite being only twenty-one when we met and with only one relationship behind me. Even though reason, not impulse, was my natural guide, I was spellbound by Boris. It wasn't even sex, the usual judgment-obscuring agent. From my fathomless depths, an inner voice insisted that a man like Boris should not be missed – he was one of a kind.

A week after we moved to our new abode, Boris turned up from his evening shift with a bottle of French champagne and a jar of black Caspian Sea caviar. Given the elite clientele at the Astoria and his charming manner, he often received tips in foreign currency, and he visited a *Torgsin* every time he got his hands on some. And 'saving for a rainy day' was not his thing. Living for today was Boris's natural outlook. I was in bed, just about to doze off with a book in hand. It was not late, just about my winter bedtime.

'A new *Torgsin* close to the Astoria, and very well-supplied too! Just discovered it!'

He pulled a dark bottle with silver foil around the cork out of his bag high above his head, sporting a wide grin, just like a magician pulling a white rabbit from a hat.

'Taa daa!'

'Oh, you are crazy! But that's well known! As a matter of saying something not so obvious, do you expect me to drink champagne and eat caviar in my pyjamas ... thick flannel pyjamas ... ?'

'If that's not an appropriate evening entertainment attire for the young lady, she can take it off.' He bowed politely. 'I personally cannot think of a better evening attire than Eve's costume ... if only she did not eat that apple and start feeling shame!'

'Oh, shame is not my problem Boris Antonovich, you know that! Only, I think it must have been warmer in the Garden of

Eden than in our apartment in November!'

'I'll keep you warm!' He kissed me and squeezed me tight onto his chest. 'I cannot believe I scored such a girl! I won a lottery!'

He was still in his overcoat that retained the outside chill and damp.

'Go take that coat off and wash your hands, you flatterer! And put on your pyjamas, so we're equal.'

'Equality of the sexes, of course, Comrade Francesca! In our socialist homeland nothing less is good enough!'

'For me, it's always been thus! I was eight when the revolution swept through the land.' I winked.

Boris pulled a face. Then he spotted the book on the bed.

'In bed with *The Idiot*, huh, wife? Although a prince, Mishkin is not much competition . . . surely less than the three *Brothers Karamazov* would be! That morose atheist Ivan would be the best in bed, I reckon!'

'Shhh, you loony . . . you'll wake up the neighbours.' I was kicking the bed laughing. 'I guess we'll never know! No sex in classical novels. Or any Russian novel ever, in fact! All that high-minded stuff . . . is there a God or not . . . is it okay to be a nihilist or not . . . it's kind of sad, don't you think? As you came through the door, I was on the page where Nastasya Filipovna throws a hundred thousand rubbles into the fire . . . to prove that she is not for sale!'

Boris lowered his voice. His face turned serious. 'Francesca, the old couple next door is not having much sex . . . or fun of any kind. I'm sure they are interested in what we are saying . . . and doing.' He jumped onto the bed and winked. 'I saw Mrs Hohlakova chatting cordially with the concierge last night. They stopped talking and greeted me *very* politely as I passed by. I had a feeling they didn't want me to hear . . .'

'Probably gossiping about us! We're new; they've been collecting data. We shouldn't make their job too easy, though!'

# 6

Boris thought one should love and live without fear, without
calculation, without thinking about tomorrow, regardless of
what anyone else thought. I was not entirely convinced; we had
to be at least a rough fit in conventional society – my family, the
too-close-for-comfort neighbours, our workplaces. I never had
the courage to fully abandon the reality principle; in my world,
it had always trumped the pleasure principle. My father's
ascetic influence! But the play principle, the one that ruled
Boris's personality and therefore his life, was dear to me. In the
life of adults, the play principle contained, inevitably, a degree
of pushback to the reality principle, a degree of indifference
about the consequences of one's actions. This could hurt us. In
the Russia of the 1930s, it was important not to be conspicuous,
lest one attract the attention of the powers-that-be, suspicious
of any creativity – except perhaps that of engineers.

It was my unpleasant duty to clip the wings of Boris's inner
child, or the extra-terrestrial pebble. I did this without real
conviction; the supremacy of the play principle might be the
ultimate wisdom and Boris was the *homo ludens* incarnate.
Sensing my ambivalence, he appreciated my role. Sometimes
I thought that, in some ways, we were not that different from
most couples: having found someone to take care of 'reality',
the husband could playfully, and often irresponsibly, pursue
his vocation, or passions, or just seek his pleasures. Was this
what was going on? No, no, Boris was not like that, he was not
like others! His playfulness was not irresponsibility. He was

not dumping the mental clutter of everyday life on me, as my father did on my mother, choking her mind. She was more intelligent and creative than him, but her imagination could never soar, pinned to the ground by her wifely and motherly duties that she took extremely seriously.

Boris was never going to be a typical Russian husband. He was not domineering, and he did not take me for granted after we married. But he was jealous. Often, he'd make up a story about me having spent the day in the arms of some university hunk from my 'Materials' class, with whom I had sex in a lab, sitting on an edge of a sink and holding onto a tap, breaking a few glass tubes and bulbs in the throes of passion. I laughed at his stories, which often ended with the two of us kissing and caressing while the story continued. I thought it was just a game, but sometimes it felt real, as if he really thought I could run away with the most attractive young engineer-to-be or a university tutor, who, in Boris's estimation, all drooled over me.

What concerned me more was that in rare quiet moments, I could sense Boris possessed a solid, even though deeply buried, core of self-destruction. Underneath Boris Antonovich's sparkling personality there was a deep sediment of gloom, which rose to the surface only on rare occasions. His enchanting playfulness was his way of keeping the existential anguish at arm's length. Sometimes I could read this visceral tragic sense on his handsome face and it was instantly contagious: a deep, inarticulate melancholy would grab me like a tight metal hoop around my heart. But love for Boris also opened the bottom drawer of my mind, as he once put it, where I could rummage through its self-repositioning content: enthralling thoughts, moments of unprovoked mirth, one-liner poems which I could orate to Boris and in return be given a look of pure love in his deep blue eyes.

## 7

The abrupt end of Boris's ballet career at the Bolshoi was a huge waste of his talent and years of hard work. It was unjust too; it was what happened to genuinely gifted people who were outspoken but unprotected by influential family networks. For many months after we got married, I insisted he try joining the Soviet Ballet in Leningrad, a venerable house with a long tradition in spite of its new name. Its original name, the Imperial Ballet, could not survive after the real regicide was carried out. Ballet itself, as an art form, nearly became a victim of the new times; it was seen as a bourgeois pastime. After a few years' hiatus, Comrade Stalin luckily realised this was something Russia – the Soviet Union – could use to show off its cultural prowess, indeed its superiority, internationally.

After my repeated entreaties, Boris eventually relented. We put together a letter and sent it to the impresario of the Soviet Ballet. Uncle Vasily had a third-degree connection with the man so the strings he could pull were quite weak. In an ideal world, Boris would not need this. In 1931, only in his mid-twenties, miraculously fit just from waitering and sex for exercise, his dance fitness could be quickly regained. It took many years of discipline and sacrifice to create a ballet dancer, a short career with uncertain prospects post-dancing, apart from the certainty of joint and tendon aches. They should have rejoiced upon seeing his offer and take him back with gratitude. Instead, they sent a curt 'thank you for your interest, we are not recruiting new dancers at this time' letter in response. It made me sad and frustrated. I felt as if I had poked into Boris's wound and made the scab bleed again.

Only after this did Boris tell me what really happened at the Bolshoi. After the promise of a leading role was withdrawn, he had decided to inquire with the Bolshoi's general manager.

'I knew this was not going to be a popular move but I did it anyway. I was not given a plausible explanation. I learned shortly afterwards, through the grapevine, that the dancer who got my role was well connected in the Central Committee. At the same time, a story was launched about my late father being . . . well, not a proper communist and patriot, but rather a "bourgeois element". I refused to take the minor role in the production and left. After parting in such a way, no-one would give me a good reference, and no other troupe would take me. Not a metropolitan one, anyway.'

'Let's go to France and you can join the Ballets Russes! Uncle Vasily knew Serge Diaghilev; perhaps he could find a connection with his successors in Monte Carlo. He could possibly get you an audition.'

'Stop dreaming, Francesca! Would you really leave everything you have here and move to France? In case I was actually able to travel for an audition and also satisfy the Russo-French ballet bosses! We would have to escape. Your family would suffer. They would find my mother too.'

He was right. For once, I was the dreamer and Boris was firmly on earth; the cold, hard, dry earth that could not sustain an exotic flower like him. I had to give up that battle before our first year of marriage was over.

Boris was not naïve. In political matters, he was more astute than me. His feelers were out and I trusted his judgment. His parents' fate, his experience at the Bolshoi, and his employment at the Astoria, all meant he was far ahead of me in understanding the Soviet Russian version of humankind. I was still a student, in a world of theory and science, equations and engineering calculations; still innocent of the rough world of work and unpredictable politics.

What worried me, though, was that wise as he was about

the society out there, he was always prepared to act against his better judgment. His flamboyant waitering reflected his passionate and fearless nature and it was essentially risky. Often, he did not know who he was talking to among the guests at the Astoria, but he would not curb his tongue when chatting with strangers. Recently, he had been invited to join OGPU as an informer for a 'handsome honorarium, all while doing your first job'. He flatly refused, then added that he did not plan to be a waiter for much longer. This seemed to me a good excuse. But was it good enough for OGPU?

For my parents, it was hard to accept Boris as a son-in-law. A good waiter, a great waiter – this did not cut it with them. 'What is a "great waiter"?' My mother scrunched her face in distaste. 'He should go back to university. You should encourage him. Uncle Vasily can help.' My mother mourned Vanya's disappearance for a while, but she eventually relented and accepted Boris. For my father, dropping out of university was plain lazy, perhaps also irresponsible. He expected Boris to complete his economics degree and achieve the status of an 'academic citizen', and he made this clear in a one-to-one conversation with Boris. I did not ask for details, but I knew such an encounter could not have the desired effect with Boris.

After Boris and I got married, it became clear to me that no-one really believed in the 'classless society' slogan, not even my father, a true, pre-1917 Bolshevik. Having been born and raised before the revolution, my parents' generation were Russians with a thin Soviet veneer. At the age of twenty-one, I realised my father was a hypocrite, just like everyone else. At that point, Uncle Vasily rose in my estimation; he turned out to be truer to his outward persona – always a bit of a snob, drawn to pleasures and not endorsing the revolution and the 'just society' beyond what was humanly believable.

To his further credit, Uncle Vasily liked Boris, who often invented funny coinages and silly rhymes that a linguist could appreciate. 'You may well have some hidden literary talent, my boy.' I thought the statement would be better without 'some hidden' and 'my boy', but I knew the intention was good. Boris returned Uncle Vasily's affection and never refused a drink with him, even though he was, thank God, not betrothed to vodka. Yet Uncle Vasily thought Boris a bit of a tearaway; he told my mother that our marriage was 'a better deal for Boris Antonovich than for our Francesca'. Of course, she hurried to pass on my favourite uncle's judgment.

'Isn't every marriage a better deal for the husband than for the wife?' I retorted. She averted her gaze and stayed silent. We both knew the world was full of marriages and husbands that made us feel sorry for the wives. I was not quite sure whether she thought her marriage was like that. She never complained and was deeply loyal to my father. I too was sure I had an excellent deal, in spite of my family's unanimous ruling to the contrary.

# 8

As a married couple, we were entitled to 'couples accommodation', and quite quickly, only three months after we submitted our application, were allocated a flat. Well, it was not really a flat. After the revolution, larger city apartments were divided into two, three or even more separate lodgings, in a hurry and often shoddily, by veneer partitions painted white, pretending to be solid walls. My university and Boris's grand hotel both issued certificates stating that we were proper Soviet citizens in full-time employment or study. This, on top of being a married couple, meant that the State Housing Commission was required to house us in separate 'private' accommodation. I suspected my father pulled some strings, but I did not ask.

Our new home was not private in any sense of the word. The flat, which we managed to furnish with donations from my parents and the Nevskys, did not fully shelter us from the prying eyes of other people – only the most deserving citizens were spared from having 'co-tenants'. Boris called them 'uber-neighbours': neighbours with whom one had to share a toilet and a bathroom, even a kitchen in some cases.

Older people referred to their co-tenants, often whole families who shared utility rooms with them, as 'co-lodgers'. True to the word, we had all been given a place to live that the all-powerful state could take away from us at any time. We could be ordered to move on any pretext, usually to do with the housing commission having 'secured a more appropriate accommodation to suit our new circumstances', even though the said circumstances might be exactly the same as before. Given the corrupt and haphazard nature of housing allocation and the chronic housing shortage in large cities, we were not unhappy with what we were assigned.

Our flat was in an old, seven-storey city building in the Admiralteysky District, not far north from the city centre. Boris could walk to work, and I could catch a short tram ride to university. I was in my last semester, busily writing my graduation thesis, and I did not have to commute regularly, but I liked working in the main library, insulated from the outside world, which was rarely fully possible at home, in a subdivided apartment. The mid-nineteenth-century design meant high ceilings and a poor floor plan, made worse once a large apartment was partitioned into several living quarters. We had two rooms, a bathroom to share with two other families, and a small kitchen installed in the bigger of two rooms, close to the balcony door. Yes, we had a balcony, hooray! For this luxury we paid by our bedroom, half of an earlier large room, not having a window.

The building had an old lift with an ornate scissor-grid iron door that creaked ominously when the lift was passing between the second and third floors. After we brought in our suitcases and crates, and a couple of muscular young men sent by my father managed to cram our couch and some smaller pieces of furniture into the lift, I never set foot in it again. It was only three floors up anyway! Boris laughed at me; he did not care. He was not scared of anything.

Next to the ground floor lift entrance was a concierge alcove, separated from the entry corridor by a polished wooden counter that lifted like a drawbridge. The concierge was a man pushing forty who could not have been any worse at his job. He rarely delivered messages, parcels addressed to tenants disappeared, keys left with him got lost. Our co-tenants advised us to avoid asking anything of him. From his wanton lack of care to do anything right and to the satisfaction of residents, Boris and I suspected he was an OGPU informer. Perhaps he was meticulous at his *real* job!

Each large city building had a full-time concierge service from 6 a.m. to midnight, with a telephone that all residents were entitled to use. From midnight to 6 a.m. the buildings were locked but unmonitored. The concierge officers across the city must have been police informers. No better opportunity for spying on people: seeing who comes and goes, who visits who, who telephones who and what they talk about. There were always people among the residents who unwittingly became the informers' assistants. Some of them also knowingly, no doubt.

The building originally housed bourgeois families and each apartment had three or four spacious rooms, a large entry hall with hooks and hat stands, tall mirrors and umbrella stands, a large kitchen adjacent to the dining room, with a slot through which the cook could pass food to the serving staff. Each apartment had at least one small servant room, often with no windows. A story we were told, but never had a chance to verify, was that the apartment above used to have two bathrooms with gilded taps and other fittings. It had belonged to an elderly Jewish widow who was apparently sent to live with her son's family not too far away, under the pretext that she was old and needed assistance. Her flat was confiscated by the local housing commission and her two maids 'freed' into factory work. Now these large flats housed the revolution's intelligentsia – teachers, engineers, musicians, architects. Boris and I were not of this class, not yet anyway, but I was guessing we were given an advance because I was Admiral Andrey Ivanovich Mendel's daughter and an engineer-to-be.

A thin partition separated our rooms from our co-tenants, a couple in their mid-forties with a son about to complete high school. The boy was given the other half of our partitioned bedroom, and his parents slept in the lounge.

'The assumption was,' Boris mused, his eyes turned upwards, 'that they, married for twenty years, lost all interest in each other and could not be caught in the act by their son.' The boy of seventeen had to walk through his parents' room if he wanted to get to the toilet, or anywhere really.

Boris was on one of his favourite tangents: 'He can also hear what is happening in our bedroom if we're not careful. But perhaps we should not be ... he might enjoy hearing things ...' He smiled his usual wide, mischievous smile and his blue eyes were sparkling at me, seeking agreement. The idea that someone might be listening turned him on. We often made love during school hours, when the teenager was away; Boris had varied work shifts and I was a student. If it happened at other times – and Boris's erotic imagination was never switched off, so it often did – we tended to switch on the wireless to drown our sighs, groans and whispers. At times, Comrade Stalin's speeches were a background of our passionate pairings, but Boris knew how to make me forget them, whispering much more exciting things into my ear.

One day, only weeks after we moved to 6th Krasnoarmeyskaya Street, Boris brought home a phonograph and a few vinyl records. Sombre Shostakovich music was not the greatest noise curtain for our lovemaking, but among the accidentally acquired music collection there was also a French comic operetta, dominated by a glass-shattering soprano.

'Not my choice,' Boris explained. 'They came with the machine.' He would not tell me any more about the origin of our new possessions.

'I'm impressed you could carry it all.'

'I'm a man,' Boris declaimed in his deepest voice. He lifted me up and turned me a full circle round the room before throwing me back onto the bed.

'And a crazy ballet dancer!' I squeaked, surprised, before bursting into laughter.

Subdivided flats were not conducive to receiving and entertaining guests. Our life there was rather secluded; we socialised outside. It was a long time before Uncle Vasily and Aunt Sonya paid us a brief visit. Seeing the phonograph, Uncle Vasily offered to bring some French records from his next trip to Paris, the latest *chansons*. 'And some American jazz, perhaps?' he inquired.

'Yes please, Uncle Vasily, jazz is really sexy; jamming, improvising, long playful stretches, crescendos . . .' Boris was playing an imaginary trumpet.

This was followed by Uncle's famous guffaw. 'That's very

true, young man! You've obviously had a chance to listen to it. The modern black American music is passionate, playful and creative! Just like the two of you, I'm sure.' Uncle Vasily winked at me mischievously.

'Of course we are, Uncle Vasily!' I responded flatly, noticing that Aunt Sonya did not approve of the men's innuendo. 'Why don't you sit down and have a snack and drink with us? It's nearly time to eat...'

Aunt Sonya quickly glanced at her husband. I thought this meant 'No'. Our kitchen table was not a salubrious setting for two people belonging to Leningrad's intellectual elite, dressed in their finery.

'Thank you my dear, but we have to go. We're actually off to see the premiere of Shostakovich's *Lady Macbeth of Mtsensk* at the Mikhailovsky Theatre. An opera on Russian peasant life. Pre-revolution. Must be bleak. Sonya has to write a review.'

'We just wanted to see your new place and make sure you settled in well, not missing anything...,' Aunt Sonya added.

'But we can surely have a quick drink, Boris Antonovich.' Uncle Vasily relented. 'One for the road, Sonya? It will make it easier to get through several hours of Shostakovich.'

The last remark must have convinced her. 'Oh, all right – a small one for me, please!'

As soon as we saw them off to the creaky lift, Boris turned around and whispered: 'Do you think they still enjoy some bedroom fun, our Sonya and Vasily?' His hand slipped down my back.

'I think they do, in fact. Uncle Vasily is too much of a *bon vivant* to let that area of pleasure die. But then, he has enough opportunity to do it elsewhere... but no... I think he still admires Sonya.'

Boris laughed at the musings he led me into and kissed me

passionately before we even entered the flat. His erotic imagination included how other people did it, or not. Every couple was under scrutiny. The Astoria's guests, people walking in front of us in the street, our co-tenants, politicians and their wives. Who's on top, who is the horny one, is she noisy . . . ? Does he sweat, does he grunt, what is their favourite position? Do they talk while doing it? Since he had revealed this odd habit, I caught myself with the same thoughts quite a few times. It was an innocent enough amusement, no harm done to anyone. We concluded that, in spite of declarations of 'free love' and 'shedding bourgeois morality' in the years following the revolution (Uncle Vasily told us about it at length), in 1934 Russians were more sexually repressed than ever, not least because of living in shared accommodation with thin walls. Boris was ready to admit that not everyone found a lack of privacy a turn-on.

A retired couple upstairs, both violinists at the State Philharmonia many years before the revolution and a few years afterwards, had a different privacy issue. I had met them on the stairs shortly after moving in – they did not like the creaky lift either.

'A *barabashka*, or even a few of them, were making noises overnight,' Mrs Petrova confided.

'Um . . . I didn't hear them. I must have slept quite soundly.' I thought playing along might be more fun than trying to oppose the popular superstition about house spirits.

'Oooh, you know, one pinched me in my sleep and woke me up. Then I heard them dropping things on the floor.' She quickly crossed herself every time she mentioned *barabashka*. 'I think, my dear, that the *barabashkas* are angry.' Mrs Petrova was pleased to have my ear. 'They are declared a superstition and people are now reluctant . . . afraid to leave offerings for them. I also think the old owners' *barabashkas* fight with the new ones that moved in with us. It's not good. Not for tenants, or the building.'

Mr Petrov nodded all along but said not a word.

I was kind of glad that the minds of Soviet citizens did not dry up into pure rationality in our 'scientific socialism'. Boris loved the *barabashkas* story.

# 9

Against the odds, coming from different backgrounds, Boris and I clicked at a level much deeper than physical attraction. Sex was good, even great, but that was not the reason why he was unmissable. It seemed odd that he was so eager to marry me. Was I so great? It would have been flattering to accept this version of events, but I could not fully convince myself of that. I thought that on top of any personal quality he might have admired in me, I also represented stability; I was level-headed and my family, including the extended one, replaced the family he had lost.

Sex was never far from his thoughts, but Boris was not a predator or a pest. He was a talker, a seducer, and spectacularly good at it; he had no problem persuading me to action. Both his sexual appetite and prowess were only second to his erotic – or should I say pornographic – imagination, which was bottomless, and in fact part of that prowess. Over time, the stories got wild-er because he did not like repetition. One time, a story about his mother and her friend started with these two middle-aged women knitting over a cup of tea and biscuits, and finished in a late afternoon threesome with *him*. The story was so utterly absurd that I burst out laughing in the middle of the act and he had no choice but to join me.

'You were leading yourself into an impasse with that story, right? Can you describe your own mother having an orgasm?' I laughed.

'Of course I can – why not?' he replied. I thought Boris was also exploring how far he could go with his porn fantasy. Was there a limit to what he could say? He was pleased to find out that there was not. I was not squeamish – words were not deeds. It was clear to me that sexual fantasies were not reality, not even real desires that one would enact if given an opportunity. I did not see anything wrong with the sex fiction on tap spicing our love life. His jealous stories must have been just that, the overflowing of his feverish imagination. I tolerated the stories of my infidelities because they were outrageous and amusing; their twists and turns overshot the realm of possible by a considerable margin. His jealousy was purely verbal; he did not sulk, he did not try to check up on me, and it did not seem that his jealous imagination caused him any pain. The knitting ladies story was not the only occasion when I burst out laughing in the middle of our passionate coupling, which, of course was the end of it. Laugher is a great bonding force but, as I also learned with Boris, the muscular contractions involved in laughter were physically incompatible with lovemaking.

In September 1936, we celebrated our fifth wedding anniversary with a bottle of Italian prosecco from the nearby *Torgsin*. I was happy to notice – but somehow shy to say it aloud – that we had not succumbed to sexual and emotional wear and tear. It was mostly to Boris's credit; his devotion to our marriage and his talent in beating stultifying routine were exceptional. Nearly six years on, our sex was a source of undiminished joy and pleasure. Each time we got entangled on the spacious bed in our windowless room – and sometimes elsewhere – our bodies and souls melted into one. Once we had sex at the nearby Novodevichy Cemetery. It was close to midnight, a white night of early July, when he got a sudden inspiration to 'go for a walk'. He chose a dress for me but forbade underwear. The concierge was just packing to go home when we rushed past him, hand in hand and giggling. We were married – no-one could object! It was barely properly dark; the sky was a Parisian blue. The stars looked closer from the darkness of the cemetery and a floral scent lingered in the humid air.

'I can smell roses . . . and death.'

'The beautiful death! Love and death, Francesca. *Lyublyu i smert*. All poets know they are an excellent match. Come, sit here.' He lifted me up on a small platform, part of an imposing monument to some no doubt important man. The marble was cold under my backside.

'This must be very rude and disrespectful, Comrade Boris Antonovich!'

'A man with such a huge . . . and phallic, incidentally . . . monument got enough respect during his life. Probably more than he deserved.'

Boris had an idea that we should 'explore', that is, make love *al fresco* in all city parks within walking distance. In Leningrad, the annual season for this was short and balmy nights rare. And when they happened, we would not be the only people there. Cemeteries were a safer bet; people avoided them after dark. After the first cemetery experience, Boris and I agreed that the spirit of *memento mori* had a sensual charge. I strongly suspected that Boris' creative spirit needed another outlet, beside the erotic domain. And indeed, not long after we put his ballet career to the final rest in a box of painful unfulfilled dreams, a new artistic path opened before my adventurous spouse.

## *10*

'I am invited to a secret writers' meeting. The day after tomorrow – Friday. A poetry reading. You should come too. To put ourselves in the right mood, I wrote a poem for you. It was a quiet afternoon at the Astoria.'

Boris pulled out a white roll of paper. The whole length of the cash register roll was written over. He let it unroll on the floor and took the pose of Cicero in front of the Roman Senate.

'It looks like a long poem – up to five metres, I'd say!'

'Shhh!' He started reading:

> *Francesca! My beloved kitten*
> *By you, I am utterly smitten*
> *Fire in my loins, honey in my heart*
> *Without you, I'd never make art*
> *With you, each day is a wonder*
> *Only when I'm dead we'll be asunder . . .*

A loud knock on the veneer partition stopped the performance.

'Excuse me! It is past ten p.m. Please be quiet.'

'Terribly sorry Mrs Hohlakova! We lost track of time,' I yelled back.

'I'll read it myself . . .' I whispered and took the scroll from Boris's hand, which was frozen up in the air. Still frozen in the position, he fell on the bed next to me.

'Do I have talent?' he whispered, grinning.

'Not a slightest doubt about that, Virgil of Petersburg, my beloved pebble!'

The Friday night poetry meeting was in a house at the southern outskirts of the city. It was a large patrician house that had seen better days, surrounded by a spacious garden. Tall pines blocked the view from the outside. When we entered, a thin man with a greying goatee introduced himself and offered us chairs. He then introduced us to a dozen people in the room. Two were Russian language students who, it turned out, were taught by Professor Nevsky. The thin man was an established poet in the *samizdat* circles, and we were offered his work tucked in a paper folder. We had two days to read it, and then Boris was to pass it on at the Astoria, to a specific guest, at an arranged time. The folder could be easily hidden in a copy of *Pravda*; several copies of *Pravda* were always on the newspaper stand in the Astoria Café.

From that evening on, Boris started writing poetry in earnest. He stayed up late most nights; it was as if someone opened the floodgates. I thought he had real promise. His poems were full of existential angst mixed with eroticism as a way of forgetting: 'consolation of the body'; 'seeking shards of sparkling bliss in the morass of being'. This was decadent individualistic poetry that could never get an imprimatur from Stalin's censors; it could also get the author in trouble. Only positive, victorious literature was published; building a new world, perhaps encountering some obstacles on the way, overcoming them, and a happy ending for the proud socialism-builders; or an unambiguous critique of the rotten bourgeois society. Nothing else could pass a *Glavlit* review; their boot prints were all over theatre repertoires and publishing houses' decisions. According to Uncle Vasily, Comrade Stalin, himself a poet in his youth, sometimes personally read work awaiting publishing permission.

Uncle and Aunt Nevsky were good people to show Boris's early works to – a linguist and a journalist who often wrote art reviews. They both took interest, and their feedback was encouraging. They knew the Russian literary scene as well, both the approved state writers and the most prominent among those whose work was only circulated underground, in *samizdats*. Uncle Vasily passed many Western books, acquired on his academic trips to Europe, on to us.

'The whole edifice of civilisation has been built on the foundations of sexual repression, Comrade Francesca Andreyevna. It is now official – the whole world knows it!' Boris proclaimed on the evening of our wedding anniversary.

'Yes, Comrade Boris Antonovich, this is quite a plausible proposition! No such repression in your head, so no civilisation there either haha! I wish Uncle Vasily would not pass on all the fashionable books he smuggles from Paris and London for you to cite from.'

However, where we lived, *Anno Domini* 1936, Boris's unrestrained nature meant walking a tightrope day after day. I understood that talking to guests at the Astoria about topics one would be well advised to avoid with strangers made the humdrum job bearable. He made friends or enjoyed cordial acquaintance with artists – poets, writers, musicians, painters – that frequented the Astoria's café. Some people knew of him before they even met him as a waiter. He was known as the 'dancing waiter', Uncle Vasily learned through his networks. This local fame was flattering, but also dangerous.

His manager, a well-meaning woman, was pleased that he attracted clientele, but warned him against being too conspicuous, for his own good. Police informants visited regularly. Boris argued he could always recognise them – they were dull people, usually sitting alone, trying to engage him in conversation about the hotel and its visitors. They eavesdropped on other people's conversations and often walked to the toilet or to the cloak counter to 'retrieve some forgotten item' from their overcoat, in order to have a better look at the patrons. I was not convinced it was so easy to recognise them. There surely must have been intelligent people among informants? Boris reckoned that the smart ones were recruited into the higher caste of spies on international missions.

We sometimes spent a weekend with Uncle Vasily and Aunt Sonya in my parents' dacha at Irinovka. My father rarely had enough free time to leave Leningrad and relax, but he was willing to lend his car, so the four of us travelled in style in the sturdy black Moskvitch.

We could talk more freely there, and Boris often told us about his poetry meetings and the underground publications he secretly distributed at the Astoria. One weekend, Aunt Sonya told us she had moved jobs. When we asked who she now wrote for, she replied, 'Luckily not for *Pravda* any longer.' We were all ears, hoping this was good news.

'*Pravda* makes and breaks people; more often breaks these days. Being part of this political machine is a source of great moral responsibility and often anguish ... and, I don't need to say, *Pravda* journalists are under high pressure and the watchful eye of censors. You can ruin people you write about, or yourself be blacklisted, or worse. *Glavlit's* censors can be unpredictable, depending what member of the nomenklatura is whispering in their ears. Even musicians and painters have to be careful, let alone writers and poets. But then, however careful, one can never tell ... Our neighbour Dmitri Dmitrievich's first publicly performed work was expected to be a great success, but instead it was savaged by the regime music association. Luckily for the young man, he has a powerful patron, so he pulled through.'

'And yet, no patron is a guarantee against the chief comrade's mood swings, even for Shostakovich, let alone the smaller fry,' Uncle Vasily added.

Shostakovich's dacha was four houses down the gravel road, on the edge of a small oak grove, a leftover of a larger old forest. In summer, Boris and I loved to run into the grove and along its shady tracks. We often dropped into a little wooden church on a hill, close to the edge of the forest, with a small cemetery on one side. It looked ancient and largely abandoned. There were no regular services but sometimes a pious local woman lit a candle. I loved the quiet and the smell of candles and incense that permeated the walls and threadbare rugs covering wooden benches.

Naturally, Boris had an idea how the church's use could be further expanded; this prompted a mock theological seminar on sin, sacrilege and the holy sacrament of matrimony, ending in a somewhat rushed activity which among good Christians could only be pursued within marriage, but not necessarily inside a church. We made it on time to Aunt Sonya's special lunch of locally caught carp with potatoes and leeks from our garden. For Boris and me, weekends and summer holidays in Irinovka were something we looked forward to very much.

## 11

It was an unfortunate coincidence that Boris's new career as a poet took off as the Party's control over our lives hardened. In 1937, 'repression' became a word commonly mentioned in our circles, in whispers. People were paranoid, with a good reason; we had a feeling we were spied on constantly, at work, in public spaces, even at home with thin walls and curious concierges. My father, who was closest to the source of the increasingly malignant power, seemed to be as powerless as the rest of us. He paid little attention to anything but his work in the navy, but his work seemed to be the cause of his growing despondency. My mother had mentioned it; I think he oppressed her with his relentless gloom, but he never explained himself fully, never let her help him. He probably did not want to burden his wife with politics, now a dangerous topic; the less she knew, the safer she was.

No-one knew what was coming next. Often, we first heard through the grapevine and then would come an article in the *Pravda* elaborating on the ignominious activities of a disgraced government official, a hapless academic, an artist who fell out of favour. Not even economists and factory directors were safe. Some cases were out in the open on the pages of *Pravda*, as a means of control by fear. The latest victim was a renowned musicologist, Professor Zhilyayev, exiled to Irkutsk, according to an official communiqué, but then we heard he had already been executed in the depths of Siberia. If an arcane trade such as musicology could lead to the gallows, no-one was safe. In fact, it was enough to be someone's wife, or a grown son or daughter; how could one be involved in an elaborate conspiracy without family members knowing?

There were people who denounced others in the hope of currying favour with the regime or saving themselves. It never worked. Discoveries of 'anti-revolutionary conspiracies' and 'Western spies' proliferated. With them came trials, betrayals, exiles, executions. The confessions of the accused were often followed by repentance which never prevented being found guilty and sentenced. The children of the 'enemies of the people' were put in orphanages. Their relatives could not adopt or even visit them. They were meant to forget what happened to their parents. This was for their own good, according to the authorities, so that they would not be burdened by the stigma of the crimes of their fathers ... and mothers.

Boris and I were young and unimportant. Me, a maintenance engineer with the regional railway authority; Boris, a colourful waiter in a grand hotel. However, I was also the daughter of an admiral, and the niece of a university professor who travelled

279

to Europe a little too often. Boris Antonovich was also an underground poet, by now well known in Leningrad's *samizdat* circles. I often lay in bed at night expecting to hear the whirr of the lift machinery, then the scissor-grid iron door opening, then the heavy footsteps of at least two men approaching. It did not happen.

Instead, one night Boris did not come home from work. I fell asleep before midnight and woke up a couple of hours later; he was not next to me, or in the old servant room we turned into a study where he often wrote late at night. I felt terror growing in my belly. The concierge's phone was only available from 6 a.m., but what good could come from calling Uncle Vasily and telling him Boris was missing in front of a police informant? No, I had to go to the Astoria first thing in the morning and see if I could learn anything useful there. They only opened at nine. It was an anxious wait. I forced some breakfast down my throat, put on my oldest, most comfortable boots and rushed the few blocks to the Astoria on foot. I had to wait for a few minutes until a waiter unlocked the entrance.

'Good morning, comrade! I am Francesca Andreyevna Vorodina, Boris Antonovich's wife. Do you know him? He did not come home last night.'

The slim, slightly hunched waiter paused for a moment before answering.

'Of course I know Boris Antonovich! I saw him yesterday afternoon; my shift was ending as his was starting. He was his usual jovial self. I do not know what happened afterwards.'

'Can I see the manager? Comrade Steigerova, isn't it?' Boris had mentioned her many times.

'Sure . . . she is in the office.' He hesitated a little. 'Let me take you there.'

'Thank you so much!'

He knocked and a small bespectacled woman with a kind face turned and looked at us over her glasses.

'Comrade Steigerova, excuse the interruption, the young lady ... this is Comrade Vorodina, Boris Antonovich's wife.'

'Good morning, Comrade Steigerova. I am sorry to interrupt. Boris Antonovich did not come home last night. I am very worried. I wonder if you know anything.'

'I left the office at four in the afternoon, during his shift. Everything was in order. Perhaps it's something innocent? He had too much to drink after work and had an impromptu sleepover somewhere? These things happen.' She half-smiled.

'Not to Boris Antonovich. He is barely a drinker. Thank you! I'd better go. Not sure where, though.'

'I wish you luck, Comrade Vorodina. I hope Boris Antonovich is well and will be here again this afternoon.'

I felt in my gut, tight with worry, that this was unlikely.

I decided to take a long walk to my parents' house. My father had been 'temporarily transferred' to the port of Murmansk, one thousand kilometres north. My mother was concerned, but he phoned home weekly, and apart from him sounding listless, things seemed regular. If he was at home, he would have been able to engage some connections so we could at least learn what had happened to Boris. But from Murmansk, this was much more difficult.

My mother knew something was amiss as soon as she saw me. It was not usual for me to pay her a visit first thing in the morning, without letting her know beforehand, and by myself.

'Francesca, my dear! How nice to see you! Excuse my hair in disarray – I was just about to do something about it. Are you alone? Where is Boris?' She poked her head out of the front door, as if he could be hiding in the corridor.

'I wish I knew, Mama! He didn't come home last night ...'

She opened her mouth to say something, but I signalled her to stop. 'No, it's not anything casual, if this is what you wanted to suggest – he's always home on time. If he were alive and free, he would at least call the concierge. There were no messages – I asked this morning. I went to the Astoria too; he was last seen at work.'

'People like him are bound to get in trouble. Times are tough. He never wanted to keep his head low. And then those poetry circles ... Vasily told me about his underground success.'

'Are you blaming him, Mama? Is it his fault we live in this terror? It's like a nightmare. What other nation lives like us? Miserable, in terror and fear? Perhaps the Germans under Hitler. But his murderousness is more predictable: Jews and communists. With Stalin, everyone's neck is potentially under the axe. He is killing the elite of his own nation. Not even his own really – he's Georgian. The chief madman Dzhugashvili!'

'Tone it down, Francesca, you don't know who's listening! Let's wait until tonight; if there is no sign of Boris, I'll speak to your father next time he rings. I cannot call him – he could not provide the phone number of the Murmansk naval base. You know everything around him is military and secret!' She sighed.

'I cannot wait that long. Can I call Uncle Vasily?'

'Let me call him. Our phone is almost certainly monitored. It will raise no suspicion if I call. I'll find an innocent reason to invite him over at once.'

Uncle Vasily and Aunt Sonya were also among the small elite with a home phone. Sonya answered.

'Sonya, good morning! Marya here. I am in a small trouble – can you put Vasily on, please? He may be able to help me.'

'Good morning, my dear Mashenka, what is troubling you?'

'Oh, Vasily, I'm embarrassed to bother you, but you know Andrey is away ... I had a dizzy spell this morning after getting out of bed and I fell in the bathroom. I might have damaged my wrist. I am feeling quite woozy. If you are free this morning, could you drop by and take me to Dr Dvorkin's surgery? Andrey's car is here, we can use it.'

'I have a lecture to give at eleven, but I can be a few minutes late for my dearest sister! I'll leave shortly, so see you before ten I hope.'

Uncle Vasily arrived as promised, before my mother could force me to eat. I accepted a strong cup of tea. He was genuinely surprised to see me there.

'Francesca, my dear! What's happening?'

My mother signalled him to speak quietly.

He sat between us at the dining table. The conversation proceeded in a low voice.

'You are not dizzy, Masha, are you? What is wrong?'

'Boris has disappeared.'

'Well, not disappeared,' my mother interjected. 'He did not come home from work last night.'

I gave her an exasperated look.

'Hmm ... let me see. People do disappear these days. What can be done? Sonya knows a man called Sorokin, whose wife is also a journalist, a good friend of Sonya's in fact. Comrade Sorokin is Yezhov's right hand ... one of his top henchmen, a 'Commissioner of State Security First Class' or some such. I hear from Sonya he is a pig, but a powerful one. Sonya may be able to get information about Boris Antonovich – if he is in their clutches.'

'Thank you so much, Uncle Vasily!'

I gave him a big hug as he was getting up to leave.

'Do not worry too much, my darling girl. Perhaps one poem is not enough to get a person into a gulag ... if there is any common sense left in this country!' He put his arms around my mother. 'I have to rush now. But I will speak to Sonya as soon as I can – this afternoon.'

My mother turned to me. 'What did he mean, one poem? What has Boris done?'

'It's a poem called "The Russian soul under socialism". The title references that Oscar Wilde essay from 1891, "The soul of man under socialism", inspired by Russian anarchists. Boris's poem was well received . . . in the *samizdat* circles of course. Uncle Vasily thought it was very good, but also dangerous.'

'Yes, I can well imagine. Boris is not a candle burning quietly to the end – he's a firecracker!'

I stood up to leave. 'I'm off too, Mama. I'm going to the university library. I cannot bear to sit at home alone or go to work and pretend all is normal. I'll drop by our place just in case there are any news or messages.'

My mother sighed deeply. 'You can stay here if you like, honey. I'll have to go to school shortly, back by mid-afternoon. There's food in the kitchen, you can have some lunch, just warm it up. A nice beans and sauerkraut soup with smoked bacon pieces that you used to like.' She smiled. 'You're thin as reed, Francesca.'

'Thank you, Mama, that's kind of you. But I cannot focus on anything, and anxiously wandering through your house all day . . . I'll pick up some books and sit in the library. I can imagine myself there for a few hours. I'll be back here in the afternoon. We should hear from Uncle Vasily by then, and I'll have some of your yummy food. If Mitya does not clear it off beforehand.' I attempted a smile.

## 12

The university library reading room was beautifully furnished and lit by elegant table lamps, a remnant from tsarist times.

I could not focus on the thermal characteristics of steel used in railways and tramways. I stared into space, across the large hall. With an open book and notes in front of me, I was the picture of a hardworking student, but in fact I was imagining the most plausible scenario of Boris's disappearance.

⁓

Boris is leaving the Astoria through the staff entrance on Voznesensky Avenue. It is about ten fifteen at night, pitch dark in early March. The entrance is shaded from the streetlight. Two agents step out of the shadow.

'Comrade Boris Antonovich Vorodin?'

'Yes ... ?'

'Please come with us. You can assist in an inquiry. We are from NKVD.'

'Right now? I'm tired and quite hungry, comrades. Can this wait until the morning?'

'Definitely not.'

They approach abruptly and grab him by his upper arms on both sides. He could escape; he is stronger and faster than them. But they are armed no doubt. And even if he managed to escape their grip and their bullets, what then? Live like an animal, run and hide? So, he tenses up but does not try to escape. The agent on his right-hand side clips handcuffs onto his wrist. They do not know he is left-handed. All the same, he is attached to one of the agents.

They push him into a car. A third agent is at the wheel. They drive through empty streets. After turning the first corner, the non-attached agent blindfolds Boris. After fifteen or twenty minutes they stop and enter a building. Once inside, they remove his blindfold. The foyer is dimly lit and quiet. They proceed to a brightly lit examination room. He squints. He feels no fear, just his stomach rumbling. All that is on offer in the room is water. He asks for a glass and drinks. Just water, no vodka! They have not figured out yet that it would be easier to get drunk people talking than the sober ones! They do not know this because they've never been sober in the company of drunks.

A medium-height, thickly set man enters the room. He is wearing a uniform. A combination of buttoned-up black jacket and the usual olive-green breeches. Tall black riding boots. Quite smart, but also menacing. He sits at the large table opposite Boris. He does not introduce himself.

'What did you mean to achieve by this collection of poems, Comrade Vorodin?' He slaps a paper folder down on the table. 'And specifically with the poem titled "The Russian soul under socialism"?'

'I wanted people to read it ... those who like poetry.'

'This is a *samizdat*. It is illegal to publicly distribute literature that did not receive *Glavlit's* approval. You surely know that ... even though you're just a waiter.'

Humiliation #1.

'We all contribute to our homeland according to our abilities. All jobs have equal dignity, we are often told.'

'Not a point for you to make! You were a ballet dancer who arrogantly left the Bolshoi six years ago; the troupe that everyone would be proud to belong to. We also know that your waitering is camouflage for spreading anti-socialist propaganda.'

'Oh, is it? I had no idea!'

'Do not be impertinent, Comrade Vorodin. It is late and my patience is growing thin.'

'I suggested we did this in the morning, but my suggestion was rejected.'

'Stop offering free comments! You're not in the position to suggest anything, do you understand?'

Humiliation #2.

'This is not an underground poetry reading society!' The officer's raised voice reaches a threatening pitch. 'Answer my question!'

'Why did I write the poem? And other poems? If that's the question, well, I like writing them. They are my version of truth ... of meaning.'

'Your version of truth, is it? So everyone has his own version of truth, huh? What chaos! Are you an anarchist? A nihilist? There is only one version of truth that guides the Party, that in turn guides society, for the benefit of everyone. Simple!'

'I thought it was more complicated. That's why I wrote this.'

'Is that so?' The interrogator yells into Boris's face. He smells of alcohol. He jumps on his feet and starts pacing across the room. Then he opens the folder and waves a handwritten page on top towards Boris.

Boris stays quiet. The agent he is handcuffed to tenses up.

>'*Russian soul: grown men crying over a poem.*
>*Russian soul: marinated in vodka; pure but incoherent ...*'

'Et cetera, et cetera! You ridicule the Russian people! What is complicated about that? It is a series of simple insults. Or you pity them from your artistic heights: "*Russian soul: dignity crushed by whip and mud ...*"'

'There's more ...' Boris tries but gives up.

'"Soul" is a religious, bourgeois category! Isn't it? Why not "the Russian man"?'

'Because the "Russian soul" has been discussed in literature for centuries. Even outside Russia. I've just joined the discussion ...'

'We have parted with the past! This is a new world, a new society. Why resurrect fruitless old debates, Comrade Vorodin?'

'"Resurrect" is a religious term too. The title of a Tolstoy novel also ... which we still read nowadays ...'

The interrogator slams his meaty palm on the table. The handcuffed agent twitches. 'Do not try to give me lessons, you arrogant nitwit. Our debate may end sooner than planned and this is not going to be good for you ... and your pretty face!'

The interrogator belches the last words into Boris's face, too close for comfort. Boris can smell alcohol again, and garlic. He stays impassive. The interrogator pulls a bunch of handwritten pages out of the folder and tosses them in front of Boris.

'And these other poems ... anti-revolutionary, bourgeois rubbish, offensive to every honest, hardworking Soviet citizen! Bourgeois decadence! Writers are the engineers of human souls! Russian art, literature and music should enlighten people. People cannot be duped by abstract paintings and atonal music! And why would they read poems that humiliate them?'

My nightmarish daydream was interrupted by a student arriving next to me. He threw his books noisily on the desk and checked me out unflinchingly, but did not say hello before he sat down; an unusual behaviour among the usually timid and polite bookworms. An informer? Perhaps I was paranoid because of Boris's disappearance. I collected my books and notes, got up and squeezed past the ostentatious neighbour. I thought it better to have a long walk and get some fresh air. I walked to my parents' place. Perhaps there would be news from Uncle Vasily?

Mitya was at home, listening to the wireless. He had just had lunch and was happily ignoring me. I ate a little, alone. Soon after I finished, Mama came home. She didn't even manage to warm up her food before the phone rang.

'Mashenka, it's Vasily. Sonya has already delivered the

question to Comrade Sorokina. She will let us know as soon as she manages to talk to her husband.'

I spent the night at Mama's place. I could not see myself going home alone. Even Mitya took an interest after he realised the issue was rather serious. He reckoned I was safer in the bosom of the family.

In the morning, just as Mitya left, the phone rang again. Mrs Sorokina delivered her husband's office phone number to call at 3 p.m. Not before, not after: 3 p.m!

It was true! Boris had been arrested. I could go home and ring from our concierge phone. The informer concierge might already know what happened, and if he didn't, he'd be pleased to learn. At this point, no harm in it; the deed was done. At 3 p.m., Comrade Sorokin's secretary advised me that he would see me at 5 p.m. sharp. I returned to our flat and chose a serious, modest outfit. I thought about the forthcoming meeting. What would he ask? What could I say to get Boris back? How many people were released from NKVD's clutches? I've never heard of people returning home. Once they were arrested or they simply vanished, there seemed to be only two paths: to Siberia or to the gallows. It took a longish tram ride to reach the Bolshoy Dom, the NKVD headquarters on Liteyny Prospekt, which gave me too much time to fruitlessly mull over things. A security guard took me to Comrade Sorokin's office on the first floor. The secretary's antechamber was empty.

Comrade Sorokin was sitting in a tall leather chair, behind a massive desk, with his palms folded over his bulging stomach. He waved towards the chair across from him and slid a bit lower in his own.

'*Pozhalysta*, have a seat, Comrade Vorodina. The wife of Boris Antonovich Vorodin, the ballet dancer turned poet . . . ? He peered at the dossier opened on the table. 'And a daughter of Admiral Mendel? Beautiful, beautiful. Great indeed! A good family. I would like to help if I can.'

'Thank you . . . thank you for making time to see me.' My mouth was dry and refused to extend into a smile.

'You father was a good Russian patriot, a military man, an important man. A little taciturn, a bit curt sometimes. We were not always sure what he thought, but he was always good at his job, diligent, punctual, respected by his officers. A patriot. It's a shame he lost his political compass lately . . .'

'Do you mean to say my father is also in trouble . . . ?' My heart began to race.

'Let's stick to the matter that brought you here, young lady. How did your father allow you to marry this . . . clown? It was reported he often finished his poetry readings by a somersault, or a spin, then a bow.'

'Boris Antonovich is not a clown, Comrade Sokorin. A somersault never offended anyone. No harm in being athletic or cheering people up, is there?' I felt heat spreading through my body. My cheeks were burning.

'Your husband was too prone to bravado!' He peered into the dossier again. 'He used to start his poetry readings with "Comrades, ladies and gentlemen, Comrade Informant!"'

I noticed that he referred to my father and Boris in the past tense.

'Well, there always was one there. How else would you know this . . . ?

'That is correct. We need to know how people feel and think . . . and who our enemies are; the enemies of the people, not just the Party. Party and people are one.'

'I am here because of my husband, but you say my father has been apprehended too . . . ? In Murmansk . . . ?' I persisted.

'Too many questions, young lady.' He raised his voice

slightly. 'I cannot discuss your father's case. He's a military man. A different department.'

'Can I see Boris Antonovich? Is he here – I mean, detained in Shpalernaya Street?'

Comrade Sorokin straightened himself in his chair and pulled a cigarette out of a packet of Belomorskys. He lit it up and inhaled deeply and slowly, looking at a point above my head. His pleasure was obvious.

'Let us collaborate on this matter, Comrade Vorodina. You could help them both, and yourself . . . and me. Let's have a win-win situation.' He smiled.

I waited for him to continue without any clue about what might be coming. Me helping him . . . ?

'Come closer, young lady.' He beckoned with his hand, sporting a friendly smile. Reluctantly, I got up and walked a few paces towards the desk.

'Come, come closer, you can help me with something here.'

I walked around the desk and stood next to his tall leather chair. I was marginally taller than him seated. He suddenly wrapped his arm around my waist and drew me closer to him. I froze.

'Come, come, you're a married woman! You know how to best help a man once he's done his honest day of hard work . . .' He started unbuttoning himself. His breath smelt of vodka and tobacco.

My mind raced. Can I do this? Would it help? Would they free Boris because I was ready to do whatever pleased Comrade Sorokin? Can a man like this be trusted to honour his word? No, no, no . . .

'No!'

'No? I have not heard such a response to my friendly request yet. Don't you want to help your husband . . . your family? You may even enjoy it . . . it has happened before.'

I was still in his grip.

'Would you like a glass of vodka, Comrade Vorodina? It may help you relax. You are tense. I understand. You could tell me what kind of husband was your Boris Antonovich . . . ? Young, fit no doubt . . . a dancer . . .'

'Isn't it all in your dossier?'

'Not quite, not quite . . . but it would be interesting to hear.'

He removed his arm from around my waist and reached for the bottle of vodka on his desk. I stepped back.

'I have to go, Comrade Sorokin. I am sorry you wasted your time to see me. Goodbye.'

I rushed out of the room, desperate to leave the forbidding building. The guard at the first floor did not try to stop me. I ran down a wide stairwell. Another guard at the main entrance did not show any interest in me either. Once on the street, cool dusk reminded me I'd forgotten my coat in Sorokin's office.

I shivered at the tram stop. The dark was falling on the city and despair was filling my heart. What could I do? Where could I go? To Mama again! She might have news from my father . . . or some idea about what awaited us. She would give me a hug. I needed it more than ever.

# 13

We are now the 'enemy of the people'. Me, Boris, my parents, Uncle Vasily, Aunt Sonya. Who are the 'people' we worked against, I wonder? The ordinary folk, the people marching into factories before dawn and out of them mid-afternoon at the sound of three loud siren whistles? They work hard but life is better than in their villages, where starvation is a real possibility each winter and spring. With their stomachs full of simple greasy food and vodka at subsidised prices, they do not see a reason to protest. For them, Stalin is God and Tsar in one person. Yet, the army-administered plunder caused villages in southern Russia and Ukraine to erupt into revolt. The remaining *kulaks*, which now means anyone who owns enough land for a decent life, are sent to Siberia. They are beaten with sticks and rubber straps, tortured, far away from anyone but their torturers. Still, stories have reached Moscow and Leningrad. Those who dared to rebel openly against their land being 'collectivised' were executed. Thousands of people! We, the city folk, have been on thin ice all along; we can be disposed of on the lamest of pretexts.

The bad people, the 'counter-revolutionaries', are those called 'intelligentsia': university students, lecturers, writers, artists, and people in government positions who are not able to turn a blind eye to the orgy of shameless sycophancy and unrestrained power. The 'intellectual' is not a respectable title any longer. The people whose tool of trade is words are now suspect and they must be careful about how they use them. The notorious Article 58 introduced 'counter-revolutionary activity' as a crime punishable by death. Stock revolutionary phrases became the only safe option, but not everyone can stomach them, especially after it became clear that professing revolutionary faith and loyalty to our great leader could not guarantee a long life.

The revolution has taken a cannibalistic turn and not even the high secret police officials are safe. It is a small consolation that some of these high inquisitors have themselves been executed after sending many other people to the firing squad. Vodka has much to answer for in people denouncing their colleagues, neighbours, even family members. While sober, most people had the good sense not to elongate the chain of reckless destruction of lives and families; churches are empty but Christian tenets live on in people's minds. The 'progressive proletariat' in Russian cities and towns chant slogans in support of Stalin, the Party and a bright future when told to do so; deep down, they are still the God-fearing Russian peasants, most born and bred in villages where their survival was in God hands, while the Tsar claimed his taxes regardless. Vodka can make these meek people belligerent and hateful; once alcohol removes inhibitions, it is harder to believe in equality where some people could naturally enter a grand hotel and others could only dream about it.

A week after Boris disappeared, I heard the whirr of the lift stopping at our floor and footsteps in heavy boots, then a resolute knock on the door. I was not sleeping much anyway; I was waiting for them. Only days later Boris and I were transported south to Luga by train, then eastwards, towards the wetlands, on trucks.

In a large barn, a group of about a hundred people huddles around four braziers. Boris and I are lucky to be together. This is because the commander of Operation Mshinskoye Forest knows my father. A small privilege, spending our last days together, being killed together.

When I last spoke with my mother, she told me my father managed to organise Mitya's escape to Finland on a military ship. I hope he made it to safety. He will have to grow up at once. My father probably knew they were coming for him too; he was well connected. But he would not try to escape himself. Neither would Mama. Whatever happened to her? I hope they are together ... somewhere. Papa is a soldier, he can cope with anything, but I cannot imagine Uncle Vasily in prison. Who knows where he is, is he still alive? And Aunt Sonya? Entire families have been wiped out, leaving no-one to seek justice or revenge, or tell what happened once this is all over. Only small children, the orphans of the revolution, are spared because they will not remember.

My eyes fill with tears. We will be erased from the face of the Earth, as if we never existed.

'They are just keeping us alive through the subzero nights, so they can kill us properly, in an organised way, rather than us accidentally freezing to death,' Boris observes loudly. Perhaps his gallows humour can cheer people up a little? Several people turn their heads, but no-one makes a sound.

Most people in the room are 'intelligentsia' but they seem stolid, tongue-tied. Are they dumbstruck with terror? As we warm up, bodies start to give off odours of life and decay. Acrid armpits, rotten teeth. Always together: life and decay. Life and death. Luckily, our detention will be short; we are not going to be turned into beasts by prolonged hunger, filth, freezing, back-breaking work, illness. We have not been tortured, just rudely interrogated and intimidated. We'll die as human beings, more or less. Class differences in death, as in life? Ironic, given that we have been brainwashed by endless sermons about equality. We are not going to be the regime's exemplary spectacle; our expiation and contrition are not needed. Too many of us need to be liquidated and the revolution is in a hurry to eliminate its detractors. Revolution! What a joke! Lame but deadly. The revolution dissipated long ago in the trot of history. It is about our paranoid Chief Comrade and people who can whisper into his ear until they too fall from grace. Thousands of rank-and-file police and soldiers are 'following orders', killing their compatriots, peers, neighbours. What wretched people we are, the Russians! When will this horror stop, and who will stop it?

Before dawn, we are ushered out of the shelter into the milky fog. Lake Vyal've is close and the fog is thicker here in the wetlands. Once the fog lifts a lovely spring day will emerge, birds will chirp and flower buds push on fruit trees, soon to become white or pink blossoming crowns. We will not see them. At the time we are ordered outdoors, it is still eerily quiet and misty. Only soldiers' heavy boots crunch on the gravel. In a couple of minutes, rime forms on Boris's beard. It makes him look grey and much older. He has not shaved for weeks and his hair is dirty. His eyes are clear but they look darker blue than usual. He is expressionless.

I must look like a shadow of my earlier self after several uncomfortable nights, my lips cracked by cold, my eyes swollen. I do not cry when they try to scare me. Faced with cruelty and brutality, I am able to turn fear into anger. But when Boris tried to comfort me last night, when he embraced me on an uncomfortable bedroll spread on the rough wooden floor and whispered words of love into my ear, I dissolved in sobs. Exhausted, I eventually fell asleep. I woke up with a start, remembering in an instant where we were. Now I turn towards Boris. He takes my hand and gives me a weak smile. For a few brief moments I rest in contemplation of our love. Our seven happy years together. We had more than most and I'm grateful.

Once we are outside, no-one talks. What is there to say? What do people think about in the last minutes of their lives? About their loved ones? Their children if they have them? Do their lives really flash in front of their eyes? Some people seem bewildered; some resigned. A woman close to me is shaking with fever chills. She seems alone. There are no spare blankets. People huddle up against the cold. My nostrils ache from the thick, frigid air.

Two trucks arrive. No-one seems eager to climb up a small wooden step attached to the back of the truck. I squeeze Boris's hand and nod towards the truck. It seems all the same to me whether we take this one or the next. He squeezes my hand in return, pulling my arm down, meaning to say: 'wait'. What are we waiting for? To hear a distant – probably not too distant – volley from multiple guns? Receive a last moment pardon? It happens in novels, but not in real life. In fact, yes, Dostoevsky received a last-minute amnesty and was sent to hard labour in Siberia instead. Is that story true? Uncle Vasily said it was, so I've always believed it. If he had been executed then, as a young man, the same age Boris is now, all those great novels would not have been written; the novels that have not been mentioned in recent years, or reprinted, considered 'reactionary'. Especially *Bésy*, my favourite, a premonition of the revolution, nearly an oracle. And what an experience for a writer, a close shave with execution – almost like a well-planned field trip. These thoughts distract me for few moments and bring a flash of relief, like lightning momentarily illuminating the night.

The moment is thick with reality. No hiding in the bottom drawer of one's mind! The only choice left: to climb on the first truck or wait for the next one, delay one's death by a few minutes, perhaps half an hour, an hour. Boris looks at me again and smiles. We climb onto the truck. We hold hands tight. I am so happy we are together, but Boris's presence also makes me soft, emotional. Alone, I'd call up my tough side, the anger. Perhaps.

'Can the same thing make you happy and sad at the same time?' I ask Boris in a whisper.

'Yes.' He readily replies, as if he knows exactly what I'm talking about.

The trip on the back of the truck on a bumpy road is uncomfortable but short. A file of horsemen lines both sides of a cosy clearing that is now an execution yard. Stationary horses neigh and stomp. At the bottom of the clearing, at the very edge of the pine forest, there is a small chapel with a derelict tiled roof; a tiny bell tower is still standing. This bell is not going to ring for our souls. I liked the sound of church bells as a child so much, before the revolution silenced them. On Sunday mornings and on holy days of the Orthodox calendar, the city would be enveloped in a warm, soothing music; for a few moments, it transported even the unbelievers into a transcendental realm. The chiming of bells would take us to a serene space outside our everyday worries and vanities and deliver a moment of peace and togetherness.

Five of us are separated from the group. There are ten soldiers in the firing squad. This must be the ratio to make sure we are all properly dead by the time the echo of the gunfire dissipates above the lake. The soldiers have Asian faces. They are brought from Kazakhstan, Kyrgyzstan, the distant parts of the empire, to shoot us and not feel sorry for us, the light-haired, blue-eyed, European-looking Russians. Perhaps they take it as revenge? No, they are too young for such thoughts and feelings! Barely twenty, some look even younger, indoctrinated into loving the Soviet Union, speaking Russian from an early age. They are sure to lose their innocence manning the firing squad ... but then, who knows? They are just obeying orders! They blindfold us, tie our wrists together and lead us to our places. Through the blindfold, I can still see the world lighten up as the sun breaks through the wispy fog; I feel a ray of thin April sunshine on my face.

'On your marks!' Crunching of boots on the gravel again. 'Cock your guns!' The soft sound of a body falling precedes the double click of rifles getting ready to fire. Someone fainted. Not Boris, he is the last on the right, next to me. In a moment, the space pebble will return to his native planet. Where am I going to go ...? '*Strelyat!*' A burning pain fills my chest. The darkness first, then silence, and my body floats free.

## Post Fabulam V
## Melbourne, 2021

S o there you are. My past lives have been committed to paper. Ten months of dedicated work, a state of immersion I've never achieved before, not even in the most absorbing days of my working life. My laptop never far from me, I perfected a method of typing in bed. A few months left to live focuses one's mind. I have turned a large volume of notes and recordings into a prose that others could appreciate; you be the judge, dear reader – if a publisher can be found. I'll have to leave that with Bertie, I won't have time. Will he persist?

The voices of children are coming in through the window from a nearby park. From behind the trees, the shrill sounds are muted, almost calming. They transport me back to my childhood, or rather that moment at age eleven, maybe twelve, the moment when unselfconscious childhood finished and the troubled universe of the self, the glass cage of the ego, set in to occupy my head for the rest of my days. Is this the same for everyone? Somehow, that point in my life when I became who I am is associated with the early spring. Late February in Europe. Crisp, sunny, still cool days, snowdrops, primroses and hyacinths pushing through in the neglected green patches between apartment blocks. All of us, children from the neighbourhood, coming out to play after school, run after a ball screaming, play chase, climb trees, hang off monkey bars in playgrounds. Not fancy Australian playgrounds, just a seesaw, monkey bars and a couple of swings, often damaged. Us older ones rode our bicycles aimlessly through small suburban streets and irritated drivers who had to be extra careful around us. The budding young self, suddenly self-conscious, anxious, ruminating, melancholy without an obvious reason, sleepless at night. Puberty, hormones, self-awareness, the human condition.

What is the truth of it all, I'd like to know? Have I just told you a sad, even tragic, tale of a woman whose life was brutally cut short five times? Or, perhaps, of a woman who was repeatedly spared old age and its distressing decline that ends in the final betrayal of the body, the 'natural death'? Was this a tale of cosmic justice: being given another chance after dying young? In Buddhism, reincarnation is a punishment for bad karma, but here in the West we prefer to misunderstand it as a story of hope, even immortality. Francesca lived, worked and loved; she bit into life with a healthy appetite each time, sometimes more than she could chew. She never had time to finish the feast. I'll finish it this time and therefore this should be my last life.

Laying it down in front of you feels like the hardest task: choosing the episodes, passing judgments. Just like public ones, personal histories are a matter of choosing certain episodes and interpreting them in a certain way. In comparison to an enormous, messy pile of memories of my past fifty-eight years, the short previous lives seem like neat stories with a clear point, or points, that emerged from the narratives naturally, effortlessly. What has been the point of my current life? I know that very early, sometime at the end of high school, something I chose to call 'autonomy' started to feel like the ultimate value. Early on, I developed a gauge, a gut feeling, definite and clear: which people and which situations truncated it, endangered it, when I needed to run away. The first runaway was to Bucharest, then to marry Filip in Croatia, then to Australia, then a runaway from the marriage. Now perhaps, I'm running away from the illness and its inevitable dependency, and the only way out is death ...

As a young woman, I decided I was not going to be 'just a woman'; I would hold the helm of my life firmly. Surely, I was reminded I was (just) a woman often, daily perhaps, covertly and overtly, deliberately and inadvertently. But I tried to keep my course, like a man would, without apologising. I was reprimanded along the way, but never unbearably, never fatally; not burned at a stake, not executed by a firing squad, not killed by a husband who assumed his right to control me. The problem was that a 'proper woman' squatted inside my head, loving, caring, wanting to put others before herself. The price to pay for being a woman and a man at the same time was much work! A relentless effort. I was a mother but also earned my own living all along and others recognised, respected this as independence. I never found myself in a total impasse, surrendered to the will of others. Is this success? Perhaps 'the truth' will somehow leak out of my fingertips. Isn't this the hope of every writer?

Over a decade ago I greatly enjoyed a novel titled *The Household Guide to Dying*. In anticipation of her death, the protagonist cooks and freezes meals for her family. Feeding them beyond the grave – that's the spirit! A female spirit. That irresistible, masochistic dedication to others. I recognise it; in my life, it has caused much internal confrontation with the other, arguably more natural instinct, selfishness. Could a terminal diagnosis be a belated licence for a woman to be selfish – the privilege men acquire by birth? I will allow myself to die without accomplishing a cooking marathon; my gender-neutral writing marathon is gruelling as well, but it suits me a great deal better. And decluttering is kind of fun, finding pieces of myself, my life, in thousands of objects, and putting those pieces to rest.

# VI: *The Natural Death*

## *Francesca (1962–2021),*
## *Romania – Croatia – Australia*

I CAN EASILY RECONSTRUCT MY MUCH younger self. Always a scribbler, I left evidence behind. Diaries, poems, letters and impromptu little essays with adolescent musings on life, love, other people, society. Reaching into the top shelves and bottom drawers of my memory is hard work. I kept my diaries for decades, they travelled across the world, but I never looked at them. I am having a look now, skipping through lines and pages, saying hello and goodbye to my past selves in quick succession: a child, a teenager, a young woman.

When Bertie is here, I'm decluttering; another fine task for the end of one's days. It's handy to have a more precise timing for one's death, where the margin of error is not years or even decades, but only months or weeks. One can prepare, get one's affairs in order. Yet it is still difficult to decide what to keep, what can be left behind that is of any value to others.

In my current state, decluttering is physically taxing, not to mention carrying heavy stuff to recycling bins. Bertie's help is invaluable. Books are a real burden, bookshelves bursting, weighing tons. Finding a charity or a second-hand bookstore that wants any is no mean feat these days, and the recurring lockdowns complicate it further. I have cherished books all my life, and my last act is to write one. I had planned to return to books in retirement, but I miscalculated. There won't be any retirement, just a long sick leave leading to my neatly planned date with the Grim Reaper. So the books have to go, one way or another; Bruno is not of a generation that cherishes inheriting a large dusty library.

The hardest decision of all: the photographs. Many thousands of them in old glossy paper format. I pick up a photo of two smooth-faced nineteen-year-olds, posing in front of a horseman monument in a Bucharest park: Monica and me, besties from week one of university; it's late spring, long sunny days, the end of our first year as journalism undergrads. No-one else in the whole world is interested in this photo. I cannot send it to her. Perhaps she has a copy anyway. I hold it, leave it on the desk, come back, toss it onto the paper recycling heap, then pick it up again and look at it with superstitious reverence. I cannot toss people in the bin, especially dear, close people, it's like killing them symbolically, purging them out of my life. I want to keep that lovely spring day when we wandered through the park, young and hopeful, slaphappily clicking away with my father's camera.

The sea was my pre-pubescent writing inspiration, then came boys. My childhood ended at age eleven, with the first diary entry about my sister's boyfriend. My parents both worked full-time, leaving me in the care of eighteen-year-old Michaela, a devil-may-care teenager. It was 1973 and I was infatuated with Marius, a fashionable, long-haired 21-year-old on a motorcycle. A Vespa, to be more precise, an imported Italian scooter. Wow! His father was *someone*, I cannot remember who exactly. Back then, this might have been the only Vespa in Constanța. Marius was super-cool!

He took me for rides sometimes, on a whim, all to my sister's chagrin, and treated me to ice creams and cakes. In his favourite *cofetărie*, he introduced me as his girlfriend to a group of his mates. They chuckled and I of course knew it was a joke, but I was still chuffed. Michaela must have been an uninspiring girlfriend given he preferred to ride about town with a skinny kid with square, silver-rimmed glasses in tow. Being pressed onto his back with my arms wrapped around him gave me a proto-sexual pleasure while wind was forcing tears out of my eyes. I was aware of his male scent, an early premonition of desires of the flesh. I don't think he felt anything of the kind from me being pressed onto his back. I was a flat-chested, bookish eleven-year-old, nothing like a proper Lolita.

I was devastated when Michaela and Marius broke up. She quickly mended her broken heart with another lad who paid no attention to me. The indifference was mutual. He was nothing like Marius: uncool, no Western gloss. Michaela married him two years later and had a couple of children before she was twenty-five.

At twelve I became a fully formed neurotic, and aware of my sexuality; the two could have been connected. I knew women menstruated, because I shared a bedroom with Michaela, and she always grumbled about the nuisance of her periods. Some-times she stained her bedsheets overnight. At thirteen, my nearly permanent sulking could only be helped by the company of my friends or being left alone with books. At that time, I switched from comic books to 'real' books, including books about love, some of them esteemed literary classics, that put ideas about romantic love into my head. A girl, a woman, would be better off without it; but more on that later. My family was just a bother, especially Michaela. I was over the moon when she moved out of the family home. I was fourteen and I had a room of my own. Not everyone did. Bingo!

My older brother, the middle child, was meant to be the star of the family – after all, he was the only son. But Florian was caught by the last outbreak of the polio virus that lingered ominously over Romania in the 1950s. His withered leg and prominent limp made him an outsider at school, and later it kept girls at bay in spite of his otherwise great looks. He grew into a bitter, sarcastic teenager, neglected his university studies and devoted himself to Western rock music. He was a connoisseur with a respectable collection of LPs in his room and a guitar he played alone. At twenty-seven, just as our parents gave up all hope, he completed his degree in economics. In his early thirties, he moved to Cluj. He avoided family visits and reunions. What became of Florian? He must be alive, because no-one ever told me he wasn't. Michaela would tell me, even though we only communicate via text messages at birthdays and Christmases. After the death of my parents, my connection with Romania faded.

I left home before Florian, at eighteen. I was pleased to leave Constanța, not because of my hometown's industrial features, I didn't mind those. I loved to watch the world from above, from my room on the ninth floor of our apartment building: the flat Black Sea coast, sprinkled with oil refineries and chemical plants. The hum of a large shipyard; buzzes of drills and bangs of sledgehammers invaded my teenage bedroom from six in the morning until late. I watched a tall crane rotating, lifting, lowering. On clear days, I could see workers, ant-size, milling on metal surfaces of emerging ships, their welding tools sparking. I did not know back then that a view of a shipyard was not 'great' and that sulphuric acid from a nearby chemical plant was leaking into the sea. With its changing colours, the sea was an enchanting backdrop to my young life: sparkling blue, aquamarine, greyish-blue, grey, lead grey, black. Marea Neagră. The Black Sea.

My hometown, personified in my conservative mother, became too small-minded and controlling. Bucharest was large enough and far enough. I was outside my parents' reach; I remember the exhilarating sense of freedom. To get there, I had to choose a course of study not offered at Constanța's Ovidius University. My father, an education fanatic, let me go. I had always made him proud at parent–teacher interviews, so he owed me this. To study journalism under Ceausescu was probably silly, but what did I know at eighteen? I did not feel the communist oppression then. In high school social studies classes, we criticised Western consumerism and the 'false liberties' of capitalist countries, with conviction. Nonetheless, Western products were status symbols with special allure. The 'elite' of my class had something 'foreign' to cherish and show off: a pair of jeans, a little bottle of perfume, a piece of costume jewellery, a pair of Nike or Reebok sneakers. We did not see a contradiction.

## 2

I've always thought my undergraduate years were the happiest of my life – a pretty face, a taut body, all the adult rights but not yet all the adult responsibilities. But then, just yesterday I found a diary from that time full of gloomy thoughts and self-doubt. My love life, with its emotional intensity, dominated. The diary helped me remember that only a knife's blade separated my youthful joys from melancholy, which could be triggered by a mere rainy Sunday afternoon. I could be the life of the party, but some days I glumly avoided people. Was I emotionally unstable in my youth? It must be the issue with the occasional diary, a scribbler writing to unburden her weary soul; when she was happy, she just lived.

Once in Bucharest, I was awakened, excited, elated. My

little private freedom eclipsed the repression and poverty that descended onto the nation like a sullen, heavy cloud. The 1980s, Ceausescu's austerity decade, made the food in the student canteen, previously mostly edible, revolting. Pork-chops-and-chips that were always in high demand soon disappeared from the menu. Thin soups, where much was made with little, thickened by flour fried in pork lard, became regular items on the menu. A year or two later, even pork lard became a luxury, at least for the city folk. 'Power reductions' were at first being announced, but later became increasingly random as well as more frequent. People grumbled but did not dare to complain openly. The district central heating worked only for a couple of hours in the morning. We shivered in our student rooms and studied mainly in bed, under a duvet, one arm outside holding a book, the hand acquiring a bluish hue.

Libraries were poorly heated, too. Hot water in the shared bathrooms was available two evenings a week. Yet at nineteen, bathroom queues were not enough to kill the joy of being alive. In the evenings, we read with torches, if we could procure batteries; shared student rooms had squinty forty-watt bulbs on the ceiling. In lecture theatres, we sat on uncomfortable wooden chairs wrapped in our winter coats and scarves. My parents' incomes shrank and with them my monthly allowance. Their earnings were still too high for me to be able to claim the state-provided stipend, so I was in a financial clinch. I needed a job.

My first job, short but unforgettable: Monica and I apply through the student employment service. We're called to start immediately; ominously, there's no competition for the job. At 10 p.m., a special bus takes us to a night shift in a detergent factory. As we reach the industrial zone on the edge of the city, the city lights, already dimmed by electricity reductions, disappear altogether. We never learn where exactly the factory is. We are dropped at the entrance of hell and follow the scrum of women into the factory hall. Our job is to hold large plastic bags upright and wrapped around the opening of a tube coming down from the ceiling, while white powder flows down into the bag. In spite of the gauzy face masks we are given, our noses and throats are full of detergent dust within minutes. The factory in-joke is that we can make soap bubbles right out of our mouths.

At 2 a.m., we have a short break in a cramped locker room; there's nowhere else to go. On our second night at work, two women's dispute turns into a punch-up. One has accused the other of stealing money from her purse. Monica and I sit holding our half-unwrapped sandwiches and watch, stunned and speechless.

'You dirty thieving Gypsy,' the accuser mutters threateningly as she confronts a slight woman with raven-black hair. 'I'll break your sticky fingers.'

The hatred on both women's faces is intense.

There's nowhere for us to escape to, except to the smelly toilet or back to the factory floor. Women around us sit on low shoe lockers munching their food, looking into the middle distance, expressionless; the way of distancing when no physical distance is possible. Yet they twitch, alert to the proximity of punching and kicking limbs. Someone calls the supervisor and a short, sturdy woman waddles in and separates the brawling parties in a matter of seconds.

Monica and I left the job after a week. During that week we learned a great deal about our country's social stratification.

Some women did this job for years, perhaps their entire lives.

Having heard the story, my parents approved my resignation. The carefree youth, with that precious innocence of taking things and people for granted: parents, grandparents, life itself, whose end is in the incomprehensible, hazy distance. Whatever happens, one is hopeful and spared the worst thing; parents insert themselves between oneself and the trouble, in Romania at least. It's different here in Australia. Whenever I see a homeless youth on a Melbourne street, the Romanian in me thinks: 'Where are his parents? Do they know their child is sitting on the pavement with a handwritten cardboard sign, begging?'

# 3

My weekend visits home: at least once a month, with a student discount on the *rapid*, a train not as fast as the name may suggest. I walk from the railway station to my parents' apartment through the dark, brooding streets of Constanța. The use of electricity is rationed; only street corners are lit up. I have told my father not to pick me up, as petrol is severely rationed too. It's only a short walk anyway, and the streets are safe. The worst thing that can happen is to encounter a hungry stray dog, but I have some biscuits with me. The stray dogs are too weak and too scared to be aggressive. People are barely able to feed their children, so they have abandoned their dogs. Dogs eat meat and meat is expensive. Stray cats fare better, searching the rubbish bins and catching mice.

I arrive in front of the building undisturbed. I ring the bell downstairs, then I push the heavy wired-glass entrance door and out of habit, walk to the lifts. Bummer! The lifts cannot go up without electricity. The bell doesn't ring either. I walk nine floors up with my little suitcase – a decent amount of exercise.

My mother opens the door and I hug her, breathing heavily. My dad squeezes me tight against his chest and kisses me on both cheeks. The lounge room is candlelit. It's not romantic; they look serious and withdrawn.

It is hard to pretend all is well while sitting in a cold, dark room. The long radiators under the windows are stone-cold. A little blue light is flickering in the corner of the room. My father, a naval engineer, managed to get a *butelie*, a gas bottle, from his shipyard.

'So glad we took this heater from the old flat instead of selling it for peanuts as you had suggested.' My mother turns to my father, then towards the gas heater on wheels. 'I told you, one never knows.' Mama has always been pessimistic about the future and during the 1980s she is right increasingly often. That afternoon, she stood in a queue to get cooking oil and sugar, and 'coffee' made mainly of oats.

Mama sighs. 'It would be nice to have a proper cup of coffee instead of this insipid horsefeed.' She sheds her slippers and lifts her feet up on the coffee table. She complains about her varicose veins. One candle burns on a tall shelf, on top of the bar, illuminating a wooden carving of Ceausescu's bust, of dubious artistic value, next to the red leather-bound *Illustrated Youth Bible* my father bought when I was twelve, and an even thicker, dark green volume of *The Dictionary of Foreign Words and Phrases*. A heavy metal bust of Karl Marx serves as a bookend. I wonder why they keep Ceausescu in their living room, but I don't ask. Politics is a depressing subject these days.

They wait for my news, something to distract them from the bleak present. Ah, I know!

'I met a nice Yugoslav boy at the volleyball tournament in Novi Sad last weekend. In fact, I first met him in the Universiade in Bucharest last summer, so this was our second meeting. We stayed in touch. He's in the senior Yugoslav team. Two years older than me.'

Mama and Tata stay quiet for a few moments. I cannot see their facial expressions properly: approval or disapproval? It's January 1982, I'm a year and a half into my degree, and my mother's fear I'd go wild when not under her watchful eye has abated. Did you like Novi Sad, my father asks.

'A really nice town, but they have some restrictions over there, too. Not as bad as ours. This year's May Day volleyball tournament is to be held in Constanța and his team is coming, so we'll meet again.' I pause. 'His name is Filip.'

They wait for more.

'I can speak with him in Serbian,' I brag. 'He sometimes laughs at my sentence construction, and my declensions, but he understands me. He is Croatian, from Zagreb. He says Serbian and Croatian are the same language. "Serbo-Croatian". But we mainly speak English. He speaks Italian quite well too, so he is able to understand some Romanian.'

'Meeting every six months, well that's something! It may not be often enough to . . . to . . .' Mama is at a loss as to how to finish the sentence. 'You may forget about him. Or he about you.'

'Forget about *me*? Not a chance!' I spread my arms in jest and smile. 'We're staying in touch by letters. And by telephone. His mum works at the phone exchange so he can speak interstate and internationally for free.'

'Their coast is nice!' My dad joins the conversation. 'I've been there several times on business trips, to the Rijeka, Pula and Split shipyards, a few years back, in 1975 and 1976, I think. A fantastic coast, many islands, and I am sorry to say, much nicer than ours—'

'Oh, don't be silly, Bogdan . . . !' My mother interjects. 'It's nice here.'

'—and they earn more than us. A better standard of living.

Most of my Yugoslav colleagues have German or Italian cars. They can travel abroad as they please ... Do keep in touch with your Croatian boyfriend, Francesca. What's his full name?'

'Filip Kolar. His father is from Bosnia, and mother from the coast. One grandma is Italian. I forget the island's name ... it was hard to pronounce.'

'Brač? I've been there. They took me there on a boat trip from Split. They have several smaller shipyards on the island. We had an excellent seafood dinner in a town called Milna and lots of local red wine. They make great red wine, those Dalmatians.'

'I bet they do! Business trips were invented for that purpose, for eating and drinking, if not worse!' my mother quips. 'And just as well.' She suddenly softens. 'You can only dream about it now, travelling abroad or even just eating well.'

'No, it was not the island of Brač. "Brač" is easy to pronounce, it sounds almost Romanian. It was some impossible name with no vowels. You'd need a speech pathologist to help you say it properly.'

I smile at my mother, a speech pathologist, but she is not cheered up by my banter. My father is remembering good times and I am hinting at fleeing westwards, but she is sleepless with worry about the future and tired of waiting in queues. She feels responsible for us all, and she cannot forget we are sitting in a poorly heated room smelling of gas, in the candlelight, and that her monthly salary is just enough to buy food for the family. Florian is not helpful; he hides behind his full-time student status, plucks on his guitar and ignores everyday problems. 'Tightening the belt' is the government's order; Ceausescu suggested Romanians would be better off if they ate less, as the nation had started to get plump. Luckily, my father earns substantially more than Mama, so they can just make ends meet and still partly support my studying in Bucharest.

Eventually I manage to distract them from their candlelit gloom. We have a cold supper with a glass of cheap red, and my dad tells a couple of jokes. We go to bed early. I try reading in bed using my faithful torch, but the previous conversation has created a whirlpool of thoughts and I cannot focus on the book. I think of Grandma Cosana. She spoke to me in Serbian. I spent much time with her and Grandpa Ilia as a pre-schooler. Grandma Cosana died of cancer when I was fifteen, may she rest in peace. Her mind was sharp, her manner fierce, but she was always gentle with me. She hugged me and kissed me at every opportunity until I became too big to sit on her lap. When I was a little older, a teenager, she told me: 'There is a better country out there, where the sun sets. Serbia. Yugoslavia.' Is this why she spoke to me in her old country's language? How did she know what was happening in her old country? She never spoke about it, or her family.

Grandma Cosana met Grandpa Ilia in Timişoara in the 1930s, when he was a young soldier. She was a teenager, barely eighteen. She never revealed much detail, and I was too young to be interested. My father did not seem to care about where and how his parents met. My mother was cryptic about it: 'I do not know much. People from Banat were selling their produce in Timişoara. There were big livestock fairs there back then, before the war. Grandma Cosana did not speak much about it. And Grandpa Ilia, you know him – he never spoke much about anything.'

I look up at their wedding photo on my bedroom wall. I think Grandma Cosana was a Gypsy. A light-skinned, fine-boned, green-eyed one. In the photo her hair is dark and shiny, her eyes and lips extra shapely, slightly exotic. She loved horses and knew how to calm them down and make them do what she wanted. She must have been a beautiful and spirited girl.

A young, sex-deprived soldier would have been head over heels with her at the first sight. She probably plotted her escape and when Ilia was discharged from the army, she ran away with him in her best outfit, carrying only a small wrap of spare clothes. They married in a hurry and that was it. She was now Român, a Romanian, rather than a Romani, a Gypsy woman: a very important difference. That's how I imagine it happened, but I may be wrong. I like the idea that I'm one-quarter Gypsy.

# 4

The correspondence with Filip intensified and became much more personal after our second meeting. He seemed to pay attention to my long letters even though his were shorter. He was smart and perceptive but not a natural writer. Phone conversations were still a bit awkward, perhaps his mother might be listening. Someone was always listening. We didn't have phones in our student rooms; there were three open phone booths in the foyer of our dormitory wing. I had to arrange a time for him to call. This did not allow for much spontaneity or privacy. When we talked, Filip would switch from Croatian to English quite often. He wanted me to practise my 'Serbian', but English was easier for me.

He was in the final year of his degree, a top student. As a young Tito's Pioneer, a decade earlier, he had been a gymnastics champion. I had joined the senior national selection recently, so both of us were in the first volleyball teams of our respective countries. I liked to watch him play. He was tall, slim but strong, and had the shapeliest legs a man ever stood on. He was one of the team's two main shooters. His movements were languid, but he was always fast enough to jump and smash the ball hard across the net; like a snake slithering slowly and then suddenly soaring into a high precision attack. He said he was looking forward a lot to seeing me again in May, which made me feel a little giddy.

The Yugoslav senior men's team beat the Hungarians and Romanians in Novi Sad. It was better that way. Hungarians and Romanians hated each other, and Yugoslavs were a neutral party of a sort.

We meet again at the May Day tournament, brimming with pent-up desire. In Novi Sad, we shyly held hands while watching others play, but now it's a different story. The teammate who shares Filip's hotel room has agreed to stay out until 11 p.m. I am so glad I lost my virginity during my first university year in Bucharest; I would not have wanted *that* to be in the way of this much-anticipated lovemaking.

I am grateful to Flaviu, who was relentless in his pursuit. He was twenty-four, a mature age student, a passionate and adventurous type, but I could not fall in love with him. Yet he was so persistent I eventually relented. The sex was good. Learning sex is easier when one is not 'in love', as there are no gushing emotions, no breathless excitement, no stage fright. There was no fear of pregnancy either, because Flaviu had a low sperm count. With him, I got a good deal: satisfying, unadulterated sex combined with almost fatherly care. Flaviu thought it was a big deal that I 'gave him my virginity' but I did not think much of it. I found his old-fashioned attitude, limited to this specific issue, half amusing, half irritating.

But now with Filip, it is different. I am in love. He is a gentle lover, not as expert as Flaviu, and a little ... absent-minded ... ? But the deed is done, all went well, and I am relieved. I feel as if we have passed an important test.

Later I ask him to come to my parents' place for lunch.

'Now that you went to bed with me, I must meet your parents and marry you, huh? Is this how you do things in Romania?' he jokes.

'Well, you're only here for three days and who knows when again, and they are curious. I told them about you. They are long married and have been doing the same jobs for decades, and life is a little monotonous. Meeting you will be their excitement of the month,' I joke back, but it's the simple truth. 'Don't worry, my mother is a good cook. And you'll be across the border in two days, where we cannot follow you and make you marry me.' I laugh. He smiles.

The lunch is scheduled for the last day of the tournament, after the morning finals. Luckily, that's a day when we'll have electricity. His team is due to fly back home in the evening.

On the evening of the second day, I sneak into Filip's hotel room again. The second time, we are more relaxed. He admires my breasts and plays with them a lot, kisses them gently. I enjoy being pressed against his almost hairless, chiselled chest.

'All that training!' I smile as I run my fingertips across his six-packed stomach. 'Do you think sex will diminish your performance in the finals tomorrow morning?'

He guffaws. 'No, I don't think so! Perhaps, if it were a hundred-metre race. But it's only volleyball.' He kisses my nose while gently holding my head.

I teach him how to say 'good day' and 'nice to meet you' in Romanian, so he can impress my parents. Introductions are quite awkward. My mother has made a special effort: schnitzels in a cream sauce – decent meat is hard to come by and expensive – and potato croquettes. Filip is an occasional beer drinker, and my father has had the foresight to have some in the fridge. I can see they approve of Filip. Tall, good-looking, top sportsman, well-educated, from a country due west: he ticks all the boxes. He even accepts my father's invitation to smoke with him.

I take him out on the balcony to 'see the view'. Mama hates it when people smoke in her lounge room, making her curtains and couches stink of cigarette smoke. Over an ice cream dessert, the conversation that started hesitantly develops freely in various languages. My father speaks some Serbian, my mother a little English. Inevitably, we discuss the Nadia Comăneci phenomenon. I often have to translate. We all smile and laugh a great deal to compensate for the absence of multilingual finesse. Florian is out and I am glad my siblings are not mentioned.

I see Filip off to his hotel. We share a long, full-length hug in the foyer. 'Take care of yourself, Francesca. Keep in touch.'

'You too! Have a good trip.'

Neither of us are into declarations of love. I've always disliked sentimentality. I prefer 'show, don't tell' and I think he does too. And I'd hate to appear a needy, clingy lover. I hope the distance will make our hearts grow fonder. And there is no chance we'll get bored with each other!

Filip has three flights home – to Bucharest first, then to Belgrade, then to Zagreb – and he'll only be home in the early hours of the morning. As an afterthought, I say, 'I've never been on a plane.'

'You're too long to be folded into a suitcase, but we'll fly you to Zagreb one day . . . soon.'

I like the promise. It'll keep me going.

## 5

That May I did not get my period. At first, I was just a little nervous; my period had been late before, even weeks late. Then came June. Each time I went to the toilet I hoped to see a stain on my underwear. The anxiety in the pit of my stomach was almost constant. If I forgot it for a few moments, it surged back into my consciousness violently, like a blow.

In late June my exams started, but I could hardly concentrate on studying. By then, I was sure I was pregnant. I told Sofia, my volleyball buddy. She was two years older than me, four years into her medical degree. She explained that a woman could lose her reproductive function, and hence her period, if her body fat dropped too low because of hard physical training. She already talked like a doctor. That was a glimmer of hope, but it had been nearly two months and I had to be sure.

I had to confide in my sister. Michaela and I had never been close, but there was a practical reason. Michaela was a lab assistant and could do a pregnancy test for me on the sly. Abortion was banned, and the penalties for illegal abortions were draconian: prison and a loss of medical licence for doctors, prison for women.

I call Michaela from a public phone at the Cișmigiu Gardens, where no-one can hear me. I often go for a walk there or take book to read or study on a bench when it is warm.

'Bring the first morning urine to my place, not directly to the lab,' Michaela tells me. She lives in a new suburb, quite far from the city centre, but there is no other way but to go there.

'I beg you, don't tell Mama, she'd panic.' I'm not sure Michaela will do as I ask. 'At least don't tell her before it is all over,' I add.

'Let's see what the test says first. Have you had any morning sickness?'

'No, but some foods I normally like now smell repulsive and my breasts are tender for weeks now, like before my period . . . which is not coming.'

'Hmm,' is all Michaela says as she nudges her two pre-schoolers through the front door. We leave them both, a four-year-old girl and a toddling boy, in a nearby kindergarten, then travel downtown together. Her lab is not far from my faculty. A crowded bus is not a great opportunity for a catch-up. I'm not too sorry about that.

'Call me after three in the afternoon.' Michaela waves and gets off the bus.

At 3 p.m. I am back at the Cișmigiu Gardens. A male voice answers the phone. Michaela picks up a few moments later and talks about our mother, pretending we haven't seen each other for a long time. Someone must still be in the office with her even though work finished at three. A minute later she whispers: 'Positive.'

A jolt in my gut.

'Thank you so much, Michaela. Say hello to Petre from me.'

'What are you going to do?' she says a little louder.

'Oh, I don't know, Michaela! I have two years of university left. I'm not having a child in a hurry.'

'Take care of yourself. I have to run to pick up the kids. *Ceau!*'

I talk to Sofia again. She'll know somebody who knows somebody.

'Oh no! Are you sure?'

'Yep, done the test.'

Sofia groans. 'And what now ... ?'

'Well, you met Filip at the May Day tournament. This was when it happened. I've thought about it. He's in Yugoslavia and we are not even a mature couple. I'm not having a child at twenty! I have no choice ...'

'Less than two months. There's still time.'

'Do you know anyone?'

'I've heard a rumour about a gynaecology nurse. I may inquire through a third person. Perhaps Imre.'

Imre is Sofia's colleague and boyfriend *in spe*, a final-year medical student. He'll have a vested interest in keeping the secret. Asking him probably means Sofia plans to succumb to his advances. It is risky even to ask around about abortion. One has to be sure not to ask the wrong person. *Securitate* informers are everywhere.

'Imre can lend you money, he has enough savings.'

'Sofia, you are my salvation!'

'Did you tell Filip?'

'No. I spoke to him, and I was a little tempted ... but I stuck to my decision not to tell him. He could think I did it deliberately to "get him". And even if he would be happy about it and want to have a child, that's not what I want. Not now. No way! Then what would he say? That he was sorry? Offer me half of the doctor's fee? Or the whole amount? If he was here with me, of course, we'd talk about it. But at this distance, over the phone ...'

'Yes, it is an emotional minefield,' Sofia concurs.

'A relationship Russian roulette. It could easily kill it,' I add.

'Yes, this would not necessarily bring you closer together. Difficult.'

'Sofia, we sound like two wise old women, don't we?'

She just squeezes my hand.

I feel intensely sorry for myself.

I should have known better: I did not want to ruin the so-much-anticipated lovemaking with Filip with *coitus interruptus*. There's no legal contraception in Romania, but he could have brought condoms from Yugoslavia. The thought had occurred to me, but how could I have asked? I could not! I counted on my luck and now I am paying for it. Flaviu's infertility lulled me into a false sense of security. Filip's sperm count was obviously better.

I will have to stick it out. I need some luck, and some money.

Two days later, Sofia comes back with a report. 'Some nurses do it for roughly their monthly salary . . . which is not huge money . . . but it is risky. I know of a woman who died. You don't hear about it, but it's happening. Nurses do not study medicine. Some learn the ropes by assisting gynaecologists but . . . you need a proper doctor, a gynaecologist. Which I'm guessing will cost more.'

'How do I find one? How much will it cost?'

'I don't know. You could do it safely and legally in Yugoslavia, but you need permission to leave the country, a convincing reason. And as a foreigner there, you'd still need to pay.'

'Sure thing. There is another tournament in Zrenjanin in early July, just before the summer break. It's a junior competition and I was not going to go. I have exams too . . . but I can talk to the coach, and he'll include me on the list. He's an easy guy and he likes me. He knows I have a Yugoslav boyfriend so a nudge and wink will do. That'll be over two full months of pregnancy, not too late, is it?'

'Pregnancy is counted from your last period. That'll be ten or eleven weeks, still well within the recommended parameters.' Sofia looks serious but pats my hand encouragingly.

A desperate thought occurs to me: I could flee after that, ask for asylum in Yugoslavia. Then what? Call Filip? Tell him what happened? Expect him to welcome me with open arms, take me under his wing, marry me . . . ? I'd be damaged goods, a woman after an abortion. Perhaps he'd hate me aborting his child? No, no, no! That is all silly. He should not know. I'll come back home, finish university. I hope Filip and I will last. I don't want to ruin it.

～✑～

It is all done efficiently and professionally by a woman doctor. Sofia has dug out a name and a hospital's phone number through her connections, bless her! The doctor is about forty, a serious but warm face, warm hands, supportive attitude. She earns a bit on the side after hours, Romanian customers. She is not a villain and her fee is not exorbitant. She helps desperate women. She was impressed by my knowledge of Serbian when I first called to arrange a meeting. Thank you, Grandma Cosana!

I come to her surgery after 8 p.m. The doctor locks the door and gives me a local anaesthetic. No anaesthetist to put me to sleep as is usual for registered procedures, she explains. She suggests I take a tranquiliser immediately and gives me one for later, in case I need it. *Apaurin*, printed on the silver foil cut out of a larger panel.

The procedure does not take long. I am frightened, but the pain is successfully dulled. The doctor is careful and focused. Lying there with my feet high up in stirrups and legs spread, I am pleased the doctor is a woman. It just makes more sense. She can empathise, perhaps. She tells me I am likely to have mild, dull pain afterwards and a brownish mucous secretion for a few days. However, any serious bleeding or painful cramps will require an urgent medical intervention. Avoid cold water and wet bathers until your next period, she says.

She drops me off at my hotel. 'The taxis are expensive even for us.'

I take a strong painkiller and an *Apaurin*, just in case, and fall into a deep, dreamless sleep from which I am awakened by my roommate shaking me by the shoulder. The ten-hour bus trip back to Bucharest is scheduled for 7 a.m. I stretch from a foetal position and rush to the toilet. Everything looks under control inside my undies; a huge sense of relief. If I had needed medical attention, all would have been revealed. An even stronger sense of relief comes from the knowledge that I am back in the land of the non-pregnant.

⌒∂⌒

At the end of July, I was ready to resume normal life. Only one of my exams had been moved to the autumn exam period because of the trip to Zrenjanin. It was comforting to have Sofia, who knew what happened and cared. She thanked me for telling her about the whole thing in as much detail as I could remember. I didn't mind contributing to her medical knowledge this way. Her support was crucial, before and after.

Sofia became a professor of medicine and we have remained close friends to this day.

# 6

My parents spent the second half of July in our holiday house. I excused myself with university work and the exam coming up in autumn. I got my next period at the start of August, an entirely normal one. A huge relief, once again. Thank you, body, for not making any dramas! Mama and Tata returned to work in August and I headed for my vacation. There was a part-time job on offer for a month in the tourist office, replacing a woman on maternity leave. I was suitable because I spoke English and Serbian. It was a good opportunity to earn some money and return the debt.

The job left enough time to loll on the beach, close to an old stone cottage built by my great-grandparents, and renovated into a holiday house by my parents, in better times. Monica was coming with me. It had been hard to persuade her father to let her come.

323

'What's his problem?' I asked.

'He thinks I am going to return home pregnant. You know, ruin my future.'

Monica didn't know about my recent drama. Was pregnancy the worst fear of all parents of young unmarried women? In Romania at the time, quite possibly.

'But you're still a virgin!'

'He doesn't know that. We don't talk about such things.'

I sighed. 'Your parents are so conservative. Your father, anyway. My mum is too, but not quite as bad. What about your mum?'

'I don't know. She doesn't seem to have opinions. She's not expected to have them, maybe not even allowed! My dad is a tyrant. She had plenty of opinions about you coming to lunch in a T-shirt with no bra though.' Monica rolled her eyes dramatically. 'You know, looking like that in front of my brother and father!'

'Oh! I'm sorry to have caused trouble. In fact, you know what, I'm not sorry at all. They should step into the twentieth century! It's 1982!'

'Not a hope!' Monica concluded.

'Is this bra incident the reason why we all had to beg your father to let you have a summer holiday with me, including my dad phoning him?'

'Oh, I don't know. He's like that, a pain in the arse. Crusty old military man. The only thing that convinced him was that your father was an engineer. As if that's relevant!'

That summer, after my abortion in Serbia, Monica and I were going to have a quiet holiday. But it turned out a 'quiet holiday' was not possible at age twenty.

❧

Another photo: my hardworking, super-handsome Gypsy boy, Luca. I remember the hot August afternoon when we first spoke.

After plunging into the shallow sea to refresh, still dripping, I hurriedly tiptoe across hot pebbles and buy two *înghețate la cornet* from a visibly bored woman servicing the ice cream trunk fridge. One of the last luxuries Romanians can still afford in 1982: an ice cream on a hot day.

Upright and smiling, wearing a dazzling white T-shirt, Luca is leaning on his souvenir stall tucked between the fridge and a newspaper kiosk. I smile back and stop on a whim.

'Hello, how is it going? Boiling hot today, hard to walk barefoot!' I jump on a cool patch of grass.

'All good here *chez Oncle Luca*, thanks for asking – keeping in the shade, and the trade is not going badly!'

'Oh yeah? Authentic local handcrafts? Popular with the foreign tourists, are they?' I wink and nod towards a legion of shiny wooden storks and cigarette boxes mass-produced in an inland factory.

'You'd be surprised. Foreigners who holiday at the Black Sea Riviera love this stuff.' Another flash of white teeth. I know him, by sight; he's been here for years but we've never spoken before.

'Maybe you're just a great salesman.'

I am flirting with a Gypsy! Perhaps the thought of Monica's conservative parents is inspiring me?

'I'm Francesca, nice to meet you.' I stretch my arm across and knock over a couple of tall storks.

He laughs and shakes my hand. 'We kinda know each other, don't we?'

'Indeed.'

A pleasant scent reaches my nostrils as he stretches forward to tidy up the stall. After another minute of small talk, he asks me what I am doing that night. Not wasting his time! We quickly agree to meet for a drink, which includes Monica, of course. He offers to pick us up – he has a car! My father only managed to buy one in his late thirties, just as I was starting school.

'Oh no, no need to, honestly. My house is a skip and a jump from the beach promenade.'

The ice creams are getting soft in my hand. I rush back to the beach.

'We're going out with a Gypsy tonight? People will talk,' Monica says matter-of-factly, outstretched on her beach towel.

'They sure will!' I expect a flurry of gossip among my many relatives and feel a strange excitement about the transgression. I am not concerned about my local reputation; I don't even live in Constanţa, let alone in this small coastal village.

That night, the three of us sip our drinks, trying to have a conversation despite a noisy live band playing sugary tunes under the trees. Luca sounds smart in spite of never even attending high school. Roma boys in Bucharest are expected to start earning money as soon as possible, he explains. At twenty-four, he has ten years of full-time work behind him, buying, selling and cab driving. His uncle, with a stall at a beachfront nearby, owns both the souvenir business and the cab.

It is close to midnight when he drops us home in his sturdy Dacia. I invite him in. Monica wishes us good night and retires to her upstairs room at once. Bringing a man home on the very first date is another transgression, this time of my own rule.

Later that night, we establish that Luca's belly is a lighter colour than my tanned skin.

'So much for the racial differences,' I say.

'I have no time to lie on the beach, like some nice girls I was lucky to bump into.' He laughs and gives me a peck on the lips.

'My paternal grandmother might have been a Gypsy from Yugoslavia.' After hearing the story, he thinks it likely.

The following weekend my parents arrived. There was tension in the air; they suggested we 'talk'. It started politely. Yes, it was true I was dating a Gypsy and sometimes driving his car. Yes, he had stayed overnight. My parents looked increasingly agitated by my lack of contrition.

'Luca is smart and kind and he earns more than you, Dad…'

My father turned red in the face.

'Listen, Francesca,' – he only called me by my full name when he was cross with me, which was rare – 'even if he had a PhD and a million dollars, he would still be a Gypsy.'

A stinging disappointment: my father was an ordinary, garden-variety racist! I knew most people would feel the same as him, but I had imagined he was above the fray. His blunt declaration strengthened my resolve. War bugle! Rebellion! Luca wasn't just a pretty face, he was honest and reliable. It was lust that brought us together, but trust and respect developed quickly. The streetwise boy who had been navigating adult life since the age of fourteen entrusted all the proceeds of his sales – a large yellow envelope stuffed with various currencies – to me after a week's acquaintance.

'It's safer in your house than in my rented room in town,' was all he said. I did not count the money. I don't think he did either.

In early September, the holidaymakers were gone and the beaches grew deserted. My part-time job ended. Monica had left a couple of weeks earlier. It was time to leave, me back to university, Luca to his cab driving in Bucharest. Early one morning, we left in his Dacia chock-a-block with bags and boxes.

As we were driving into Bucharest, Luca asked me whether I'd move in with him, instead of sharing my student room with another girl.

'If I did that, my parents would cut off my financial support.'

'You don't need them; I'll support you until you finish university and get a job.'

I did not know what to say. In Luca's world, girls were married with children at twenty. Luca would have been married himself by now, but his fiancée turned out to be 'no good', whatever that meant; I did not ask.

'No hurry. Think about it,' he said sensibly. 'I'm staying with my grandma, but we could rent a small flat together. Let's go to Oksana's place first, she'll be delighted to meet you.'

'How odd! Almost the same name as my Serbian grandma, Cosana – just jumbled letters.'

'Yes, that's the Serbian way; they spell it with "K" though.'

Luca kept impressing me. On top of his many virtues, he was a careful and skilful driver, not fatigued by the long trip. I felt a rush of love for him. Should I move in with him after all? I thought of Filip. Who knew what he was up to this summer? He might be in another girl's arms.

Oksana was a diminutive woman of seventy. She treated me as one of her own from the get-go, with the same warm but not uncritical devotion she bestowed on Luca, her oldest grandson. She was illiterate but her mind was sharp. Under her gaze, one felt transparent.

I am not sure where exactly in Bucharest we are; it was already dark when we meandered through a network of small streets. Luca's teenage half-brothers, nicknamed Albu and Negru, White and Black, make an appearance to say an awkward hello. Albu has blue eyes; Luca explains this was because his father is Român. Not a Gypsy. Oksana's place is a small granny flat. Only a curtain divides the kitchen and three sleeping alcoves, one for the boys, one for Luca and one for herself. There is no bathroom, just an outdoor toilet.

'The boys often disappear for a day or two to stay with Mama or with our uncle.'

While we're having Oksana's pilaf for dinner, Luca's mother drops by before work. She is a woman of forty with beautiful features and a hesitant manner, a folk singer, entertaining in the pubs of Bucharest. In spite of heavy make-up, she looks like Luca's older sister; she had him at fifteen. Luca addresses her by her first name, Elena. Oksana treats her brusquely. Elena is the black sheep of the family, twice divorced, and with Albu born out of wedlock. Gypsies are traditional about sex and family, even more so than other Romanians. A pub singer must wear too much make-up and revealing décolletage, but mingling with heavy-drinking, lustful men night after night inevitably stains a woman's reputation. Her brother, Luca's uncle, is an energetic and short-fused man in his mid-forties, the clan's patriarch. His brick-and-tile house in a 'white' suburb and a banana-coloured Mercedes sedan, a mid-1970s model, are hallmarks of success. Like many of Bucharest's Roma people, he has a knack for business.

I soon realise that a woman aspiring to a professional job cannot be a proper Gypsy bride.

'Eat some more, you're too thin,' Luca's aunt remarks. A few other women nod their heads. The social life of the clan is intense and mostly takes place in this house. The concern is about my fertility, Luca explains afterwards. The enquiries about our wedding plans are regular, and marriage means having babies. A few. I keep saying I am still studying. Luca is in denial of the obvious problem: I'll never fit in.

We are at the crossroads. How can I explain to him why I think we are not meant for each other? Regardless of his

ethnic origin, I cannot see myself married to a Bucharest cab-
bie, trapped in a small city flat with a few children. I cannot
tell him this.

I am also nervous about falling pregnant again. We have
been careful, but I know *coitus interruptus* is not bulletproof.
Luca would love it if I fell pregnant, but I dread it. We don't
have much opportunity for sex at any rate; my student room
when my roommate is out, and Oksana's place, with curtains as
dividers, is equally awkward. For me, this adds a certain thrill
to our coupling, but the reality of our mismatch dims the spark.
Luca is devoted, but never pushy. It is hard to find much wrong
with him. In Roma society, he could be a perfect husband, but
I know I can never be a good Gypsy wife.

In early November, a frigid drizzle set in for days. As the university year heated up, Luca fitted into my life less and less. One
day, with a nagging feeling of guilt, I sat down determined to
write a letter; explain that I was not the woman for him, for
his world. My grandma Cosana would have approved of this
decision. She escaped the Roma society herself. She would
want me to be as free as a woman can be.

Luca was a proud and reasonable man, and after one failed
attempt to see me, and my second letter, a message really, asking him politely but firmly to give up on me, he obliged. He
left a brief note under my door: 'I thought we could be happy
together, but if this is what you decided, I wish you luck. Love,
Luca.' This cemented my high opinion of him.

# 7

In that kind of mood – a little sad, a little guilty, but too busy to dwell on it and determined to move on as quickly as possible – I phoned Filip and left an upbeat but urgent message on his answering machine. 'Hello Filip, Francesca here, how's everything? I haven't heard from you in a looong time, since July! Do you care to call me back? By-e!' I was slightly surprised when he called back the next day. I was not waiting anxiously for his call, and I was glad I felt that way. But it felt good to be in touch again.

Filip declared all was fine, as always. He was guilty of not keeping in touch, but he thought of me often, he said. He had spent three months at a sport teacher/coach internship, most of it outside the city. No phone handy. Sounding enthusiastic, he suggested I should move to Zagreb before I finished university. It was too long to wait for another two years. I could transfer my study to Zagreb University. He'd ask about the exam recognition at his first opportunity. I should bring a full, official transcript of my marks with me. If I meant to work as a journalist, I'd need time to brush up my Croatian anyway.

These were all good points. Moving westwards from the increasingly desperate Romania was an attractive prospect. Yugoslavia was a free country in comparison, and richer by several notches, especially its western part, where Filip lived. We agreed to do some more research at our respective ends and talk again in a couple of weeks. Filip and I understood each other; we grew up in different countries, but we belonged to the same social universe.

When we spoke again, he sounded like he had thought it through quite carefully. We agreed I would complete my third year of university in Bucharest, so that would be another seven or eight months. We could wait that long, he proposed, and I agreed wholeheartedly. It was a big move! Getting out of Romania might be difficult, I reminded him. Might it be simpler to not return from the next international tournament, he asked; one was coming up in spring. I could ask for asylum; my sporting prowess and a basic knowledge of the language would get me a foot in the door. Another way to get a free exit from Romania and Yugoslav citizenship down the track, was to declare ourselves engaged to be married. Marriage was just a formality, we agreed, perhaps naïvely – we were young.

Filip summed up the situation clearly. 'You see, Francesca, I am not going to move to Romania. If we want to be together, this is the only way.'

My parents went quiet when I told them about the plan. Tata nodded a great deal, visibly pleased with the prospect of my moving West, to an open country with a better standard of living. For my parents, this was also a definite proof my Gypsy affair was over, and I could imagine they were relieved. Mama worried that the refugee path to Yugoslavia was too radical and could block us from seeing each other in the future. She suggested that Filip send a letter of intention to marry me and I could try to get an individual passport based on that. As usual, she was right. Tata knew some people who could smooth the process. I was going to speak with Filip again.

I was not sure whether Tata's connections intervened, but the Romanian authorities were sympathetic. In December, they promised to issue an individual passport in my name. We normally travelled to international tournaments on a 'group passport' handled by the tour leader: a piece of stamped and signed watermarked paper with team members' photos and identity details, each photo stamped, the list checked by border police against our identity cards. While abroad, we were not allowed to separate from the group, apart from in a very small, agreed-in-advance perimeter, usually to the closest supermarket.

Getting a passport was slow. I was finally called to the passport office for an interview in May, just before starting my third-year exams. They asked me whether I still wanted to marry the Yugoslav. They had a point; the relationship might have not survived the six-month delay, but this one had. Filip was not fickle; in the serious business of emigration and marriage, this was an important virtue. I was looking forward to my great adventure, confident that Filip and I were a good match. In June, I finally collected my passport. We agreed I'd come over when I had cleared as many exams as possible in the spring exam period. I cleared all but one, Media Management in Socialist Romania. I thought the University of Zagreb might not mind that particular omission. There was only the last, fourth year to complete in Zagreb.

We met in the meantime, at yet another May Day international volleyball tournament, in the Hungarian town of Pecs. This time I asked him to bring condoms. Given the plan, we could now act like an established couple. I swooped on him with an avalanche of questions about the city of Zagreb, the university, Croatia, politics, media, his family, his house, travelling by plane, supermarket supplies. He answered patiently and with a great sense of humour. I felt very lucky. I wondered how all this was even possible; we had only dated a couple of times, as a side show to playing volleyball. But somehow it all felt right and natural. I felt peaceful around him. Apart from his perfect legs and excellent physique, he was well educated and quite cultured. What attracted him to me? Was it my exotic value? It was a momentous decision to import a foreign wife.

～⌒～

Filip sent me an air ticket Bucharest–Belgrade, as was his light-hearted promise a year earlier. I vividly remember the hot day in mid-July, when I stepped off the Belgrade–Zagreb train with one large suitcase, the other behind me at the train door. Filip grabbed both and took me to his father's car, which he had borrowed for the occasion. A silver Renault 5.

'Welcome to Zagreb, Miss Francesca Ionescu! It's hot and humid, but we'll soon head for the coast. To the unpronounce-able island of Krk.'

We drove to his home in silence. I was a little nervous about meeting his parents. We were there in ten minutes, along a wide, straight, partly cobblestoned road on which blue trams also ran, noisily and threateningly close. Filip had his own quarters on the ground floor of a family house surrounded by a shady garden, in the western outskirts of the city. Filip's father shook my hand and welcomed me with an intense expression on his face, then disappeared to another room, while his mother, a tall blonde with motherly curves, gave me a hug and kissed me on both cheeks. She then fussed over me for what seemed a long time. Was I hungry? Thirsty? Tired? Would I like a coffee? Did I need a shower? I smiled, saying as little as possible in my awkward Serbian.

I had a large glass of mineral water and went downstairs to unpack. I was now in Filip's hands and, contrary to my usual instincts, I was not concerned about it. Already at first sight, Zagreb looked much better than Bucharest. I had a great sense of freedom once again, the feeling I had when I left Constanța for Bucharest three years earlier. The austerity measures were on in Croatia too, and unemployment was high, but the city was full of Western cars and well-dressed people. Zagreb was cleaner and much less grey and worn-looking than Bucharest. There were no stray dogs. We could go to Italy anytime. Or

Austria. The real West was open to us. The only thing that felt oppressive was the humid summer heat.

We settled into the life of two students sharing a small flat, rather than the life of a cohabiting couple, which suited me fine. Our sex life was somewhat sparse; we were both busy and did not see a great deal of each other daily. I did not mind; we had long miles to walk together and we could 'keep ourselves for later'. I was aware our student lifestyle was only possible thanks to the support of his parents. His mother supplied cooked meals most days and took care of our laundry. I was highly appreciative of this, but Filip took it for granted. He was the only son and I thought he was a little spoiled by his doting mother, but I was too young and busy with learning the ropes of my new life to worry about this.

After his graduation, he enrolled in a master's degree and worked hard at his studies, while continuing his volleyball career, with training taking hours each day. I quit volleyball and studied diligently; failure was not an option. Brushing up my Croatian, including complicated declensions and conjugations, was tough brain gymnastics. Yet my studies proceeded without glitches, and I graduated with a degree in journalism by the end of 1984. I had to sit some extra exams, but the international transfer slowed me down only by a few months.

No-one was in a hurry to see us married, but we tied the knot in 1985, when Filip started his full-time job as an assistant lecturer. His parents were pleased with the prospects it offered him. I was chuffed when my first article in Croatian was published even before I graduated, a book review commissioned by my print media professor, who was impressed by my written exam. I gradually established a small network and started earning pocket money as a freelancer. Professor Ungar had a vast network of high-profile connections and was helping me find work. I was grateful, and hopeful; things were going well.

A few months after we married, I secured a steady 'external collaborator' position at a Zagreb weekly, and less than a year later, I was writing a weekly column on social and political issues in Eastern Europe. In comparison with Romania, Yugoslavia always came out looking good, even though both countries were living through their difficult austerity decade.

The Universiade took place in Zagreb in 1987, and I got to cover it for a local radio program. I was self-conscious about my accent, but everyone thought it was charming and made me stand out. I was memorable. To my surprise, my foreignness turned out to be a bonus. Was it a small-nation habit, being fascinated by foreigners? The following year, I started working part-time as an assistant coach with the Croatian women's junior volleyball selection.

We were now, three years after I stepped off the train at the Zagreb's main railway station, a financially independent, grown-up, married couple. We shared Filip's parents' house rent-free, which was an entirely usual set-up there and then, and still is. We were lucky to have our own floor in a family house rather than tripping over each other in a small high-rise flat, which was how most city people lived.

# 8

In 1990, after Filip's parents retired and moved to the country-side, graciously leaving us alone and in charge in our Zagreb home, we renovated it and spread to the first floor. A year later, our son was born. After two miscarriages, this was a great relief, a happy ending. Everyone's emotions were heavily invested in Bruno, the only son, the only grandson. A boy had been my secret preference, and probably everyone else's, not necessarily for the same reason. I was convinced men had easier lives and more freedom, and this is what I wanted for my child.

I was twenty-eight by then and gradually getting a clear idea of what being a 'complete woman' was like. Exhausting: one never stops juggling balls. But we were young and it was a good life by anyone's measure. Days, weeks and months rolled past in a flurry of activity. Friends admired our renovated house and its tasteful furnishing, and people patted me on the shoulder over my budding journalistic career. Bruno played in the garden with our friends' children. The results of my labours were palpable. My mother-in-law liked me and praised me often in front of other people – this had to be the ultimate proof of my virtue, we often joked. My first varicose veins coincided with Bruno's birth, and my first grey hair, which I spotted with a mixture of horror and pride.

So there I was: a wife, a mother and a mistress of a proper family household.

*Household!* It sounds innocuous enough, but soon after Bruno was born, I realised it was the place where a woman's brain gets irretrievably cluttered with the trivialities of life. It was my problem to have the shelves in the kitchen free of grease and those in the bedrooms clean of dust. It was my job to fluff up the cushions on the couch and take feather duvets out for airing. Not that anyone cared; Filip didn't seem to notice such details, but I did! Bruno had to be clean, happy and fed home-made meals, and that's always going to be the mother's job. Because she had a full-time job, the Eastern European woman of my vintage lived under an illusion that she could keep a compartment in her brain for herself, free of the quotidian clutter, devoted to higher-order, even creative pursuits, among which might have been her career, if she was lucky. But she was mistaken!

The household's tentacles grew out, the creepers of household thoughts entangled, unstoppably, the farthest reaches of my brain. Conducting a radio interview, a thought invades my consciousness: I need to buy some vegies for dinner on my way home. Will the open-air market still be open when I get out of the studio? A load of washing tomorrow morning early, so it gets dry during the day. The electricity bill may be overdue. I'll have to queue in the bank tomorrow. I lose track of my interlocutor, but I'm experienced enough to fake my way back into the conversation.

A woman is bound to lose this battle: the whole world supports the household colonising her brain.

After two years of assistantship, Filip became a full-time lecturer. I had good prospects as a journalist. Jogging in breaks between work, mothering, shopping, cooking, cleaning. I was not sure that Filip would ever notice how hectic my life was if I didn't tell him. I started telling him and he was taking it gracefully, promising more help and professing his love for me and Bruno, but little changed. We talked the talk of a modern couple but walked a rather traditional walk.

At the time Bruno was a sweet little boy of two or three, Filip started irritating me by his mere presence. Not his fault. He was a good man. It was marriage. From day one, the wedding day (she must look perfect, what terrible stress!), marriage is hard work for a woman. For a man too, most of the time, but he doesn't get emotionally bogged in the aggravations of matrimony. Things other than marriage make men tick: work, career, status, golf, football, hobbies, derring-do, women other than their wives, DIY, you name it!

Filip loved me in his lightweight, calm, uncomplicated way. He did not demand anything. If I didn't cook dinner, he'd find something in the fridge. If he ran out of clean underwear, he'd put on a load of washing, probably mixing whites with colours ...

But this never happened. In truth, I could have downgraded the role of a conscientious mother and housewife, but my inner woman could not tolerate that. There was a child; I would feel guilty.

Motherhood, the site of woman's oppression: the feminists surely got that one right. You may object at this point, dear reader: motherhood is beautiful, noble, you love your child unconditionally, experience all those indescribable feelings . . . Oh! Yes, you sure love them. They are your biggest investment. You invest your body in the pregnancy, childbirth, breastfeeding, the sleepless nights and the rest of the physical slog. Then there are emotional stakes, as the worst fear settles in your soul, about your children. If you're an Eastern European mother, it never goes away. By becoming a mother, I lost the pure, priceless freedom to keep the focus of my life within myself, rather than painfully decentred in another person. Because you care, you always care. Care is what you do.

I'll say again: Filip was a good man; gentle, undemanding, reasonable. But a good man, a good husband, is defined negatively: he's not a drunk, he does not brawl, he does not beat his wife, he does not chase other women, he does not waste money gambling. He does not have to *do* anything to be nice. But that's not enough to make a good woman. Oh no! To be a good woman, you must work hard for it: be helpful, loving, generous with your time, a good mother, devoted to family, supportive of your husband, self-sacrificial, forgiving. Caring. Doing, always doing.

Resentment set deep in my soul. I was beholden to others. Filip seemed content; he was happy to stay where he was, follow his routines day after day, year after year. His apparent peace was like a mirror showing my face distorted in a Munchian scream.

Good women let their talents become stunted, shrink their dreams into hobbies, careers into jobs. The world supports their indentured servitude sealed by love and devotion. I tried hard, but I could not quite fit into the mould.

There was also an angst harder to define. I could not just live and be grateful for what I had. An existential neurosis was gripping me, a demon flogging me: there's more to be done, gained. More of what? I knew it was not about the conventional spoils, money and fame, but I didn't know what it was. I still don't. There was someone inside my head from whom I could not escape, someone who was perhaps me, or perhaps not. Perhaps my father, the superego.

The state of grace eluded me.

A thought haunted me: what now? Would I just do the same day after day, then die? There had to be more to life, whatever 'more' meant. Yet a contrarian, pleading little voice persisted inside my head as well: why not *just live*? Friends over for dinner, hiking on weekends, theatre a few times a year, exhibition openings, career progression, a decent life. Filip could do it, helped daily with a glass of wine, or two, or three.

We were different.

A rational reason to flee had been on the horizon for a while, and it gradually assumed clear contours. The country was increasingly unsettled. After the spectacular fall of the regime and the breathtaking execution of the Ceausescus, Sofia, Monica and my parents were telling me Romanians were leaving the country in droves. Yugoslavia had galloping inflation, whooping unemployment, economic depression. The country was going to dissolve; in my journalistic circles a war was being mentioned as a realistic possibility.

Emigration was my project; perhaps it would be possible to find that 'something more' in another country. Filip accepted it unenthusiastically. The thought of leaving Yugoslavia – by then the independent Croatia in fact – would not have crossed his mind. Why upend everything and have it tough starting anew? He would have much preferred to be left in peace. He was easy to live with: no alarms and no surprises. An 'easy to live with' person is also a 'hard to work with' person, and marriage is work, especially with children, so that was a problem.

Poor man! I pushed him along, I felt him burdensome, and I felt genuinely sorry for him at the same time. Perhaps he deserved a better wife, not a well-rounded neurotic like me. Those possessed by the demon of not-wasting-time are never able to relax and let others do so, and always full of doubts that they've done enough.

To Australia then! Canada was too cold, South Africa unsettled, in Western European countries one felt like an immigrant forever, and to get to the US we had to play immigration lottery – not my thing. To apply for an Australian visa, I had to collect a formidable pile of documents, translated into English and certified. I worked even harder, slept even less, but in a few months, it was done; our application for permanent residency was submitted.

In Australia, I encountered the protestant ethic first-hand. I fitted into it nicely. There's something heroic, self-denying and almost touching in this focus on work, money and delayed gratification. Is southern European hedonism more selfish, more irresponsible, or just more rational? Filip sat down with his glass of wine, or two, now on an Australian couch drinking Australian wine, and looked perfectly peaceful, just like before, happy to watch a 'feel-good' movie. I observed him with a mixture of horror and envy. My movie-watching was purposeful, it was work: an

Australian movie could help me understand things around me, perhaps, or help brush up my third language. I could never unwind. Is this why I got cancer?

Our marriage soon disintegrated – it was just a matter of time. Filip and I slept in separate rooms and waited for the situation to somehow resolve itself. Here, it was much easier to divorce, but I had no energy and no money to leave. Leave where? Bruno was barely in primary school, too young to lose his father. So, I was married, but in fact I was single, aged thirty-six and celibate for over a year.

And then, straight from this marital stupor, one hot, windy, sluggish Sunday afternoon, I was delivered to a violent tumult of emotions. How could I suspect, while half-heartedly getting ready to see a local art exhibition, that I'd walk into a person who caused a turmoil in my heart, body and soul three hundred years earlier?

# 9

The drone of a dozen whirling ceiling fans creates a hypnotic atmosphere in the exhibition hall. Overheated visitors mill about in all directions like disoriented ants. I have agreed to accompany my old friend Marianne, who has just completed her fine arts degree and wants to suss out the local scene. I immediately lose her from sight, and I wander about distractedly. I randomly stop at a stall showing a half dozen modern paintings reminiscent of Matisse. A resonant man's voice addresses me from behind.

'I can tell you more about the group if you like.'

I turn around with a pre-adjusted all-purpose smile. There is a man, not young, mid-forties perhaps, dressed in black jeans and a white T-shirt with an inconspicuous logo above his left nipple, which shows through the thin, soft cotton. 'Southern Artists Collective.' His curly hair, silver in front, black at the back, sits on his shoulders. I become aware of my unwashed hair and perfunctory make-up. But it does not really matter – what has to happen, happens just the same.

'Yes, sure ... you must be part of this ... collective?'

'I am.' He steps closer and smiles. I suddenly feel even hotter; my hairline getting damp with sweat. There is a plant smell about the man, reminiscent of sage, and not a trace of a smell of sweat, remarkable in the heat. He has a striking face, not easily placed in any particular global location: not Indian, not African, not European, not Asian. His green eyes shine; bright eyes, no capillaries. His forehead is gently lined and two long curves around his mouth deepen when he smiles, revealing a line of white teeth. Clean shaven, with a small, fashionable goatee just under his luscious lip. Not a face one could forget. Have I seen it before?

'Are any of these paintings yours?'

'Yes, this one: A woman in the bath.'

'Is this your signature? Di-ego Mo-ore ...'

'Yes, that's me. Nice to meet you!'

'Nice to meet you too. I'm Francesca.' I point to the woman in the bath. 'She looks like you. Isn't that your face?'

He chuckles. 'I have two daughters. Perhaps it is one of them. It was not intended.'

The feeling of déjà vu deepens. Something is tugging on my memory, but I cannot put my finger on it. I feel so hot now I need to wipe my forehead. But I only have my wallet with me, men's style. I wipe my forehead with my forearm.

'It's very hot in here.' Justifying my inelegant behaviour.

'Yes, sorry, only the ceiling fans, no air-con in here ... You look unusual,' he says suddenly. 'Where are you from?'

I laugh. 'Looking unusual? Me ...? I am usually asked where my accent is from.'

He guffaws. 'Okay: where is your accent from?'

This question bores me to tears, in fact, but in this particular case I did ask for it.

'Romania. Croatia. It's complicated. You do not sound like an Australian either.'

'I am South American. Chilean, to be more precise. Here since age eighteen.'

A young man approaches asking for information on how to join the Collective. Diego scribbles his name and phone number on a piece of paper and hands it over to me, apologising.

'Let's have a chat in peace ... over a coffee. Please call me ... Fran.' He abbreviates my name to one syllable without my permission, as many Australians have done before him. He smiles at me sweetly. The face of the woman in the bath, definitely. The same enchanting eyes.

I stuff the piece of paper into my pocket and return to reality. The ceiling fans drone on, drowning the hum of visitors' voices. I spot Marianne at one of the nearby stalls and join her.

Diego looked like no-one else, I told Marianne. His face was not just cross-racial, having picked the best of everyone; it was timeless, ancient; further back from a Roman emperor's profile on a gold coin. It hailed from the pharaohs.

At this point Marianne lifted her eyebrows and looked at me askance from behind the wheel. (In Australia, one invariably spends much time in cars.) 'You seem *very* impressed ... and so quickly! Did he ask you for your phone number?'

'No, he didn't. But he gave me his.'

Marianne chuckled and upturned her hand into a 'told you so' gesture.

I pulled out the phone number weeks later, while checking my trousers pockets before washing. It's not that I had forgotten Diego Moore, but perhaps I sensed trouble. I thought I had lost the scrap of paper and was sorry and pleased about it at the same time. But now it seemed like fate. I had to call him.

Diego answered the phone quickly. He remembered our brief encounter at the exhibition, or at least so he said, convincingly. We arranged to meet later that week for an afternoon coffee. Heading to university that morning, I chose my outfit carefully and I put on my prettiest Italian sandals. I spent more than the usual five minutes on make-up. During the day, I was distracted, and my work progressed slowly.

I arrived first. Diego was late. In those eight minutes I became aware I was waiting for a man I knew nothing about and with whom I probably had little in common. Why did I want to meet Diego? I did not know. We were a poor match. He was a local *personality*, according to my friend Rose's intelligence. Whatever that meant. I was going to find out. I did not think of sex. It takes more than three minutes with a handsome bloke for me to start thinking of sex. I think this is true for most women, or perhaps I'm just subconsciously prudish? Men are simpler creatures: see an attractive body, desire it. Women are more complicated, more sophisticated. Or just more *soppysticated* perhaps, mixing love with sex too readily, to their own detriment. In hindsight, I was probably desperate for a distraction from a dead marriage.

Diego arrived in the same old pair of jeans and another simple, clean T-shirt. I was definitely overdressed. The 'coffee strip' was full of dressed-down, relaxed people.

His face surprised me again. A strong, perfect nose, full lips, the upper protruding a little over the bottom one. Beguiling green eyes and a smile that could make anyone but Jeanne d'Arc swoon. As he walked, effortlessly and flexibly like a cat, his slim body wafted beauty and harmony. Diego was not good-looking; he was beautiful, bewitching. When he sat down, muttering some apology for being late, the background sights and noises paled away. It was now only him and me. After less than five minutes, I was imagining what it would be like to kiss that mouth and smell his fragrant hair.

It was all too easy to extrapolate his exceptional looks to his character. But that proved wrong in about half an hour. Diego was not a man eager to defy convention. He was pragmatic; cheating at the game was easier than trying to change its rules. He pretended to respect monogamy ('Oh, you're married,' he said seriously) while juggling several lovers, who came and went without him trying hard, I was pretty sure. What woman would not want to have this man for a lover? The combination was incongruous: an Australian suburbanite looking like an Egyptian pharaoh. His artistic persona made more sense. There seemed to be some ancient wisdom behind his smile, his deep green eyes, but I was reading too much into his pauses, silences and the sweet, almost feminine smile. He was a natural at the art of seduction.

I left the café nearly two hours later utterly infatuated. Not because we had a fantastic conversation, we didn't. It was something else, something deep, undefinable, primordial, that bypassed my brain. No man had ever had such an effect on me before.

We were to meet again in six days, and I counted them off one by one. He invited me to his place. Not exactly his place, he explained; he was house-sitting. I did not care. I came there mid-afternoon and we made love. I could not wait. My advances were warmly welcomed, with a smidgen of irony perhaps. He must have been used to women throwing themselves at him. His smell, free of any cosmetics, made any resistance impossible. The way he made love, with a seductive nonchalance yet passionately, his proud uprightness, his unique gait, his elegance: he was above all leagues. A demon disguised as a human male.

My torture started three days later when he called to postpone our third date. 'I'll call you.' So here I was, deep in my thirties, waiting for the phone to ring hour after hour, minute after minute, like a besotted teenager. The rhythm of our dates was unpredictable, he called, then he didn't, we met, then I would not see him for weeks. We made love and I thought 'this is the meaning of life, no doubt'; he cancelled the following date and I was left in a painful state of desire. As a lover, I was appreciated, but my infatuation was not reciprocated. The attraction was mutual, but clearly asymmetrical; he desired me from time to time, no doubt as *one* of his casual liaisons, while I wanted him every waking moment. In rare moments of closeness, I was promoted from being just a female body to be penetrated for pleasure to being a casual confidante. 'I am hoping some meaning will come out of all this,' he told me, waving his arms around, pointing to dozens of paintings stacked along the walls of his studio. Diego was a talented artist, but his paintings of women were usually nudes, often headless. They were bodies, not people.

Fifteen years later, after a vivid dream about being detained in a Palermo dungeon, it dawned on me: Diego Moore was the Black Moore, reincarnated. This was why I had a premonition when I first saw him. I recognised his smell, his touch. I had many déjà vus, but of course, I could not know. He did not show any sign that he had known me in 1693, even though he had promised at my execution that we'd meet again.

I was easily seduced both times. What wretched detained witch could resist him and why would she want to? The Black Moor was a benefactor of a sort: a fascinating and respectful interlocutor who reinstated the dignity of a woman in chains, in the final months of her life, and an amazing lover who revived and reawakened her tortured body back to life and pleasure, before it was committed to fire. And at the end of the day, he was a good employee of the Spanish Inquisition, sending witches to the stake. I am sure he did not believe in witches; he played the game but cheated in it, back then and again three hundred years later.

He was just using me then and he was using me again now, in 1999. The second time round I didn't have any doubt about it, but it did not matter. I was spellbound again. Having been subjected to the obstacle course of Diego's silences and absences, my state of aching desire lasted beyond its natural course. I managed to maintain my pride though: I did not call him, chase him, beg him. He did not know the depths of my obsession. I was often tantalisingly close to doing stupid things, but I always resisted. It was of paramount importance to preserve my self-respect; this was a tiny patch of dry land, often flooded but still possible to stand on, saving me from drowning in the morass of almost unbearable longing.

Eventually, the teeth-grinding, groaning desire lessened in my body. A married colleague was only too happy to act as a conduit, as a puncture through which the lump of pain in my chest, and my groin, slowly fizzled out. My body relaxed from the spasm over Diego. Were the short, flaming ecstasies worth the long, intense agony? Being in his arms was the ultimate bliss, but I experienced enough pain to supply an anthology of romantic poetry. What was it, this burning passion? Perhaps my hormones, the final call of fertility?

Once the passion was finally snuffed out, dead and cold, after nearly two years, I was not at all sorry. I was free, cured. I felt like a person who walked out into a sunny, breezy day after weeks in hospital. I was not sorry about having known Diego, either. Without him, without the Black Moor, I would not know such a storm of feeling, an anti-marriage, was possible.

## *10*

The story of my infatuations could be titled '*A feminist in love or how Proust can ruin your life.*' Would I ever have felt like I did, had it not been for reading Proust at the tender age of sixteen? Hundreds of pages devoted to intricate descriptions of how he felt in the presence of Gilberte, who he was 'in love with', then a little later, Albertine. It's not natural; one needs to learn how to be 'in love' and how one should feel about an unrequited love. A mad and utterly unnecessary sexual obsession with one particular person when they don't reciprocate, and mainly because they don't.

But perhaps Proust was not where I first learned about being 'in love'? I knew how to be in love already at thirteen, or even earlier. At that time, I read *Angélique, Marquise des Anges*, a hyper-romantic French adventure novel in a pink binding, translated to Romanian, that I found on my parents' bookshelf. I pored over its several volumes with breathless attention, forgetting to eat and deaf to my parents' calls and requests: 'You're going to ruin your eyes!' I did ruin my eyes. I turned into a short-sighted bookworm even before I hit puberty.

But eyes were easy to deal with: glasses, contact lenses. Greater damage is a life marred by falling in love, repeatedly, where one person, often undeservedly and almost completely accidentally, becomes the focal point of the universe to which one's thoughts compulsively travel. The total absorption, the pain of not being noticed or not given enough attention, then a blind, stubborn hope of perfect happiness. The natural imperative to reproduce, packaged as poetry! What else? Once you're infected by the virus of romantic love, by reading, watching movies and listening to silly discourses of 'more experienced' people, it does to your mind the same as the herpes virus does to your body. You have it inside you, and at irregular intervals it bursts out and painfully reminds you of its presence. There is no cure. Diego was the paroxysm of my learning to be in love. I loved Filip in this heart-fluttering way too, for a while, but marriage soon took care of that. Overall, he was a wiser, more rational choice, thankfully, given we had a child together. I didn't feel Diego was a choice at all in fact, just like the Black Moor wasn't. It was like tripping on a rock and falling into the abyss.

Proust's harmful lesson lost most of its power by my early fifties. I had never been fully convinced that 'being in love' was something special and worthwhile, let alone the supreme experience. But a firm conviction based in incontrovertible logic could not kill the germ. In school, I was that hapless youth who earnestly believed that the messages of literary classics were the ultimate wisdom. I took them seriously and I wish I hadn't, I wish I could have avoided the infection somehow. I wish my teachers knew better. I wish they had told me Dostoevsky, Tolstoy, Joyce, Shakespeare, Sartre, all of them, were not gods, but deeply flawed human beings – selfish, vain, neurotic – who made their wives and lovers unhappy and neglected their children so they could ease their existential pain by writing, oblivious of what they were doing to their nearest and dearest.

What's the good in peeping across the hedges of years? Can worthy discoveries be made by treating one's life, one's things, one's memories, as an archaeological site? Proust believed so – he searched for the lost time, furiously writing his gigantic novel, locked in his cork-padded room. What a weirdo! He would have loved the lockdowns! What does it say about me, then, that as a teenager I read *À la recherche* from cover to cover, the whole gargantuan oeuvre written by a super-neurotic mummy's boy, and not at all riveting in fact? Fifty pages a day was my self-imposed quota, while my friends dated and partied, just like Proust himself did in *fin de siècle* Paris before he locked himself away, after his mother died.

I cannot say Proust ruined my life, but I'd certainly ban *À la recherche du temps perdu* for anyone under twenty-five, maybe thirty; these days people mature later. Stay innocent, sleep well at night, leave those unsettling classics alone! Push your boulder up the hill over and over, in vain, just don't think about it.

## 11

My natural death is around the corner: it's too late to learn from the past. Is excavating it a hobby of choice for people whose lives are nearing the end, once they stop caring about 'wasting time'? Fossils are dug up, dust brushed off them with utmost care, exhibits looked at carefully; they are then described, interpreted, inserted into a system. Committing the six lives to paper creates a semblance of order and meaning, like turning an unruly swarm of butterflies in the field into a tidy collection in a natural museum. Come to think of it, creating order has been one of my passions. A female urge, perhaps: cleaning, tidying up, fighting entropy to the last breath. Ironically perhaps, I feel like I finally *have time*, protected from the glare of life with its many demands in the penumbra of my illness. Am I allowed to say that perhaps I've reached some sort of conclusion, and therefore I don't mind dying? I've tried many things, I lived,

I loved, I was not fearful, I dared here and there, and perhaps *je ne regrette rien*. Bertie and I have not been *un grand amour*. We have not spent much time looking deeply into each other's eyes or lying together in a post-coital swoon. In return, he has not caused me too much pain either. Or me him, I think. At least, I hope not. Compared to the violent emotional seesaw over Diego – one part ecstasy, forty-nine parts agony – Bertie has been an excellent deal, a quiet and sensible attachment, my most neurotic moments excepted.

With Bertie, age must have dulled the intensity, and thank God for that. Slowing hormones, probably, rather than wisdom acquired through pain. Whatever it may be, these days I prefer to use the intensity of feeling, my life energy, what's left of it, for things other than romantic illusion. However, every now and then I feel that pain again for a few moments, when something, the way he looks at me, or more often the way he does not look at me when I'd like him to, recreates a faded but still discernible contour of the pathetic longing for that impossible kind of love, for the giddy depth of feeling of oneness in our bodies and souls. I know, that's not even love, and yet . . .

Will Bruno miss me? I am not sure whether to want a 'yes' or a 'no' to be the answer to this. I want him to remember me sometimes, maybe twice a week, with pleasant sadness, like I remember my recently deceased father. But I reckon that's more than his current rate of remembering his mother. It's not likely he'd remember me more often after I'm dead, is it? He's far away in California, absorbed in his quantum computers. But who knows? Perhaps he will quote me sometimes. 'My mother used to say . . .' I don't want to burden him with my illness. All he knows is that I have cancer but am feeling okay, for now. He never asks beyond what I tell him. Like his father. The blessed souls. No worst fears in their hearts. But

I am not sure; one never really knows what's deep in other people's hearts. Not even in one's own – Doctor Freud may have gotten that one right.

Not long ago, I had to face my age. Mirror, mirror on the wall, suddenly spoke differently, just like in the tale of Snow White. Only now I know what other people see when they look at me. Gaunt, faded. Abruptly, overnight, I see a woman in her late fifties – and that's what I am. I knew the eternal 35-year-old was an illusion, especially after people stopped addressing me as 'Miss' a few years ago, and one schoolgirl even gave me her seat on the train. But it was a pleasant illusion. A foreign mirror, in a restaurant, in other people's houses, occasionally startled me by flashing my real, ageing face back at me, but I was able to forget it.

Not that the illness has made me look sick; at least, not yet. Rather, the diagnosis brought it home that I was at the threshold of old age, the time when people's bodies start betraying them. But don't be sorry for me, or anyone else knocking on heaven's door; we'll all get there one day, our last and everlasting day.

I have accepted my fate. Goodbye reincarnation, welcome eternal peace! I am mortal, multimortal even. Which is a great consolation, in fact.

## I am, I was

*Six women*
*A midwife procuring life and death.*
*A lady teaching orphans to write.*
*A peasant girl whispering to her donkey.*
*A student thirsty for all knowledge.*
*A lover dying with her beloved.*
*A wide-eyed traveller wishing herself fearless.*
*And more*
*I laugh and cry the same hour.*
*I mend, I ruin, I help, I fail.*
*My thoughts slither about like a family of snakes.*

# Acknowledgements

Apparently, everyone has a novel inside themselves. I was pregnant with this one for twenty years before my water finally broke and I started writing it in earnest – in 2020 when I quit my full-time academic job and finally had enough time for creative writing.

I would like to thank all the people – friends, colleagues and editing and publishing professionals – who monitored my early and more recent labours, and helped bring the manuscript to the final stage by providing comments, suggestions, corrections, advice on historical detail, proofreading and encouragement: John Inverarity, Gordana Crnković, Adrian Flitney, Peter Waxman, Jan Prislin-Planinc, Adrian Planinc, Charlotte Williams, Laura Ciutina, Laura Tomescu, Gavin Wood, Melek Bayram, Geert de Vries, Anke van der Veen, Zdenka Karakas, Carol Marković and Rachel Matthews. I am grateful to Sylvia Balog for her initial structural editing and her generosity in providing feedback and advice on the manuscript and beyond. *Grazie mille* to Vassilissa Carrangio for helping to obtain permission for the use of the cover image. *Hvala* to my cousin Zach Colic for putting me in touch with Romanian proofreaders.

The final push that brough this novel into the world has been ably assisted by Susan Young of Ashwood Publishing, whose patience and humour made the editing and publishing process a pleasure, and whose close attention to the manuscript and excellent advice honed the final product.

The finishing work on the manuscript coincided with moving to rural Tasmania, to be uplifted and inspired by its dramatic landscapes day after day, and often remembering, as a recent 'blow-in', the palawa people who have lived here for millennia.

# Selected Sources

The following sources were useful in researching historical and other detail for this work of fiction:

Braudel, Fernand (1992) *Civilization and Capitalism, 15th–18th Century* (Vols. 1–3), Oakland, CA: University of California Press

Brown. Archie (2009) *The Rise and Fall of Communism*, London: The Bodley Head

Camilleri, Andrea (2017) T*he Revolution of the Moon* (a novel, translated from Italian by Stephen Sartarelli), New York: Europa Editions

Chaplin, Charlie (1966) *My Autobiography*, Penguin Books Ltd.

Hastings, Selina (2010) *The Secret Lives Of Somerset Maugham, A Biography*, London: John Murray Press

*Het Kleine Weeshuis* (The Little Orphanage), An exhibition, 2018, Amsterdam Museum, Kalverstraat 92, Amsterdam

Hobsbawm, Eric. J. (1996) *The Age of Extremes: A history of the World 1914–1991*, New York: Vintage

Hobsbawm, Eric J. (1996) *The Age of Revolution: Europe 1789–1848*, London: Abacus

Huisinga, Johan (1996) *The Autumn of the Middle Ages*, Chicago: Chicago University Press

Lane, Joanne (2007) *Sicily: Adventure Guide*, Edison, NJ: Hunter Travel Guides

Mak, Geert (2001) *Amsterdam: A brief life of the city*, London: Vintage Books

Meyers, Jeffrey (2005) *Somerset Maugham: A Life*, New York: Vintage Books

Orwell, George (1931) The Spike (Chapters 27 & 35 of *Down and*

*Out in Paris and London*), at https://www.orwellfoundation. com/the-orwell-foundation/orwell/essays-and-other-works/ the-spike/

Orwell, George (1946) 'How the Poor Die', in *Fifty Orwell Essays*, at http://gutenberg.net.au/ebooks03/0300011h. html#part39

Orwell, George (1946) 'Decline of the English Murder', in *Fifty Orwell Essays*, at http://gutenberg.net.au/ebooks03/ 0300011h.html#part39

Volkov, Solomon (1979) *Testimony: The Memoirs of Dmitri Shostakovich*, London: Hamish Hamilton

*The Times Atlas of World History* (1984) (revised edition), London


Websites:

Google Maps, https://maps.google.com

Museum of the Holy Inquisition in Sicily (Carceri dell'Inquisizione), by Laura Leonardi and Per-Erik Skramstad, at https://www.wondersofsicily.com/palermo-museum-inquisition.htm

... and many others, including of course, Wikipedia!

www.ingramcontent.com/pod-product-compliance
Lightning Source LLC
Chambersburg PA
CBHW030514120726
47904CB00005B/1460